Cassie [illegible] in Colo[illegible] for many years and has now moved to Oregon. Her [illegible] is an hour from the rugged Pacific Ocean and an hour from the Cascade Mountains—the best of both worlds—not to m[illegible]s in Portland and awa[illegible]ette Valley. She's look[illegible]cific Northwest and fin[illegible]Mills & Boon romances

New York Times and *USA TODAY* bestselling author **Cindy Dees** is the author of more than fifty novels. She draws upon her experience as a US Air Force pilot to write romantic suspense. She's a two-time winner of the prestigious *RITA*® Award for romance fiction, a two-time winner of the RT Reviewers' Choice Best Book Award for Romantic Suspense and an *RT Book Reviews* Career Achievement Award nominee. She loves to hear from readers at www.cindydees.com

Also by Cassie Miles

Mountain Retreat
Colorado Wildfire
Mountain Bodyguard
Mountain Shelter
Mountain Blizzard
Frozen Memories
The Girl Who Wouldn't Stay Dead
The Girl Who Couldn't Forget
The Final Secret
Witness on the Run
Cold Case Colorado

Also by Cindy Dees

Navy SEAL's Deadly Secret
The Cowboy's Deadly Reunion
Special Forces: The Recruit
Special Forces: The Spy
Special Forces: The Operator
Undercover with a SEAL
Her Secret Spy
Her Mission with a SEAL
Navy SEAL Cop

FIND ME

CASSIE MILES

COLTON 911: DESPERATE RANSOM

CINDY DEES

MILLS & BOON

First Published in Great Britain 2021
by Mills & Boon, an imprint of HarperCollins*Publishers* Ltd
1 London Bridge Street, London, SE1 9GF

www.harpercollins.co.uk

HarperCollins*Publishers*
1st Floor, Watermarque Building,
Ringsend Road, Dublin 4, Ireland

Special thanks and acknowledgement are given to Cindy Dees for her contribution to the *Colton 911: Chicago* series

ISBN: 978-0-263-28358-7

1021

MIX
Paper from responsible sources
FSC™ C007454

This book is produced from independently certified FSC™ paper to ensure responsible forest management.

For more information visit: www.harpercollins.co.uk/green

Printed and Bound in Spain using 100% Renewable Electricity at CPI Blackprint (Barcelona)

FIND ME

CASSIE MILES

To Matt and Lauren, fantastic cooks.
And, as always, to Rick.

Chapter One

The dark blue delivery van chugged across the motel lot and parked beside her Toyota hatchback sedan. Though the logo on the side of the van—Valentino's Bakery and Wedding Cakes—seemed innocent enough, Isabel D'Angelo suspected trouble. Today, she was supposed to meet with a couple of the top honchos from Denver's most extensive crime organization to talk about a job, but they hadn't contacted her. Not a text or an email or a simple phone call. Why not? Had the deal gone sideways? Did they find out that she was undercover for the FBI?

Angie shook off her doubts. If she hoped to convince anybody that she was a math whiz with a special talent for money laundering, she had to totally believe her own cover story. More than confidence, she needed swagger, and she had to get it right the first time. Posing as a criminal wasn't really a far stretch for her. Though she'd graduated number one in her class at Quantico, she'd been a delinquent teenager. Her natural talent for deception was one of the main reasons she'd survived in the foster system. Lying came easy.

Peering through the slit between the cheap motel curtains and the cold window frame, she watched two guys—one in a suit, the other in a black leather jacket—leave the van and approach her room. A gust of October wind flipped back the older man's suit coat, and she saw a holster. He was armed. Nervous tension heightened her senses as she slipped into a leather jacket of her own—pink and studded, of course. A long time ago, she'd learned to use style, sparkle and flash as distractions. She tightened her long, sleek, white-blond ponytail and applied a fresh coat of fiery red lipstick.

She whipped open the motel room door and confronted the men. "You're late."

"The boss didn't tell you when we'd be here," said the man in a gray business suit with an open collar blue shirt. He was nondescript, bland and about five feet nine inches tall, which matched her height without shoes. In her specially designed platform combat boots, she was close to six feet tall.

"It's after four," she said, as if criminals kept regular business hours.

"Let's go, Angie."

"I didn't catch your name."

"Carlos."

"Nice to meet you, Carlos." She closed the door to her motel room and went forward, brushing past the two men. "I'll take my car and follow you."

"You ride with us."

From the corner of her eye, she saw the guy in the black leather jacket reach toward her in an attempt to grab her upper arm. *Did this dope really think she'd allow him to manhandle her?* Angie's self-defense moves were practiced and precise. She yanked his thick wrist behind his back and twisted hard. After a chop to the back of his leg, he dropped to a knee. While keeping pressure on his wrist, she flipped open the monogrammed switchblade she'd taken from a special pocket in her skinny jeans and waved the razor-sharp edge in front of his face.

Though her pulse was racing like a jackrabbit facing a rattlesnake, she stifled any sign of nerves. It was important to establish her identity as a dangerous person, even though she was cute, skinny and female. "Your name?"

"Murph." His ID sounded like the bark of a mumbling mutt...*murph, murph, murph.*

She released him and took a step back in case he decided to lash out. "Here's the deal, gentlemen. I don't want trouble. If it's important that I ride with you, fine. Just ask nicely."

"Sure," Carlos said. A smirk twisted his thin lips, and she had the impression he'd enjoyed her confrontation with Murph. "Please, Miss Angie, would you join us in the van?"

"Don't mind if I do."

She climbed into the rear. This windowless area wasn't meant for passengers. A lingering scent of vanilla and sugar, plus a couple of white pastry boxes tied with string indicated that the vehicle actually was used to transport baked goods. She perched on the edge of a bench seat on the wall. Murph—still cradling his wrist and acting as though she'd hurt him—slid behind the steering wheel.

In the passenger seat, Carlos turned so he could see her. "I have one more request. Until we know you better, the boss insists that you wear this."

A black hood dangled from his forefinger, and she stared at it in disgust. "Why?"

"This isn't negotiable." His smirk deepened. "Would you, pretty please?"

She snatched the hood from his hand. "I'll do it, but this is a waste. I'm new to Denver and don't know my way around. I couldn't tell you where we are or where we're going."

The lie rolled easily from the tip of her tongue. When

she was fifteen, she'd spent six months living on the streets of this city after she ran away from her foster home in Utah. That was eleven years ago, but there were parts of this town she'd never forget. Since yesterday, she'd been studying maps and computer images of Denver and the surrounding area. Knowing various locations and resources could be vital to her survival.

Riding in the back of the bouncy van with the black hood over her head provided an opportunity to plan and to focus. Her goal today was to get hired by the sprawling crime business that had taken root in Denver during the post-WWII population boom. Her entry point would be through their gambling and money laundering operation, but her endgame involved gathering enough information to destroy a brand-new start-up project that might turn into the biggest human trafficking ring west of the Mississippi.

Unlike her other undercover assignments, mostly in California, she had a personal stake in bringing down the patriarch, Nicolas Lorenzo. During her stint as a runaway in Denver, she'd lost a friend who had been swept up by criminals involved in the sex trade and never seen again. Angie didn't have many friends, and she'd loved Marigold. She'd sworn that someday she'd get even.

Someday was almost here.

Though she was unable to see, she could tell a few things about their route from shifts in direction and changes in the light that filtered through the hood. They'd gone southwest, hadn't taken a highway. She really hoped they weren't headed into the mountains. Angie wasn't a fan of the unmapped hills and forests. After a few bumps and a downward turn, she guessed that they were driving down a ramp into an underground parking structure.

After they parked, Carlos pulled open the door to the

van and took her hand to help her climb out. "I need for you to keep that hood in place until I tell you to take it off."

"It's hard to walk."

"Don't worry. I won't let you bump into the wall."

Without vision, she was thrown off-balance. Instead of facing Lorenzo with her head held high, she'd be forced to approach tentatively, clinging to Carlos like an invalid. No doubt that had been their plan: make her feel helpless so she'd be more cooperative.

Carlos guided her into an elevator. When they emerged, she shuffled her feet and felt carpeting on the soles of her boots. Carlos guided her through a door, taking care so she didn't run into anything. He seated her in a padded chair before he whipped off the hood.

Angie blinked at the late afternoon light pouring through a wall of windows into a conference room. As soon as she could focus, she found herself staring into the most crystal-clear blue eyes she'd ever encountered. Deep set and framed by long, dark lashes, those piercing eyes dominated a square-jawed face with high cheekbones. His scrutiny disrupted her composure more than the van ride or the black hood. He seemed to be assessing her, taking her measure and making a judgment.

Dragging her gaze away from him, she checked out the other two men seated at a round table. To her disappointment, neither was Nicolas Lorenzo. Carlos took the empty chair to her left and dismissed his partner. As soon as the door closed, Carlos regaled the others with the story of how she'd bested Murph in the motel parking lot.

While he talked, she watched their expressions. The man with the incredible eyes barely reacted. Who was he? The other two were familiar from her research into the Lorenzo family, but she knew nothing about this guy with the rugged features and thick, curly, dark blond hair.

He continued to watch her, and she endeavored to match his cool resolve. She busied her hands to keep her fingers from trembling. From a pocket of her pink jacket, she took out a lipstick. There was a mirror on the side of the tube, and she used it to apply a fresh coat of bright red. When she pursed her full lips and smoothed her platinum hair, she saw that the men had stopped talking to watch her. She had their attention.

"Gentlemen, I'm Isabel D'Angelo. I go by Angie. Some people call me a genius when it comes to numbers. Hire me and I guarantee to boost your profits."

"How much is this going to cost?" asked an extra-large man who barely fit into his chair.

"Not a dime," she said. "I take a commission from a percentage of the profits."

"You come with high recommendations, if you know what I mean," said the man opposite her.

"I think I do."

"Our associates in San Francisco like you. I'm Nolan Zapata. This big ape sitting next to me is Valentino the Baker. And that's Julian Parisi, otherwise known as the Professor."

She could have sworn that Julian's firm handshake ignited an electric spark that sizzled up her arm and elevated her core temperature by several degrees. All the while, he never broke eye contact. "We have a mutual friend," he said, "Manny Harris."

"Not a friend of mine," she quickly responded, tossing out another lie. Harris was with DEA and had successfully infiltrated a drug cartel before recently being reassigned. Why would Julian mention him? Was he testing her? She tried to pull her hand from his grasp but he didn't let go.

"Where did you learn your math skills?" he asked.

"MIT." She'd been telling this lie for so long that she

almost believed it herself. “I had an uncle in Reno who showed me how to put all that academic data to use in gambling.”

“Handy.”

“Why do they call you Professor?”

“For one thing, I got brains.” He reached into the pocket of his dark blue blazer, took out a pair of black frame glasses and perched them onto his nose. “When I’m wearing these, people tell me that I look like I should be standing in front of a classroom.”

Angie never had a teacher who had blue eyes that could stare into her soul. If she had, she might have been more motivated to stay in high school. “I’ll call you Julian.”

“Now that we’re all friends,” Zapata said, “I want to make you an offer, Angie. We can use somebody with your skills, but you’ve got to prove yourself. I’ll give you one week to reorganize our OTB operation.”

“Horses?”

“That’s what off-track betting means.”

Her dislike for the massive beasts was pure truth. Animals were as unpredictable as children and almost as annoying. “I’d rather handle sports betting, even soccer.”

“It’s not your choice, honey.” Zapata gave her a dismissive nod. “I’ll check in with you, and I will expect higher profit after next weekend.”

“It’s already Thursday,” she pointed out. “I can’t make big changes in such a short time. Give me a month.”

“Ten days,” He emphasized the finality by whacking the flat of his hand on the table. “I hear you’re a smart girl. You’ll figure it out.”

There was an implied threat behind his words. The Lorenzo organization wasn’t about to open their books to just anybody. “You won’t be disappointed.”

"I need to take your cell phone," Julian said. "Security reasons. Don't worry, I'll give it back."

She'd expected as much. All her contact numbers had already been cleared and sanitized. She took the red-gold phone from her jacket pocket and placed it on the table. "I want it back as soon as possible."

"Your password?"

With her manicured and polished index fingernail, she punched in four numbers so he could see them. "I don't know why you're digging around but don't be rude, okay?"

Carlos snorted. "She likes for everybody to be polite."

"Nothing wrong with manners," Julian said.

Though his voice was friendly, she didn't make the mistake of thinking that he was ready to accept her. Behind his glasses, his mesmerizing eyes narrowed slightly, reminding her of a cat playing with a mouse. Julian was arrogant—the type who'd allow her to make a move and lead her to hope that escape was possible before he knocked her over with a swipe of his paw. She wouldn't let her guard down. Angie wasn't anybody's easy prey.

She addressed the men at the table. "Time's short. I ought to get started right away."

Julian stood. "May I offer you a ride?"

Being alone with him in a car seemed risky, but she didn't have a choice. Murph wouldn't want to take her and calling a rideshare service for a pickup after a meeting with known criminals didn't seem prudent. "I don't need to wear a hood this time, do I?"

"I wouldn't want to hide that pretty face."

The fact that she managed to suppress her natural tendency to blush at his compliment was a testimony to her skill at falsehood. She was attracted to him but couldn't allow herself to be disarmed. She returned his fake smile with one of her own and followed him out of the boardroom.

In the underground parking structure, she took a quick inventory of parked vehicles that ranged from flashy sports cars to humble delivery vans like the one from Valentino's to a tanklike Hummer. Julian Parisi's high-end, silver SUV managed to combine the rugged power of an off-road vehicle with the luxe of a limo. The vehicle suited the man with starry blue eyes and muscular shoulders. He was tough and smart, a dangerous combo. She needed to figure out where Julian fit into the Lorenzo organization and why he'd been the one to offer her a ride.

She climbed into the passenger side and snuggled into the smooth leather seat that fit her like a very expensive glove. Passing the first hurdle and getting herself hired had been easy, but there would be more to come. She suspected that the Professor would be administering the next test, and failure could have lethal consequences.

With her seat belt fastened, Angie turned her head and studied the man behind the steering wheel. *Damn, he's hot.* In profile, his features were chiseled. His dark blond hair gave the impression of being unkempt, but she figured that his style was the result of expensive barbering. He glanced toward her and quickly looked away, avoiding eye contact. *What are you hiding, Mr. Adonis?*

She asked, "We're headed back to my motel, right?"

"I think there's someplace else you'd rather go."

"Where's that?"

"You'll see."

She was wary and irritated. He had no right to make decisions for her. She glided her finger along the secret pocket in her bedazzled jeans where her switchblade was hidden. "I have a better idea. You tell me where we're headed, and I'll decide if it's okay."

"It's better than okay." He didn't seem threatening, but

she'd heard that most sociopaths were charming. He continued, "When we get there, you can tell me if I'm right."

As they emerged from the garage and drove west, she tallied up the facts she'd learned today. The FBI dossier she'd been given for this assignment hadn't mentioned Julian Parisi—a gross oversight since he seemed to be a major player. The other men she'd met had been described with emphasis on Zapata, a high-ranking number cruncher who had a reputation for crunching bones when debts weren't paid on time.

She knew that the six-story square office building they'd just left was used mostly for accounting, real estate, investments and other relatively legitimate businesses. Most of Lorenzo's other enterprises were in central Denver, not the mountains. Where was Julian taking her?

After a long drive on the highway, the SUV exited onto a curving two-lane road that led deeper into the pine-covered foothills. Her anxiety kicked up. A seed of panic took root in her belly and sprouted branches as she remembered horror stories about fierce grizzly bears, rockslides and flash floods. Nature was dangerous. And the man behind the steering wheel might be equally lethal. He could throw her off a cliff or drown her in the rapids of a river. Since she was undercover, nobody would miss her…not for months.

Without inside info, she could only hope that he was a decent guy. In her undercover work, she'd run across many criminals—especially those involved in white-collar crime—who resembled corporate executives more than felons. They wore expensive clothes, had good taste and sent their kids to exclusive schools. Julian might be one of those guys…an MBA who took a wrong turn.

Or he could be a stone-cold killer.

Chapter Two

Angie fidgeted in the passenger seat. This drive seemed endless. "Here's a thought. You don't have to tell me where we're going, but I want to guess."

"Take your best shot."

"A restaurant?"

"There's food."

For an instant, hunger overwhelmed her anxiety. Coming from LA, she'd been driving for the past couple of days, living off burgers and chicken nuggets. "I wouldn't mind a nice meal."

"There's also dancing."

"A cowboy bar," she guessed, "with a mechanical bull."

"We're not going line dancing." The two-lane road swerved into a thick forest. The golden glow of sunset filtered through heavy boughs and dappled the scenery. "I'm taking you to a private gentleman's club."

A fancy name for a strip joint! In her teens when she was bouncing around in foster care and desperate for cash, she'd pole danced in one of those places that was supposed to protect the women who worked there. They didn't.

Why was he driving toward a place that was obviously inappropriate? This might be some kind of test, like being ordered to wear that black hood when Carlos was driving. Julian might think the degrading locale would show that her position in the Lorenzo family was precarious. Not that she needed a reminder. Living undercover with the constant threat of danger was growing more difficult with every assignment. "Take me back to my motel."

"We're almost to the club."

Rounding a twist in the road, the SUV came out of the forest. On the opposite side of a wide meadow, she saw a stone-and-cedar building with a flagstone terrace and a deck jutting from the front. Seven-story wings rose on either side of the center section. From the windows and rustic balconies, she guessed that the wings were used for hotel space. On the left end was a half-full parking lot. A neon sign over the entryway said Nick's. No doubt, Nick referred to Nicolas Lorenzo, the bastard who had taken Marigold.

A flood of emotions whirled inside her. She was scared about what might happen, excited for a new challenge and eager for revenge. Why hadn't her FBI handlers told her about this place? She covered with one word: "Impressive."

"Not what you expected?"

"Most of the gentlemen's clubs I've seen are super sleazy. This place is actually kind of wholesome."

"The times are changing."

"What's that supposed to mean?"

"Las Vegas advertises fun for the whole family. They've got roller coasters and water slides and petting zoos."

The gambling capital of the world looked like a touristy playground with activities for every age and taste, but that wasn't the Vegas she knew. Angie was more familiar with the dark underbelly where desperate gamblers squandered their last nickel, hookers offered group discounts and vice was readily available.

He pulled onto the shoulder of the road and parked. When he turned toward her, he took off his glasses and slipped them into the pocket of his blazer. "I know your secret, Angie. You're not who you say you are."

Masking her surprise, she hid within her undercover identity and got ready to avoid trouble by lying. Her deceptions followed a few simple rules: keep your adversary off-balance by confronting them; start with the truth—make the lie plausible; and reveal as little as possible. "Why would you say that?"

"Your online identity starts three years ago. Before that, you didn't exist."

She scoffed. "I thought professors were supposed to be smart."

"Why don't you explain it to me?"

"Obviously, I'm not using the name I was born with. In my line of work, I need to change my identity." She'd also transformed from a mousy brunette to a flashy platinum blonde but he didn't need to know that. "Three years ago, I wiped the slate clean."

"Does your line of work have anything to do with the feds?"

He leaned a few inches closer. Without the glasses, the shimmer in his eyes was nearly devastating, but she kept her focus. "Are you asking about Harris?"

"Maybe I am."

"Yeah, we dated, but as soon as he grew a tail and turned into a rat, I dumped him."

"Let me give you a warning, Angie. You seem like a decent person."

"Do I? That's not the look I was going for." With her long ponytail, red lipstick and studded jacket, she thought she'd been doing an excellent impersonation of Badass Barbie.

"Denver seems like an easygoing place where the kids play guitars and ride bikes and the sky is not cloudy all day. But don't underestimate the Lorenzo family. Once you're part of their business, it's hard to get out. Here's my advice to you, back away while you still can. Hop into your Toyota and drive back to California."

"I'm not a quitter." She'd studied the odds and figured that she had a shot at derailing a human trafficking operation, not to mention the possibility of taking revenge against Lorenzo for the disappearance of Marigold so many years ago. Her risk was worth the reward. "Is there food at your fancy gentlemen's club?"

"Four bars and three restaurants, one is gourmet."

She sensed there was something he hadn't told her. "What else?"

"This is where you'll be working. The OTB venue is on the lower level."

Surprise, surprise. She hadn't expected to be stashed away in the mountains. How was she going to dig into the inner workings of the Lorenzo organization from this remote location? Somehow, she needed to get back into the thick of the city.

Without another word, he started the engine and drove to the front entrance where a deferential valet took his car keys. Julian thanked the young man by name.

"You must come here often," she said.

"I ought to. I'm the general manager." He accompanied her to the front door, which another valet whipped open for them. "I don't handle the details of the day-to-day operations, but I oversee the building."

"Does that mean you're my supervisor?"

"No."

He was starting to annoy her. "You should have told me from the start that I'd be working here. Then, I wouldn't have spent the whole long, very long, drive worrying."

"Worrying about what?"

"For all I knew, you could be some kind of serial killer weirdo. And you could have been escorting me to a shallow grave where my bones would be picked clean by coyotes."

"How do you know I'm not?"

She took a moment to look around. "This place is too classy for a serial killer."

The large, three-story-tall lobby was an attractive space with flagstone floors and woven carpets. Rustic staircases on either side led to an upper level and downstairs. The tasteful decor combined antiques and heavy wooden furniture arranged around two moss rock fireplaces. A front desk for the hotel stretched along one wall.

He asked, "Are you still impressed?"

"There's more natural light than I would have expected."

"Glass ceiling." He looked upward at the A-frame skylight high above them. "A number of contractors told me that feature would never work, but it does. The other lighting is geared to create an open atmosphere."

He sounded proprietary, and that attitude made her wonder. "Did you build this place?"

"For the past three years, I've been working on renovations."

She pointed toward the balcony that encircled the second story. "What's up there?"

"There's a coffee shop and a bar that opens onto the deck. At the rear is a gourmet restaurant. Behind that is a members-only casino with poker, blackjack and roulette. No slots."

"I thought gambling was illegal, except in certain cities in Colorado."

"We get around the restrictions because Nick's is a social club. The gambling is a diversion we offer our members—not a significant part of our operation."

Halfway down the lobby to her right was the entrance

to the strip club that she'd expected to find. A tasteful sign read Nick's Burlesque. At the closed door, two muscular bouncers stood guard and checked the ID's of a couple of guys in baseball caps. When the door opened, the echo of a country western song slipped out. She recognized the tune as "Save a Horse (Ride a Cowboy)." And she cringed at the unbidden memories of her time on the pole.

When she turned in the opposite direction, she recognized a tall, tanned man with silver hair combed back from his forehead. It had been eleven years since she'd seen him. Nick Lorenzo hadn't aged at all.

When Julian introduced them, she fought to hide her explosive surge of pure rage. She forced herself to shake his hand. "I've heard so much about you."

"Likewise." He treated her to a slow scrutiny. "Your hand is shaking."

"I must be hungry." She looked away, fearful that he'd see the hatred boiling inside her. She wanted to claw his face with her fingernails, to slash her blade across his carotid, but violence would only be a temporary satisfaction. Building a case against Lorenzo would be far better. She focused on her assignment. "I spoke to your man Zapata, and he gave me ten days to punch up your profits."

"I trust his judgment."

"You won't be disappointed."

She forced herself to confront him, eyeball to eyeball. The last time she'd seen Nicolas Lorenzo, she'd been a bow-legged, gawky fifteen-year-old with stringy brown hair and scraggly teeth in need of braces. He'd been so captivated by Marigold that he hardly noticed her. Now he was staring.

"Have we met before?" he asked.

It took all her considerable skill at deception to mask the truth with flirtation. She flapped her fake eyelashes and gave a husky laugh. "I could never forget a man like you. Wealthy, powerful and..." she reached toward him with her painted fingernail and traced the lapel of his sports jacket "...and sexy."

Had she gone too far? She'd waited so long for vengeance that she was momentarily thrown off-balance. *Get it together.* She had to succeed in putting this snake out of business—for the sake of her best friend.

AS SOON AS Angie and Lorenzo met, Julian sensed trouble. He observed them with the sort of morbid fascination usually reserved for the moment before a locomotive crashes into a stalled car on the railroad tracks. A major disaster was imminent, and he doubted that he could slam on the brakes. In the short time he'd been with Angie, he deduced that she wasn't a woman who backed down. She'd told him that she wasn't a quitter.

And Lorenzo was worse. If he got angry, there was no stopping him. In the three years it had taken to build Nick's, Julian had learned that his boss didn't listen to advice, even when the suggestions were prudent. Lorenzo ran his business based almost entirely on ego, and his instincts were often wrongheaded, especially when it came to women. If he considered them to be potential lovers, he rolled out the charm. If they were worker bees, he barely wasted a glance in their direction. Angie presented a problem for him because she didn't neatly fit either category. Not only was she pretty enough to be a lover but she came with a set of skills that would benefit the organization. And she was sending out mixed signals, licking her lips and flirting. Her voice was breathy when she claimed to be delighted by this opportunity to spend time with *Lorenzo the Great.*

Her sarcasm was too subtle for his boss who preened at

being referred to as "Great." Julian guessed that in Lorenzo's one-track mind he thought he'd discovered a truly elusive, mythical creature: a woman who would make sweet love all night and earn money during the day. Before he could take a stroll down that fantasy lane, Angie sent him on a detour, talking about a mutual acquaintance in California who'd made a pass at her.

"Almost ripped his fingers off," she said with a too-loud laugh. Her pouty smile turned feral as her lips pulled back to bare her white teeth. "Nobody coerces me. Nobody commands me to do something I don't want to do."

Lorenzo took a backward step but didn't give up. "As long as you're going to be working here, I want you to stay in the hotel."

"Or maybe not." Julian wasn't thrilled with the idea of having Angie here all the time. He didn't know what game she was playing but was certain that she was trouble. "Most people don't like to live where they work."

"Not like you," Lorenzo said.

"What does that mean?" Angie asked.

"My man Julian is on the job night and day." He reached over and patted Julian's shoulder. The boss was one of those guys who liked to poke, stroke and jab…all in good fun. He continued, "When he first started working for me, he was nothing but a contractor in a hard hat and a tool belt. Look at him now. His blazer is tailored, and he's wearing eight-hundred-dollar custom-made boots."

Not true. Though Julian knew carpentry, he had training as an architect. And he didn't believe in throwing away money on clothes. He attempted to steer the conversation away from Angie's housing situation. "I was on my way downstairs to show Angie her new office."

"Wish I could join you," Lorenzo said, "but I have a business dinner. Angie, I insist that you stay in a hospitality suite on the fourth floor. You'll have daily maid service, access to 24/7 room service and a much better view than the parking lot of your cheesy motel."

"Thank you." She was cool and polite. "How could I say no?"

"I'll send Murph to pick up your luggage."

"Not Murph. I'd rather not have him pawing through my things."

"Of course not."

Lorenzo snapped his fingers toward the hotel reservations desk where Tamara Rigby was in charge. She glared as she came toward them, and Julian didn't blame her for being annoyed. Tamara was too qualified to be considered a worker bee. She had a degree in hospitality management and an MBA. Julian knew he was lucky to have her working here.

While she and Angie made arrangements to pick up her car and luggage from the motel, Julian contemplated how his afternoon had gone to hell. The downward trajectory started when he failed to convince Angie to quit. Then Lorenzo invited her to stay in one of the hospitality suites. And now, Tamara was shooting angry glares in his direction. He didn't think the day could get worse until Lorenzo said, "One more thing…"

Julian watched a young man with a beak-like nose, black hair and dark eyes shuffle across the lobby toward them. He wore a shoulder holster under his blazer. His name was Rudy Lorenzo.

While they shook hands, his uncle explained, "Rudy is moving into the office next to yours, Julian. He'll be your assistant."

"I like to do my own hiring. No offense, Rudy."

"This is a done deal," Lorenzo said. "My sister's son works for you."

Julian didn't want or need an assistant. He had efficiently delegated the major responsibilities at Nick's, and the place was a smooth-running machine that managed to provide access to several vices without actually breaking any laws. From the start, Julian had known that this delicate balance couldn't last forever, but he wasn't ready to give up control. Something big was coming, and he wanted to be in on it.

Nick Lorenzo clasped Angie's arm and planted a light kiss on her forehead. "You're invited to a cocktail party at my place on Saturday night. Wear something nice."

"I'll be there," she said through clenched teeth.

Her eyes flashed a warning that Lorenzo didn't see. The boss had already moved on, striding across the lobby to meet his dinner partner—the newly elected mayor of a nearby mountain town.

"Let's get to it," Rudy said, rubbing his hands together. "I'll hang with you guys."

"Not necessary," Julian said. "I'm showing Ms. D'Angelo around, and you're already familiar with the place."

"Yeah, I've spent time with the pole dancers and at the poker tables, but I ought to see the offices, especially the sports betting. I want to meet Leif Farnsworth, the ex-Bronco quarterback who runs that operation."

"It's late. He's probably gone for the day."

"So, does he have a sense of humor? Would he think it was funny if I called him by his nickname—Falling Leif? I mean, that's a hoot on account of he got sacked so many times."

For the first time in hours, Julian felt the tension lift. A real grin spread across his face when he contemplated the literal fallout when Rudy insulted the quarterback. Leif hated his nickname. Whenever anyone mentioned it, he threw whatever happened to be at hand—a stapler, a coffee cup or one of the smaller computer programmers. "You might want to rethink that plan, Rudy."

Beforc they could descend to the basement level, the door to the burlesque club opened a slit, and a skinny, young girl slipped out. When she spotted Julian, she ran across the flagstone floor, jumped into his arms, and wrapped her arms and legs around him.

He patted her back. "What's wrong, Cara?"

"My mom needs you. You gotta come right now."

He glanced at Rudy, who seemed confused, which just might be his usual state of mind. Nothing Julian could do to repair Lorenzo's nephew. Likewise, he couldn't immediately fix the problems that came with Angie. The woman was a puzzle that required concentration to assemble.

Cara came first. Her crisis took precedence over the other disasters of the day.

Chapter Three

The girl who clung tightly to Julian looked over his shoulder, and Angie caught her gaze. Though the kid couldn't have been more than seven or eight years old, her eyes expressed a sad resignation that was typical of a much older person. Angie knew that attitude, and she guessed that Cara had seen enough of life to understand how things worked and, more important, how to get what she wanted. The girl's tense lips and clenched jaw showed her stubborn tendencies. Again, Angie understood. When she was growing up, her foster parents and her teachers and her social workers often complained that she was willful and disobedient. *Of course I was! That's how I survived.*

She gave a wink, which Cara returned. They were kindred spirits. If Angie had been twenty years younger, they would have been buddies, pals and partners in crime.

Unlike Angie in her youth, this kid didn't look like she'd been physically abused. Her jeans and yellow turtleneck were clean. Her sneakers were neatly tied, and her shiny brown hair fell halfway down her back in two tidy braids. It took someone with a personal connection—someone like Angie—to see the neglect.

Cara needed attention. She'd bolted through the doors of the burlesque club at a time of day when most families were sitting down to a dinner of meat loaf and mashed potatoes. Did people actually do that anymore? Cara had made a beeline for Julian's arms. He was her target. Angie suspected that the girl had been waiting for Julian, watching through a crack in the door or from some other secret vantage point. The way she attached herself to him made it clear that she never wanted to let him go.

Still holding the kid, he returned to where Angie was standing. He spoke into Cara's ear. "Here's the problem. If I go into the club to talk to your mother, I can't bring you along. Kids aren't allowed inside."

"But I was already there."

"It's not appropriate. Don't make me lecture you, again."

Though he set Cara's feet on the floor, he couldn't break the connection. The kid latched on to his hand and pleaded. "Please, Julian, let me come with. I won't get in the way. I mean it, cross my heart and hope to die."

Angie heard echoes of her own misspent childhood and the many empty promises she'd made to authority figures. Cara was smart and clever. She might have a wealth of useful information she'd be willing to share…if Angie could make it worth her while. *A seven-year-old confidential informant?*

"I have a suggestion," Angie said. "You can leave Cara with me."

The kid's head whipped around so fast that her braids twirled. Cara focused hard, looking her up and down, sizing her up. "Who are you? Julian's new girlfriend?"

"I'm a new employee," Angie said. "I'll be working downstairs in OTB."

Cara nodded. "I like your jacket."

"Want to try it on?"

"Sure." She dropped Julian's hand. Apparently, he wasn't as appealing as shiny, pink rhinestones.

"It's settled," he said with palpable relief. "There's a coffee shop upstairs. I'll meet you there in a few minutes."

"Cool," Rudy said. "I'll go with Julian."

Angie had been so caught up in the unexpected appearance of Cara that she'd forgotten the big lug that Nick Lorenzo left with them. Not so for Julian. Without skipping a beat, he tapped Rudy's heavy shoulder and said, "Your job as my assistant starts now. You need to accompany Angie. This is her first time at Nick's. Show the lady around."

"You got it, boss."

"Don't call me boss." He turned to Cara. "Stay with Angie and do what she says."

Wearing the too-big jacket, she sashayed ten steps as though walking the runway at a Paris fashion show. She pivoted and gazed at Julian with her brown, Bambi-like eyes. "You better hurry. My mom needs you."

The little girl watched every step Julian took as he headed toward Nick's Burlesque. When he disappeared behind the doors, she exhaled a deep, heartfelt sigh that made Angie wonder if the kid wanted Nick to be her new daddy or her boyfriend. Either way, it was creepy.

In normal circumstances, Angie tried not to get involved in other people's problems, but Cara was different. The kid was bright and resourceful. She had the appealing waif act down pat, but Angie could give her a couple of pointers on how to manipulate the grown-ups. A cute smile was good for drawing people close and making them want to help you, but a quivering lower lip would melt their hearts.

Before they really started talking, Angie needed to get Rudy out of the way, and she had to find a place where she and Cara wouldn't be observed on the multitude of surveillance cameras she'd noticed at Nick's. She asked, "Are you hungry?"

Cara preened in the pink jacket. "I could go for some sushi."

"Seriously? You like raw fish? How old are you?"

"Seven and I just started second grade." She tugged on Angie's hand. "We can eat at the Gourmand restaurant. The chef knows me."

"That's okay by me," Rudy said, "as long as I ain't paying."

"Or we could do something else." From what Julian had said, it seemed obvious that Cara wasn't allowed free rein of Nick's. She might welcome an opportunity to explore. "Where's your favorite place? Not the casino because they'll chase you right out. And I'm guessing the shops are too pricy."

Rudy reminded her, "We don't have time for shopping. We're supposed to go to the coffee shop."

"I've never been good at taking orders." She exchanged a knowing glance with Cara. "Besides, I don't think Julian will mind if we take a look around."

"There's a barn behind the hotel," Cara said. "I really love the horses."

Perfect! A barn might be the only place on the premises that didn't have surveillance. "Rudy, I have a job for you. Please tell Julian that we went to check out the barn."

He balked, placing his considerable weight between them and the door. "I mean no disrespect, but the boss wants you to go to the coffee shop."

"No disrespect." Where did that attitude come from? She made a guess. "Have you been talking to Murph?"

"He told me you like things to be polite."

"And you get it. Good! We're going to be friends, Rudy." She flashed a smile—a drop of honey to catch this fly.

"Look through the window. Pretty soon it's going to get dark. If we want to see anything, we should go right away."

"But the boss said—"

"Cara and I will take a quick look at the horses, and then we'll go to the coffee shop. Please tell Julian. Can you do that for me?"

Rudy looked across the lobby at the entrance to the Burlesque with eager eyes. Obviously, he'd rather be mingling with the scantily clad dancers than tromping through the horse barn. He gave a nod. "Yes, ma'am, I'll do it."

The "ma'am" struck an odd note of deference. Angie figured she was only a few years older than Rudy. "Thank you."

She and Cara went out the front door, descended the three stairs from the verandah and followed the wide asphalt pathway to the right. The last rays of sunlight speckled the forested hillsides. The temperature was cool but not chilly enough that she needed her jacket. Angie inhaled a deep gulp of air that was so clean and crisp that she coughed. Maybe the mountains weren't so bad, after all.

Cara looked up at her with undisguised respect. Apparently, the little girl approved of the way she'd gotten what she wanted from Rudy. Angie grinned back at her. Children weren't her thing, but she might have to make an exception for this one.

"You handled him," Cara said.

"You could have done the same." Angie probably shouldn't encourage such willful behavior. She changed the topic. "Did you go to school this morning?"

"Sure did. In the afternoon, Mom picked me up. Usually, we go home and hang out until my babysitter shows up. She stays until my mom gets off work. I knew today was gonna be different as soon as I saw my backpack and sleeping bag. Mom brought me to work with her. She said I could sleep in her dressing room."

Angie wasn't familiar with the arrangements for this burlesque show, but she knew that most strip clubs didn't provide private rooms for the dancers. Cara's mom must be a star. "Tell me about your mother."

"Her name is Jane, and she goes by Calamity Jane because she does Wild West stuff. She's really popular and has a bunch of fans."

Hence the dressing room. "Tell me about her act."

"It's really cool. She uses throwing knives and bullwhips. In one routine, she snaps her whip at one of the other dancers until all her clothes are off. I mean, *almost* all her clothes. Nobody gets totally naked at Nick's."

"Sounds like a reasonable policy."

"Uh-huh." Cara shrugged her skinny shoulders. "Julian has a lot of rules."

"Like what?"

"No kids backstage. No drugs allowed. No performers are allowed to go out on dates with the customers or the staff. Stuff like that."

Angie had heard that story before from other strip joints that touted their operations as a humanitarian effort for young women who were down on their luck. She wouldn't press Cara for details. Angie wasn't here to investigate the burlesque show, which sounded like a legit operation, especially when compared with human trafficking. "Where did your mom learn how to use a whip?"

"She grew up on a ranch. She's also a sharpshooter, but Julian has a rule about real guns at work. Sometimes, she'll bring one anyway and leave it in the car."

Calamity Jane sounded like a potentially dangerous

stripper. No wonder Julian was quick to respond to her problems. "Did she bring a gun today?"

"I dunno."

The asphalt path rounded the south wing of Nick's and led past a windowless cedar wall below five stories of hotel rooms. Angie wondered what kind of activities went on at this level where there were no windows. Was it the off-track betting operation or a walk-in vault or a secret, illegal casino? It might be a good place to hide victims of human trafficking. She and Cara strolled past a cellar door built into the rear section. Angie noticed two surveillance cameras. At Nick's, someone was always watching.

A delivery truck loaded with beer drove along a road beside the pathway and circled past them toward the rear of the building. Earlier, when she and Julian left his SUV at the front door, she'd seen the parking lot at the other end but not this road. She'd thought there was only one access, but a rear entrance made sense. With all the restaurants and bars, there had to be a steady stream of deliveries, plus garbage pickup and laundry services for the hotel. All this coming-and-going made a good cover for criminal activity.

The rustic landscaping at the front melted into a part-dirt and part-asphalt yard that was over fifty yards wide and stretched all the way around to the loading dock in back of the hotel. Cara grabbed her hand and pointed to a long building with a corral attached. "There's the horse barn. Right over there."

"I see it." Four other outbuildings of various sizes surrounded the area.

Cara tugged Angie's hand. "We gotta hurry. It's getting dark."

"There's time." Thus far, they'd been satisfying Cara's

demands. It was time for Angie to get some payback. "Can I ask you a couple of questions?"

The girl rolled her eyes. "Okay, but we've got to keep walking."

"Why do you think your mother was so upset?"

"She didn't say, but she told me to stay close to her and not go running off."

Angie came to a halt. She squatted down so she was eye to eye with Cara. She wasn't surprised that the kid had disobeyed but wanted to understand why. "Did your mom explain why she was breaking the rules and bringing you to work?"

Cara lowered her gaze and stared at the toes of her sneakers. "She doesn't have time to give me a bunch of reasons. She's a single mother, always tired. When she gives me an order, I'm not supposed to ask why. I just do it."

"But you didn't do what she said. First chance you got, you went running to Julian."

"I'm not stupid. I could see that Mom needed help, and Julian is good at fixing things."

"Was your mom scared?" When Cara pinched her lips together and shook her head, Angie could tell that she'd hit the bull's eye. Something had frightened Cara's mother. Angie asked, "Is it dangerous?"

"She asked me if I saw a man with a black beard and a scar on his forehead." She tugged again at Angie's hand. "There's nothing else. Let's go to the barn."

"First, I've got to tell you a secret. Okay, here it is. I don't much like horses. They're big, stinky, slobbery and not very smart." She shuddered. "When we get to the barn, don't expect me to pet these animals."

Cara rolled her eyes. "Now who's the big, ol' scaredy cat?"

"Am not." Somehow she'd fallen into a grade school

conversation pattern. *Not good.* "Okay, maybe I am a teensy bit scared. Don't tell anybody."

As they approached the barn, Cara added a bounce to her step. She waved at a rangy man wearing jeans, a plaid shirt and a beat-up cowboy hat. His bowlegs didn't disguise the fact that he was limping. As they approached, Angie noticed the cowboy's black eye.

"That's Waylon," Cara said. "He's my friend."

"Hey, cutie-pie," Waylon said with a friendly wave. "Who's this lady?"

"Her name is Angie, and she's scared of horses."

So much for Cara's ability to keep a secret. Angie shook the cowboy's outstretched hand and said, "Pleased to meet you."

"Y'all don't need to be ashamed," he drawled. "Horses can be dangerous."

"Agreed."

"In my years of working on ranches, I've come to believe that the main reason for fear is unfamiliarity. If you let me take you out for a ride, you'll learn to appreciate these animals."

Inside the horse barn, she saw a row of six stalls on the left side and six on the right. A total of seven were occupied with horses that peered over the half doors. No doubt, the beasts were calculating how they could get her alone and trample her.

Cara bounced up to him. "Have you seen my friend, Gigi?"

"Nope."

"Who's Gigi?"

Cara rolled her eyes again. "He's gonna tell you that Gigi is imaginary, but she's really real. I met her a couple of weeks ago when I was picking up pinecones behind the barn. She was silly, told me she lived in the forest like a chipmunk. Then Mom called for me, and I had to go."

Angie had to wonder if the imaginary playmate was somehow involved with human trafficking. This topic deserved further conversation, but not right now. Cara was on edge, and Angie didn't want to set her off. "We'll look for her."

"Good." She whirled and glanced up at Waylon. "Can I saddle up and take a ride?"

"Afraid not," Waylon said. "It's almost bedtime for these ponies."

"Can I feed them?"

"You know where the apples are. But you better take off that fancy jacket. With all those sparkles, the horses might think you're wearing their dessert."

She peeled off the pink rhinestone jacket and tossed it toward Angie, who was grateful to Waylon for rescuing her clothing from a bath in horse slobber. She watched as Cara dragged a small bench toward one of the stalls, grabbed an apple and fed the big brown horse. Then she petted the muscular neck and cooed.

Angie looked around the barn. She didn't see any cameras, but still she worried that they were under surveillance. Cameras were everywhere. Her earlier thought that they might avoid surveillance in the barn was wishful thinking.

"Are the guests at the hotel allowed to ride the horses?"

"Someday, we might have a program for horseback rides, but right now, they're private property and belong to Mr. Lorenzo."

That gave her another reason to dislike the beasts. The smarmy presence of Nick Lorenzo hung over every part of this place like an ominous, dangerous thundercloud. Her hatred for him had grown after seeing him again today.

She'd almost forgotten the permanent sneer to his mouth and the greasy smugness that radiated from him.

She phrased her comments carefully. "It looks like you have room for expansion. What are all these outbuildings used for?"

"Mostly storage, and there's a garage for ATVs, snowmobiles and the Jeep we use for a snowplow in winter." He pointed toward a long, ranch-style building at the back of the lot. "That's a bunkhouse. In the summer, I usually have ten cowboys working for me. In this season, I only need five or six part-timers, and everybody goes home at the end of the day."

A vacant bunkhouse would be an ideal place for holding the victims of human trafficking. They could be brought here and tucked away until arrangements were made for their final destination. But was Waylon the sort of man who would go along with that scheme? He seemed kind and decent, but her radar for detecting villains wasn't working well. From the moment when she gazed into Julian's azure eyes, she'd been willing to believe that he had more in common with a smart, handsome professor than an upper-level thug in Lorenzo's operation.

She watched as Cara moved her bench to the next stall and greeted a black horse with a blaze of white on his forehead. She motioned for Angie to join her. "Come on, you can feed him the apple."

"No thanks." She put on her jacket, glad for the rhinestone armor to protect her from horses and other dangerous creatures.

"Are you going to be working here?" Waylon asked.

"I think she should be a performer at the Burlesque," Cara said.

Oh, hell no. But she didn't want to say anything that would insult Cara's mother. "I don't have any special talents."

"But you're pretty," the little girl said.

"Can't argue with that," Waylon said. "You're pretty enough to be a headline stripper."

Cara hopped off the bench, stamped her foot and glared at him. "How many times do I got to tell you? They're not strippers. They're performers."

Angie shot her a thumbs-up.

Waylon touched the brim of his hat in a sign of respect. "I'll try to remember. Young lady, it appears to me that you've got one more horse to feed."

While Cara got back to her task of distributing apples, Angie looked up at the cowboy. "That's quite a shiner you've got. What happened?"

"Tripped and fell into a fence post." He shifted his weight from foot to foot, then he looked up and to the right—a nonverbal sign that he was lying…or trying to. He wasn't good at deception. "Guess I'm just clumsy."

"Is that when you hurt your lcg? I saw you limping."

"Must have been at the same time." He hobbled across the barn toward Cara. "I don't rightly recall."

"Maybe you had a concussion. Did you get checked out by a doctor?"

"I ain't got no need for doctoring. Besides, I'd have to drive all the way into Denver. It's too far and a waste of time."

And Waylon wouldn't want a doctor to examine him and discover other bruises that showed he'd been in a brawl. "Aren't there local clinics?"

"This here is a small mountain county without a lot of special services."

Also, she figured, there probably wasn't much of a police presence. Nick's was a nearly perfect location for transporting illegal goods. They were close to Denver but separated by county lines that limited jurisdiction and investigation from big-city law enforcement.

When she took on this assignment, she thought she'd need to spend a couple of weeks investigating the organization and determining the location that would be used for trafficking. Her intuition told her that there was no need to look any further. The trafficking operation was certainly being funneled through Nick's. She'd fallen right into the middle of Lorenzo's spiderweb.

She was determined to put an end to it…an end to him.

Chapter Four

The snapping of two bullwhips—louder than gunfire—echoed against the silver striped walls inside Nick's Burlesque. Calamity Jane was dressed in a denim thong, a holster, a skimpy fringed vest and red cowboy boots. She'd already taken off her red cowgirl hat, and her curly brown hair bounced around her shoulders as she went through her routine with a whip in each hand.

Julian watched impatiently. Not that Jane's act was boring. She took aim at beer cans on a ledge onstage. One by one, she tore through them while never losing the beat to "American Woman." After a strut down the spotlighted runway, she used her whips to extinguish candles on two of the tables close to the stage. The small but enthusiastic audience applauded. Most of these guys had seen the show before and knew what was coming. They cheered when Jane pulled three wooden targets onto the stage and drew one of the throwing knives from her holster. Other knives awaited her on a special table. After a sexy bump and grind, she took aim at the first target that outlined the shape of a man. Three throws. *Thunk-thunk-thunk.* Three hits. Head, heart and crotch.

She was deadly accurate. He couldn't imagine that Jane was afraid of anything, but Cara had implied fear when she told him that her mom needed him. Julian would stand on his head to help Jane out, definitely didn't want to lose her. She was a draw, one of the most popular acts at the Burlesque. She'd worked at some of Lorenzo's other clubs in Denver but preferred Nick's because of Julian's rules prohibiting full nudity and fraternization with the customers. Some of the other dancers didn't mind showing more skin and picking up bigger tips. Not Jane. She'd told him that being a good mother was the most important thing in her life. She adored Cara.

The kid was bright, no doubt about that, and she had ten times the street smarts of most adults. That little girl had been clever enough to know that her mom couldn't chase after her while she was onstage. Cara must have waited for that precise moment before running out the door of Nick's Burlesque. This marked the third time he'd caught Calamity Jane bringing her daughter to work, and he couldn't let it slide.

Julian made his way around the club to the stage door, where he slipped inside. From the stage, he heard renewed cracking from Jane's whips. At an outdoor event, he'd seen her light a couple of specially treated whips on fire which made a spectacular effect in the darkness but was against regulations for the club. Near a long backstage table covered with a sparkling array of makeup and glitter, he motioned to Lola—a tall brunette in a flamenco-style dress who had a surprisingly operatic mezzo-soprano voice.

"I know why you're here," Lola said as she adjusted the ruffled skirt that she'd rip off during her aria from *Carmen*. "It's Cara, right?"

"Bringing a minor child to the club is against the rules."

"Maybe those rules ought to change. I've got a couple of kids myself, and I'd be willing to pay if you set up some kind of day care."

"Not a chance." Was she blind? Couldn't she see the obvious? Nick's was an adult establishment with drinking, gambling and sexy performers. Though he wanted to believe that these were victimless crimes, he knew that lines sometimes got blurred. People got drunk. Fights broke out. "I can't guarantee it would be safe, even if the day care was in a separate area."

"Why not?" Lola tapped him on the chest with the long-stemmed paper rose she always held between her teeth during her performance of the "Pole Dance of the Toreador."

"Number one, our patrons don't want to be bothered by children. Number two, this isn't a good environment for kids. And number three, I'm glad you feel like you can come to me with your concerns, but I'm not your caretaker. I'm your employer."

"So?"

"No day care, Lola. Now, tell me what Cara is so upset about."

"No idea. She probably just wanted to get your attention."

He hoped that was the only issue. The sooner this situation was taken care of, the sooner he could get back to Angie. She was up to something, and he needed to figure out what was going on. Her background references from sources in California didn't tell the whole story about Ms. D'Angelo. She'd already admitted that she erased her past and gave herself a new identity. What else was she hiding?

He heard the sound of Jane's act coming to a close with a flurry of swirling whips. She dashed backstage holding her red cowgirl hat filled with tips. As soon as she caught her breath, she confronted him. "I know you're mad."

"Yes."

"I can explain."

The backstage area offered zero privacy. In addition to the dancers and crew milling around, there were hidden cameras and mics, supposedly for the protection of the performers but the surveillance also gave an insight into potential hustles these ladies could be planning. No cameras in the bathrooms, but there was audio surveillance. The three private dressing rooms, including Jane's, were discreet. He followed her into the room and closed the door. The scent of leather from her whips and holster mingled with a woodsy perfume.

"I'm listening," he said.

"Just before I went onstage, somebody told me that Cara ran off, and I'm guessing she went looking for you. Where is she?"

"Don't worry. I left her with a reliable adult."

"Are you sure this person is responsible?"

There were a number of reasons that Angie couldn't be trusted, but Julian couldn't imagine that she'd harm a child. "She's a new hire, assigned to revamp the OTB operation."

"You left her with a woman? Good! Cara tends to get attached to men. She sees all of them as potential father figures, but I don't have to tell you that."

Jane unfastened her holster and hung it on a peg before she stepped behind a screen to change. Not wanting to accidentally ogle, he trained his gaze on a photo of Jane and Cara that sat on her dressing table. They were riding on a sorrel horse with mountains in the background. "You can't keep bringing her to work."

"I'm sorry."

He noticed that the apology didn't come with a promise to never do it again. "Cara said you needed my help. What's going on?"

"I saw something I probably shouldn't have, and now this jackass is following me. I don't recognize him." She was babbling, nervous. "He's got a dark beard and a scar on his forehead. Does he work here? I'm sure there's a simple explanation. Maybe he just got a job in one of the kitchens?"

Her obvious tension worried him. Jane wasn't the sort of woman who got easily frightened. "What was the jackass doing?"

"I don't want to get anybody in trouble." She poked her head out from behind the screen. "Can you promise that you won't fire anybody or put them on leave or dock their pay?"

"I'll do whatever is necessary if there's real danger. Tell me what you saw."

She dove back behind the screen. When she emerged, she was wearing jeans and a plaid flannel shirt. Except for the glitter and exaggerated stage makeup, she looked like somebody who worked at a ranch. "Yesterday, I got here early and went out to the barn. Waylon lets me take the horses out for a run so they'll get exercise. When I was getting back, I heard a commotion from inside the horse barn. Somebody with a deep voice yelled a bunch of threats."

"Do you remember what was said?"

"A whole lot of cursing and stuff like, 'You'd better not tell. Keep quiet or else.'"

"What were they supposed to keep quiet about?"

"I don't know." She plunked down in the chair at her dressing table to put on her sneakers. "I rode closer. That's when I spotted this guy storming away. If I'd been armed, I would have nailed him. But I got distracted by what I saw in the barn. Waylon was bleeding and struggling to stand. He'd been hurt bad, and I rushed to help him."

Jane shuddered, clearly upset by this incident. Later today, Julian could check yesterday's video from the horse barn. "Did Waylon tell you what the fight was about?"

"He said it was just a scuffle, told me to forget I'd ever seen that guy. And I probably would have done that. But this afternoon I saw him again. Oh, damn, what am I going to do?" She dabbed under her eyes with a tissue, wiping away tears before they fell and smudged her mascara. "He was standing on the sidewalk across the street from my house in Denver. He knows where I live, where my daughter goes to school."

"Did he say anything?"

"I didn't give him the chance. I picked Cara up from school and drove here." She looked up at him. "What if he comes after us?"

"Is there anybody else you told about this?"

She shook her head, sending ripples through her brown curls. "I told Cara to watch out for a guy with a beard and a scar, but I didn't want to talk to anybody until I knew what was going on. Julian, what should I do?"

"You and Cara stay here tonight on the concierge level."

"Is it safe?"

"The guys who work on that level are trained bodyguards, former Marines."

"That means they're sharpshooters."

"They'll protect you." He rested his hand on her shoulder. "And if the first line of defense fails, you've got your guns, your knives and your whips. You'll be fine."

"Why did that man with the scar come after me?"

"I'm not sure." *A giant understatement.* He was aware that something big was going down in the next couple of weeks, but Nick Lorenzo hadn't seen fit to brief him on the details. Julian was responsible for what happened at Nick's but knew very little about the rest of Lorenzo's operations.

He hoped the man with the scar was nothing more than a bully with a grudge against Waylon, hoped their fight had no deeper significance. But he suspected deeper problems were on the horizon. The gentlemen's club was relatively successful but didn't make massive profits, not even with the casino. Sooner or later, Lorenzo would get greedy. There would be demands.

He heard a heavy knock on the dressing room door. “Can I come in?”

It was Rudy. His uncle Nick had probably assigned this kid to be Julian’s assistant so that Rudy could keep an eye on him. Trouble was in the air. “Get in here.”

Rudy stuck his head inside. His heavy, dark eyebrows raised and his beak of a nose twitched from side to side as if sniffing. “Hi, Miss Jane.”

“Howdy,” she drawled. “What are you doing here?”

“You’re going to be seeing a lot of me. I’m Julian’s new assistant.”

Julian stepped toward him. “You were supposed to be watching Angie.” He purposely avoided mention of Cara. The last thing he needed was an explosion from Calamity Jane.

“Don’t worry, boss. Everything is okay.” He swaggered into the dressing room, hitched his thumbs in his pockets and surveyed the whips, knives and skimpy, sparkly outfits. “Anytime there’s trouble backstage, Miss Jane, you can call on me to help. I’m your man.”

“Angie was supposed to wait for me in the coffee shop,” Julian said.

“Well, sir, she and Cara changed their minds. They went to see the horses before it got dark.”

Jane bolted to her feet. “My daughter is at the horse barn?”

“Yes, ma’am.”

“The one place I told her *not* to go.”

She darted from the room and headed toward the rear exit. Julian followed.

Rudy brought up the rear. “Did I do something wrong?”

“You’ve seen Jane’s act,” Julian said. “Once I saw her

snap the buttons off her boyfriend's jeans with her whip because she thought he was cheating on her. You'd better hope nothing bad happened to her kid. Run and keep up with her."

Rudy blew past him like a nervous tornado.

Chapter Five

With his phone pressed to his ear, Julian made his way through the back hallways of Nick's. His first call was to Tamara Rigby to check on the progress of picking up Angie's luggage and to reserve a suite on the concierge level for Jane and Cara. Then he called the concierge desk to alert them to the arrival of new guests. Then he contacted the tech expert in the surveillance room and asked him to pull up footage of the horse barn for the last two days. He slipped his phone into an inner pocket of his blazer. The situation was under control.

He exited through a door by the loading dock where cases of beer were being off-loaded. A dark blue van for Valentino's Bakery and Wedding Cakes nestled into a parking spot by the kitchen door, which didn't necessarily mean that fresh bread was being delivered. Valentino the Baker preferred using his vans for personal transportation. If the Baker was here, he might be dining with Nick Lorenzo. Julian reminded himself that he needed to move fast if he hoped to catch the big boss and get some straight answers, assuming that Lorenzo would be honest with him. *Not good odds on that bet.*

A cluster of kitchen workers gathered at a picnic table by the fence to taste the beer and have a smoke. The normal bustle at Nick's seemed to be moving forward at an unperturbed pace, but he sensed undercurrents of trouble.

Night had fallen. The outdoor LED lights spread illumination across the asphalt road and parking area. Julian strode toward the horse barn. After working three years at Nick's, he'd become more than a manager. He'd learned to walk a fine line between efficiency and empathy. His duty was to keep the various businesses running, but he cared about the people who worked for him and their needs. Lorenzo warned that Julian was too approachable, too soft. Lola felt comfortable about demanding a day care center. Jane confided in him. Waylon needed his protection.

Julian couldn't turn away, but he couldn't hold this delicate balance forever. Sooner or later, he'd have to leave Nick's. But not today...today he worked for Nick Lorenzo and was doing a good job.

As he approached the barn, a tableau unfolded under the lights outside the open double doors. Jane squatted down in front of Cara, alternating hugs and kisses with severe scolding. Rudy rested his hand on his shoulder holster and scanned in all directions, obviously looking for something to shoot. Waylon pulled down the brim of his hat to hide the bruises on his face. And then, there was Angie in her sparkly pink jacket with her long platinum ponytail draped behind her like a flag. Her slender fingers covered her lips, and he had the distinct impression that she was holding back laughter.

When she spotted him, she gave a nod of recognition and a conspiratorial grin, as if to say: *Good luck with this mess, glad it's you and not me.* She tapped Cara on her skinny little shoulder and pointed out that Julian was almost here. All eyes turned toward him.

He inhaled, breathing in the scent of hay and horses that

reminded him of his youth in Wyoming. He pushed his glasses up on his nose and inserted himself into the scene.

"Are you okay, Cara?"

She bobbed her head. "I'm good."

"Jane?"

She positioned herself behind her daughter, holding Cara to keep the girl from dashing off somewhere. "Thanks, Julian. We're going to be fine."

"You and Cara will stay here tonight. I just talked to the guys on the concierge level, and they have a suite for you. Order room service from any of the restaurants."

"Can I get anything I want?" Cara asked.

He imagined the little princess calling for platters of sushi and lobster followed by ice cream sundaes. "Your mom will place the order."

"I really appreciate this," Jane said. "Before we get settled for the night, I ought to go backstage to pick up a few things."

"It's better if you and Cara go directly to your room and stay there. Rudy will escort you. If you need anything, tell the guy at the concierge desk, and he'll take care of it."

The five bodyguards who shared the concierge duties were among his most trusted employees. Using their training as former Marine sharpshooters and experts in hand-to-hand combat, they kept the concierge floor safe for those who might be in peril. On the flip side, they might also be called upon to contain Lorenzo's enemies. On one occasion, they spent a week guarding an ex-wife who needed to be removed from the property and sent far away. Sometimes, Nick Lorenzo extended hospitality to other crime organizations and cartels that were represented by dangerous people—animals that couldn't be left unchecked.

This particular assignment—guarding Jane and Cara—was a winner for the concierge team. Julian was fairly sure that his bodyguards would be happy to spend time with Calamity Jane. They could exchange tips on gun handling and whips.

"What about Angie?" Cara asked. "Is she going to stay with us?"

"She'll also have a room on the concierge level. After I finish showing her around, I'll bring her upstairs." He shot Rudy a glance. "Make sure they get to their suite."

"I'm on it." He herded Jane and Cara toward Nick's.

Julian's first problem was solved: Jane and Cara were no longer in harm's way. Next, he needed to find out why the man with the scar had attacked the old cowboy. Julian glanced toward the barn door. Waylon had disappeared. Why? Was he hoping to avoid the inevitable conversation? Julian muttered, "Where the hell did he go?"

"He's back by the horse stalls," Angie said. She placed her hand on Julian's forearm as if she could restrain him with a touch. "Waylon probably doesn't want to talk about getting beat up. It's embarrassing to admit, especially to the boss. Not that it's any of my business."

"You're right about that." He patted her hand and deliberately removed it. "What happens between me and my employees is not your problem."

His plate was full. He had a load of other things to worry about, including the sexy blonde who stood beside him. He wasn't sure he should be talking in front of Ms. D'Angelo until he knew her real identity. Was she going to mess up everything he'd worked so hard to build? Creating this gentlemen's club hadn't been easy. Now that everything was up and running, he hated to see it fall apart.

Turning away from her, he took a stride toward the horse barn. Getting rid of Angie wouldn't be easy. She fell into step beside him. "Waylon hasn't done anything wrong. He told us that he feels terrible about putting Jane and Cara in danger."

"Maybe you should wait out here."

"If there's really any danger, I'd rather not stand outside like a pink rhinestone target," she said. "Don't worry. I won't get in the way."

Since she'd already heard everything Cara, Jane and Waylon had to say, there wasn't much point in trying to keep her out of the loop. Inside the barn, he approached the old man. "If you don't mind, Waylon, I want to see your face."

Reluctantly, he took off his hat. Gray hair matted on his forehead, and his complexion was waxy and pale. The dim light inside the barn masked his bruises, but he still looked like he'd wrestled with a lawn mower. His left eye was black-and-blue. His jaw was swollen. Bandages covered a couple of cuts on his face, and he'd hidden any damage to his hands with worn leather work gloves.

He lifted his chin and said, "My noggin got banged around, but it ain't bad."

"Did you go to a doc?"

Waylon shook his head. "I don't need anybody poking and prodding and taking X-rays. I'm okay."

"Stubborn," Julian said under his breath. "Here's the deal, Waylon, I can't force you to seek medical attention, but I strongly suggest it. In the meantime, you're taking two days off with pay, starting now."

"No, sir, that doesn't work for me. I'm starting a new project."

"What project?"

"Me," Angie said. "Waylon agreed to give me horseback riding lessons."

"I thought you hated horses."

"I do. This is an opportunity to get over my fears. I

mean, as long as I'm running the off-track betting operation, I should know something about the animals."

Her logic made sense. Apparently, Waylon agreed, because he puffed out his chest and braced himself to take a stand. Julian had bigger things to worry about. "Fine, you two can plan your timing for Angie's horseback riding lessons, but I still want Waylon to take off two days at least. The other cowboys can fill in for you."

"Then it's settled," Angie said as she headed for the door. "Let's get back to our tour of Nick's. I can't wait to see my office."

"I'm not done," Julian said. "I have a couple of questions for Waylon…if you don't mind."

"Sorry for the interruption."

She was polite; he had to give her credit for that. Bossy *and* polite made a dangerous combination. He couldn't get mad at her but couldn't allow himself to be railroaded. She took a step backward and went silent as though she could fade into the woodwork. *Impossible!* No matter how hard she tried, this flashy woman would never be invisible.

He turned to the battered cowboy. "What was the fight about?"

"I caught the guy sneaking around by the garage and told him this area was off-limits and he needed to leave. I thought he might be a member of the club so I was careful not to be rude. He seemed to understand, gave me a nod and took off. But he wasn't gone, not for long. About an hour later, I saw him again. This time, I yelled for him to get away from here, and I might have cussed a little."

"Was anybody with him?" Julian asked.

"Not that I could tell."

"Did he give you his name?"

"He did not, and I never saw him before."

"After you yelled the second time, what happened?"

"He came after me like a rabid badger, charged into the barn and started throwing punches. I'm not much of a fighter, but I could tell that this guy knew where to hit and make it hurt. He slammed me up against the stalls and kept hollering about how I better not tell anybody about this or else. That's when Jane rode up, and the guy took off." His hesitant eye contact was both sad and courageous. "That son of a bitch better not try to hurt her."

"Don't worry about Jane and Cara. Nothing bad is going to happen to them. I'm more concerned about you, Waylon. Maybe you ought to stay in Denver with your sister."

"I won't bring trouble to her doorstep," he said. "My cabin is safe. I've got alarm systems and firearms. The guy with the scar got the jump on me once. Ain't going to happen twice."

Julian realized that Angie had analyzed the situation perfectly. Waylon felt responsible for Jane being threatened, and he was more embarrassed than hurt. "Next time—if there is a next time—I want you to call me first thing. Now, you should head on home."

"I was just about to do that. Larson is working the night shift, and he ought to show up real soon."

"You go," Julian said. "We'll wait until Larson gets here."

Before Waylon left, Angie gave him a hug and promised to call about the riding lessons. Then she joined Julian to watch as the old cowboy limped across the grounds to an area where cars were parked. "You handled that well," she said.

"I have my moments."

He strolled outside and led her to the whitewashed corral fence attached to the barn. Standing here in the shadows, he could look up and see the stars coming out. Nightfall in the mountains was amazing and beautiful.

The inky black sky filled with stars—a thousand times more than were visible in a city. To the east, the glow from Denver's lights was visible. He pointed to a bright star. "That's Vega. Behind that is the jaw of Draco the dragon. That square shape to the north is supposed to be the body of Pegasus the flying horse."

"Where's Scorpio?" she asked. "That's my birth sign."

"I don't know." He wasn't into astrology and not an expert in astronomy, either. He just liked stargazing. "When I was growing up in Lander, Wyoming, me and my brother sat on the porch every night after dinner. He'd play his guitar, and I'd look up and dream about the future."

"Did your dreams come true?"

Not yet. He looked down at her face…so beautiful in the starlight. This conversation had gotten too personal for his taste. He needed to keep his distance from her…and everybody else for that matter. "So, Angie, do you have any questions?"

"Tons," she said. "Where do you want to start?"

"Give me something easy."

"I think I already know the answer to this one. Waylon was assaulted, but it doesn't sound like anybody contacted the local police."

She had to be kidding! According to her résumé, Angie had worked for other crime organizations in California and Nevada. She wasn't naive, couldn't possibly think they'd knowingly invite a cop into their house. "We prefer to deal with lawbreakers ourselves."

"That's what I thought. While we're on the topic of investigating, I noticed cameras in the lobby and also here in the horse barn. Do you have eyes and ears everywhere?"

"I do," he said without apology. "And my equipment is state-of-the-art. The cameras out here are designed to keep an eye on the horses and the expensive machinery in the garage." As soon as he had the chance to get to his surveillance room, he'd rewind backward in time to the fight with Waylon. If he was lucky, he'd be able to figure out what the man with the scar was looking for. "Surveillance is necessary. Nick's has a lot of cash businesses, especially with the casino. We need to be able to check what comes in and what goes out."

"Are there cameras in the hotel?" she asked.

"In every hallway." He could guess what she really wanted to know. "Don't worry about privacy. Nobody is going to take pictures of you in your room."

"It wouldn't be the first time." Her full, ruby-red lips frowned at what had to be a bad memory. "I don't like being spied on."

"Nobody does. Next question."

"Is Nick's open all night?"

"We sure are. Since we're a private club, we're not hampered by rules that govern other establishments. Some of the restaurants and the burlesque show close at midnight, but nobody wants to shut down a casino or pull the plug on a high stakes poker game when somebody else is losing big."

"What's your game?" she asked.

"Don't have one."

"Come on, Julian. Everybody has a favorite. Blackjack?"

She didn't know him, didn't know his background and didn't realize the significance of what she'd just said. Angie had just stepped over the line into forbidden territory. Julian didn't gamble and didn't drink. He'd lost four years of his young life to addiction and never wanted to relapse. Though he no longer attended AA meetings, he'd been sober for six years.

He stepped away from the corral. "Here comes Larson. I'll fill him in, and we can finish our tour."

He could feel the intense focus of her dark eyes as she walked beside him. "Something wrong?"

He didn't respond. This was his life and his problem. He didn't let anybody climb inside his head and poke around, especially not a pretty California girl with a mysterious past.

She gazed up at him. "Was it something I said?"

He tapped the face of his watch. They were wasting time. He had things to do, places to go. "I'm running late."

"No problem, I'm capable of exploring by myself."

Not a chance. He didn't want Angie wandering through the hotel, stirring up trouble. "I'll contact Tamara to finish your tour. When you get to your room, feel free to order anything from room service."

"Will I see you later?"

He didn't trust himself to visit her suite late at night when she'd changed from her sparkly jacket into a silky gown and unfastened her long, straight, platinum hair. "Tomorrow. If you have a problem, call me."

Switching into high gear, he briefed Larson, rushed to the hotel front desk and turned Angie over to Tamara. He entered his office on the second floor, closed the door, leaned against it and exhaled a long, ragged breath. She'd gotten inside his defenses and tweaked his nerves. And she'd done it so easily, as though she made a regular habit of shredding a man's life and skipping off to a riding lesson with her ponytail swinging behind her.

He went through the stack of papers on his desk. By the time he was done with the sorting, shuffling and signing, Julian felt like he was more in control. He put in a call to Nick Lorenzo, failed to reach him and left a text. Talking to Nick might give him all the answers he needed about the man with the scar.

Down a short hallway, Julian entered the surveillance room where dozens of camera feeds showed the activities taking place at Nick's. Gordon, the tech genius who helped build this system, sat in the midst of these screens and flashing lights. He swiveled his bobble head on his skinny neck and looked up at Nick. "What do you want to see?"

"The cameras at the barn and surrounding area. I need to go back two days." He gave Gordon an idea of what to look for. "There have been reports of a man with a scar lurking around in that area. I want to see where he goes and what he's after. Also, let's zoom in for a tight close-up so we can use our facial recognition software."

"Give me a minute."

Julian took a seat. There was a bit of private business he wanted to handle. When he'd told Angie that there would be no secret photos of her, he'd meant it. But there were, in fact, two cameras and mics in her bedroom suite. He punched a series of buttons to access those cameras. His intention was to shut them down…but there was no harm in taking a peek…just to be sure she was all right.

Both screens were dark.

He checked the microphones. Dead.

A spark of panic fired up inside him. He didn't want to believe that something bad had actually happened to her. The problem had to be in the equipment. "What's going on with this thing?"

Gordon popped up at his elbow. "Let's run it backward and see what's up."

They went back five minutes, then eight and then he saw Angie. She gazed directly into the lens of the camera and held up a sheet of hotel stationery with a message scrawled in lipstick. "Bye, bye, bye."

Gordon snorted a laugh. “I like her.”

“I’ll let you check out her phone and return it to her.”

Angie reached up with the lipstick and painted over the camera lens.

Julian stared at the darkened screen and shook his head. *I like her, too.*

Chapter Six

After spending two days reinforcing her cover story by digging through spreadsheets, calculating algorithms and reprogramming computer software in her OTB office, Angie was eager to get out of the windowless basement at Nick's and attend a party. The occasion was the sixtieth birthday of Nolan Zapata, and lots of important people from Lorenzo's shady businesses all across Denver and the surrounding area would be there. Mingling with this crowd might shed light on her investigation, which was something she desperately needed.

Since her work in OTB relied on computer data, she had access to cyber records for Lorenzo's businesses. She'd hacked, studied and scanned but had found nothing definite about the size of the human trafficking operation, how it worked and when it was supposed to start. A few disturbing threads of data connected Lorenzo with coyotes known for transporting illegal immigrants and with a cartel involved in the sex trade. One of the main players in that cartel was named Zapata—just like Lorenzo's chief number cruncher.

She'd expected to find more details about payments. Trafficking in human beings required negotiation and cooperation. There should have been more records and detailed plans, but her cyber search had been mostly futile.

Tonight at the party, she planned to sneak into Lorenzo's office and download data from his personal computer onto a flash drive—a risky scheme. She had a better chance of getting info by chatting up Lorenzo's associates at the cocktail party. If she played her cards right, she might get these guys to blab about the impending operation.

One thing was for sure: that blabbermouth was *not* Julian. During the time he'd spent with her over the past couple of days, he'd been funny, polite and—*God help me!*—sexier than any man had a right to be. He'd told her nothing. She wasn't sure what it would take to make him open up to her. Maybe they'd never connect. Maybe she'd finally met the man who could resist her teasing and her lies.

Until she had details, there was no point in contacting the local FBI. She had to know enough to catch Lorenzo's guys in the act, which meant keeping her eyes and ears open at Zapata's birthday party. Tamara Rigby, also invited, advised her to dress up—the glitzier the better. But Tamara showed up at the door to Angie's suite on the concierge level wearing a blah cocktail dress with long, lacy sleeves. The beige of her dress was almost an exact match for her straight, chin-length hair.

When she looked at Angie, her eyes popped. "Wow."

Angie's jumpsuit was glistening white, strapless and streaked with gold threads. Her jacket and belt were metallic gold. She'd twisted her long platinum locks into a knot on top of her head which was fastened in place with decorative hair chopsticks, one of which doubled as a weapon. The other was a lockpick. "Am I overdressed?"

"You're perfect. I'm the one who needs sprucing up."

"No problem." She went to her closet and selected a curve-hugging red sheath with a plunging neckline. "You can't go wrong with red."

Tamara hesitated for less than a minute. “Do you think it’ll fit?”

“I’m sure it will.” Angie grabbed the dress and led Tamara into the landing outside her room where one of the hunky bodyguards sat behind the concierge desk. After a wave to him, she knocked on the door to Jane and Cara’s suite.

As soon as Jane opened the door, Angie said, “We have a problem. Tamara needs to get totally glam before Julian picks us up in fifteen minutes.”

Jane welcomed them inside. “You came to the right place. Come with me, Tamara. We’ll start with your makeup.”

“Shouldn’t I try on the dress first?”

“That comes after I fix your face. I don’t want to get makeup on your clothes.”

Jane escorted her to the big mirror outside the bathroom, sat her down on a dainty little stool and flipped open a makeup box with a rainbow array of highlights, shadows and rouge. While Jane launched Tamara’s makeover, Cara took Angie’s hand and pulled her across the room to one of the windows. Cara’s long brown hair hung loose past her shoulders.

“How are you doing?” Angie asked the little girl.

“Bored,” she said. In case Angie didn’t catch her frustration, Cara repeated, “Bored, bored, bored.”

“You’re not allowed to run around outside the room.”

“It’s like being in jail.”

“Not really. This is a classy place.”

These rooms were a mirror image of her suite. Designed for comfort but with a touch of luxury, the sitting room—furnished with a sofa, two overstuffed chairs and a table—was equipped with a big-screen TV, sound system and video game console as well as a kitchenette. The bedroom was in a separate chamber to the right.

With a dramatic sigh, Cara pivoted away from the window and flopped into the chair behind the desk. "Mom has a thing for one of the concierge dudes. Tomorrow, he's gonna take us out for target practice."

"I saw Waylon today." Angie had her first riding lesson, which meant she'd gotten up on the horse but hadn't gone anywhere—kind of like her undercover investigation. "He wanted me to say hello to you. As soon as everything is safe, he promises to take you out for a ride."

"Whatever." Cara rolled her eyes.

Angie recognized the attitude; this little girl had already learned not to count on promises from well-meaning adults. "Why did you want me to follow you over here? Is there something you want to tell me?"

"Look out the window."

Squinting into the darkness, Angie could see four stories down to the loading dock and a rear door from the kitchen. A couple of guys were sitting outside on the steps and talking. Across the road and to the left was the light outside the bunkhouse. The horse barn wasn't visible from this angle. "If there's something I'm supposed to see, I don't get it."

"After lunch, I was looking out and I saw her. I saw Gigi, my friend."

Her imaginary friend? "Where was she?"

"On the hill behind the bunkhouse. She dodged behind bushes. I think she's hiding from somebody, maybe the guy who punched Waylon."

A possible scenario unfolded inside Angie's head. If Gigi existed, she might have been part of a group being trafficked through this location. She might have escaped and gone into hiding at Nick's. "Can you remember the first time you played with her?"

"Exactly two weeks ago. I remember because it was a Saturday so I didn't have school. Waylon was supposed to babysit me but he was busy with the horses." She twisted a strand of hair in her fingers. "I didn't mind that he wasn't paying attention. Hanging out in the barn is cool. That's where I met Gigi. She's funny, but I think she might be a liar because she says she's nine and she's no bigger than me. She made herself a nest in one of the empty stalls."

Finding Gigi took on a new importance. The child could be in danger of being taken again by Lorenzo's men. If Angie could convince Julian to run the video from the surveillance cameras at the barn backward, they might see evidence of Cara's story. If she told him that Gigi might lead to the guy who punched Waylon, Julian might go along with her plan…or he might totally reject it. She just wasn't sure where she stood with him. When they first met, he seemed suspicious but friendly. And when they were standing outside the horse barn under the stars, he warmed up to her, let down his guard and talked about his childhood in Wyoming. Then she pushed too hard, and Julian shut down.

He hadn't been rude over the past few days, but he kept their conversations short and to the point. He didn't seem to trust her, which was pretty much the way she felt about him. But would he help her find Cara's mysterious friend? "Have you seen Gigi again?"

"Nope."

"If you do, have your mom call me."

"Okay." Cara popped out of the chair, suddenly brimming with restless energy. "I wish you didn't have to go to that stupid party. You could stay here and play with me."

"Here's the deal," Angie said. "If you haven't seen Gigi

by Monday, I'll take you with me on my riding lesson, and we'll look for her."

The kid grabbed her around the waist for a clumsy hug that really felt good. Angie stroked her fingers through the girl's smooth brown hair, and Cara snuggled against her. Their shared warmth reminded her of hugs with Marigold. Their time together on the streets of Denver had been scary but also hopeful. Marigold had been a true friend.

"We're done," Jane announced as she escorted Tamara into the room.

The makeup—including an expertly done smoky eye—was gorgeous, and Jane had used some kind of product to make Tamara's hair shine with a soft luster. The dress was fantastic, as Angie knew it would be—bright red with a deep-V neckline and a cinched waist. "Fantastic!"

"I look good," Tamara said with a note of wonderment.

"Better than good. You look amazing, and we've got to run before Julian gets impatient and leaves without us."

Tamara gave Jane a hug and thanked her.

"No kisses," Jane said, "you'll smudge the lipstick."

"Got it," Tamara said with a giggle.

And then, they were off.

JULIAN PARKED AT the entrance to Nick's, got out of his SUV and walked around to the sidewalk. Though he wasn't usually a fan of Lorenzo's parties and did everything he could to avoid them, he had a mission tonight. Somehow, he had to snag a few minutes of private time with the boss. Lorenzo hadn't returned any of his calls or messages, and Julian needed answers about the man with the scar.

Leif Farnsworth, the former Bronco quarterback who managed the sports betting operation, sauntered over and joined him. Blond, tall and handsome, he wore a brown leather jacket tailored to fit the span of his wide shoulders. Because Leif was a jock and good-looking, many people assumed he was a slab of brainless beefcake. They were wrong.

Not only did Leif have an encyclopedic memory for sporting statistics, he could calculate percentages and odds in his head. He played violin and regularly watched performances of Opera Colorado. When he'd attended Stanford on a football scholarship, he'd actually gone to classes and learned something. Julian enjoyed spending time with him.

"Where's the rest of our carpool?" Leif asked.

"The ladies are running late. No surprise. We're going with Tamara and Angie."

"Angie's a hard worker. She's been keeping her pretty little nose to the grindstone."

"Zapata gave her a deadline."

"Got it." Leif nodded. Zapata had a reputation of being dangerous. Not even a semifamous former athlete dared to cross him. "What's the story with Angie? What makes her tick?"

"She's single, spent the last couple of years in California, hates horses and is good at hand-to-hand combat. She had Murph on his knees in two minutes."

"Dangerous and beautiful, that's a scary combination, like a Venus flytrap."

The two women came through the exit side by side. When Julian spotted Angie dressed in shimmering white and gold, his heart flip-flopped inside his rib cage, which was not the reaction he wanted. Being attracted to her would, most likely, lead to trouble.

Beside him, Leif seemed to be having heart palpitations of his own. His voice caught in his throat. "I've never seen Tamara look like this. Red is good on her."

In her vivacious dress with the neckline that plunged all the way down, Tamara Rigby transformed from the uniformed supervisor for hotel operations to a creature of passion and maybe even desire. Julian had thought for a long time that Leif and Tamara would make a good couple. Both were smart; Tamara had an MBA in hospitality management. And both were cultured. Both had talents that were wasted at Nick's. Though Julian paid them well and promoted them quickly, he knew that these two could do better.

He nudged Leif's shoulder and said, "Let's make sure she's sitting in the back with you."

As soon as the women were seated with Angie in the passenger seat beside him, Julian pulled away from the curb. He tuned the radio to a classical station that was playing Rossini's greatest hits. The couple in the back seat of the SUV chatted intelligently about lyric opera in the early 1800s and this piece—a favorite of Tamara's—from *The Barber of Seville*.

Angie peered into the rear of the SUV, listened to them and then looked at him. "You must have known that Leif and Tamara were both opera fans. I think maybe you were playing matchmaker."

"I just set up the carpool."

"And I appreciate the ride." As she reached up to smooth her already perfect hairstyle, the glow from the dashboard highlighted her delicate profile. "Did you want for us to ride together for some kind of protection, like a safety-in-numbers thing?"

"Why would you think that?"

"After we talked to Waylon, you upped the security. Employees—especially the women—are escorted to the parking lot after dark. Cara and Jane are still living on the concierge level. While I'm on that subject, I approve of those concierge guys who have got to be former military and obviously know how to handle lethal weapons. Anyway, I'm guessing you never found the man with the scar."

He tried to brush her off. "I have the situation under control."

"Do you?"

There was an edge to her voice, and he wondered about her underlying motives. "My precautions are to make sure nobody else gets hurt. If you don't mind, let's drop it."

"Okay, but I'm still a little nervous. When you looked at the feeds from your surveillance cameras, did you find anything that might lead to the guy who attacked Waylon?"

"Not a thing."

He didn't have to repeat his request for her to drop the topic because Leif and Tamara had launched into a sing-along with the radio—a karaoke performance of the "Figaro, Figaro, Figaro" aria. If he'd told Angie about the surveillance feeds, it would have been a short conversation. He'd seen the man with the scar attack Waylon. There had been no audio to show what they were saying to each other but the video gave a clear picture of a bully attacking an old cowboy.

Over and over, Julian had studied the tapes. He'd memorized the physical characteristics of the man with the scar, learned how he walked and how he gestured with his hands. He and Gordon put together a facial recognition package that would alert them if the man with the scar showed up again at Nick's. It was important to find out what this guy was after.

The assailant had been lurking around outside the barn and the bunkhouse, which might be significant. Right now, that bunkhouse was unoccupied, but it was furnished with ten bunkbeds, a propane heater and stove. It was big enough for people to live there. Perfect for human trafficking.

As he drove through the western outskirts of Denver,

his fingers tensed on the steering wheel. For the past couple of months, he'd been worrying about subtle changes in operations that would affect Nick's. He'd become aware of a cover-up. Conversations would shut down when he joined the group. His receipts had been audited by Zapata's team of accountants…twice.

After putting together bits and pieces of information, his best guess was that Nick's was about to be turned into a hub for human trafficking. He hated that idea. The victims of these operations were little more than slaves—young women used for sex, indentured day laborers, forced housekeepers and nannies. When they were first hiring at Nick's, he'd been adamant about green cards and fair wages. He'd made his opinions known, and a lot of the guys weren't happy about his strict rules governing the women who worked in the Burlesque.

Tonight, he had to talk to Lorenzo and get answers. Not knowing what to expect was killing him. The only thing worse would be to learn the ugly truth.

Chapter Seven

"We're almost there," Julian announced. "Over there, on the right, you can see the house."

From the back seat, Tamara said, "I've heard a lot about this place. People call it the Glass Palace."

Angie leaned forward in the passenger seat of Julian's SUV and peered through the night, trying to get a better look at Lorenzo's unusual mansion. The upscale neighborhood in an area southwest of Denver consisted of sprawling properties of two, three or five acres that were landscaped for privacy with a combination of conifers, cottonwoods and aspens that blended into the rocky hillsides of a national forest. In this season—early October before the first major snowfall—the aspen leaves flashed gold in Julian's headlights.

He drove the SUV into a line of cars on a long, winding, two-lane road leading to the entrance. The closer they got to the house, the more spectacular it was. Dramatic spotlights defined the sharp angles of a modernistic design. The towering front of the house was floor-to-ceiling windows. Inside, Lorenzo's guests milled throughout, talking and drinking on three different levels. There were staircases, and a transparent cylinder that housed an elevator. For sure, this was a palace. Incredible!

She reminded herself that this remarkable structure had

been built with the profits of gritty, sleazy crime, which really wasn't a valid reason to find fault with the building. Instead she aimed her hostility at the residents of the house who were fair game for criticism. "You know what they say about people who live in glass houses."

From the back seat came the rumbling baritone of Leif Farnsworth. "They shouldn't throw stones."

"And they shouldn't walk around naked," said Tamara. "And they can't have secrets."

"I'm not so sure about that," Angie said. "Lorenzo has secrets."

"Everybody does," Julian said. "Tamara was commenting on the transparency of a glass house. The secrets are there, but it's hard to keep them hidden."

"I guess you're right. We all have secrets," she mused. This might be an opportunity to gather information from the others in her carpool. Not that she thought Tamara was hiding something that might pertain to her investigation. She didn't know whether Leif deserved closer scrutiny, but Julian had secrets that had baby secrets of their own. "I've got a game for us. We go around the car, and each one of us tells a secret."

"Okay," Tamara said. "Here's mine. I was married and divorced before I was twenty-two. And it wasn't for the reason you might suspect. I wasn't pregnant...just a bad judge of character."

"I never would have guessed that you had a wild side," Leif said.

"I don't, not really. After that, I learned to be even more careful."

"Tell that to your sexy red dress," he said. "Here's my big secret. This is actually something that bothers me. I never graduated from Stanford. I'm four credits short."

Angie heard the pain in his voice, and she was glad

when Tamara leaned over to console him. Those two had bonded like Velcro. She turned her focus on the man in the driver's seat. "Your turn, Julian."

"After you, I insist."

She wasn't constrained to the truth. Every trace of her real background had been erased. No one could tell if she was lying her ears off, which made her urge to share something of herself seem odd and unnecessary. For just this once, she wanted to bypass deception.

"I grew up in foster care," she said.

Honesty spilled through her lips and spread around her like a goopy puddle. Her wall of defense was melting.

"What happened to your parents?" Tamara asked.

"The system lost track of my father when I was a kid. Mom was an addict who was in and out of jail. I suppose I could find her if I wanted. But I don't."

"Was there anyone else?" Tamara said. "Any family."

"There was a girl who was my age." This was the second time she'd thought of Marigold in just a few hours. Being this close to Lorenzo must be sparking dangerous memories. "We were closer than sisters but life tore us apart. I miss her every single day."

Tears welled up behind her eyelids. *This is crazy! I don't cry.* This kind of uncensored reaction was why she avoided the truth. Sure, she had a lousy childhood and missed Marigold with all her heart, but those factors wouldn't help her solve the human trafficking issue. Her personal heartache wasn't enough to land Lorenzo in prison.

"What about Julian's secret?" Tamara asked. "Come clean, boss."

He shifted position behind the steering wheel, and Angie could tell that he was reluctant to open up. The fact that they had that defensive attitude in common made her wonder what else they shared. "Here goes," he said.

"It's no secret that I'm not a drinker or a gambler, but very few people know that I'm an addict. I've been sober for six years."

"Were you in AA?" Leif asked.

"Hell, yes. I did years of group meetings and one-on-one therapy. It's not easy to restart your life…nothing about addiction is easy. Every time I hear a dealer shuffle or a roulette wheel whir I get that prickly feeling across my shoulders. The cash in my wallet is ready to play. The worst part is that I can't drown my desire to gamble in booze or pot or any other high."

"Why on earth do you work here?" Tamara asked.

Angie knew the answer. To defeat your demons you had to face them. That was the reason she had joined the FBI. She needed to study and comprehend the many ways law enforcement had failed her as a child, and then she needed to do something about it.

Julian shot her a glance. "Maybe I like to play with fire."

"I get it." She finished his thought. "Be careful that you don't get burned."

AS JULIAN GUIDED the SUV in the line of cars leading to the front entrance of Lorenzo's house, his anxiety expanded inch by inch. Talking about his addiction was hard. Old fears and frustrations raked up and churned inside him. He hadn't been to a meeting in over a year. Maybe it was time to start again.

Angie huffed. "Why are we going so slow?"

"My guess," Julian said, "is that there's a metal detector at the door, and the valets are holding the cars until they're sure the guests are clean."

Apparently, he wasn't the only person who was serious about security. Frisking a bunch of gangsters was bound to take a while. He wouldn't be subject to a search. As manager of Nick's, Julian was above suspicion. He adjusted the bulge of his shoulder holster under his jacket, confident that he wouldn't be asked to disarm. He glanced between the seats and made eye contact with Leif. "Are you carrying?"

"Not tonight."

"Ladies, how about you?"

"Oh, please," Angie said. "Weapons make lousy accessories."

Since they weren't armed and therefore wouldn't run into trouble from the guys with the metal detectors, Julian could slip the SUV out of this interminable caravan and detour around to the rear of the house. He eased onto the shoulder of the road and drove to a one-lane dirt road—a path, really—that took a couple of quick turns and disappeared into the trees.

"Where are we going?" Tamara asked.

"The service entrance in the back."

He'd visited the Glass Palace several times and had taken every opportunity to study the architecture. The central structure was built in the 1920s when Frank Lloyd Wright's clean, modern style was popular. The house had been upgraded and expanded two or three times, including the replacement of much of the glass with quadruple-pane, bulletproof sheets that maintained the appearance of transparency but were as strong as a fortress.

The SUV bounced along the unpaved path as it curled through stands of trees and massive, granite chunks. Lights from the house glittered through the forest, enticing them to come closer. The sounds of conversation and laughter mingled with an undercurrent of music from a piano.

Finally, he drove into a clearing outside the house where several other vehicles from the caterers and waiters were parked. Julian would have to jockey around to find a space to leave his SUV that wasn't in the way.

He slipped the car into Park. "You three might as well go inside. After I find parking, I'll join you."

"Are you sure you don't want company?" Angie asked. "I'll wait with you."

"Go, I'll catch up with you later."

He shooed them away, glad to have a moment of solitude before he entered Lorenzo's den and confronted him about the man with the scar. Leaning back in his seat, Julian turned off the headlights and inhaled a breath, hoping to center himself before he made his next move. From where he was sitting, he could see the kitchen area that fitted into the hillside behind the house. Toward the front, he saw three stories of glass and an acrylic staircase with steel gray steps that matched the polished marble on the floor. The people moving through this scene appeared to be floating. He noticed Angie melting into the crowd as she talked to Rudy and Carlos. Her glittering white-and-gold jumpsuit contrasted the men in dark suits. Not a surprise. No matter where she went, Angie would stand out.

His gaze was drawn to a guy in a silk shirt and a black vest who wore a baseball cap. His outfit was more casual than most of the other guests but not enough to make him too obvious. The thing that caught Julian's attention was the man's gait. As he moved across the second floor level and descended the staircase, his stride matched the figure Julian had been studying for two days on the surveillance feed from the barn. The scar on his forehead was hidden by that baseball cap and he'd shaved the beard, but the way he moved was familiar. When the guy tapped somebody else on the chest, Julian swore under his breath. He'd seen that gesture a hundred times, had memorized the shape of those stubby fingers. No doubt about it. This was the man who attacked Waylon.

Though his SUV was blocking two other cars, Julian didn't have time to search for a good parking spot. This might be his only chance to nab this guy. He threw open his car door and charged toward the house just as the man in the baseball cap stepped outside.

Trying not to alert the guy, Julian slowed his pace and ducked behind a blue delivery van from Valentino's Bakery and Wedding Cakes. When he peeked around the edge of the van, he saw the guy with the baseball cap staring directly at him.

Fine. Julian wasn't in the mood for games. He stepped into the light, no point in trying to hide. He was ready for this showdown.

The thug yanked off his cap and pushed back the hair on his forehead to show the jagged outline of his scar. His upper lip curled in a sneer, taunting. He stuck the cap back on his head and took off running, dodging through vehicles and diving into the forest.

Julian sprinted after him. While he ran, he drew his Glock from the shoulder holster. Though he couldn't see clearly enough to take aim, he needed to be ready. Slapping aside the low-hanging branches and stepping around rock formations, he went deeper into the forest.

As they got farther away from the Glass Palace, the darkness intensified. The moon was on the wane, and starlight barely penetrated the overhead branches. His pursuit was based more on instinct than vision. He stumbled and came to a stop amid a circle of rugged pine trunks.

Trying to ignore the noise from the party, Julian listened intently. He cast back in his memory to his youth in Wyoming when he'd gone hunting every weekend. In the dark, he couldn't use his ability as a tracker, not when it was important to move fast. He took off his glasses and closed his eyes. When he opened them, he saw the faint trail leading into the forest. Far ahead, he saw the leaves on a chokecherry bush rustle.

He figured the guy wouldn't go right because that direction led to the road and the endless line of cars approaching the house. Uphill to the left was the most likely direction. Did he see branches shaking? Did he hear the heavy breathing of a man on the run?

From behind, he heard someone approaching. Had the guy doubled back? Julian slipped into the shadow of a tree, raised his weapon and waited. Leif Farnsworth staggered forward.

Julian blocked his path. "What are you doing here?"

"Don't shoot. I thought I could help."

"Why are you here?"

"I dropped off the ladies, and then I went outside to find you. It didn't seem right for you to miss the party because you were parking the car." Moonlight spread across his shoulders, emphasizing a shrug. "I saw you running after a guy."

"And you jumped right in."

"Good guess, Professor. I know there's something weird going on at Nick's, something weirder than usual. If you let me, I'll help."

Julian didn't know how much he trusted the big man, but he knew Leif wasn't an idiot. He had a temper and was aware of the ethical problem of working for Lorenzo, but wasn't foolish.

Julian lowered his gun. "You go right. I'll go left. If you see him, yell."

"I'm on it."

The former quarterback darted through the trees as though evading a pass rush from the defensive line. Julian tried not to think of how Leif earned his nickname of "Falling Leif" because he'd been sacked so many times. Their chances of catching the man with the scar were minimal at best.

He had better odds talking to Lorenzo and getting him to explain what was happening. Was the man with the scar working for him? Or was he an enemy?

Chapter Eight

Inside the Glass Palace, Angie mingled with many guests from different strata. Solid-looking politicians rubbed shoulders with cowboys, rock musicians and divas dripping with diamonds. The attendance had to be over three hundred, and she doubted that most of them had come for the stated purpose of celebrating the sixtieth birthday of Nolan Zapata. They were here to enjoy the Glass Palace and maybe to curry favor with Nick Lorenzo. People didn't seem to care that he was a criminal who was about to sink to a new low in depravity with his human trafficking operation.

With her background and the constant deceptions that were the foundation of her life, Angie couldn't claim righteous indignation. Most definitely, she didn't think she was better than anyone else. But she hated to see Lorenzo get away with his crimes.

Rudy and Carlos joined her almost as soon as she entered. Rudy's somber outfit of black suit with black shirt and tie didn't disguise the blush of excitement that colored his cheeks. If Angie had to guess, she'd say this was the first time the kid had been invited to a grown-up event. Carlos was blasé, unflappable. He snagged a champagne glass from a passing waiter and handed it to her.

"I'm not much of a drinker," she said. Her thoughts immediately went to Julian and his sobriety. Functioning in environments like this without an alcohol buffer had to be difficult. "I don't suppose one glass will hurt."

"I'd like to hear your opinion," Carlos said. "This sparkling rosé comes from a winery on the western slope that I'm considering for an investment."

"Investment?"

"I might buy the place," he said with casual ease, suggesting that the purchase of a vineyard was no big deal.

She had to revise her opinion of Carlos. When he picked her up at the motel, she'd thought he was a low-level gofer which was terrible and inaccurate stereotyping on her part. *I need to be smarter.* She should have realized that he had status when he took a seat at the table with Zapata, Valentino and Julian. Finding out more about him would be wise, starting with learning his last name.

After a sip of bubbly, she wrinkled her nose. "It tickles my tongue, and it's kind of sweet and yummy. I'd say you should go for it. All you need is a name for the label. Maybe your family name."

"Zapata? No." He shook his head. "My *familia* has a history of controversy, even though we're now farmers and businessmen, like my uncle."

She should have known, should have done more research. Carlos was related to Nolan Zapata, and their *familia* had ties to a cartel from Colombia. She definitely needed to pay more attention to Carlos—a guy who tended to fade into the woodwork. "Whatever you call your wine, I'm sure it'll be a winner."

Rudy leaned close to her ear. "Who's the chick in the red dress you came in with?"

"Tamara Rigby, the woman who runs the hotel operations."

"No way," he said. "That mousy little worker bee is the lady in red?"

"Why don't you tell her you like the dress? I'm sure she'd appreciate the compliment." And Angie wouldn't mind time alone with Carlos. She turned to him. "How long have you been working for Lorenzo?"

"Ever since I graduated from college. My uncle wanted me to be an accountant like him, but I'm into real estate and investment. Colorado is a good place to buy and sell property."

"I'm sure that's true, but I've never seen anything like this house. Tell me about it."

As he described the layout and special features, they glided across polished marble floors toward a long table where a five-tier cake from Valentino's bakery stood waiting to be cut. This dining area had an open ceiling that was three stories high. On the second level, she spotted Tamara leaning against the clear acrylic half wall on the balcony. From the way she gestured and tossed her head, Angie could see that the lady in red was enjoying herself. On the third floor above her was Nick Lorenzo, looking down like an evil gargoyle.

She pointed him out to Carlos. "What's up there?"

"An art gallery," he said. "Behind the wall of art is the private area. That's where you find the bedrooms, bathrooms and offices."

Lorenzo's office was her targeted destination. After skillful hacking on her computer, she'd studied blueprints and also learned that there was a way to approach the office without being seen on any of the surveillance cameras. She dropped a comment that might be used as an excuse if she got caught sneaking around on the third floor. "I'd love to see the art."

"Not without an invite. Lorenzo is protective of his favorite treasures."

"The house is huge. Does anybody else live here?" In

her dossier for the case, Angie had learned that Lorenzo had been divorced for years but stayed close to his three adult children. "Maybe his kids?"

"They have their own houses and condos," Carlos said. "The only other person living here right now is Marion."

"A girlfriend?" Angie had very little info on Lorenzo's mistresses. The women seemed to drift into and out of his life like waves on a shore.

"She's an artist and actually acquired some of the masterpieces hanging on his upstairs walls, but I don't expect to see her around much longer. She's getting to that age, if you know what I mean."

She knew exactly what he meant. Lorenzo liked his women young. She looked up to the third floor where he'd been standing. He was gone, which meant it was time for her to get busy.

She couldn't politely detach from Carlos who directed her toward a maroon sofa where his uncle sat like a king waiting for the peasants to come forward and kiss his ring. Nolan Zapata twirled a flute of champagne between his bejeweled fingers. The only other time she'd seen him was that first casual meeting, and Angie was impressed with how well Zapata cleaned up. His thick black hair was combed back from his forehead, and he was so clean-shaven that his jaw gleamed like marble. He wore a silver brocade jacket with tuxedo trousers. Graciously, he rose to greet her.

"Congratulations on your birthday," she said.

"Thank you for the gift. I assume you're part of the group from Nick's who chipped in to buy me that trim little motorboat."

"That would be a rational assumption." She had *not* contributed. "Have you had a chance to look over my suggestions on how we can change the off-track betting operation?"

"No talk of business tonight," he said. "I'll look at your numbers on Saturday of next week as we agreed."

She knew her first ten days would be successful. With help from the forensic accounting department at the FBI, she had perfected a computer program that upped the profits. All she really had to do was install the new algorithms and let them run.

"Carlos has been showing me around," she said. "I didn't realize that you two were related. Is your whole family from Denver?"

"We come from a small town in New Mexico by the name of Ojos Caliente."

"Hot eyes," she translated.

He lowered himself onto the sofa and patted the space beside him, indicating that she should sit. His hard-edged gaze sliced through her like a blade. "I heard you were taking riding lessons from Waylon," he said.

"I thought learning about horses would help me with the off-track betting. I'm not really fond of barnyard animals."

"Racehorses aren't like the old gray mare in the barn," he said. "Those animals are Thoroughbreds, worth more than most people."

Spoken like a man who was about to embark on a human trafficking scheme. She suspected Zapata knew all about the attack on Waylon, and she carefully eased into the topic. "Poor Waylon got into a scuffle the other day,"

"Who was he fighting with?"

"I have no idea." She lied easily. "Julian said he'd take care of it."

"And I'm sure he will," Zapata said.

Digging for information, she asked, "How many of the employees at Nick's report to you?"

"A few." He brushed off her question.

"What about security men and women?"

"Excuse me, Angie."

Abruptly, he stood, which indicated that their conversation was over. Uncle Nolan wasn't anywhere near as chatty as Carlos. She'd only known him for a few days but was fairly sure that she had the rough outline of his profile figured out. Zapata wasn't a friendly boss, beloved by his employees. More like a stern, angry father, he laid down ironclad rules and meted out harsh punishment for failure. Her best bet was to keep her distance and stay on his good side.

She worked her way across the first floor toward the staircase. On the second floor, she saw that Leif Farnsworth had joined Tamara. The gang of adoring Bronco fans who always seemed to be following him were getting in the way of his conversation with the lady in red.

Angie ascended a staircase that followed a twisting acrylic path similar to the disappearing stairs in an Escher lithograph. With all this glass and plastic, she felt like she was wandering in circles. On the third floor where she'd seen Lorenzo looking down, there were fewer people. To her right, she saw the artwork. To her left, there was a subtle door that blended into the decor. She knew that plain entrance would lead to the bedrooms and offices.

Though she could have used her ornate hair decoration to pick the locks, she'd rather not if it wasn't necessary. It wasn't. The handle turned easily in her grasp, and she slipped inside a well-lit corridor with doors on either side. According to her blueprints, there weren't supposed to be surveillance cameras down this hallway, but she didn't want to take unnecessary risks. As long as she didn't break into a room, she could claim that she'd been looking for a bathroom.

At the end of the hallway, the door was opened a crack. Angie pushed the door with her shoulder and entered an opulent bedroom. This might be a good time to back out, but she'd come this far. She saw a small desk with a laptop that might be Lorenzo's private computer. The information she needed might be on that very hard drive…or not.

Angie cleared her throat. "Hello? Is anybody here?"

She heard a rustling on the far side of the room. A floor-to-ceiling window slid open and a woman stepped inside. As she stared at Angie, she didn't seem frightened, merely curious.

"I knew it," she said. "I knew someday we'd be back together."

"Marigold. It's you."

In that moment, everything changed.

JULIAN CREPT DOWN the hallway to the bedroom at the end. He hadn't intended to spy on Angie, but he was curious about why she moved through the crowd at the party, avoiding conversation and ignoring the lavish buffet. Her attention focused on the staircase leading to the third floor. When she ducked into the door to the private quarters, he followed. Finally, he might be able to figure out what kind of game she was playing.

From the first time he gazed into her dark, beautiful eyes, he'd suspected that she had some kind of secret agenda. With all her criminal connections and computer training, she might be part of an extortion or money laundering scheme. He doubted that she knew about the possibility of human trafficking; smuggling and transportation weren't in her wheelhouse. When she entered Lorenzo's bedroom, he moved close to the door so he could overhear what Angie was saying. The other woman in the room had to be Marion, Lorenzo's long-term mistress. No matter how many others came and went, Lorenzo kept contact with her. Marion was special to him.

Why did the two women keep saying "Marigold"? One of them was crying.

From behind his back, he heard the door to the corridor click and open. He pivoted and saw Lorenzo. The boss wasn't going to be happy about having Angie break into his private quarters. She could get fired…or worse. Julian had a better chance of survival. He was also annoyed by the way Lorenzo had ignored his calls and texts.

Before Lorenzo could speak, Julian confronted him. "I've been trying to get in touch with you for the past couple of days."

"Congratulations," Lorenzo said with an expansive gesture that displayed the tailored cut of his burgundy jacket. "You've caught up with me."

"Waylon was assaulted. I reviewed the feed from the surveillance cameras and saw his attacker sneaking around outside the barn, the garage and the bunkhouse."

"So what?" Lorenzo dusted his manicured hands as through he was disposing of the problem. "Waylon must have gotten protective about the barn and tried to chase the intruder away. The old cowboy isn't as tough as he used to be."

"I'd tend to agree with you." It was never smart to directly contradict the boss. "I'd almost decided this was nothing to worry about, but then I saw the guy here at your house, mingling with your guests as though he had every right to be here."

Lorenzo's eyes narrowed. He didn't like what he'd heard. "You're mistaken."

"Not likely. This guy has a distinctive scar on his forehead. When I approached him, he took off running."

"Did he get away from you?"

"He went into the national forest." The slimeball had planned his escape from the start. After crashing through the trees, Julian and Leif had discovered a stack of branches that had probably been used to hide a dirt bike or an ATV. There were also tire tracks. The final touch was the baseball cap he'd been wearing. Julian took the cap with a Nick's Burlesque logo from his pocket. "He left this behind."

Lorenzo snatched the cap, stared at the logo and threw it on the floor. "Son of a bitch."

"The guy is bad news," Julian said. "The way I figure, he's working for you or working for your enemies."

"He was so stupid that he got picked up by the cameras. Then he called attention to himself by getting into a brawl. How can this jackass be working for me?" Agitated, he raked his fingers through his silver hair. "I don't recognize him."

It had long been Julian's opinion that Lorenzo wasn't an effective manager. His success was based on two factors. Number one: he had a nose for sniffing out talented employees and didn't mind paying them what they were worth. Number two: he frequently came up with decent ideas for improvements.

However, when it came to the day-to-day grind of running the operation, Lorenzo checked out. As soon as he'd put Julian in charge of Nick's, he'd stepped aside. If he was, in fact, starting up a human trafficking operation, Lorenzo would pass the major responsibility to somebody else, probably Zapata.

"He might be a new employee," Julian said. "You can't be expected to know everybody who works for you."

"True." Lorenzo paced down the corridor and back. "I'll talk to Nolan. He keeps track of new hires."

"Is there some new project you're working on?"

"Don't worry about it, Professor."

Julian pressed his point. "The guy with the scar was

creeping around by the barn. Anything going on out there? Was he looking for something?"

"Hell if I know."

Julian shifted gears. "He also threatened one of the performers at the Burlesque."

"Which one?"

"Calamity Jane."

"The cowgirl with the whips and knives?" He barked a laugh. "She can handle a threat."

"If there's a new project at Nick's, I need to know." Changing direction again, Julian used an aggressive tone. "You've got to tell me so I can be prepared."

They faced off. Julian wasn't going to back down. If Lorenzo was going to jump into the dark, cruel world of trafficking and slavery, Julian couldn't stand by and let it happen. There were steps to be taken.

"Next week," Lorenzo said. "Zapata will fill you in."

Or kick me out.

The bedroom door swept open and Marion stepped through. Her ice-blue outfit sparkled with crystals, and her wavy blond hair cascaded down her back. She gave Lorenzo a peck on the cheek and then wiped off the imprint of her lipstick.

"Nice to see you, Julian." She smiled at him then turned back to Lorenzo. "We need to get downstairs. It's time to cut the cake."

"They can wait." His arm snaked around her waist, and he pulled her close against him.

"But it's time. I don't want Zapata to feel like we're disrespecting him on his birthday. He might get hungry and bite my head off."

"We can't let that happen," Lorenzo said. "By the way, Julian, nice job on the motorboat birthday present."

"Thank you, sir."

Julian followed them down the corridor. With every step, he tried to think of a reason to go into the bedroom and check on Angie. Leaving her here alone worried him. Not only did he want to be sure she got away safely but he was also curious about her connection.

At the door leaving the corridor, the lovely Marion turned to him. "I've forgotten my phone. Would you go back to the bedroom and get it for me?"

"Of course."

"Thanks so much. We'll see you downstairs."

She'd given him an excuse to check on Angie, and Julian grabbed the opportunity with both hands. He rushed into the bedroom, looked around, checked the walk-in closet and peeked into the attached bathroom. Angie was nowhere in sight.

He knew the blueprints for this house. There were no other exits from the bedroom…but there was a balcony. He opened the sliding glass door and stepped outside into a cool evening breeze. Angie crouched on the floor beside the acrylic wall that stretched the length of the balcony. Her face was buried in her hands. Her shoulders trembled with silent sobs.

Chapter Nine

Julian gathered Angie in his arms and held her while she wept. Though she barely made a sound, her body shuddered in violent bursts. Her breath hissed through clenched teeth. Whatever happened between her and Marion had shredded Angie's composure. He wanted to let her cry until she ran out of tears, but they needed to hurry and get the hell away from here. Half the people downstairs were criminals, and most of them worked for Lorenzo. All the boss had to do was give the word to make her disappear.

He stroked her shoulder under the gold jacket. "You need to calm down, please calm down. It's important for us to get to the car."

"I can't." She swabbed at her eyes with the back of her hand, smearing her eye makeup. Pieces of hair had come loose from her topknot and twisted around her face in messy disarray. "Just leave me alone."

"You can't stay here."

"And I can't go back to the damn party." With both hands, she shoved against his chest, creating space between them. Grasping one of the sleek chairs on the balcony, she dragged herself away from him. When she tried to stand, her legs crumpled and her shoulders drooped. "I look awful. It'll take forever to repair my face. People will notice."

"I have another idea." He stood. "Take off your shoes."

Too upset to question or complain, she did as he said. "Now what?"

"I've studied every inch of the blueprints for this house."

"Why?"

"The design and the architecture are fascinating. Anyway, I know this place better than Lorenzo, better than almost anybody." He took her hand, shocked by how cold she was. Her fingers felt like ice. He pulled her to her feet. "First, you're going to borrow a pair of Marion's sneakers. Then we're going to go down the fire escape."

"Are you joking?"

"It was installed in the 1950s as a safety feature," he said, "accessible only from the roof where there are no surveillance cameras."

"Well, why not?" Shaking her head, she stumbled toward the closet. "With all the amazing stuff in this house, I wouldn't be surprised if you told me we were going to fly into the forest on a magic carpet."

If Aladdin's technology had been available, Lorenzo would have bought it. Julian grabbed Marion's phone and slipped it into his jacket pocket. "Let's go. Shoes first, then we're out the door."

"We've always worn the same size. Since we were twelve, long before we ran away."

"What do you mean?"

"Nothing." She tucked her feet into a pair of black-and-white Converse high-tops from a wall of shoes in the walk-in closet.

He led her from the bedroom. At the far end of the corridor, he opened the door to a short hallway. They hurried past boxes stored on shelves and went up a flight of stairs. He paused at a metal door and looked down at her. Her makeup was a mess and her platinum hair looked like a bird's nest. He saw her innocence and her vulnerability. "Before we go outside, I need to know that you won't fall apart. Once this door closes, it's locked. We can't go back."

She lifted her chin. "I can do it."

He had to believe her. Finding another escape route was risky, and he didn't want to slip up and attract attention.

The door to the roof was stuck—probably hadn't been used in years—and he had to use his shoulder to get it open. Early October was chilly in the mountains. He took off his jacket and helped her put it on before guiding her across the roof to a ladder that hung over the edge of the parapet.

The front of the house and most of the right side were glass, but these back walls revealed a more utilitarian purpose. The fire escape from the roof was painted light brown. Otherwise, it was similar to something that might be found on an apartment building in Brooklyn.

He stepped over the edge and held on to the railing. "I forgot to ask if you're afraid of heights."

"Too late now." A weak smile flickered across her lips.

"I'll go first. If you need to stop, just let me know."

He descended backward, watching her move down the fire escape. The wind rattled around them, but the metal fire escape held firm. There were no direct lights in this area, but the glow from the rest of the house lit the trees and rocks in the forest. The farther they went, the stronger she seemed. By the time they reached the last step and he lowered the ladder, she had recovered much of her strength.

When her foot in the Converse sneaker touched the earth, he felt a whoosh of relief. They just might pull this off. "Here's the good part. We're closer to where I parked the car."

"I'm sorry I fell apart," she said with a nod. "I almost never cry. It's not like me."

"It's okay. I won't let you get hurt, I promise."

He led her around the back of the house, passing the kitchen and heading to the place where he'd parked. Fortunately, no one had pulled in behind his silver SUV and blocked the exit. They could be out of here in minutes.

First, he put through a phone call to Leif asking him to meet at the door where he'd originally dropped him off. When thc former Bronco appeared, Julian handed over Marion's phone. "Make sure she gets it right away."

"Where are you headed?"

"Angie's sick. I'm taking her back to Nick's. Can you get a ride?"

"You bet, and I'll be real happy to take care of Tamara."

He drove to the front of the house and exited on the long driveway. As the SUV put miles between them and the Glass Palace, his tension ratcheted down. Not that he was relaxed, far from it.

"I have some questions," he said. "You had to be eavesdropping on what I said to Lorenzo. How much did you hear?"

"Some," she admitted. "You said something about chasing the man with the scar into the forest. Are you sure it was him?"

"I've been watching him on tape for the past couple of days. When I saw him in the house, he was taunting me, peeking out from under the cap before he made his run to a dirt bike he'd hidden behind a stack of branches. Leif joined me."

Leif's unexpected appearance seemed too convenient, maybe even suspicious, but Julian wasn't about to discuss his feelings with Angie. She owed him multiple explanations. "Another question," he said, "Why did you go to the third floor private quarters?"

"To see the artwork," she said.

That was a lie and not a very believable one. She'd been on the opposite side of the art display inside Lorenzo's bedroom. There must have been something else she went looking for. "Who's Marigold?"

"I don't know what you're talking about."

Another obvious fib? She was really off her game, and he wasn't about to waste time digging through layers of deception. "Might as well tell me."

"Or what's going to happen?"

"I'm not going to threaten you."

"Good, because we both know that never works."

"I want to help you," he said. "Just trust me. Who is Marigold?"

"Someone I never thought I'd see again." She stared through the windshield, concentrating intently on a vision he couldn't see. Was she examining her own past? "I don't like to talk about what happened to me when I was growing up. Too much sadness. Too many people who failed me. For me, foster care was horrible, but it's not like that for everybody. I was a behavior problem."

Not a surprise. "Earlier tonight, you opened up."

"Which is not like me," she said. "Usually, if somebody asks about my past, I'll make up something about winning a surfing contest in Hawaii or stealing a Van Gogh from a heartless billionaire."

"You'll lie," he said.

"It's easier, and people tend to believe me."

"You're a good liar."

"Damn right, but not tonight. When we were all telling secrets, I talked about a girl who was my closest friend. We were in the same foster homes, starting when we were twelve. We ran away from a foster home in Utah together and came to Denver. Our first job was at a strip joint."

"What else?"

"I was fifteen, and she was almost seventeen but looked younger than me, except for her breasts. She developed early. Her name was Marigold."

Julian's pause was just a second too long, but she noticed. "Don't feel sorry for me. My mistakes when I was with Marigold were motivation for turning my life around."

A picture began to form inside his head. "You said you'd lost touch with her."

"She was taken away from me. The guy who ran the strip joint took her and a couple of others to a private party. I'm guessing the event was similar to the one we just attended with a lot of booze and shiny surfaces to hide the decadence."

"Decadent? Zapata's birthday party seemed innocent."

"Now who's lying?" she scoffed. "We both know that the real excitement doesn't start until after midnight. That's when they bring in the pretty girls to dress the place up."

Julian didn't usually stick around for the late-night lap dances. Being sober brought out the ugliness. "Your friend Marigold was selected but not you. Why not?"

"I wasn't a party girl. I was a gawky fifteen-year-old, flat-chested with dull brown hair and scraggly teeth in need of braces. I didn't know how to dress, didn't know how to put on makeup. I wasn't pretty." She lifted her chin and looked down her nose. "Make no mistake, Julian. It takes a lot of effort to look the way I usually do."

"What happened to Marigold?"

"She hooked up with the big boss, and I bet you already know that his name was Nick Lorenzo. Marigold came back to me a couple of times and showed me jewelry he bought for her. She thought it was love, that he was her prince. I couldn't blame her for turning her back on me."

"She wasn't eighteen," he said. "It was rape."

"That was what I tried to tell the cops. All that got me

was a big, fat nothing. I got shipped back to the foster home in Utah."

The pieces of her story were falling into place. His instincts about her were correct; she had underlying motives. Starting a new job with Lorenzo was only part of the reason she'd come to Colorado. Needing to give her his full attention, he took advantage of the solitude on this curving mountain road by driving onto a wide space on the shoulder and turning off the headlights. As night settled around them, he turned to her.

"Let me see if I've got this right," he said. "Marigold is the real reason you took this job. You wanted to find out what had happened to her."

"I need to know. Marigold was my dearest friend, and she vanished without a trace. It was like her existence had been erased. I did a ton of computer research and even came to Denver twice to look for her. Nothing!"

"And you thought if you infiltrated Lorenzo's organization, you'd figure it out."

"Do you know what it's like?" she asked. "To lose someone you love hurts, but to never know what happened to them makes it worse."

Threads of anger wove through her voice. Having already spent the tears and sadness of grief, she'd moved on to rage. Her tangled hair and smeared makeup gave him a hint of the gawky teenager she once had been—the young woman who had been abandoned by Marigold. Gently, he held her hand and waited until she was ready to continue.

"I blamed Lorenzo," she said, "and I hated him. I thought he'd funneled Marigold into some kind of trafficking operation, turning her into a high-priced escort or a sex slave. I even thought he might have had her killed."

"What was your plan tonight? Did you go to the third floor to confront him?"

"That's a hard no. Guys like him never confess."

"Why were you there?"

"Investigating," she said. "I'd done a computer search of my own, looking for Marigold, but I thought I might learn something different if I could download the hard drive from Lorenzo's personal computer."

"A long shot," he said.

"And I didn't follow through. I saw his laptop but didn't snatch it."

"Why not?"

"I never expected to walk through that door and see her standing there." Angie's fingers twisted in his grasp as though her hands had a life of their own. "When we were kids…she chose to stay with him. She wanted that life."

"And now?"

"She says she's ready to leave Lorenzo, and I've got to believe her. Marigold is done with him. She promised to meet with me on Monday night. Then we'll figure out what to do."

He knew that her escape wasn't a simple matter of walking away. In her role as Lorenzo's mistress, Marigold had been privy to the inner workings of the organization. "She's been with him for eleven years."

"I know." Angie nodded sadly. "Think of everything she's witnessed. Her testimony could probably put Lorenzo, Zapata and a dozen other guys in prison."

He hated the idea of Angie meeting with this woman. "Marigold isn't the teenager you remember. How do you know you can trust her?"

"I don't."

"It might be smart for you to step aside and leave it to the cops to rescue her. The only way she can be safe is if she's a protected witness."

"She'll never go for that." Angie wrung her hands. "Protective custody is just another type of prison. She needs to be free."

He suspected Angie was correct. His acquaintance with the woman who had been with Lorenzo for years and went by the name of Marion was limited, but she didn't strike him as someone who would quietly fade away. She was trouble, and he wouldn't let that danger spill onto Angie. She deserved better.

Chapter Ten

A little more than twenty-four hours later, it was close to midnight, and Angie had recovered. She'd showered, slept for a full ten hours, gotten dressed, splashed on a coat of bright red lipstick and come up with a plan of action. Not only would she free Marigold from Lorenzo's slimy tentacles but would also complete her undercover mission of shutting down a human trafficking ring. *That's right, I'm a superstar!* Angie liked the symmetry of linking Marigold, who had once been the victim of a predator, to saving countless other women from a similar fate at the hands of traffickers.

Dressed in a dark leather jacket with a knit cap covering her shiny platinum ponytail, she crept toward the parking area near the loading dock behind Nick's where she knew a blue delivery van from Valentino's Bakery and Wedding Cakes was parked. She'd been watching from the window of her suite and had seen Valentino leave his van, which was when she put her plan in gear. Hidden in shadow, she flattened her back against the wood siding and peered through the night, trying to calculate the angles she'd have to follow to avoid being seen on the surveillance cameras. Her intended strategy had been to fasten a tracking device onto the van, but that wouldn't be possible. She couldn't tiptoe across the space without being spotted on camera.

The alternative was old-school; she'd have to tail his van in her car. Following the sidewalk around the building, she picked up her hatchback from the lot and drove to a position where she could follow Valentino when he left. Finally, her investigation was making progress...or was it?

After seeing Marigold, Angie had gone through more mood swings than an aerialist on a flying trapeze which was a particularly apt comparison because she, too, was working without a net. Of course, she was happy, elated, delighted to find her friend. But she couldn't forget the pain when she'd been abandoned. Her thoughts ranged from a deep-rooted desire to call for help from an FBI task force to the extreme opposite—forgetting she'd ever seen Marigold. Why should Angie risk her life and her career for a woman who had chosen to stay with Lorenzo and had made zero effort to contact her for eleven years? Marigold didn't deserve her friendship or her loyalty.

Slouched in the dark behind her steering wheel, Angie closed her eyes. Memories swarmed through her mind. She thought of their adventures when they'd hitchhiked across the Rockies and worked for a few days on a river raft on the Roaring Fork. In Denver, they'd done a bit of juggling on the street as buskers. Most of all, she remembered the warmth of having somebody who loved her no matter what.

She opened her eyes. Today, she'd come to the conclusion that the best way to help Marigold was to fulfill her undercover mission and expose the trafficking operation. Who was being taken? How were they being used? Where were they dropped? Obviously, money was involved, a lot of money, which led her to the conclusion that Zapata was the mastermind, using his position in the Lorenzo organization and negotiating with his cartel connections. In her gut, she knew he was the evil genius, but she didn't have evidence to obtain warrants and didn't know when the full-scale operation would start. She suspected trial runs were already underway.

Oddly, it was Julian who pointed her toward investigating. Since last night, he'd been hovering around her, watching for signs of mental collapse. When he took her to lunch in the coffee shop, she felt his electric blue gaze sliding over her like some kind of cool, sexy, mysterious caress. *Not the way I want to think about him!* Julian was smart and incredibly good-looking, but he was also a crook and would be swept into the same net as the others when arrests were made. She needed to be more guarded around him. Last night, she might have let something slip that made him think she was a cop.

At lunch, he couldn't stop talking about the man with the scar. Julian was obsessed and worried that this guy was part of a larger operation. *Like human trafficking?* She poked around the edges of that scheme, but he wasn't thinking that way. He sensed that she was in danger and wanted her to quit working at the OTB and go home to California. As if he could protect her? The idea made her laugh. As a trained FBI operative, she shouldn't require help from him or anybody else for that matter.

As she waited for the van, she checked her phone and saw a text from Julian. Not surprising that he wouldn't call at eleven thirty on a Sunday night. It was much too late. She read his message: Surveillance cameras pay off. I have facial recog on man with scar. He's in the casino. This may be over soon.

Though tempted to call him back and join his investigation, she decided to stick with Valentino. Earlier today, she'd overheard him telling Zapata that the fleet of delivery vans belonged to him, and he gave the orders. A disagreement between these two powerful men might lead to evidence that she could use. After a bit of computer research, she learned that Valentino had eleven vans and operated bakeries in five different locations, including Colorado Springs. His business seemed tailor-made as a cover for smuggling people throughout the state.

Though she wasn't an expert when it came to collecting forensic evidence, she hoped to find a clue in his vans—fibers, fingerprints, a discarded tissue, an article of clothing or a toy. She hated that children were part of trafficking, and she still hadn't forgotten her promise to Cara. Tomorrow, they'd search for Gigi in the hills behind the bunkhouse. Tomorrow night, she'd meet with Marigold.

The dark blue van drove past the spot where she was parked. The game was on!

Angie waited until the van was almost out of sight before following. Near midnight on a Sunday, the traffic on these mountain roads was almost nonexistent so she didn't need to worry about blending. Her challenge was to keep him from noticing that she was behind him.

Living in Southern California for years, she'd spent hours every day in a car, had learned how to maneuver through eight-lane highways and had developed skills in pulling 180-degree turns, sudden stops and reversing directions. Car chases and vehicular pursuit were pretty much her kind of thing. She kept her distance on the curving mountain roads. There was really only one route that went directly into Denver. Occasionally, she'd speed up to make sure the van was still on the same road, and then she'd drop back.

When they got to the outskirts of Denver, there was more traffic. From the direction the van was traveling, she figured that Valentino was headed toward his bakery in a southwest Denver suburb—a location she'd looked up online and programmed into her GPS.

She exited a main road and drove south two blocks to

the small strip mall with the bakery. A half block away from the mall, she parked and killed the headlights. At this hour, all the shops were closed and locked. Outdoor lights shone on the asphalt parking outside the dry cleaner, electronics store, hair salon and a couple of others. Valentino's Bakery and Wedding Cakes was on the end. She saw him drive around to the back. *Time to make her move.* Since she didn't know how long he'd be at the shop, she hustled. There was no need to bother with being stealthy. No witnesses were on the street, not even a late-night walker with a dog.

She tried the handle on the van. It was locked. This utilitarian vehicle didn't have a fancy security system, and she was confident that she could break in. While she was digging in her small purse, the back door from the bakery slammed open.

"Who's out there?" Valentino bellowed.

Silhouetted by light from inside the bakery, Valentino took up nearly the entire doorway. His height wasn't much above average, but his extra-wide girth showed the result of consuming too many cakes, cookies and fresh baked breads. Not that he was soft. He had the shoulders of a Brahman bull and looked like he could lift a delivery truck.

Though she had a friendly relationship with him, she was in serious danger. Valentino had a reputation for violence. His nickname—the Baker—came from an incident when he crammed one of his enemies into an oven and set the temperature to 400 degrees. He glared at her with tired, red-rimmed eyes. In his right hand, he brandished a heavy marble rolling pin.

Her instinct was to run, but he'd already seen her. Even if she managed to escape, he knew where she lived and could bring down the wrath of Lorenzo upon her. As always, she was prepared to protect herself. There hadn't been time to subtly hide her weapons before she took off to follow his van, so she'd slipped her snub-nosed Beretta Tomcat into the small plaid purse she wore on a strap across her chest. She placed her hand on the purse's flap, ready to draw if necessary. In spite of his legendary temper, she didn't want to shoot the man. Valentino had a wife and four children.

Angie straightened her shoulders and confronted him. "We need to talk."

"How the hell did you find me?"

"I followed your truck from Nick's. I thought about tooting my horn and getting you to pull over. And I tried to signal you while we were driving."

He smacked the rolling pin against his left palm. "It's late. What the hell do you want?"

"Please don't be angry." Hoping to defuse his hostility, she played to his ego. "I need your advice. You're smart. You know how this organization runs."

"Go on."

"Over the past couple of days, I proved to Zapata that I could boost the profit margin for OTB, but he's going to fire me unless I do better." She amped up her appeal by snatching the knit cap off her head and letting her long, platinum ponytail swing free, which was usually an effective distraction. "I have an idea that I want to run by you."

"You got two minutes." When he leaned toward her, his scowling face—with downturned mouth and heavy, black eyebrows—seemed as big and round as a full, angry moon. "Talk."

"I was in my suite, looking out my window, and I saw your truck, and I thought of...cake. Not just any cake, oh, no, but a spectacular cake with a track and horse racing decorations. I wanted to tell you, and I ran downstairs to find you. But you were already driving away. So I hopped in my car and followed."

He nodded, apparently believing her lame explanation. "Tell me about the cake."

"I want to host a reception for all the members who placed bets with OTB this year." Thinking fast, she was creating this plan on the fly. Actually, an exclusive party wasn't a bad way to promote more gambling, which meant more losses and more income. "Can I come inside and talk about it?"

Now that he seemed appeased and unlikely to kill her, she wanted to press her advantage and check out the interior of the bakery. Though Valentino's name was emblazoned across the front and customers visited during the day, this location might be a good stopping point for trafficking. The area behind the shops was hidden by a tall fence and shrubs, and the street in front had very little traffic.

"You're full of crap," he said.

"So I've been told."

"But as long as you're here…" He pushed the door open and stepped aside. "Talk fast. I only stopped by to pick up some paperwork and leave notes for the morning crew. Then I go home and sleep till noon."

Inside the large kitchen, the stainless steel ovens, refrigerators, mixing vats and cooling racks gleamed under bright lighting. The delicious aromas of sugar, chocolate and baking dough scented the air. The countertops, worktables and chopping blocks were clean and organized. Everything was spick-and-span as befitted a professional bakery, which wasn't a surprise to her. Every time she'd tasted his wares, she'd been impressed by the luscious, rich quality. The Baker was a pro when it came to his craft, but that didn't mean he was a decent human being.

She kept a wary gaze on Valentino while meandering toward the open doorway that led to the customer entrance and the display cases at the front of the shop. Though she was fairly certain that the delivery trucks were being used to transport illegal cargo, this shop probably wasn't a destination. There wasn't enough extra space to hide much of anything, and the strip mall probably rested on a concrete slab with no basement. "So this is where the magic happens."

"Magic?"

"I've had your cakes. You are a magician."

He didn't smile or preen at her compliment, but he did set aside his marble rolling pin, which she considered to be progress. "This shop is mostly for doughnuts and breakfast goods. My wife thinks I should add tables so people can sit and have a meal, but that's not for me."

"I understand. You're a baker, not a chef."

"Exactly, and I've got dozens of regular outlets for my product all over town. My trucks are running all day." He lumbered to a cubicle office with glass walls on the upper half and started shuffling through paperwork. Unlike the pristine area dedicated to baking, the office was cluttered. "This big party of yours, did you run it past your boyfriend?"

"Boyfriend?"

"Come on, Angie. You know who I'm talking about. Half the strippers at Nick's are heartbroken that Julian has the hots for you."

Cara would have wanted her to remind him that the women working at the Burlesque were performers not strippers, but Angie didn't want to offend the Baker. She moved closer to his glass office. Learning his schedule would be useful. He might keep notes on where his delivery trucks were supposed to make pickups and drop-offs.

"I'm still thinking about the timing for my party. Could we do it week after next?"

"That's close to Halloween. We usually have special cakes for parties and sugar skulls for Dia de los Muertos. But I can try to fit you in."

She sidled around the glass wall and entered his office. "Maybe I could take a look at your calendar."

"Don't crowd me."

A rattling noise, like a door handle being shaken, came from the front of the store. She took a backward step and craned her neck to look in that direction. "What was that?"

In the few seconds it took for her to turn back toward the Baker, he'd whipped open a file cabinet beside his desk and taken out a semiautomatic AK-47 that made her Tomcat look like a kid's toy. The barrel of the gun aimed at her gut. *No, no, no, no...* "What are you doing?"

"Somebody's at the front," the Baker said. "If it's a friend of yours, you'll be sorry."

"I don't know who it is, I swear." Moving fast, she backpedaled across the kitchen, avoiding the stainless steel tables and cabinets. Should she take the gun from her purse? She was afraid he'd see it as a threat, and she didn't want him to retaliate. "I'm on your side."

The rattle became the crash of glass shattering. The front of the store was dark, and she couldn't see anything. On the side of the kitchen opposite Valentino's office, she ducked under a table. The Baker hid behind a refrigerator.

When she saw the man who swaggered through the door and entered the kitchen, she gasped. He had stubble and a scar across his forehead. It had to be the guy Julian was searching for. Why was he here? What did he want? Julian was supposed to be watching him at the casino. His semiautomatic weapon was a match for the one Valentino held. She could tell that he wasn't alone.

The man with the scar gave the orders. “Show yourself, Baker.”

“I got nothing to say to you.”

“Zapata isn’t happy. He doesn’t think you can handle more responsibility.”

“He should tell me himself, and you should get the hell out of my bakery.”

“Are you threatening me, Baker?”

“That’s right, Damien.”

Damien worked for Zapata. As soon as she got clear of this situation, she could use that information. A thug like Damien had to be wanted by the FBI, which meant she could call on their resources to pick him up without compromising her investigation.

She ducked lower and froze in place. Damien hadn’t noticed her. He kept his attention focused in Valentino’s direction as he took a few tentative steps into the kitchen with his weapon at the ready.

“You made a mistake,” Damien said. “Your men let that little girl get away. She could cause all kinds of trouble.”

A girl who escaped? Gigi?

“Not my men,” Valentino roared. “Your guys messed up. They were so busy jabbering at each other that they lost track of what was going on with her.”

“Not a chance. My men are pros.” He moved closer. “There’s no need for us to have a problem. Put your hands up and come with me. I don’t have to hurt you, Baker.”

She didn’t believe him.

Neither did Valentino.

The Baker stepped out from behind the fridge and sprayed bullets at Damien, who managed to get off a blast of his own before he fell. His blood splattered the appliances and stained the spotless, tiled floor. Angie pulled her

Beretta Tomcat from her tiny purse. She'd gone through weapons training at Quantico but had never killed anyone.

A second man dove through the door. He dodged across the floor in a frantic dance and ducked behind a giant mixing vat. He raised his weapon, but Valentino fired first, and the second man went down.

Angie watched the one-sided battle with a terrible combination of fear and awe. Her pulse raced. She wanted to move but didn't know where to go. A third man slipped through the door into the kitchen. In a crouch, he ran between the mixing tables, coming in her direction. Neither of the other men had taken any notice of her, but he seemed to sense her presence. He was too damn close.

She braced her elbows on the stainless steel table to steady her aim. Her weapon fired one shot at a time, and she couldn't afford to lose a single bullet.

The third man squinted as if actually seeing her for the first time. He swung his semiautomatic in her direction. She should shoot now. *Now!* If he got off the first volley, she'd be dead before she had a chance to return fire. She didn't want to kill him. A dead man couldn't give her any information. Aiming at his shoulder, she squeezed the trigger.

He took her bullet without falling down. Her shot was inconsequential. He barely slowed his pace as he continued to come at her. On the other side of the kitchen, she saw the Baker take advantage of the momentary distraction caused by her shot. He blasted the third man.

She sank to the floor, gasping for breath and trembling. When she looked down, she saw that the sleeves of her jacket were speckled with the third man's blood.

Three were dead,

There were no more.

Chapter Eleven

There was movement from the front of the shop and the sound of someone kicking through the broken glass from the window. A voice called out, “Hold your fire. It’s me, Julian Parisi. Are you all right?”

The Baker aimed his weapon at the open doorway. “Are these bastards with you?”

“You know they aren’t.” His voice was angry. “I overheard you yelling at each other. You knew that Damien worked for Zapata. I’ve been chasing all over the damn place, looking for him. All the while, you knew I was wasting my time. You knew who he was.”

“Maybe you’re not so smart, Professor.”

This was only the second time she’d heard anyone use Julian’s nickname, and she didn’t miss the sneer in Valentino’s tone. In spite of Julian’s intelligence, he didn’t have much in the way of street smarts.

“Here’s my question,” the Baker said. “If you weren’t working with Damien, how did you end up here in the middle of the night?”

“I saw him at Nick’s, picked him up with facial recognition on the surveillance cameras. Instead of grabbing him, I followed him when he left the casino and got in his car. I didn’t know he was coming here, didn’t know he was gunning for you.”

The Baker heaved a heavy sigh. "You got anybody else with you?"

"Rudy and two other guys," Julian said. "Are we done talking? I need to get in there and clean up your mess before the cops arrive."

"Yeah, you can come in."

He stepped through the door with his hands raised over his head, which was smart because Valentino was still armed and ready to shoot anybody who irritated him. When Julian looked in her direction, she could tell he was surprised to see her and angry, very angry. "Good evening, Angie."

The sound of his voice comforted and disturbed her at the same time. Even though he'd given an explanation for why he was here, the timing of his arrival felt strangely coincidental. Not that she thought he was working with the cartel like Zapata, but she knew that Julian was an important cog in Lorenzo's machine.

She looked from the dead men on the floor to Julian. Both sides of this battle were criminals. There was nobody to root for. She tried to force a smile but failed. "Glad to see you."

He turned his back on her and asked the Baker, "What's she doing here?"

"Buying a cake."

"At midnight on a Sunday?" He shook his head in disgust and disbelief. "That's what I call a half-baked story."

Valentino chuckled. "Good one."

Julian leaned over Damien's body, felt for a pulse and shot her a glance. "Did you kill him, Angie?"

"She tried." The Baker illustrated by making his thumb and forefinger into a gun. "Blondie has a little pop gun in her purse."

How could he make jokes? She stared into the lifeless

eyes of the man who had fallen only a few feet away from her. Blood stained his pale yellow shirt, his face and his hands. In death, his fingers still clutched his weapon. She'd seen dead people before. A few years ago in Reno, she'd witnessed the aftermath of a bloody battle with six victims, but this was the first time she'd seen a man take his last breath and die right in front of her.

Julian came closer and placed his hand on her shoulder. She jerked away. *Don't touch me.* She didn't want to be lulled into false security, not with three murdered men on the floor. Her brain needed to stay sharp.

"You've got spatter on your hand," he said. "Were you injured?"

"This isn't my blood."

"It could very well have been."

He was right! She could have been killed by Damien and his men or by the Baker. The smart thing to do right now was to get away from here as quickly as possible. Maybe she ought to drive straight to the FBI headquarters, admit defeat and end her undercover assignment. For the first time, she considered quitting in the middle of an assignment. On her phone, she had a highly protected app that she could activate with a three-digit code. The signal rang through to the FBI and notified her handler that she was in need of immediate backup. Special agents could track her location using her phone's GPS.

Never before had she thought she'd need those buttons. Calling for help would knock her down a few rungs on the career ladder, and she wouldn't have her choice of assignments. But getting killed on the job wasn't a good alternative.

She wanted to stick with this investigation. Damien had dropped new information that she should check out. He'd mentioned an escaped girl, which indicated that they'd already started the trafficking operations—at least, trial runs—using Nick's. Angie had to stay on the job so she could rescue that girl who might be Cara's playmate. Until Gigi was safe, Angie couldn't quit, but that didn't mean she had to stay right here in the middle of a crime scene. "My car is parked down the block. I'm leaving."

"You're in no condition to drive." Julian pulled a stool over beside the stainless steel table and patted the seat. "Sit. Catch your breath."

"I'm fine. I don't need help." Her standard response. She'd made that claim so many times that she actually believed it was true. She didn't *want* to be dependent, didn't *want* to need him or anybody else.

In an unexpectedly gentle tone, he said, "Let me take care of this."

If only she could believe him! She wanted to take a step back and let her brain rest while somebody else took the initiative and the responsibility. Gazing into his intense blue eyes, she felt safe and reassured.

From her perch on the stool, she watched as Julian checked the other two men to make sure they were all dead. He took out his cellphone and had a conversation. She wondered if he was talking to Lorenzo to get instructions. Or was Julian important enough that he didn't need to consult with the boss?

The Baker lumbered over and stood beside Julian. "This wasn't my fault," he said.

"Okay."

"Damien broke in here. This was a clear case of self-defense. You can ask Angic on account of she saw the whole thing. She's my witness."

"It's all right, my friend. You don't need to worry about witnesses or self-defense," Julian said. "We're not going to tell the police about this."

Ice-cold dread surged through her veins. *No police?* With numb fingers, she checked the safety on her Tomcat to make sure it was ready to fire in case she needed to shoot her way out. As if she could? Running away was a much better idea. If she could slide out of this room and make it to her car, she wouldn't stop driving until she reached the Pacific shores.

Rudy entered the shop from the front. "Hey, Baker, it looks like I missed all the fun."

The young man's bravado wasn't convincing. She noticed a twitch near his eye and guessed that he was nearly as nervous as she was.

"About the other two guys who came with us," Julian said. "Can they be trusted? Before you answer, keep in mind that your uncle will be very disappointed if your buddies start bragging or shooting off their mouths to the cops."

"They're cool," Rudy said.

Julian spoke to the Baker. "Go home and clean up. Take a shower to get the gunshot residue off your skin. Then you should burn your clothes. Your wife will give you an alibi, not that you need one. We will never speak of this night again."

"What am I supposed to do?" Rudy asked.

"You and your crew are in charge of cleanup. There's not much time before Valentino's morning bakers come in to start work. Wipe everything down. Use bleach on the blood. Repair the broken window in the front door."

"Got it," Rudy said. "What's your job?"

"Not that it's any of your damn business, but it's what I always do," Julian said calmly. "I get rid of the bodies."

He stalked across the kitchen toward her. With every step that brought him closer, her heart beat faster. "You don't need to tell me what to do," she said. "I know the drill. I go home, take a shower, burn my clothes and forget this happened."

"You're coming with me."

She most definitely did *not* want to ride along while he dumped the bodies. "But I need to clean up. I've got blood on my jacket."

He took off his glasses and leaned closer. His blue eyes—a liar's eyes—cast a mesmerizing glow, but she had to be immune. She couldn't take a chance on going with him. "You ride with me, Angie."

Turning off her apprehension was impossible, but there was a part of her—the FBI-trained sector of her brain—that told her she needed to hear what he had to say. Julian was a major player in the Lorenzo organization. He might give her information that would unravel all these twists and turns. No matter how scared she was, she had to go with him.

Climbing off the stool, she stood before him and stared up into those incredible eyes. She linked her arm with his. "Lead on."

WHEN JULIAN ESCORTED Angie to his SUV and held the door open for her, he saw her reluctance in the way she fidgeted. This lady was ready to take off like a jackrabbit, and he couldn't let that happen before they had a few things straightened out. "Please wait for me in the car," he said. "And I need to see your purse."

"Why?"

"Maybe I want to freshen up my lipstick."

"Not funny and not the right timing. We're only a few steps away from a murder scene." She did a *tsk-tsk* like an old lady. "You and Valentino share a very weird sense of humor. Now, tell me why you want my purse."

"To dispose of your gun," he said. "I'm guessing that

your cellphone and car keys are also in that tiny purse, and I'd feel better with both of those items in my possession."

"So I can't run away?"

"Correct."

"You don't trust me."

Before she could make another objection, he lifted her purse from her lap. "Stay here. I'll be back in a minute."

He returned to the bakery and gave more detailed orders to Rudy and the other two stooges. They'd found a storage closet at the back of the shop, and it contained the supplies they'd need, including painter's drop cloths to wrap the bodies and a pane of glass to repair the broken window in the front door.

"Use all the cloths," Julian instructed. "I don't want to get too much blood in my car."

"You got it, boss." Rudy stepped up. He was in charge and clearly enjoyed giving orders. "We'll take care of the mess. You tell my uncle I'm doing a good job."

Julian returned to his SUV, got behind the wheel and turned toward her. "Here's your purse, and I brought you something else."

He handed her a small white box printed with the Valentino logo. She immediately opened it. "A cupcake?"

"You're welcome." He started the engine and drove around to the back of the shop where Rudy and his guys could more easily load the bodies. Valentino's van was already gone.

"I don't believe this," she snapped. "Do you really expect me to forgive you because you brought a cupcake?"

"It's chocolate icing."

"In the future, please don't grab my belongings and treat me like a child. If you really needed for me to stay in the car, you could have explained. Like an adult." She flipped open the purse and dug through it. "Where are my car keys?"

"I gave them to Rudy." He maneuvered the SUV so the rear was near the back door of the bakery. "He's going to drive your car to Nick's so we don't have to come back into town to pick it up."

"Totally unacceptable," she said. "I want my keys and my car. And I don't want to ride along with you to dump the bodies." He saw her reach for the door handle and tapped the childproof locking system. She yanked the handle twice before she realized she couldn't get out. "Open this. Open it now."

"For the next hour, I need your undivided attention. I owe you an explanation, and this isn't something I can rattle off in a few quick sentences. It's complicated, and it's important that you understand. Things can get serious when you're working for Lorenzo. Tonight, you saw how bad it can get."

"Three murders. It doesn't get much worse."

"Last night, I promised that I'd protect you. That's what I mean to do."

The side door of the SUV slid open, and Rudy stuck his head inside. "Where do you want them?"

"In the back, and you'll need to collapse the rear seat to make room. I'll pop the lock."

Angie turned so she could see what was going on behind her. In a quiet voice, she said, "What if I don't want your protection?"

"I'm not trying to insult you or say that you're weak. But you're new in town and really don't know what you've gotten yourself into." The car bounced as the first body was loaded into the back. "You might get hurt while you're figuring things out."

"Thanks for your concern but you don't know what's

best for me. I've been making my own decisions for a very long time, and I know what I need." She swiveled around in her seat and focused on the windshield. "You might have gotten the wrong impression last night when I was all weepy. I'm not like that."

"I never said you were."

"You think I should stay safe. What does that mean? Wait, let me guess. You think I should keep my head down and do my job at OTB and not make waves. I should be a good girl, an obedient girl. Take no risks. Then I won't get hurt."

In the dim light behind the bakery, he studied her determined expression. When she looked at him, her dark eyes blazed. "I'd never try to tell you not to make waves. That's not your nature. Angie, you're a tsunami."

"You bet I am."

The back of the SUV bounced again as corpse number two was loaded inside. "Give me the chance to explain. Afterward, the decisions are up to you."

"And you'll take me back to my room at Nick's?"

"If that's what you want."

She flipped open the lid on the cupcake box and scooped a bite of frosting. The rumbling sound from the back of her throat sounded like purring. "I love chocolate."

TELLING HER THE whole truth might not be the smartest strategy he'd ever come up with, but his decision was made. He'd meant it when he said she needed to know what kind of mess she'd stumbled into. A clear picture was necessary, but he wasn't anxious to get started with his long, complicated story and wasn't sure how she'd react.

"Question," she said. "When do I get my gun back?"

"Not as long as it can be tied to the murders. Are you attached to the Tomcat?"

"It's a handy size." She licked her lips, savoring every taste of chocolate. "I can't actually remember the last time I fired it."

The third body was dumped inside and the back of the SUV closed with a final click. Rudy tapped on the driver's side window and Julian lowered the glass.

"We're done," Rudy said.

"Good." The kid was proving to be a useful assistant, after all. "When you're finished with the rest of the job, take photos on your phone and send them to me."

"Got it." He stepped out of the way as the SUV pulled forward.

Driving west toward the mountains, Julian should have felt more relieved. The issue of the man with the scar had been permanently settled with Damien's death. Evidence from the crime scene would be erased. And he knew Zapata was not to be trusted.

"I'm ready," Angie said. "Tell me your complicated story."

The truth would shock her. He couldn't just blurt it out. "I'm going to start with what happened three years ago when I joined the construction crew working on the building and renovating at Nick's."

She popped the last bite of cupcake into her mouth and gave another chocolate purr. "I don't suppose you grabbed another one of these."

"I should have grabbed a dozen." Glancing over at her, he wished she'd invite him to lick the icing from her lips. Thoughts like that made it even more difficult to be honest with her.

"Back to your story," she said. "Once upon a time..."

"This isn't a fairy tale. There's no moral to the story, and I'm pretty sure there isn't a happily-ever-after."

He didn't want to drop this bombshell while they were

so close to the bakery and might be followed. Better to wait until…until what? Damn it, there wasn't a good time for him to tell her that he'd been lying from the first moment they'd met. The whole time he'd been accusing her of withholding information and being mysterious, he had his own secrets.

She might betray him, but that was a chance he was willing to take. If she didn't want to cooperate and step away from trouble, he could always have her arrested. That was one of the advantages of his real job as an undercover agent for the Colorado Bureau of Investigation.

Chapter Twelve

The primary purpose of Angie's undercover work was to dig up evidence that would help the FBI shut down illegal operations and lock criminals away. Though she hadn't been following a detailed plan with Lorenzo, she must have been doing something right because here she was, riding along with Julian, who wanted to tell her his deepest, darkest secrets. As a high-ranking member of Lorenzo's organization, he had access to information that could seriously damage the start-up of a trafficking operation.

She should have been hanging on his every word but didn't really want to hear what he had to say. What if he felt compelled to confess to her? *Oh, the irony!* She liked this guy and didn't want to arrest him.

He was driving the same route that he took on the day they met. She remembered how nervous she'd been, imagining all the terrible things that could happen to her in the mountains. Now she was calm. *Another irony!* The bodies of three murdered men were tucked into the space behind her.

"Where are we going?" she asked.

"I have a place I generally use for things like this."

The thought that he had a special body dumping site should have terrified her. Why wasn't she frantically plotting her escape from him? "That's another joke, right?"

"Here's what I want you to know," he said. "I was a carpenter before I met Lorenzo on the job site for Nick's. We discussed architecture and found out that we had similar tastes, which resulted in incorporating some of my ideas in the project. I took over the supervising of several crews. Long story short, I ended up working for him on a more permanent basis."

She understood what he was trying to tell her in his roundabout way. "You didn't intend to start out as a criminal."

"Exactly."

Not much of a defense. If he was such an innocent participant in Lorenzo's business, how did he become the go-to guy for dumping bodies? *We all make our own decisions.* That was a painful lesson she'd discovered many years ago: take responsibility for your actions.

But she didn't climb up on her pulpit to lecture him. What good would it do to make accusations or insinuate that he was a bad guy? Though she hadn't seen a dangerous side to Julian, she knew better than to poke a sleeping grizzly.

He continued, "I'm not part of the inner circle, never was. Sure, I have a lot of responsibility. Nick's is an important part of the overall business, but Lorenzo doesn't tell me everything. He and Zapata and the rest of them stood back and watched me spin while I was searching for Damien."

The SUV exited the highway on the right and followed a narrow road that she thought would take them through Morrison and then into the wide valley where Red Rocks Amphitheatre was located. She didn't like this deviation from standard procedure, and worried about the way he was constantly checking the rearview mirrors as though expecting to see the headlights of another car following them.

She glanced over her shoulder toward the rear window, trying not to look at the bodies wrapped in drop cloths. "I haven't been this way before."

"Scenic route," he said as though that explained everything. "We're actually headed back to Denver."

"What about..." She nodded toward their terrible cargo. "Don't you have to do something about them?"

"I've got it covered."

For some unexplainable reason, his vague promise didn't trigger a panic attack. Her pulse was steady and strong, which made her think that he'd hypnotized her with his electric-blue eyes and tousled hair. The facts pointed to danger, especially with the way he kept looking for a tail, but she felt safe.

Telling herself not to be an idiot, she eased her phone out of her purse. This might be the right time to punch in that code and call for FBI backup. Holding her phone at the ready, she leaned back in the passenger seat and watched the scenery unfold. Even at night, Red Rocks was impressive. Not that she was in the mood for sightseeing.

"Here's the thing, Julian. You're trying to soften the blow by easing into your explanation, like pulling the bandage off slowly. But I'm not a patient woman. I'm more of a rip-it-off-fast person. Just tell me what I need to know."

"When I took that carpentry job, I thought it was just a couple weeks' work but I'm glad it turned out the way it did. Managing Nick's is the best job I've ever had. I'm going to miss it."

"Are you planning to quit?"

"I have to." He seemed to relax behind the wheel, satisfied that they were the only ones on the road. "There's no choice."

"Is that what you want to tell me? That you're quitting?"

"That's part of it, but—"

"Tell me," she demanded. "If you don't explain real soon, I'm going to scream like a tone-deaf opera diva."

"A threat?"

"You don't want to hear my high C."

"From the moment we met," he said. "I've been lying to you. And it's not just you. I've lied to everybody."

If she hadn't been the self-proclaimed Queen of Deception, she might have been more shocked. "I'm going to need a little bit more."

"I'm not really an architect or a carpenter or a criminal. I work for the Colorado Bureau of Investigation, the CBI, and I've been undercover at Nick's. I feed information to law enforcement so they can swoop in and make arrests."

She didn't know whether to laugh or cry. He was never going to believe that she was his mirror reflection, working for the FBI. "Why tell me? Aren't you worried that I'll rat you out to Lorenzo?"

"You could." He guided the SUV onto the highway leading back to Denver. "It's a risk I'm willing to take. There's something big going down at Nick's, and I don't want you to get caught in the crossfire."

Hadn't she told him a dozen times that she could protect herself? His big confession was a little bit insulting to her. "What else?"

"The CBI can get Marigold into protective custody."

The Colorado Bureau was nothing compared to the feds. Julian might think he had all the answers, but this wasn't his call. Who did he think he was? Her irritation spiked. She had a stake in this game, and she had the juice to make sure everything turned out right—more power than he had. Maybe she hadn't been undercover with Lorenzo for three years, but she had experience. Angie punched the three-digit code into her phone and followed up with a text. It was time for Julian to meet her FBI handler.

INSTEAD OF DRIVING to a secluded mountain dump site and digging shallow graves for the three murdered men, they went to the downtown Denver morgue used by the CBI for autopsies. Angie was somewhat impressed that Julian was able to make these arrangements with a few phone calls. He parked his SUV on a subterranean level under a huge hospital complex where a gang of medical people in scrubs and lab coats were waiting with gurneys to transport the corpses—a messy process but it would have been worse if rigor had set in. When they moved Damien to the gurney, the cloth fell back from his face. His mouth gaped, revealing yellowed teeth. His skin was waxen, and the discolored scar across his forehead stood out in sharp relief.

Though Angie would shed no tears for this man who had assaulted Waylon and terrorized Jane, she silently offered a prayer that he would be at peace. No one deserved to die from violence. She looked toward Julian. "What happens next?"

"The bodies are signed in with the coroner. Autopsies will be required."

Since the cause of death was not a question, she guessed that these three would not be high priority. Still, an autopsy could yield a wealth of information, ranging from tattoos to medical conditions related to where the deceased lived. "When will they have the preliminary DNA results?"

"Soon," he said. "They need to get an ID and check the criminal data base."

"I know." She was familiar with standard procedure. "I was asking about specific timing. The autopsy doctors probably don't work at night. Does somebody else take DNA samples and run facial recognition?"

He eyed her suspiciously. "How do you know about what happens in the morgue?"

"I watch crime shows on TV." Not revealing her identity was akin to lying, and she was comfortable in this zone. Angie couldn't wait to see the look on his face when he found out she was a fed.

A tall, lean man with a full head of gray hair and tired eyes approached them. Julian introduced him as Supervisory Special Agent Shanahan, the ranking officer in the CBI. When Angie shook his hand, she was acutely aware of the blood spatter on her sleeve. Gunshot residue wasn't visible to the naked eye, but her clothes and hands must be covered with it. She didn't kill the unnamed third man, but she'd shot him.

SSA Shanahan directed them into the building past a couple of labs and into a nondescript office. He sat behind the desk and took out a recording device. After stating his name and her alias, he made eye contact with Julian and asked, "How much does Ms. D'Angelo know about your situation?"

"She knows I'm an agent," he said. "It's okay to use my name."

"Special Agent Julian Parish aka Parisi," Shanahan said. "Tell me what happened tonight."

While he described his surveillance at Nick's and how he'd picked up visual recognition of Damien in the casino, she rolled both of his names around in her head. Changing the final *i* to an *h* transformed her expectations in surprising ways. Parisi was more musical and exotic, but Parish suited him better. Julian Parish seemed like the kind of guy who sat in the front of the class and wore glasses. If that image was true and he actually was a kind of nerd, Julian was a better liar than she gave him credit for. In spite of her attraction to him, she'd believed he was a dangerous badass.

He wrapped up his narrative at the point in time when he drove into the front parking area for Valentino's bakery. Both Julian and SSA Shanahan focused on her. It only took a few moments for her to tell what had happened inside the bakery. There was really no good way to express the intensity she'd felt in those moments when she faced death and made the decision to shoot. Three men had died.

When she looked down at her hands in her lap, she noticed a slight tremor. *This won't do!* Covering her tension, she adjusted her ponytail and smoothed her hair. "That's all."

"I might have missed something," SSA Shanahan said. "Did you tell us why you went to the bakery at midnight?"

"I needed to order a cake." She glanced from Shanahan to Julian, reading disbelief on their faces. "Valentino believed me so there's no reason for you guys to be skeptical. I needed a cake for a special event."

"Had you made an appointment with him?" Shanahan asked.

"Of course not, midnight is a ridiculous time for an appointment."

"What's your relationship with Valentino? Are you close?"

Did he seriously consider her a suspect? She couldn't resist playing with SSA Shanahan. Leaning across the desk, she licked her lips, still tasting the chocolate icing. "Let's just say that I love Valentino's baked goods."

"How long have you known him?"

"I met him at the same time I met Julian."

"Okay," Shanahan said. "You had no long-term connection."

For the third time that night, she took out her phone and

checked the app that connected with the FBI. She'd been texting back and forth with her handler. His last message told her that he'd arrived and was outside this office, waiting for her instructions.

She spun around and crossed the room. With her hand on the doorknob, she said, "There's someone here who can explain."

Though she'd never met Special Agent Hemming in person, she recognized him from his online profile. In the FBI, undercover operatives didn't show up online, didn't post photos and didn't take selfies. Their real names and backgrounds were guarded. As she approached SA Hemming, she held up her phone to show him the app and assure him that she was who she claimed to be. "Call me Angie."

He shook her hand and touched the brim of his cowboy hat. "You're not what I expected."

"I'm better, right?"

"You're something."

A big guy with an easy smile, Hemming was dressed in what she assumed was the Wild West version of "men in black"—black jeans, white shirt with bolo tie and a black jacket with fringe. He got directly to the point. "How can I help?"

She ushered him into the office where she introduced Julian and SSA Shanahan. "This is Special Agent Hemming of the FBI. This unlucky man is assigned to be my handler."

"Your handler?" Julian blurted.

"Our two agencies need better communication to avoid this sort of redundancy," she said, keeping her tone calm and even. "Like you, I'm undercover."

SSA Shanahan reacted with smooth professionalism as he shook hands with Hemming. "We're always happy to work with the FBI."

Julian was nowhere near as cool. Behind his glasses, his eyes bulged like a pair of solid blue, number two pool balls. His jaw tensed, and she could tell that he was gritting his teeth. This human volcano was about to spew. She almost felt sorry for him…almost.

Chapter Thirteen

There were times in Julian's life when he wished the floor would open and swallow him whole. *I'm an ass, a total ass.* He sat in the square institutional chair in the small office down the hall from the morgue and tensed every muscle to keep from cringing. These dull beige walls were closing in and crushing him. In his mind, he replayed every dopey comment he'd made about how she couldn't protect herself. His questions about her background and whether she was dating Manny Harris, a DEA agent, must have sounded as naive as a third grader. Less than an hour ago, he'd made his great big declaration that he was CBI undercover. *What a joke!*

Angie sashayed across the office, stopped behind his chair and leaned close to his ear. "You must have had some idea that I was a cop..."

Didn't have a clue. When he'd learned about her connection to Marigold, he'd thought Angie's secret, unstated motivation for all her lies was revenge against Lorenzo.

She continued. "Right away, you knew that I wasn't who I claimed to be. That was smart deduction on your part because my online profile and data were constructed by the geniuses in FBI cybercrimes."

Was that the truth or was she patronizing him? "You're a good liar."

"So are you."

And he was done feeling sorry for himself.

Abruptly, he stood. With an emphatic sweep of his hand, he shoved away all doubt and confusion. Whether or not she played him for a fool didn't matter. He'd been working this undercover identity for three years, and he'd be damned if he allowed Nick's to be turned into a hub for trafficking. He whipped off his glasses and stared down at her. When he spoke, his voice dropped to a low, authoritative level.

"Since we'll be working together," he said, "we need a plan to avoid bumping heads."

"What do you suggest?" she asked.

"I'll continue meeting with Lorenzo, Valentino and the Zapatas—both Nolan and Carlos. Maybe I can get them to open up about Damien and his role in the trafficking operation."

"I've got ideas of my own," she said. "Tomorrow, I want to take Cara into the hills behind the bunkhouse and search for the friend she calls Gigi. If this child exists and escaped from a prior trafficking attempt, she'll have useful info. I'm also going to meet with Marigold."

"I'll come with you to search," he said.

"Not a good idea. This little girl might be scared of men."

"Sure." He sucked down an angry breath. "But won't she be frightened when confronted by a woman on horseback who doesn't know how to ride?"

Before she could snap back at him, he noticed that her handler and his supervisor had put their heads together. They were grinning, nodding and shaking hands. He doubted their alliance would bode well for him or Angie.

Hemming came toward them. In spite of his mountainous size, he moved athletically. When he sat on the edge of the desk, Julian hoped the old wooden furniture would support Hemming's weight. "You two have made errors," Hemming said, "starting with those three dead men in the coroner's office. It would have been better to take them alive so we could interrogate and get information."

"You're right," Angie said.

He appreciated the fact that she didn't try to hide behind excuses. Julian added, "While I was studying the surveillance on Damien, I noticed a skull tat on the back of his hand and three *H*s on his fingers."

"Good catch," Hemming said. "The *H* tattoos stand for a cartel that started in Colombia and now operates from Juarez. I expect we'll find similar markings on the other two men."

"It's a start," Julian said.

"You're good at your job, Parish. Shanahan tells me that your intelligence is responsible for major disruptions in black market drug sales, illegal gun smuggling and a prostitution ring." He turned his head to focus on Angie. "This woman has equally impressive accomplishments, including the recovery of eight million dollars in jewelry and art."

"But don't either of you get bigheaded," Shanahan said. "But we don't want to shut down either of your investigations. You're going to work together. And you'll stay in touch with us through dedicated, encoded apps. Got it?"

He and Angie responded with a simultaneous, "Yes sir."

They were on the same page, which was good. And the investigation seemed straightforward. This situation might not be too miserable.

SSA Shanahan said, "We've come up with an undercover story that will allow you to spend more time together and not look suspicious."

Hemming beamed. "We want you two to pretend to be lovers."

Julian's momentary sense of well-being was gone. He and Angie would be undercover lovers? This plan had disaster written all over it.

TWO HOURS LATER, they were back in the SUV headed for Nick's. Jostling along in the passenger seat, Angie didn't dare close her eyes for even a second for fear that she'd drift into a deep sleep. The coffee they'd picked up from a hospital vending machine tasted like sludge, but the caffeine jolt was welcome.

She was just alert enough to notice that Nick had taken I-70, which was the long way around. "Why this route?" she asked.

"I want to approach from the west so it looks like I went deeper into the mountains to bury the bodies."

She groaned. "Do you really think anybody will notice?"

"I like to be prepared for any and all possibilities. Whether or not anybody is watching, I'm covered. I also didn't wash the blood out of the back. Cleaning my SUV is a job for one of the valets."

"Earlier tonight when you took that weird detour past Red Rocks, did you think somebody might be following you?"

"I always drive as if somebody's on my tail, using extreme caution. That's why I've lasted three years at this assignment. I don't take chances." He glanced in her direction. "I'm not like you."

"What's that supposed to mean?"

"Come on, Angie, you know what I'm talking about. You're lucky Valentino didn't blow your head off when you showed up on his doorstep and started talking about cake."

"He bought it," she pointed out.

"He bought the whole package, believing that you're a

pretty blonde who is kind of ditzy. The act works for you, and that's not a bad thing. But there aren't many people who can pull off that kind of con job."

She preferred to think of her approach as intuitive. Based on her intelligence and training, she charged in the right direction. If she stumbled into trouble, she used her skill at lying to escape. Still, she appreciated his ability to think ahead. "Planning is good. I promise not to jump into anything without talking to you first."

"What was the real reason you went to the bakery?"

"I wanted to look for evidence in his delivery truck. Based on a bit of conversation I overheard, I think those vehicles are being used for trafficking."

"Makes sense."

An uncomfortable moment of silence stretched between them. They'd been lying to each other for days and had no basis for trust. Also, when you got right down to the bottom line, they were rivals. He worked for the state, and she was a fed.

She imagined he was protective of his turf, and she understood why he'd feel that way. The same didn't apply to her. Though she liked to finish what she started, Angie wasn't deeply invested in Nick's. "You know, if I wasn't so concerned about Marigold, I'd be happy to step aside and let you handle everything."

"You don't seriously expect me to believe your story about Marigold, do you?"

Did he think she was faking her breakdown when he found her on the balcony outside Marigold's bedroom? "It's the truth."

"I'm going to assume that every word you've said to me is a lie, including that. Now, about this undercover lover thing...we need to figure out how to handle it."

"No big deal. We'll hold hands and give each other longing looks."

"Not enough," he said. "Nick's is like a small town with everybody watching everybody else all the time. The place runs on gossip. It's going to take more than a peck on the cheek to convince them that we've got something going."

"You think?"

"Tonight, when I park at the curb outside Nick's and come around to open your door, you need to kiss me. I want a real kiss, a big one."

"With tongue?"

"You bet, and we should go to the same room as though we're sleeping together. I suggest we use my suite because it's bigger."

This had to be the most clinical proposition she'd ever received. "Sorry, Julian, but that's a negative. It's my room, nonnegotiable."

"Why?"

"I don't want to get up in the morning and do the 'walk of shame' down to the concierge level. It's a lousy way to start the day."

"But it's okay for me to do the walk?"

"Men don't feel shame," she said. "They strut."

He laughed, and she was relieved to hear his chuckle—a sign that they were beginning to adjust to the crazy new reality that had been foisted upon them by his SSA and her handler. "I want you to know," she said, "that this lover thing is new for me. I've never seduced a man as part of an undercover operation. My platinum blond hair, the jewelry and bedazzled clothes aren't meant to attract male attention. I think of my outfits as armor."

"Yeah, you're real scary."

In the distance, she could see the lights from the parking lot and from outside the seven-story wings. The neon

Nick's logo gleamed red. At this hour on a Sunday night, the lobby and entrance were still lit, but most of the hotel windows were dark. "Is the casino open all night?"

"The casino and some of the restaurants. They're open but not very busy," He drove into the driveway. "Remember, Angie, we're going to give the valets a show. Don't hold back."

Kissing him wasn't the worst thing that she'd done on an assignment. They had chemistry, and Julian was a good-looking man. Not that handsome was any guarantee of sexual talent. A great kiss needed pressure, a friction, penetration by the tongue and taste—all wrapped up in a Goldilocks package with not too much and not too little.

She dug into her purse, grabbed a tin of mints and popped one into her mouth. She offered one to him and was glad when he took two. Was he as nervous about this as she was?

At the entrance, Julian parked and climbed out from behind the wheel. As he circled the car, she watched him give instructions to the two valets on duty, no doubt telling them to scrub the interior of his car and use bleach to erase the bloodstains. Julian's posture was strong and upright. He moved with the confidence of an alpha male.

When he approached the passenger side, he removed his glasses and tucked them into the inner pocket of his jacket. The door opened, and he took her hand to help her out. Though she was perfectly capable of bounding from the car and racing him to the entrance, she enjoyed the civilized gesture. She stood on the sidewalk, gazing into his amazing blue eyes encircled by dark lashes. He might have been grinning, but she didn't know for sure. The eyes captured her absolute attention.

"Very gentlemanly," she said.

"You're my lady."

Somewhat corny, but his words twanged an unthinking, visceral response inside her. A wave of excitement rippled from her scalp to her toes as his arm wrapped around her waist. He tightened his grasp until her body pressed flush against his chest. Her head tilted back, and her lips parted.

His mouth brushed hers, tentative at first and then he connected and increased the pressure so she had to respond. When his tongue swept against her teeth, she opened wider and welcomed him inside. He tasted of mint.

The main action stayed at the mouth, but she was aware of rubbing against him. Her hands slid inside his jacket and climbed his strong, muscular back. Though he was at least six inches taller than her five foot nine, they fit together nicely.

When he ended the kiss, her knees were weak. *Best assignment I've ever had.* She needed to send bouquets of roses to Hemming and Shanahan.

Julian kept his arm around her as they crossed the lobby and went to the elevators. The door whooshed open, and he escorted her inside. Before the elevator door could close, he held her face in both of his hands and leaned close. Under his breath, he said, "Surveillance camera. Kiss me again."

She didn't need another invitation. This should have been a quick kiss, only a few seconds, but when the doors opened on the fourth floor, Julian wouldn't let them close. Using his foot, he blocked the elevator and continued to kiss her while the bong-bong-bong warning bell clanged.

When they stepped onto the floor, a husky concierge leaned against the front of his desk with his thumbs hitched into the pockets of his jeans. He watched them with a bemused grin. Taking a moment, she straightened her clothes. Quietly, she mumbled, "I forgot about all the cameras."

"That's why I'm here," he said. "Planning."

"Well, Mr. Planner, you're lucky I remembered not to

put on a fresh coat of lipstick. With all this kissing, you'd look like a clown right now."

Julian stopped to talk to the guy at the desk while she gave him a wave and continued on to her suite. The living room was decorated in a southwestern motif with a sitting area, a desk by the window and a kitchenette. The bedroom was furnished with two queen-size beds, which meant she wouldn't be forced to sleep with him. *Too bad.* She wouldn't have minded taking this charade all the way… or would she?

In the bathroom, she took down her ponytail and massaged her scalp. Tonight had been intense—from the murders to the revelation about Julian, to the new undercover assignment, to the kiss. She needed to take a step back and figure out what was going on.

Julian tapped on the bathroom door. "I'm going to sweep the suite to make sure there aren't any new cameras or mics."

"Knock yourself out."

"Are you okay?"

"Never better."

For the tiniest sliver of a second, she considered inviting him into the bathroom to share her shower, but that was a step she didn't dare take. In her line of work, she couldn't maintain a long-term committed relationship. And Julian didn't fit the profile for a fling or a one-night stand.

Chapter Fourteen

Last night, Julian had hoped for more—more physical contact, more talking and more getting to know his undercover lover. But when he entered the bedroom, he found Angie sprawled across the sheets, sound asleep. Those two hot, steamy kisses should have led to more, and it seemed like she'd been making an effort to be sexy in an ice-blue satin nightie that hugged her curves and showed off her cleavage.

He'd stretched out on the bed beside her and watched her sleep. Without makeup, her face was fresh and sweet. She hadn't tamed her hair into a ponytail or a bun, and her unbridled platinum mane spilled across the pillow. He'd kissed her lightly on the forehead but decided not to wake her. They both needed sleep.

With morning light seeping into the room, he stood over her bed, once again gazing down at her peaceful form. Though he told himself that there would be time for him to kiss her soft lips and gradually get to know her body as a lover should, he had no guarantee. Time was not under his control. The trafficking operation could spring into action at any moment, and their assignment would be over. He needed to take advantage of every minute alone with her. And yet, he stepped back.

At eight o'clock on a Monday morning, he needed to get

started on the week's business at Nick's and to shove his investigation forward. The murders last night had flipped everything into high gear. With great reluctance, he exited her suite, being careful to close the door quietly. When he turned, he saw Muscleman Matt McHenry standing in front of the concierge desk. Was he smirking? Beside him, Cara watched Julian through suspicious eyes. This must be what Angie meant when she referred to the "walk of shame," not that Julian had anything to be ashamed of. He straightened his shoulders and walked toward the concierge and his perky companion.

"Did you have a sleepover with Angie?" Cara asked.

That was an accurate description of last night's activity or the lack thereof. "We were both tired. And we slept."

Cara dismissed him with a shrug and jumped to another topic. "Angie's going for a riding lesson today, and I'm going with her."

Last night, Julian had told the concierge on duty that the guy who had been menacing Cara and her mom was dead. Still, he wanted them to stay here and have full protection. He glanced at McHenry whose sheer body mass was enough to deter most assailants. "I want you to go with them."

"I can manage that." When he looked down at Cara, his rugged features softened. Somehow, the kid had melted his firm resolve. "Yesterday, Cara and Jane and I went into the hills for target practice. I'm thinking of getting a bullwhip of my own."

A strange way to bond, but Julian had no room to judge. He said, "I'll try to join you for the lesson."

"Yes!" Cara shouted, and then she dashed toward him and jumped into his arms for a hug. "We can have an adventure."

He hoped there wouldn't be too much excitement.

AFTER JULIAN WENT to his suite, showered and shaved, and ordered breakfast from room service, he was ready to face the day. His first stop was his office where he could deal with the myriad issues that usually popped up over the weekend. No sooner had he settled behind his desk than Tamara Rigby entered with a mug of fragrant black coffee and a folder that she dropped into his inbox tray. Though she wore her official hotel uniform of blazer, slacks and crisp white shirt, she had retained some of the glamour from her night at the Glass Palace. Her lipstick was bright, and her mossy green eyes sparkled.

"I had a wonderful time on Saturday," she said. "It's too bad that you and Angie had to leave early."

"I hope Leif took good care of you."

"He was so sweet." She exhaled a heavy sigh. "Most people see him as a big, tough football star, but he's intelligent and sensitive. We like a lot of the same music and same movies. Can you believe it? I have something in common with Leif."

He sipped his coffee, which was—as almost everything Tamara did—perfectly flavored and exactly the right temperature. This woman really was a catch. He nodded, encouraging her to continue talking. Her gossip was a welcome distraction from the horrifying scene he'd encountered at Valentino's. In contrast, things had been quiet at Nick's.

Soon, he'd have to leave this job. In the course of investigation, his role as an undercover operative would be exposed. Of course, he wouldn't be able to work for Lorenzo, and it was likely that Nick's would be altogether closed down. Julian wished for a different conclusion.

When he started as a carpenter at Nick's, the plan had been for him to spend a few weeks at the job to see if he could discover inside information. In less than a week, he'd heard delivery times for a massive drug deal and enough dirt to bury a local politician. SSA Shanahan decided that he should stay on the job for another couple of weeks. Then Lorenzo offered him a permanent position and the rest, as they say, was history.

Three years was a long stretch for an undercover assignment but not a waste of time. Julian had cemented his status as one of Lorenzo's top advisors, and he had contact with most of the other criminals in the state of Colorado and beyond. When this was over, he could provide enough intel to wipe the slate clean. The downside: he couldn't possibly continue in undercover work. Too many people knew him as the Professor, Julian Parisi. Going back to his job at the CBI meant riding a desk or sitting in front of a computer screen.

He wrapped his conversation with Tamara with a final word of caution. "Don't let your common sense get swept away by a handsome football player."

"I won't make that mistake." But her glittering smile told him that she couldn't wait to sink her teeth into the former Bronco. "We have a date for Thursday night after the NFL game."

"Isn't that kind of late?"

"That's the point." She winked.

Julian didn't completely trust Leif. Though he couldn't pinpoint a specific display of disloyalty, his cop instincts warned him that Leif was trouble. If those were the same instincts that wrongly told him Angie couldn't be trusted, and was a criminal, he might be wise to ignore them. She'd turned out to be a fed. Leif might be some other breed of hero.

No more time for second-guessing, Julian needed to focus hard on the trafficking, to take a deep dive. It was time for him to swim with the sharks. After a last sip of coffee, he stood behind his desk and asked Tamara, "Is there anything in that folder that requires immediate attention?"

She shrugged. "Just the usual."

He checked his watch. At a few minutes past nine, it wasn't too early to make the drive into Denver and confront Zapata in his office. "I'll be gone for most of the morning," he said. "You're in charge."

"What if Rudy shows up?"

"I gave him the morning off. He worked late last night." After the cleanup at Valentino's, Rudy had sent photos on his phone. He and his team had done a good job, wiping away the bloody evidence of three murders. "If he shows, give him some invoices to sign. Enough busywork to make him feel important."

Before leaving his office, he called ahead to the valet station so they could bring his car around to the front. Julian was definitely going to miss the perks and privileges of being boss. Before he got behind the steering wheel, he checked the back of his SUV, which had been perfectly cleaned and detailed. He peeled off a hundred dollar tip to go with the hundred from last night.

While making the familiar drive into Denver, he considered the issues he needed to talk about. The fact that Zapata had kept Damien's identity a secret hinted at a lack of trust. Julian wasn't being informed about the trafficking operation, and he needed to find out why. What was his place in the Lorenzo hierarchy? They couldn't just dump him…or could they? Julian was confident that nobody else could run Nick's as effectively as he could, but he wasn't sure Zapata felt the same way.

His thoughts skipped to the attack on Valentino and then to his surveillance of Damien. What was Lorenzo's position on Zapata and trafficking? Julian's stream of logical thinking came to a screeching halt when he conjured up a sweet vision of Angie in her satin nightie with her hair cascading across the pillow in a platinum wave. He lingered on that fantasy, imagining her lashes fluttering open and her dark eyes gazing up at him. He should have joined her in bed last night, should have stayed in her bedroom this morning. Facing off with Zapata was a lousy alternative.

At ten minutes after ten, he stopped at the secretary's desk on the top floor of the office building where he'd first met Angie. "Is Zapata in?"

"You should have made an appointment, Julian."

He pushed his glasses up on his nose and gave the secretary a warm smile, hoping to melt her standard show of hostility. She proudly guarded access to Zapata. Nobody got buzzed into the inner office without her approval. "You're right," he said. "I apologize for not following procedure."

"There are reasons for these rules." Though the cut of her pin-striped suit was fashionable, her tone reminded him of a disapproving librarian chastising a student about a late return. "His schedule is booked all day long, and he simply doesn't have a free minute."

Ever since he'd quoted *Pride and Prejudice* to her, he had been one of her favorites. To tell the truth, he felt the same way about her. "Give me a break, Lucille."

"It wouldn't be fair," she said.

"But I drove all the way down from the mountains."

She tapped her pen on the desktop and rearranged her calendar so the edges were precisely parallel to the edge of the desk. When she looked up at him, her pinched lips loosened into a sly grin. "I suppose I could make an exception for you. Just this once."

He suspected that she'd always intended to open the door. He respected the game she played. "Thank you, Lucille."

"I hear you have a girlfriend."

How had the gossip gotten here so fast? "I do," he said. "In some ways, she reminds me of you."

"How so?"

"She's smart and tough and doesn't put up with rudeness. She nearly broke Murph's arm for being impolite."

"I like her already," Lucille said.

He went to the closed double doors and waited for the buzz before he pushed them open. The huge corner office was surrounded by a wide terrace with two floor-to-ceiling windows. One faced south and framed a distant view of Pikes Peak. The other looked east toward the skyline of downtown Denver.

Zapata sat at a glass-topped table on the terrace, drinking coffee that Julian knew would be too strong for his taste. Also seated at the table were Carlos and Rudy. Sharing morning coffee and a plate of doughnuts with Carlos seemed natural. The two of them were family. But the presence of Rudy made him think of one word: *traitor*. Dressed in the same suit he'd worn at the Glass Palace party, Rudy Lorenzo sat straight and self-important, staring into the blue Colorado skies toward the shiny outline of the city.

Julian was angry and tried hard not to show it. He strode across the terrace and stood at the railing. Last night, he'd thought Rudy might be a decent assistant, after all. The kid and his crew had cleaned up the mess without complaint. Before that, during the evening, he'd planted himself in the surveillance room with Julian and watched Damien as he meandered through the casino. Had Rudy known that Damien worked for Zapata?

Though Julian was primed to ask questions and demand answers from his treacherous assistant, he focused instead on Zapata and Carlos. They were important and responsible for decisions while Rudy was nothing more than a punk.

He walked to a chair at the table but didn't sit. His direct focus rested on Zapata, and he tempered his rage with a social comment. "Did you enjoy your birthday party?"

"I don't feel like I'm sixty."

His thick hair hadn't gotten the news. Not a single strand of gray disrupted the shiny black helmet. "You look well."

"The secret is getting enough sleep."

"I didn't rest well last night. Your boy, Damien, caused a disruption."

"You'll get over it."

Zapata sipped from his mug and patted his mouth with a cloth napkin. Today, he wore a casual jacket over a shirt with an open collar and jeans. In spite of occasional flashes from the precious stones in his heavy gold rings, he looked like the ace accountant that he was. Everything with Zapata was based on P&L statement with emphasis on the profit.

"You should have told me," Julian said. "When I first reported that somebody attacked Waylon in the barn, you should have told me that Damien worked for you. Searching for him was a time suck. Those are hours I'll never get back."

Carlos waded into the conversation. "Our association with Damien didn't work out the way we'd hoped."

"Well, it wasn't good for him, either." Damien was murdered, dead, gone.

"Let it go," Carlos advised.

He didn't expect Zapata to apologize. That wasn't the way this guy operated. But Julian needed to get him to open up and deliver some useful information, specifically the details about the trafficking. "You owe me an explanation."

Zapata jolted to his feet. "I owe you nothing."

"You've got something going on," he said. "And I understand Nick's better than anybody. Let me help."

"You make a point." Carlos looked toward his uncle. "You both have something to say, but I think we're all on the same page. Last night, we ran into a problem, a misunderstanding."

"Three murders," Julian said.

"Could have been worse. The Baker wasn't hurt." Carlos gestured for both of them to sit. "It's all taken care of now. Settle down."

Before he sat, Julian pulled back his chair, leaving room for him to bolt if necessary. "When Damien and his gang showed up at Valentino's, was he acting on your orders?"

Carlos held up his palm to block that line of questions. "We would never order a hit on Valentino. Damien worked for a group we're doing business with, and the arrogant little weasel got it into his head that he could handle logistics better than us. Basically, this was a disagreement about transportation issues."

Julian put two and two together. Angie's suspicion that Valentino's delivery vans would be used to move human cargo made sense. Damien must have figured that if he eliminated Valentino, he could take over that part of the business. "That still doesn't explain why he attacked Waylon."

"Another can of worms," Carlos said. "Damien was a troublemaker. Now he's gone."

Zapata nodded. "It's good that Damien is out of the picture."

Now they'd gotten to the meat. "Tell me about this picture, the big picture. What project was Damien working on?"

"Back off, man. Don't you ever give up?" Rudy gave a

snort that he probably thought was clever. "Zapata already told you that this is none of your business."

"I'm not talking to you, Rudy."

"That's a dumbass mistake. You need to pay attention to me."

"You want attention? Fine. Yesterday, when you and I were in surveillance together, watching Damien, did you know who he was?"

"Maybe."

"Yes or no."

"All right, yes."

"You didn't tell me. You sat and watched while I was spinning my wheels and going nowhere fast."

"So what if I did?"

"You're fired," Julian said.

Rudy jumped from his chair. For a moment, it looked like the kid intended to vault across the table in some kind of airborne assault. Julian was ready for him. He stood, balanced his weight on the balls of his feet and braced for a fight. Usually he avoided physical contact, but Rudy deserved a knock on his pinhead. Not only had he been stupid but he was also disrespectful.

Before Rudy could charge, they heard Lorenzo's voice. "That's enough."

Julian didn't know if he'd been standing there the whole time and watching or if he'd just arrived on the terrace. Either way, his timing was outstanding. He'd avoided the pettiness of the argument but knew exactly where everybody stood. When he strode out of the shadow toward the table, sunlight glittered off the silver mane that contrasted his perfect tan.

The next step, Julian decided, would be his. Since his position at Nick's was already precarious, he might as well risk all the chips.

"I'm glad to see you," Julian said. "I need answers about the project Damien was working on. If I know what's going on, I'll help. On the other hand, if you don't feel like you can tell me, I'll consider it a vote of no confidence."

"What are you saying?" Lorenzo asked.

Julian made the big bet. He went all in. "Tell me or I quit."

"Nobody ever meant to insult you." Lorenzo crossed the terrace toward him. "You haven't been part of our family as long as Zapata or Carlos. And you're not connected by blood like my idiot nephew. But I appreciate the work you've done."

"Best job I've ever had." Julian wasn't playing games and he wasn't lying.

Lorenzo stood only a few feet away. "When the time is right, I'll tell you exactly what's going on. Until then, I have to ask you to trust me."

"I can't have random thugs like Damien roughing up my employees."

"Understood, and I only need one change in your regular routine. Starting on Tuesday, the night shift in the barn and outbuildings will be handled by three men who don't work for you."

"Tuesday? As in tomorrow?"

"Do you have a problem with that?"

Julian swallowed hard. Tomorrow was too soon. He couldn't possibly get control of the situation by tomorrow night. It took every shred of his self-control to stay cool. "No problem."

"I'll have these men introduce themselves before they start. During the day, the procedure is as usual. Nothing changes. You're still the manager. Waylon takes care of day operations in the barn."

"And at night?"

"My other crew is in charge, and your employees shouldn't be anywhere in sight."

He held out his hand, and Julian had no choice but to take it. Fighting to suppress his panic, he met Lorenzo's gaze and changed the subject. "I fired your idiot nephew."

"I heard."

"If he apologizes, I'll take him back."

Lorenzo gave a nod and stepped aside. Instructions to Rudy were unnecessary. The kid knew what he was supposed to do, and he shuffled forward and told Julian that he was sorry and would never disrespect him again.

The situation with Rudy was nothing compared to the information Lorenzo had revealed. His men would be stationed in the barn at night. The change was scheduled for Tuesday, which meant he and Angie needed to be ready to deal with the traffickers by tomorrow night.

Chapter Fifteen

Angie had always preferred to work alone. Inviting other people into her sometimes elaborate undercover deceptions often resulted in confusion and hampered her ability to think on her feet. As soon as she woke and realized that Julian wasn't in bed with her, she concentrated on what needed to happen today. Her riding lesson in the early afternoon was actually a chance to search for Gigi. The murder of three potential witnesses made it even more important to find the girl who might provide living testimony against the traffickers.

After the Gigi search, Angie would meet with Marigold. Anticipation flooded through her. She'd waited eleven years for this moment, and she feared the outcome might not be what she wanted. Marigold might be the witness who could take down Lorenzo or she might refuse to turn on the man who gave her fancy houses and jewelry. This was definitely a big day, and she wished Julian were here to talk it over.

She checked her phone and saw he'd left a text saying that he was going to see Zapata and would join her later for the horseback riding lesson. She rubbed her eyes and read it again. Zapata? The man who was in tight with a Colombian cartel? The mastermind of Lorenzo's businesses? The vindictive monster who sent Damien to kill the Baker? If she hadn't been edgy before, Julian's morning agenda—which he should have discussed with her—was enough to start her adrenaline running.

What had happened to Angie the Loner? For the first time in her career with the FBI, she felt like she needed a partner, needed Julian. Though she wanted to call him or send a screaming text in all caps, she worried that someone might be listening to their communications. Reverting to her undercover role as his lover, she sent a big fat juicy heart emoji.

Her day was underway. Dressed for her riding lesson in a pair of purple Frye boots that matched a cowgirl shirt with an embroidered yoke, she took the elevator down to the OTB lounge on the lower level. Her office was behind the public area that was basically a tavern furnished with horsey memorabilia and big-screen TVs to watch every aspect of horse racing. She tapped in the code to unlock her office door, sidled inside and settled behind her long desk where a gang of computers were performing or waiting to be called upon. She waved at the screens, some of which were blank while others displayed constantly updated records of betting activity.

"Hello, boys." Her mouth stretched in a smile. "Did you miss me?"

Some people might think it was sad that her best friends were computers, but she liked her machines. If she entered the right program, a computer never betrayed her trust. When she wanted to play, they offered gazillions of games. And if she just wanted to sit quietly with her thoughts, they wouldn't interrupt.

The only facet of her life that a computer couldn't satisfy was the one that Julian had activated when he kissed her.

Last night, their time together left her yearning for

more. After her steamy shower, she'd dressed in a satin chemise with no panties and arranged herself on the bed, prepared to greet him with everything she had. Instead, she'd given in to exhaustion and fallen asleep.

There was a knock on the office door. "Who is it?"

"It's Tamara. I have caffeine."

Angie opened the door. "You guessed the magic word."

Tamara held a tray from room service. "Do you want it out here or in there?"

Angie glanced at her friendly computers and decided not to put their beautiful circuitry in danger of a spill. "I'm pretty sure there won't be a crowd in the lounge. Monday morning at ten isn't exactly a busy time for horse races."

In the lounge, Tamara set the tray on a vacant table. "I used to go to the racetrack with my dad when I was a kid. The horses were beautiful. Dad let me stand at the railing so I could get a closer look when they'd prance around the track. Then we'd go to the clubhouse, which had a really cool vibe if you didn't mind the stink of cigarette smoke. Do you prefer coffee or tea?"

"Coffee without cream or sugar."

"That was my first guess, but I brought a latte and hot water just in case." She lifted the domed plate cover to reveal scrambled eggs, bacon and hash browns. "Mind if I join you?"

"Sit." It would have been rude to send her away, and Angie realized that the last time she'd eaten was when she had the chocolate cupcake from Valentino's. "Have you recovered from Saturday night?"

"I had a wonderful time. Thanks for helping me bust out of my shell."

"It's hard to resist the power of a red dress." She shoveled a bite of silky, delicious eggs into her mouth. "Leif couldn't take his eyes off you."

Tamara inadvertently glanced through the door from the OTB to the sports betting venue where Leif worked. "We have a date on Thursday night. Fingers crossed, I hope there will be more. Now, tell me all about you and Julian."

"It seems we have more in common than we realized." *A vast understatement!* "We connected."

"Look at you," Tamara said. "You're glowing."

"Am I?" Glowing and blushing hadn't been part of her undercover disguise. Pretending to be involved with Julian was going to be easy.

"You make a classy couple—him looking like a professor with his glasses and you with your gorgeousness."

Angie concentrated on devouring her breakfast. "There's not much high-profile horse racing on today's schedule. I'm going to take advantage of the downtime to have another riding lesson with Waylon."

"How's that going?"

"It's okay." She had gotten far enough that she could mount and sit astride without feeling like she was going to puke.

Two gray-haired duffers shuffled into the lounge and settled themselves at a table where they opened their copies of the *Daily Racing Form*. These two were regulars and came to Nick's every day.

"Bert and Ernie," Tamara said as she stood. "I'll get those two some coffee. What time does your bartender come in?"

"Eleven o'clock and thanks for taking care of my guys. It's lonely down here. I want more bettors who stick around and start bringing their friends."

She finished her breakfast, sat back and sipped excellent coffee while Tamara chatted with the gruff but oddly charming old guys. Angie didn't know much about racing or off-track betting and still didn't completely understand the codes and notes on the racing forms, but she liked the atmosphere. Everybody at Nick's was easygoing and friendly. This would have been a great place to work, except for the criminal element. Last night's eruption into violence was a reminder that Nick's was more than yummy room service and lightweight legal vices.

She returned to her office to deal with the computerized aspect of gambling, which was several times bigger than the in-house OTB. Most of the members of this gentlemen's club placed their wagers online. According to her stats, the recent legalization of sports betting in Colorado hadn't affected the cash flow at Nick's, probably because Lorenzo offered advances on bets…for an exorbitant interest rate.

While she worked, Angie lost herself in a world of numbers. Her undercover identity claimed she was a math genius. Not true, but she enjoyed computations, projections and algorithms. When she finally looked up from her computers, a couple of hours had passed. She yawned, stretched and wondered why she hadn't heard from Julian.

What had happened at Zapata's office? She'd been trained to imagine alternatives and contingencies, most of which were disasters. As her colleague, Julian needed to keep her informed. In his pose as her lover, his attitude definitely had to change. He had to portray a guy who was obsessed, besotted and crazy about her, had to act like he couldn't stand being apart from her.

When she checked her phone again, there were no other texts from him. Instead, she accessed the encrypted link with her handler at the FBI. Special Agent Hemming had left details about the autopsies which provided very little new information. Damien and one of the others had the triple *H* tattoo from the Colombian cartel. The third man had a tat of Roman numerals. MMXV stood for 2015, a year that held significance for a gang that had started in Denver and spread across the Southwest. The gang called themselves the Fifteen.

Why was Damien in touch with MMXV? Had he been planning a double cross, breaking away from the cartel and doing business with a local gang? She hated to see so many other dangerous people involved with the trafficking, but that was the way these schemes worked.

From studying Lorenzo's accounts and computer files that she had access to, she suspected that the service he provided was mostly logistical. Zapata would collect payment from the cartels and gangs that smuggled human cargo, whether it was kids, maids, sex workers or field hands. Zapata would arrange contacts and transportation which resulted in a second payment. Lorenzo was pivotal to the operation but—true to his expensive taste with original artwork and the fantastic Glass Palace—he kept his hands clean. She had questions, a lot of questions, and needed to find time to sit down with Julian and compare data.

When she emerged from her office, she counted six patrons in addition to Bert and Ernie who had moved closer to one of the big-screen TVs. Waylon had joined them and was giving a low-key lecture about how to tell which horse was a winner.

"You can read all the stats you want," Waylon said, "but there ain't no substitute for experience and instinct. I spent my whole life with horses, and I can take a look at the field for this race and tell you the result. Win, place and show."

Bert and Ernie didn't agree with the old cowboy. They had a complicated system with different colored markers that checked off various aspects on the racing form. Then they factored in the history of the horse, took a look at the breeder and trainer and jockey. Their bets were generally under fifty bucks.

"Our system works," one of them said as he took a swig from his coffee mug. "Angie, tell him. It works."

Reluctantly, she admitted, "I don't quite understand how they do it, but they get results. Last week, they did 18 percent better than the house, including a bet on a thirty-three-to-one long shot."

A commotion announced the arrival of Leif Farnsworth. He wasn't a big name in horse racing, but everybody knew the former quarterback from the Denver team. He shook hands all around before he got sucked into Bert and Ernie's conversation.

"I'm guessing y'all know the answer to this question," Waylon said. "What's the best way to pick a winner? Statistics or instinct?"

Leif shrugged. "I like to go with my gut."

"Instinct," Waylon said triumphantly.

Bert and Ernie scowled in unison. One of them asked, "How often are you right?"

"More often than I lose, but not by much."

"What are the signs?" Waylon asked. "When y'all go into a game, how do you know if you're going to win or lose?"

"I always start off thinking I'm a winner. If I thought I was going to lose or get sacked or fumble, I wouldn't leave the dressing room. I never want to screw up, but sometimes it just happens." Leif shook his head. "I calculate the variables and check my level of confidence, but there's no way to prepare for the unexpected."

Not a bad way to describe life or fate or even love. No matter how confident you felt or how many calculations pointed toward success, the unexpected could rear its ugly head and wipe out any plan. When Angie heard more people approaching the OTB lounge, she craned her neck, hoping to see Julian. No such luck! Strolling through the door were Calamity Jane, Muscleman Matt the concierge and Cara, who dodged through the tables and chairs to give Angie a hug. Right behind them was Tamara, who zoomed in on Leif.

On the big-screen TV, the horses paraded around the track, giving the crowd a last look and time to place their bets. In horse racing, it seemed to take forever to prepare for a race that lasted only a few minutes. While Waylon described the gait and the energy from one of the two-year-old fillies, she went to the bar and ordered another cup of coffee.

Looking up into the long mirror behind the liquor bottles at the back of the bar, she watched the growing crowd but was still detached from it. Cara bounced across the room and climbed up on a stool beside her. Though it wasn't appropriate or legal to have a child in an establishment that served liquor, Cara was safer here than most other locations at Nick's.

"Waylon is gonna let me ride with my mom," Cara said. "I told him I could handle my own horse, but he says I'm not big enough."

And why would you want *to?* "Riding with your mom will be fine. She grew up on a ranch."

"Yep." Cara nodded vigorously, and her ponytail bounced. "We're gonna visit for Christmas, and I'll get to do more riding."

While she chattered about a pony with black and white spots, Angie could hear the love in Cara's voice. When she'd been a seven-year-old, there had been nothing or no one she cared about so deeply. Maybe if she'd had an animal companion, she wouldn't have been such a troublemaker. Marigold was the only person she'd ever trusted. And Marigold had left her.

She felt a warm hand at her waist, looked up into the mirror above the bar and saw Julian standing beside her. Tamara was right. Side by side, they were a classy couple. He dropped a light kiss on her forehead.

Cara chirped. "Hey, Julian, you gotta give me a kiss. I'm your girlfriend, too."

"Absolutely." He brushed a kiss on the top of her head and tugged at her ponytail. "Why is everybody sitting around here and drinking coffee?"

"Beats me," Angie said. "My lesson isn't until two."

He scanned the crowd. "Is everybody coming along?"

"I am." Cara's hand shot into the air.

Being accompanied by a crowd would hamper their ability to search for Gigi. This wasn't what Angie had intended. "Jane and Matt will also be joining us. And Tamara might have mentioned that she'd like to tag along."

"Why?" Julian asked.

"Checking out the gossip," Cara said with a flip of her ponytail. "They want to know if you two are boyfriend and girlfriend."

"I'll never tell." Julian checked his watch and leaned closer to her. "We're going to get a head start. Just you and me."

A good way to search without a mob! Though she liked his solution, she had a few doubts. "How much do you know about horses?"

"I grew up on a ranch in Wyoming. Is that good enough for you?"

"You're good enough for me," she said softly, "in every way."

"Yuck!" Cara shouted.

Chapter Sixteen

After a couple of quick excuses to the group in the OTB lounge, Julian took her hand and led her through the back hallways on the basement level.

"Where are we going?" she asked.

"This is part of the original structure before it was renovated into the gentlemen's club." He used a code on a keypad to open a door at the end of the hallway. When a green light gave the okay, they stepped through. "This was originally a root cellar."

"Cold and dank," she said. "That figures."

"No need to waste money keeping preserved peaches and salsa at the proper temperature. Not that there's any of that stuff down here anymore." The few bare bulbs shed a dim light. Even though it was the middle of the day, there was a creepy vibe. "Watch your step."

"A secret space," she said. "Nobody comes down here, which makes me think it might be perfect to use for—"

He silenced her with a kiss. Nuzzling her ear, he whispered, "We have to always act like somebody is watching and listening. And, yes, you're right. This is only one of many hidden places in Nick's that could be used for trafficking."

Before he was aware of what was happening, she went up on tiptoe to kiss his throat, then she caught his earlobe in her teeth. Her light nibbles sent electric fire along his nerve endings. "What kind of idiot," she whispered, "would put surveillance down here?"

"Not so dumb if they plan to use the area for storing human cargo."

She broke away from his embrace and announced to anyone who might be listening, "I was going to say that this would make a fantastic wine cellar."

"We already have a wine cellar, a big one."

When he opened the door on the opposite side of the former root cellar, they came out at the far end away from the loading dock. The bunkhouse was almost straight ahead, and the barn was across the driveway to the left. Weather in Colorado was unpredictable in October. In spite of the golden aspens, today felt more like springtime than the edge of winter.

Angie turned her face up to the sun. With her head tilted back, her long, platinum braid reached almost to her waist. He wanted to kiss her again…and then again. After spending the morning in the company of Zapata and Lorenzo, Julian needed some sweetness to erase the foul taste from his mouth. He hated to ruin the mood with the news about tomorrow night, but they had to start planning.

He ducked his head down and whispered in her ear as they strolled toward the barn. "I have important information."

"Which reminds me…you need boyfriend lessons. A lover doesn't send a vague text about visiting a supervillain and then disappear for hours. You need to tell me where you are, and it wouldn't hurt for you to use a heart emoji or two."

"I'm a guy. I can't do the smiley valentines."

"And don't be afraid to use the L-word." She smoothed her hair. "What did you learn from Zapata?"

He hedged, trying to ease into the bad news that they were running out of time. "The most important detail came from Lorenzo, who showed up just in time to keep me from throwing Rudy off the sixth floor terrace of the office building. That punk kid knew about Damien and didn't tell me. He and Zapata both refused to talk about the trafficking, wouldn't even admit that was the plan. Neither did Lorenzo but he said that an important project would be starting on Tuesday night. And he'll have his own men posted at the barn."

"Tuesday?" An audible gasp escaped her lips. "That's tomorrow."

"It could be a preliminary trial run or could be the real thing. Either way, we need to be ready."

They were almost to the barn when she came to a halt and rooted her little purple boots to the ground. "I can't believe what you just told me. What a disaster! In light of that, I'm not ready to get back on the horse."

"But I was going to help you. That was our excuse for coming out here."

"Make up a different excuse." She pivoted and marched toward the bunkhouse. "The real reason we're out here is to find Gigi. If something is happening tomorrow night, we need to get her somewhere safe."

At the corner of the bunkhouse, Angie turned uphill and hiked around to the back. The long, rugged one-story building was built after WWII at the same time as the original lodge. The structure was sturdy but not neatly finished. Angie opened a shutter to peek through a window.

"I can't see a thing," she said. "But this would be a good place for Gigi to hide if she could figure out how to get inside."

"So would the barn." Both would be good places for

the traffickers. "Didn't Cara say that Gigi made a nest in one of the stalls?"

"That's right, but I'm discounting the barn because of the surveillance and other people coming and going. Cara also said she saw Gigi playing on this hillside."

"When was that?"

"Saturday."

"Before Saturday, when was the last time Cara saw Gigi?"

Angie paused and concentrated. "Two weeks ago and maybe some other times."

He considered it unlikely that a nine-year-old child with no special skills or knowledge of the area had managed to stay hidden for two weeks. Though the weather had been mild, the temperature dropped at night, sometimes into the twenties or lower. "If she's still around here, she must have found someplace warm to sleep."

"Like the bunkhouse." She tromped around to the end where there was a stoop and a door. "I don't see a keypad. Do you have some secret way to enter?"

This ramshackle old building didn't rate special locks and devices. With no one living here, the bunkhouse wasn't worthy of special protection. He turned over a suspiciously smooth rock beside the stoop and took out the key that was tucked in a hidden compartment. "Not exactly high-tech."

"As long as it gets us inside," she said. "I hope we can find her. She'll be a good witness."

"Are you sure about that?" He fitted the key in the lock. "Most lawyers hate to use children as witnesses. They tend to be unpredictable and suggestible."

"True, but we need to put together evidence. Witness testimony is a good place to start. And I have access to another witness—someone who knows everything about Lorenzo."

"Marigold." He still wasn't one hundred percent sure

about Angie's connection to her long-lost friend. He didn't think she was lying to him about Marigold, but she hadn't seen the woman in eleven years. Marigold could have changed. Angie had been nearly hysterical when they met. But Marigold was calm. He didn't trust her.

"She's coming here at six o'clock. If we meet in my room, I can make sure nobody is watching or listening."

"I'd like to sit in on that conversation."

"This is something I need to do alone."

She pushed open the door and entered the bunkhouse. The interior was plain and unadorned with a propane heater and stove at the front and five bunk beds on either side. He flicked the switch by the door and was surprised when the electricity came on. Had someone been using this place? Had Zapata turned on the electric in preparation for the human trafficking?

"The beds aren't made." She went to a closet and unfastened the latch to a walk-in space lined with shelves. "Everything is put away, nice and neat. Blankets, sheets, pillows and towels. If Gigi used any of these supplies, she did an amazing job of cleaning up after herself. There's not a wrinkle in sight."

At the other end of the bunkhouse were toilets and showers. When he turned faucets, no water came out, which was as it should be. In winter, they drained any water outlets that weren't in use so the pipes wouldn't freeze. "She didn't come in here to clean up."

"But it's close to the hotel where there are plenty of bathrooms. Gigi could have taken a blanket and towel from the bunkhouse."

"I think we're giving our nine-year-old fugitive too much credit," he said. "In a two-week period, someone would have noticed a little girl wandering around unsupervised. Nick's isn't a place where children are welcome."

"If she's not here, then where? At the bakery, Damien said they'd lost track of the little girl. That has to be Gigi."

Julian was torn. If a child had really gone missing, they had been treating the situation badly. There needed to be an Amber Alert, plus calls to the local police, the FBI and CBI. But Gigi might be part of Cara's imagination or one of the employees' kids. Dozens of explanations were credible. He wanted to believe there was nothing to worry about, but Damien and Valentino had referred to a missing child. "We need to talk to Cara."

"I should take a pass on that conversation," Angie said. "I don't usually like kids, but Cara is different. She's special. And I have a nasty suspicion that she's playing me."

"You? You're letting a seven-year-old get under your skin? I thought you were supposed to be tough and street smart."

"Maybe I'm turning mushy." She gave a quick, ironic laugh. "Isn't that what's supposed to happen to a woman in love?"

He couldn't let a comment like that slide on by. In a few strides, he crossed the bunkhouse and stood before her. "Are you hinting that I'm making you melt?"

"Like a sunlamp on ice cream." She reached up and took off his glasses. "You're a distraction. It's hard to be rational when I'm looking into those baby blue eyes."

"Good."

He snugged his arm around her waist and pulled her close. This time, when they kissed, he took his time to savor the flowery scent of her shampoo. He glided his fingers down her spine and caressed the flare of her hips. She was as perfect as a marble sculpture but better because she moved against him and made little moaning sounds in her throat. No one could see them in here. This kiss wasn't part of the show to make people think they were lovers.

They were embracing because they wanted to be in each other's arms. He kissed her harder, imagined that he could feel her heartbeat becoming synchronized with his. They were becoming one.

When they separated, she rested her cheek against his chest. She was breathing heavily as though she'd run a marathon, and he was the same—tense from exertion and more tense from holding back. "Before the others get here," she said, "we ought to lock the door. There are ten different beds, and I think we can figure out how to use at least two or three of them."

"Not now." He wanted their first time to be more than an afternoon quickie. "Tonight after Marigold visits, I'll come to you."

"It's a good thing that one of us is rational." She took a reluctant step away from him. "I'm worried about seeing Marigold, don't know what to expect from her. I'm a little bit afraid. I don't want to be hurt."

"You don't have to face the pain alone."

From outside the bunkhouse, he heard the sound of the others approaching the barn. Cara's flutelike voice played counterpoint to Muscleman Matt's rumbling basso, and Jane added a steady note of calm. Waylon wasn't doing any of the talking, which wasn't surprising. The old cowboy generally kept his thoughts to himself.

Before he and Angie left the bunkhouse, Julian turned off the light and flipped the lock on the door. At the stoop, he stashed the key in the secret compartment of the fake rock—a hiding place worthy of a Scooby cartoon. In keeping with the kid show theme, he was about to interrogate a little girl about her imaginary friend. This morning's confrontation with Zapata and Lorenzo felt like it took place on a darker, more dangerous planet where violence occurred on a regular basis. Julian had no one to blame but himself for the amusement park atmosphere at Nick's. He'd done his best to sanitize operations by turning strippers into performers and regulating the betting limits in the casino.

When they entered the barn, Cara stamped her little foot and scolded. "You guys were supposed to already be riding."

"My fault," Angie said. "It's such a pretty day. I just wanted to walk and enjoy the aspen gold."

Cara narrowed her gaze. "Maybe you were putting off your ride because you're scared."

"Maybe."

In his head, Julian changed her "maybe" to "definitely." Angie's complexion flushed, and her hand trembled. Being around horses wasn't easy for her. Gently, he suggested, "We could put this off for another day."

"I can do it." She faced Waylon. "Where do we start?"

"Y'all saddle up. Angie, you come with me. Matt and Jane, bring in three horses from the corral and get them ready to ride."

Cara counted on her fingers. "One for Mom and one for Matt and one for Julian. We need another horse for me."

"Not today, little one. You're riding with your mom."

When she stomped out the barn door, Julian followed. Cara stuffed her hands into the pockets of her jeans and scowled at the ground beneath her feet. At the corral, she peered through the railings and watched as her mom and Matt approached a chestnut mare with a black mane and tail. They worked together well, slipping a bridle on the mare and leading her into the barn.

Julian leaned against a fence post beside Cara. "Do you know why we came to the barn for a ride today?"

She nodded. "We're looking for Gigi."

"Angie mentioned that you saw her on Saturday. Any other times?"

"A couple of weeks ago," she said, "and once after that or maybe twice. I don't get to come up here much because I gotta stay in Denver and go to stupid old school. Science is okay, but I hate math."

Cara could babble all afternoon and not tell him anything he needed to know. Julian tried to focus her conversation. "Back to Gigi. Do you think she slept in the barn overnight?"

"I dunno." Her skinny shoulders rose and fell in a shrug. "The first time I saw her, she had a cozy little hideout in the straw inside one of the horse stalls. The next day I came back, and she wasn't there."

"Did you ask Waylon if he'd seen her?"

"Not right away."

She turned away from the corral and skipped over to a plain wooden bench. She hopped up on it and balanced as she tiptoed from one end to the other. He couldn't tell if she was avoiding his questions or just didn't care. "Did you tell your mom about Gigi?"

"Gigi is my friend, and she asked me not to tell anybody. If people found out she was here, she'd get in trouble because she was running away from home."

A runaway? That was new information. The elusive Gigi might not be part of a trafficking operation. She might be a kid running away from home. "Where's she running away from? Does she live up here in the mountains?"

"I dunno."

He wasn't going to get anywhere by threatening her, but his supply of patience was running low. "How about a last name?"

"I don't remember."

At times like this, his sobriety was tested. A shot of tequila might have made this conversation easier. “Maybe Gigi told you something about the people she lives with. Were there any other kids? Did she have a mom and a dad?”

“We didn’t talk so much. We played.”

“Think, Cara. It’s important.”

She jumped off the bench, folded her arms around her middle and scowled. “Are you mad at me?”

Expecting simple, direct answers from a seven-year-old was a long shot. He sat on the bench and forced a smile. “I’m not mad.”

“Your voice sounds like you are.”

“Come over here and sit next to me.” He patted the bench. “I promise not to snap your head off.”

Her gaze glued to his face as she took a seat on the bench. “Is Gigi in trouble?”

“I hope not.” Counting to ten, he slowly exhaled. “Let’s do this a different way, okay?”

“Sure.”

“I like you, Cara, and I know you’re a smart kid. Why don’t you just tell me everything you remember about Gigi? The way she looks, her clothes, the games you played, everything.”

“Here goes,” she said. “Gigi is very pretty, has brown hair and her favorite color is red. The first time I saw her, her outfit was brown and gold. She had a little notebook and drew lots of pictures. I wanted her to give me a picture of a fairy princess, but she said she’d better not because she was running away and didn’t want to leave clues. She was scared of a big man who smelled like doughnuts. He grabbed her and put her in a van with other people.”

Julian wiped his hand across his mouth to keep himself from interrupting. This version of the story sounded more like Gigi had gotten swept up in a trafficking scheme.

Cara continued, "You probably don't believe in fairy princesses because you're a boy, but they're real and they protect kids like Gigi and me. Gigi's princess made sure she'd be warm at night and got food for her. So did I... bring her food. On Saturday when I saw her, I got a sandwich from the kitchen for her."

"Wait." He couldn't stay silent for one more second. "Are you telling me that you managed to sneak out from the concierge level?"

"It's not hard." She gave him a sly smile. "I could show you all the secret doors."

"You're amazing, kiddo."

"I know."

They both turned and watched as Angie rode from the barn. Her posture was as rigid as the stripper pole in the Burlesque, and she bounced straight up and down in the saddle. Though her horse walked slowly, she pulled on the reins and jammed her right foot down as if she was stomping on a brake.

Beside him, Cara snickered. "Your girlfriend looks dopey."

"It doesn't change the way I feel about her."

And that, he realized, might be the closest he'd ever come to a declaration of love.

Chapter Seventeen

Julian's penthouse suite on the seventh floor was decorated in earth tones and a southwestern motif similar to the rest of the hotel but with an elevated level of style. Everything was bigger: the floor space, the sofa and the TV. The walls were hung with modern artwork, and the shelves held a variety of handmade Native American pottery. Angie strolled past the fireplace to a wall of windows with a sliding panel that opened onto a wide balcony overlooking hills and forest. She pushed the door open and stepped into a soft gray dusk that smelled of pine and smoke from the barbecue outside the kitchen. The peaceful atmosphere seemed like an unlikely location for the heinous crime of human trafficking.

Stepping around the circular breakfast table, she went to the railing. He joined her and placed a ceramic coffee mug in her hand. She wanted to believe that the FBI and CBI would shut down the trafficking operation on Tuesday night, and no one would be hurt.

"You know," she said, "this balcony would be a great place for a hot tub."

He tapped his mug against hers. "Too bad I won't be living here long enough to justify the trouble and expense of installing one. There are a lot of things I would have done differently if this was going to be my permanent home."

"Like what? The art and the pottery are beautiful."

"The decor is great, but it's not mine. I like that painting with the sand dunes and the cow skull, but I don't have any personal stories about how I found an artist in Santa Fe who studied with Georgia O'Keeffe. The pottery and woven baskets came with the place. You might be interested to know that your friend Marigold, in her identity as Marian, was the decorator."

"Not surprised, she always was artistic." Angie checked her watch with the tooled leather band. Marigold was scheduled to meet with her in less than two hours in her suite on the fourth floor. If she was ready to leave Lorenzo, Angie could make that happen. Marigold would be first in line for a new life as a protected witness. On the other hand, if she didn't want to separate from the scumbag who took advantage of her when she was a teenager, the situation could turn complicated. Angie didn't want to see Marigold swept up with the other thugs. Could she arrange for her friend to escape?

Julian draped an arm around her shoulder and pulled her close. His natural aroma mingled with the scent of the forest. She leaned against his shoulder, enjoying their closeness and wishing it could last for longer than a day.

"You're tense," he said.

"I don't know if Marigold will want to say goodbye to her sweet lifestyle in the Glass Palace. How can she walk away from a closet full of designer clothes and jewelry? And all that money…it's real seductive."

"Whoever said crime doesn't pay hasn't been hanging out with the right criminals."

"You get it." She tilted her head so she could look up at his profile. "When this is over, you're going to hate leaving Nick's."

"Damn right I am! I like having room service and maid

service and valets to fetch my car whenever I want. I like the money. Most especially, I've liked being able to build this place and organize the operations. Best job I've ever had, and that includes being an agent for the CBI."

As soon as he mentioned being an agent, her senses went on high alert. "Is it safe to talk about the CBI?"

"A hundred percent safe. When we're in the penthouse, nobody can hear us or watch what we're doing. It's one of the perks I get for being in charge of security and surveillance. Plus I've constructed firewalls and other protections." He glanced over his shoulder at the interior. "We should go inside and make our contact with your handler and SSA Shanahan."

"I got a text from Hemming about the autopsy results. He mentioned a tattoo on one of Damien's friends. Roman numerals, MMXV."

"A Denver-based gang. They're bad news. I knew they were connected with Lorenzo."

When she turned in his arms and faced him, she was momentarily distracted by the scruff that roughened his jaw and the fire in his eyes. Even in the dusk, that incredible blue shone like a laser. She dragged her focus back to their work. "How do you know about the MMXV gang?"

"You know how much I hate being watched all the time."

"So do I."

"But I love being able to see everybody else. Do you remember the first night you were here and we ran into Lorenzo in the lobby?"

She shuddered and set her coffee on the table so she wouldn't slop it all over her bedazzled jeans. "Unforgettable."

"He was having a dinner meeting with a politician, which my surveillance cameras recorded. I couldn't get clear audio from the table where he was sitting, but a hidden mic picked up a few phrases. I transmitted all of it to SSA Shanahan."

"I'm guessing that you've taken video and audio of Lorenzo and Zapata with other of their cronies, including the boss from MMXV, the Fifteen."

"The boss who refers to himself as El Jefe, plus the head of the Colombian cartel that Damien worked for. I've recorded them all—from the hotshot bosses in solid gold chains and five-thousand-dollar suits to the snakeheads and coyotes covered in desert dust. When Lorenzo goes down, he'll take a network of other traffickers with him."

"Respect," she said. "I can understand why the CBI kept you here for three years."

He glided his hand down her cheek and cupped her chin. "I'd like to claim that I planned the whole undercover setup, but it was mostly luck. I happened to be in the right place at the right time to meet Lorenzo, and we clicked."

"It took more than luck to keep this operation running. Don't deny it, Professor. You're a smart cookie."

"Gotta live up to my reputation."

Quick and hot, his mouth pressed against hers. It was like being kissed by a flame. Then he escorted her through the front room to an office where he opened a hinged painting of cowboys on horseback. Behind the painting was a wall safe and inside that was a computer. He wasn't joking when he talked about the layers of protection.

He set up the laptop on his desk and, with a few strokes on the keyboard, enabled a conference chat with Hemming and Shanahan. The two agents were waiting for their call in a bland conference room—could have been CBI or FBI—with documents, maps and photos spread across the table. Her least favorite part of the job was reporting and paperwork, and she was glad to see that Julian was cool with handling those duties.

With very little participation from her, the three men discussed a plan of action for Tuesday night when Lorenzo had guards posted at the barn. Julian had sent maps of possible places where human cargo could be off-loaded and held until final destinations were arranged. The tricky part would be to rescue the people being trafficked without having anyone get hurt. Very likely, there would be frightened children and young women.

"How can I help?" she asked.

Hemming frowned at the screen. "Me and Shanahan, we talked this over and decided that both of you should maintain your undercover identities as long as possible. We've got teams of experienced field agents who are familiar with procedures for rescue and extraction missions. You and Julian lay low."

"No problem." Angie was happy to let the experts take charge. "Will you be making simultaneous arrests at different locations?"

"We'll pick up Lorenzo and Zapata," Hemming said. "Are you worried about your friend Marigold?"

"Who's Marigold?" Shanahan asked.

"You probably know her as Marion Grant, Lorenzo's mistress," Hemming explained. "Angie knew her when they were both teenagers. They were close."

"And I don't want her to be arrested," Angie said. "She's a good person who got caught up with bad people. I can get her to testify against Lorenzo."

"We'll do what we can," Shanahan promised, "but I'm afraid your friend might be implicated in some of Lorenzo's personal financial documents. By the way, you did an excellent job gathering that information."

"It was easy. They handed over the paperwork and codes so I could revamp their OTB operations."

"Between your documents and Julian's surveillance, we have a good start to our case against these guys. Picking up eye witnesses to the trafficking operation should seal the deal."

In less than an hour, Angie would have a chance to talk to Marigold and convince her to step away from Lorenzo. She had to make that happen.

"One more thing," Julian said. "A little girl named Gigi might be caught up in all this. If we can find her, she'd make a good witness."

"A missing child," Hemmings said. "Are we talking about a kidnapping? Why is this the first I'm hearing about it?"

"It's complicated." Angie tried to explain. "The only person who has seen Gigi is a seven-year-old who might have exaggerated the situation. But I agree with Julian. We need to keep looking for her."

SSA Shanahan nodded. "Let us know how we can help."

After more of a discussion about strategy, their conference was over. Julian closed the screen and returned the laptop to the safe above his desk. "I managed to pry a few more details from Cara this afternoon."

"Was that before or after you were both laughing at me?"

For a moment, he seemed to be studying her, assessing her possible reaction. Then he shook his head and grinned. "Nope, I can't deny that we were making fun of you. I never thought anyone could look so uncomfortable on horseback."

"People get killed in riding accidents." She knew for a fact that horses were dangerous creatures. "There are serious injuries."

"Not when the horse is walking slower than a turtle."

With a flick of her wrist, she wiped away his comment. "Tell me about Cara."

"She told me that Gigi likes to draw, and she has a fairy princess who brings her food and makes sure she has somewhere warm to sleep."

"A fairy princess, eh?" She cocked her head to one side. "A lot of women around here might fit that description. Every performer at the Burlesque is pretty and glittery enough to be a princess, and then there are maids, servers, cocktail waitresses and staff, even Tamara."

"You're saying that all women are princesses."

"Maybe they are. Tomorrow, we can ask around. One of these princesses might help us find Gigi."

"We're making progress," he said.

"Thank goodness I don't need to have those profit figures ready for Zapata until Thursday."

"Whoa." He took a step back and regarded her critically. "You do realize that you don't really work here, don't you?"

"Sometimes the lines get blurred. Has that happened to you?"

"More than once," he admitted.

"Like when Shanahan suggested that we act the part of lovers. That role fits."

"Undercover lovers," he murmured.

There was no reason to be embarrassed, but she felt a blush warming her cheeks. If they only had a few hours together, she needed to take advantage of this time with him and tell him about her feelings. *Honest feelings?* Since when had she been compelled to speak the truth?

"What is it, Angie?"

"After Marigold leaves, I want to come back here to your suite." In spite of her newfound dedication to honesty, she couldn't bring herself to say exactly what she meant: *I want to spend the night in your bed.*

"I'll be waiting."

The heat from his azure eyes told her that he understood what she really meant.

Chapter Eighteen

Marigold was late. Typical! She hadn't changed a bit. Punctuality hadn't been her thing when they were teenagers and still wasn't important to her. Phone in hand, Angie paced back and forth on the carpet in front of the sofa in her concierge-level suite. She paused to stare at the app-filled screen on her phone, hoping to see a text message, but there was nothing. Marigold had always been the cool one.

Angie's fingers poised over the keys. She could send her own message but didn't want to betray her excitement or anxiety. What if Marigold didn't come? Or refused to listen? So many things could go wrong.

In the small kitchenette, she opened the fridge under the counter beside the sink. The ice-cold craft beer was tempting, but she had the feeling that she needed all her wits to deal with her old friend. She grabbed a carton of cranberry juice, climbed onto a stool at the black granite counter that divided the kitchenette from the living room and helped herself to the white chocolate and macadamia nut cookies that were provided free, compliments of room service.

Probably not a good idea to cram a cookie into her mouth, but she took two anyway. The amenities at Nick's were outstanding, and she might not have this level of service for a very long time. Her next undercover assignment might not be luxurious, but that wasn't the reason she wanted to stay here. In spite of the danger, deception and horseback riding lessons, Nick's felt like home. She'd met people here who were already like family…and Julian, her undercover lover. How could she leave before she had a chance to find out if their budding relationship might bloom.

She checked the time on her phone. Marigold was officially twenty-three minutes late. Swell! She polished off the cookie and brushed the crumbs off her crimson, high-collared blouse with the low V-neck to show off her necklaces of crystals and silver. When it was half an hour, Angie would call.

There was a tap at the door, and she flew to answer. The blonde woman who pushed her way inside without being invited smelled like expensive perfume. Her makeup was perfect. Her short, faux fur, leopard-print jacket over super-skinny jeans would have been tacky on a less confident woman, but Marigold made them look fashionable. She glanced around the room as if she owned the place.

"You decorated this suite," Angie said.

"I'm good at my work."

"Are you an interior decorator by trade?"

"I've had some training, and I have good taste, which is as much of a shock to me as anybody else."

"I always knew you were tasteful. You used to read all the fashion mags." Their conversation seemed as stilted as two people who had never met before. Angie wanted to dash across the room and give her oldest pal—perhaps her only true friend—a hug. "I missed you."

"Same here."

"I never thought I'd see you again."

"When I look back at who we were when we were teenagers, I wouldn't have given good odds for our survival."

"We did okay. With no cash and no skills, we got by for six months on the road."

"Don't make it sound like we were on a grand adventure. I was there. I remember the days when we had nothing to eat but the crap we scrounged from dumpsters. My back still aches from the nights when we slept under streetlights on concrete."

Angie tended to gloss over the horror of that time when they'd meandered from Utah to Denver. They'd taken turns saving each other's life. The predators were many and fierce. Running from a massive brown bear in the forest was less terrifying than facing street gangs in the city. "I never would have made it without you."

"Me? What about you? You were ferocious, especially after you bought your first switchblade at that weird little pawnshop."

"I've upgraded since then."

"Smart move. That first blade was clumsy and ridiculous. The only thing it was good for was scaring off somebody who got too close."

"Not our best weapon," she conceded. "You were better at disarming men."

"Like this." Marigold opened her leopard jacket. Underneath the faux fur, she wore a snug, cream-colored top that revealed her shapely, well-toned body. "A blessing and a curse."

She did a little shimmy, and Angie laughed. "You've always been gorgeous."

"And you were the smarty-pants."

Angie felt herself beginning to relax. At the Glass Palace when she'd first seen the woman who called herself Marion Grant, she'd been too shocked and confused to do anything more than dissolve into a helpless puddle of tears. The last couple of days had given her perspective. "You said you were willing to leave Nick."

"I say a lot of things." She stalked across the room and came to a stop only a few feet away. "You're calling yourself Angie, right?"

"I've used a dozen aliases since I was fifteen. I'm sure you've done the same because I've continued to look for you online over the years, and 'Marion Grant' doesn't exist. I followed a number of false trails that all led to dead ends. You're the most secret of mistresses with no identification whatsoever."

"Aren't you clever?" Standing too close, she flicked the collar of Angie's red shirt. "Tell me, Angie, are you wearing a wire?"

"Of course not. Why would you think that?"

"You've been looking for me, and this afternoon I did some research of my own. The usual computer stuff was all about your alias, and there was nothing on the name I once knew you by. Do you even remember being Maxine Dubrowski?"

Maxie and Marigold. Before they teamed up, she'd been a sullen brat who kept to herself and lashed out at the well-meaning adults who tried to take care of her. Living with her drug-addict parents would have been worse, but she could never forgive them for abandoning her. She didn't thrive in foster care, didn't have a sense of herself at all until she hooked up with Marigold. "What did you find out?"

"I called a couple of the homes where we lived. One of the foster moms—a tall woman with a faint mustache—told me that you were a success story and had turned your life around."

"And Mrs. Mustache probably claimed credit, told

you that I had seen the error of my ways and become a good girl."

"It wasn't really like that."

Angie had no particular aspiration to be a good girl. Instead, her motivation for doing well in school and developing a power base was simple. She wanted revenge against Lorenzo for taking Marigold away from her. "What else did she tell you?"

"She said you'd gone to college, graduated and then went into law enforcement. Is that accurate? Are you a cop?"

Marigold locked her gaze on Angie's face. This was it: the moment of truth.

Though they had been apart for eleven years, Marigold was closer to her than anyone else. They were sisters. Lying to her was an unthinkable betrayal. Angie knew she could pull off a deception. Based on her psychological profile and her FBI training in undercover work, she was a certified, world-class liar.

And she had a solid basis for concealing the truth. Like it or not, Marigold had been Lorenzo's mistress for over eleven years. If Angie gave up the details of the FBI raid on Tuesday night, his mistress might feel obliged to tell him, and the plan to halt human trafficking would fail. Three years of undercover work by Julian would be wasted, not to mention her own elaborate subterfuge and research.

Angie stuck out her chin. "I'm not wearing a wire. Are you?"

"What?"

"If you really think I'm a cop, you might have wanted to record our conversation for Lorenzo. And before you say anything else, I want you to know that all the recording devices—audio and cameras—have been disabled in my suite."

"Does your boyfriend know about that?"

"I convinced Julian that I needed my privacy."

Marigold took a step back. "I heard that you hooked up with him. I totally approve. I worked with Julian when I was decorating, and I like the guy. He's smart, practical and has the prettiest blue eyes of all time. Don't let him get away."

Relationship advice from a woman who hooked up with a crime boss? "I might not stay on the OTB job too long."

"Why would you leave?"

"I don't like horses. Once I get the initial computer system up and running, there won't be much more for me to do." So far, she'd been honest. "I'm not crazy about Valentino, and Zapata scares me."

"Where would you go?"

"I have options." She clasped Marigold's hands in both of hers. "And so do you. You said you were tired of Lorenzo, and I can help you get away from him and start a new life. You're beautiful and talented. You deserve good friends and a family who loves you as much as I do. Come with me, Marigold, you always said you wanted kids."

Her gaze flickered, and Angie knew she'd hit a sore point. Was this about children? Was Marigold desperate to have kids? She stalked across the room to the door and paused with her hand on the knob. "I'll be in touch."

"Don't leave."

"I can't stay. I need to get home."

"Promise you'll call me or come over tomorrow," Angie pleaded. "Promise."

"I'll try."

She whipped open the door and exited.

IN JULIAN'S PENTHOUSE SUITE, Angie prowled the room like a hungry mountain lion searching for prey. Her meeting with Marigold hadn't been satisfying. The big question about whether she'd leave Lorenzo remained unanswered, and Angie sensed that her friend was troubled in many other ways.

"Anything to drink?" Julian asked. "I have wine, beer, juice, lemonade and tea."

"Why do you keep booze in the house if you don't drink?"

"It's for guests. And the craft beer is nonalcoholic."

"I'll try that." She climbed onto a high stool and rested her elbows on the granite counter that separated his kitchenette. Though the rest of his suite was much bigger than hers, his cooking area was only slightly larger and contained a full-size fridge. "I've never been much of a drinker," she said. "I hate being drunk and out of control."

"Did your parents drink?"

"I didn't know them well enough to talk about their habits. They were both addicts, so I guess they drank, snorted and shot up. I'm lucky I didn't inherit those traits."

As he took two bottles of beer from the fridge and poured the contents into pilsner glasses, she appreciated his efficiency and economy of motion. He wasn't one of those guys who fumbled in the kitchen and couldn't take care of himself. When he pushed up the sleeves on his black cashmere sweater, she admired his muscular wrists. This was a man, a real man, who knew how to build a house, program a computer and make dinner.

"I bet you like to cook," she said.

"Sometimes. How about you?"

"Never," she said.

He brought the beer to the counter and leaned across to place her drink directly in front of her. Behind his glasses, his magical blue eyes ignited fireworks inside her. "Tell me about Marigold."

"It's hard to explain." She took a moment to compose herself and sip the craft beer, which had a smooth, wheaty flavor and tickled the back of her throat. "I couldn't bring myself to lie to Marigold, but I wasn't honest. She'd done background checking on me and asked if I was wearing a wire. She thought I'd become a cop."

"Which you didn't. You're an agent."

"I knew you'd say that." She noticed that he'd shaved while she'd been downstairs talking to her old friend. His dark blond hair was still damp from his shower. "You and I are very much alike when it comes to undercover work and deception. We're professional liars."

"Somehow, we managed to spend several days together without revealing our identities. Was anything you told me the truth?"

"Some of it."

"What's your real name?"

"Maxine Dubrowski," she said without hesitation. "I prefer Angie."

"Good to know," he said. "On the day after tomorrow, this assignment will be over and we'll go our separate ways and find new undercover identities."

She was well aware that the end was near. Their relationship would be over before it started. "We may never see each other again."

He glanced toward the fridge. "Hungry?"

"You did a good job of pretending to be dangerous. When you first drove me into the mountains, I halfway expected to be disappeared and dumped in a shallow grave. And when you loaded three dead guys in the back of the SUV, I was justifiably terrified."

"I didn't have a clue that you were FBI." He took a drink and licked the foam from his lips. "When I first met you,

I almost broke my cover. You seemed like a decent person and—"

"Decent person? That's what you thought of me?"

"It's a compliment. I wanted to get you away from here and didn't want you to be hurt. Is that so terrible?"

"Not terrible but irritating." She wasn't ready to let him off the hook. "I go to a lot of trouble to look like this. Most men are fascinated and intrigued."

"If I fell apart every time I caught a glimpse of cleavage and a smear of red lipstick, there's no way I could work at the Burlesque." He scooped up their beer glasses and crossed the room. "Let's sit over here and get comfortable."

She followed him to the love seat in front of the fireplace. He set their drinks on the coffee table, dimmed the lights and lit the fire with the touch of a button. The flames scampered across the logs in a random dance that captivated her attention, but she noticed when he added background music—classical guitar. Comfy? Yes! Relaxed? Most definitely not. Her senses were on high alert. Her pulse raced.

The love seat was just the right size for cuddling. When he sat beside her, it would have been natural to slide into an embrace. She resisted, perching on the edge of the love seat and tasting her beer. "Are you sure this stuff isn't alcoholic? I'm feeling light-headed."

"That was my plan."

"This seduction scene isn't necessary," she said. "I wouldn't have come to your suite if I hadn't intended to take our friendship to the next level."

"Friendship?" It was his turn to be insulted. "After we kissed? Last night, we slept together."

"And nothing happened. We didn't make love."

An echo of the L-word hung in the air between them. She set her glass on the table and reclined on the small sofa with his arm draped around her. She didn't usually think of sex as "making love." Why had she used that phrase with him? Loving him would be crazy.

Her thoughts returned to her conversation with Marigold. "When you said you wanted to protect me and make sure I wasn't hurt, that's exactly how I feel about my friend. I want to tell her that I'm FBI and can get her into witness protection."

"But you can't compromise the assignment," he said. "The stakes are high. If we fail to break up this trafficking operation, hundreds of lives will be destroyed. I know we're not saving the world, and someone else will fill in the gap left by Lorenzo, but I believe we can make a difference."

"That's why I didn't break cover."

He smoothed the hair off her forehead and stroked her long, smooth ponytail. "Last night when you collapsed in the bed, you unfastened your hair. Can I do that now?"

"Me, first."

She stroked his granite jawline. With both hands, she removed his glasses and put them on the coffee table. Making direct eye contact, she leaned closer and closer until she could smell the woodsy scent of his aftershave. Her mouth joined with his. Of course, their kiss was a perfect fit. They were mirror images of each other—alike in so many ways and yet different.

He spun her around so her back was to him, and he unfastened her ponytail. His fingers combed through her long hair and pulled the sleek, platinum blond strands into a coil. He rotated her head so she was facing him. His kiss wasn't sweet or gentle. He was demanding, which was exactly what she wanted from him.

She had rough desires of her own. Gathering handfuls of black cashmere, she yanked his sweater and T-shirt over his head. His bared chest pressed hard against her, and he unfastened her red shirt with more finesse than she'd used.

The love seat was too small to contain their passion. He lifted her in his arms and carried her toward the bedroom. They didn't make it that far.

She didn't want to be handled like a child. If she could have thrown him over her shoulder in a fireman's carry, she would have. Angie swung her legs down and staggered back, bumping against the dining table.

Her plan had not included lying back on the table like an entrée, but she didn't object when he slowly, carefully devoured her. He kissed and caressed his way down from her throat to her breasts and lower. Heat blasted through her and torched her inhibitions. She wanted more of him—all of him. She wanted him inside her. And that was no lie.

In the bedroom, they tore off the rest of their clothes. Classical guitar thrummed in the background. Dim light from a bedside lamp outlined his lean, muscular body. She jumped onto the bed and pointed at him. "Stay right there."

"Why?"

"It's been a long time," she admitted. "I want to look at you."

Though she'd intended to slowly memorize his wide-spread shoulders, the pattern of his chest hair and his flat belly, her gaze hopped from one feature to another like a sex-starved jackrabbit.

He flexed like a bodybuilder. "How's that?"

"Get over here, stud."

She reveled in their kisses and touches. This was sex—wild, raw and wonderful. But she couldn't help feeling that they were making love.

Chapter Nineteen

The next morning, Julian wakened slowly with memories of the night before stirring his blood. His mood elevated to a natural high. For a moment, he had a craving for vodka in his orange juice. Then his rational brain kicked in and reminded him that he was an alcoholic and couldn't drink, which was why he felt good and not hungover.

Reality landed with a thud. Today was going to be difficult and the bust tonight would be worse—filled with details and potential disasters. He started with the easy stuff: arranging rooms for SSA Shanahan and SA Hemming so they could stay on top of the action. He needed to start a search for the so-called "princess" who could lead him to Gigi. And then he could deal with the complex issue of the woman who was lying in bed beside him with her long hair rippling across the pillow. What should he do about Angie?

He watched her sleep, lying on her back with her arms thrown carelessly over her head. Her breasts and torso were covered by the sheet, but one of her long, firm legs had kicked free. She flexed her leg and pointed her toe emphasizing her muscular calf and the high arch on her foot.

He caught a piece of hair between his fingers and twirled the silky, platinum strand. God, she was beautiful! He had no idea what her other undercover disguises were like, but he knew this was his favorite. Not that he was usually drawn to sassy blondes with dramatic makeup and sparkly clothes. Julian had always liked natural, outdoorsy women. Why her? She looked ridiculous on horseback, and didn't wear shoes that were suitable for hiking. All things considered, she wasn't his type.

But when they were together, he felt fulfilled. He hated being apart from her. And the sex—the lovemaking—was magnificent. He gave a little tug on her hair. There was time this morning for another round.

She rolled away, made a quick grab for the bedside table and turned back toward him with her custom-made switchblade in her hand. Staring directly into his eyes, she pushed the button and the silver blade snicked open.

"I get it," he said. "You're not a morning person."

She closed the knife. "I'm taking a shower. In five minutes, you're invited to join me."

He watched her smooth back and naked bottom as she strode across the carpet into the adjoining bathroom. If he hadn't already been hard, that vision would have done it for him. He'd never expected her to pull a knife on him. When had she gotten the blade from the secret pocket in her jeans? Why did she feel the need to stash a weapon in the bedside table? Not that he had room to talk, there was a secret panel in his headboard where he kept a loaded gun.

He waited until he heard the water running to step into his bathroom. Julian hadn't gone to the expense of installing a hot tub on his balcony, but he'd splurged on a shower sauna with eight pulsating jets. The huge walk-in shower reminded him of a car wash. He could stand in the middle and get sprayed clean from all directions. Watching Angie through the glass walls of the shower was great. When he entered the enclosure, the view was even better. Steam billowed around their slick, wet bodies.

She slid her torso against his. "I wouldn't have stabbed you."

"Do you always sleep with a weapon?"

"Do you?" She chuckled. "I found the secret panel in your headboard."

He nodded. "Maybe we're too much alike."

Her upturned face, devoid of makeup, was beautiful and fresh. He pressed his mouth against hers and then nibbled her earlobe before trailing kisses down her throat to her breasts. Her body was perfect. As he made love to her, the inside of his brain exploded, and he was incapable of rational thought. His actions were driven purely by sensation and emotion.

Too soon, the sexy part of their shower was done. She clung to him and whispered, "I wish we had more time."

"We can squeeze in another hour or so."

"More time to be together," she said. "Our assignment will be over tonight, and I don't want to leave."

"Neither do I." When his time at Nick's was over, he wouldn't be useful to the Colorado Bureau of Investigation as an undercover operative. Too many people knew him as Julian Parisi. His life would take a radical change.

She stepped from the shower and wrapped herself in a huge, fluffy towel—another extravagance. He wondered if he could take the towels with him when he left Nick's. Probably not, they might be considered evidence.

While Angie got ready to face the day, he ordered coffee and breakfast from room service. He was finished with the food and starting his second cup when she emerged from the bedroom wearing a black-and-white zebra patterned poncho over skinny black jeans and platform shoes that he knew had a spring-loaded compartment for a one-shot gun.

He looked her up and down. "Not exactly trying to fade into the woodwork, are you?"

"Oh, but I am. The poncho is reversible, and the other side is black. I switch it around and I'm invisible." She grabbed her coffee and downed half of it in one gulp. "What's the plan for today?"

"I need to arrange rooms for our bosses on a low floor with a clear view of the barn. I'm sure they'll have some issues to discuss, and I need to talk to them about making sure the people who work here will be safe during the bust."

"I wondered about that." She lifted the silver dome that covered her breakfast and made happy sounds about the bacon and eggs. "There are innocent people working here. You don't want them to get in the way if bullets are flying."

He had considered cutting back to a skeleton crew or coming up with a story about necessary repairs that meant his employees had to take a few days off. But he didn't want to do anything that might spook Lorenzo and Zapata. "The daily operations need to look normal."

She bit into her bacon and moaned with pleasure. "How about me? What should I do?"

"Aren't you supposed to be preparing a report for Zapata?"

"It's not due until Thursday," she said. "By then, everything ought to be shut down."

"But you're not supposed to know that. Zapata has people everywhere, watching you and reporting back to him."

"You're suggesting that I should fake doing the work." She shrugged. "I can pull that off. I'm good at faking it."

"I'll bet you are."

Angie raised her eyebrows, a smile slowly spreading from one side of her mouth to the other. "Here's a question," she said. "I know how I build my skills at deception.

Growing up in foster care was risky. I needed to tell lies to survive. How did you learn?"

"According to the shrinks, I have a natural leaning in that direction that goes along with being an alcoholic. I started drinking when I was fourteen which meant I had to lie to my parents and teachers. When I got older, I hid my alcoholism from my employers, my friends and girlfriends. I'm ashamed to say that I got good at deceiving everybody."

"Everybody except yourself."

Her quick, accurate wisdom didn't surprise him. She was six years younger than him but had lived hard and crammed a lot of experience into her life. "You get me."

"I do," she said. "In addition to faking OTB statistics, what else can I do?"

"We need to find Gigi's princess."

AFTER AN EARLY LUNCH, Julian went downstairs to grab Angie and start their princess quest. On the way, he stopped in at the sports betting venue where Leif hunched over a beer and scowled at a hamburger. The handful of other people in the place ignored him, which seemed odd because the former quarterback was a local hero with adoring fans.

Julian pulled up a chair at Leif's table. "Something wrong?"

"Do you live under a rock? It's Tuesday, the day after *Monday Night Football*."

Julian guessed that the Broncos had played and lost. In this part of Colorado, that was reason for mourning. "Sorry."

"They gave up fourteen points in the fourth quarter. I was hosting a party here, and I got so ticked off that

I had to leave before I punted one of those yahoos into next week."

Leif had a dark side. "I hope your day gets better, man. Have you seen Tamara?"

"Not today."

He left the sports venue and went to Angie's office. When he entered, she was playing a video game. She swiveled her chair, leaped from it and threw herself into his arms for a big, juicy kiss. He left the door wide-open, giving a view to the old duffers who bet on all the races. No big deal. He and Angie were undercover lovers, and it didn't matter who knew about their affair.

She whispered in his ear. "I got an encoded text message from Hemming. There's been unusual activity inside the gang that calls themselves the Fifteen. He's not sure what that means, but he and Shanahan are coming here early."

"How early?"

"He'd try to make it by two."

That only left an hour to debug their rooms and disable the cams. First, he wanted to interview the potential princesses who worked in the Burlesque. "Come with me. We should talk to Tamara, even though I don't really see her as Gigi's princess."

"Because she's not sparkly?" Angie gave a snort. "Rhinestones don't make a princess. Haven't you heard of Cinderella?"

He didn't bother to cite his appreciation for Tamara's inner beauty, her intelligence and her wit. It seemed like Gigi would call her princess based on clothes alone. At the front desk, he asked Tamara if Shanahan and Hemming—who were, of course, using fake names—had checked in.

"Not yet." Her forehead pinched in a frown. "Have you talked to Leif today?"

"He's sad. The Broncos lost." If that was the worst thing

that happened today, he'd throw a parade. He wasn't sure how to work around to the topic of princesses and runaway girls.

"Are you a football fan?" Angie asked.

"Not really, but I went to every single game in high school."

"Cool," Angie said. "Were you a cheerleader?"

"Nothing like that. I played flute in the marching band."

"Were you ever a prom queen? Or one of the princesses?"

"No way."

Julian noticed a difference in her. When she tossed her head and her brown hair bounced, he guessed that she was using a new shampoo or something. And she was wearing eye makeup. "Did you want to be a princess?"

"That's a childish fantasy. Not something I encourage or condone." She returned to studying her computer check-in. "Should I notify you when these gentlemen check in?"

He nodded. Earlier, when he'd made the reservations, he'd told her that the two agents were relatives, and he wanted to show them a good time. Not much of a cover story, but it was enough to assuage curiosity for a day.

As he and Angie strolled away from the front desk, he looked down at her. "Nice job in directing the conversation."

"I've got a couple of tricks I can teach you. Normal people like Tamara might feel threatened if directly confronted. But if you ask a few pointed questions—stuff about family or high school or where they grew up—they'll be happy to talk about themselves. Tamara is not our princess."

He held open the front door to Nick's Burlesque. "Maybe we'll find her in here. We're not open for another half hour, but a lot of the performers get here early."

As it turned out, nobody but the bartender was in the performance area, and he was busy prepping the booze, mixers and garnishes. Julian licked his lips. At one time, his favorite stress reliever had been whiskey. With the house lights on, the metallic wallpaper seemed tawdry. The three-foot-tall stage and runway looked plain and dull, except for the three shiny silver poles placed strategically so most of the audience had a view.

Angie hopped onto the runway, grasped one of the poles, braced her other hand on her hip and strutted in a circle around it. "Did I ever tell you that I was a stripper?"

"You might have mentioned it." His gaze riveted to her slender form as she held the pole and leaned backward until the tip of her ponytail touched the runway. Adrenaline gushed through his veins. His heart beat hard and fast.

She glided her hands down her body, and then she raised them quickly, tearing the black-and-white poncho over her head. She removed her platform shoes carefully so she wouldn't accidentally fire the weapon hidden inside. Waving to the bartender, she called out, "Gimme some background music."

"You got it, Angie." He touched a couple of buttons near the front of the bar, and the space was filled with a throbbing drumbeat.

"I've come down here once or twice to work out. It's great exercise." She hooked her leg around the pole. "Watch this."

He couldn't have looked away if he'd wanted to.

Chapter Twenty

Julian was no stranger to strip clubs and burlesque. Right here at Nick's, he'd watched and auditioned acts that ranged from a magician with disappearing clothes to a contortionist whose joints twisted like a strangely seductive pretzel. Some of these women had magnificent bodies, but none turned him on the way Angie did. Completely covered in a sleeveless black turtleneck tucked into black skinny jeans, she was sexier than a nude chorus line of high-kicking dancers.

He was her audience, and she focused her dark-eyed gaze on him. The rest of the world faded away. Matching the tempo of the heavy drumbeat, she reached high on the pole and pulled herself up with her well-toned arms while her legs coiled and flexed. She slithered higher, swung in a loop and went upside down with her legs spread.

From behind his shoulder, he heard catcalls from other performers who had responded to the beating of the drum. They applauded Angie as she slid to the floor in a split. She climbed again and supported herself in a plank position. No doubt this was good exercise, but the only workout he was considering involved the two of them, naked in his bed.

She wrapped up her pole dance with a front flip, opened her arms to welcome applause and made a sarcastic curtsy.

Gathering her poncho and shoes, she jumped down from the stage. "Once you learn these moves, you never forget."

Lola—the performer with the operatic voice—clarified her statement. "Most people have the muscle memory but haven't kept up the strength."

"Better exercise than a spin class." Angie called out a thank-you to the bartender and turned to the four performers. Dressed in street clothes, they could have passed as soccer moms with attitude. "We wanted to talk to you ladies, and I think Jane's dressing room is comfortable."

Julian knew she was taking them to a place where there were no cameras and no microphones. He was content to follow along. After watching her pole dance, it was going to take a while for him to regain his composure.

Lola closed the door and took charge. In spite of her angelic voice, she was a hard-edged leader. "What's the deal, Julian? Something's going on, and we need to know what it is."

An agile gymnastic dancer started a series of stretches and asked, "I don't get it, Lola. Why do you think there's a problem?"

"Take a look around," Lola said. "Julian doesn't usually come down here for a pep talk. Jane and Cara are still staying on the concierge level, being protected. And I saw a bad guy in the audience—someone I used to know when I worked in Denver."

"Who's that?" Julian asked.

"He calls himself El Jefe, and he belongs to the Fifteen gang. He's deep into the sex trade. While I was onstage, he blew a kiss." She shuddered. "Guys like him make me sick."

"I'll check the tapes," Julian promised. Weeks ago, he'd sent surveillance tapes of El Jefe having dinner with Lorenzo.

"You'll know him right away. He's got the MMXV tattoo on the back of his right hand," Lola added.

"Lola's right," Angie said. "We've got a problem, and we need your help. We're trying to find a runaway girl who is in danger."

He was surprised that she'd chosen to tell the straightforward truth. He watched the four women for their reactions. Lola hardly ever betrayed emotion. The gymnast was more childlike and open. The ballad singer teared up, which didn't mean anything because she wept over every little thing. In his opinion, the most likely princess was Felicity the belly dancer, who had two kids of her own.

Julian directed his comments to her. "Felicity, you might have noticed this girl. She's eight or nine, has brown hair and likes to draw."

"Why do you think I'd notice?"

"The girl said she was helped by a princess. That's why I thought of you."

She preened. "Do you think I look like a princess?"

"Sure," he said. "And you have other kids, so you'd be sympathetic."

"Not to a runaway," Felicity said. "If I caught a kid running away from home, I'd turn her around and take her back where she belongs."

Angie added, "The girl's name is Gigi."

Nothing but blank looks from the four women. Not a princess among them. After telling them to call if they saw Gigi or if El Jefe appeared again, he escorted Angie from the Burlesque. In addition to debugging the rooms for Shanahan and Hemming, he needed to run through surveillance and make identifications on any other members of the Fifteen. He was running out of time.

As they strolled across the three-story lobby on the way to the elevators, Angie tilted her head up and spoke quietly so none of the mics could pick up her words. "There has to be a reason why El Jefe is hanging around."

"To coordinate the start of the operation." The Fifteen must be more involved than the cartel that Damien worked for. He thought of the shoot-out in the bakery. Infighting among powerful criminal gangs was a problem.

His private office was one of the safe places at Nick's. In this space, no one could listen in or watch them. He paced while he talked.

"We need more intel. Obviously, we can't strike up a conversation with El Jefe or any of his minions. Zapata probably has the most detailed information, but he's not likely to let anything slip."

"Especially not to me," she said. "Being at Valentino's when Damien was killed must have put me on his enemies' list."

"I've never gotten a warm, fuzzy vibe from Zapata." The only person who was close enough to Julian and might share information was Lorenzo. "I'll put in a call to Nick."

"Are you sure that's necessary?"

"We need to find out if the timing has changed. Tonight, a combined task force from the FBI and CBI will swoop down and pick up the major players. They'll be caught red-handed and charged. If the schedule is different, the traffickers will get off scot-free."

She stepped in front of him, halting his aimless route. "I hate that you're going to talk to Lorenzo, but I get it."

"I need to have my video guy, Gordon, debug the rooms for Shanahan and Hemming. I hate to leave this in his hands, but I don't have time to do it myself. I've got to trust him while I look at surveillance tapes."

"And I'll leave you to it." She gave him a light kiss on the cheek. "Call me if anything turns up."

After an hour staring at tapes and trying to track the movements of El Jefe, Julian was relieved to have a phone call from Waylon asking him to come out to the barn. "I got something here y'all might want to see."

"Okay." He turned away from the screens. "Did you get the order to leave the barn with three new guys later?"

"You betcha I did. The Baker himself told me."

"I'll be there in a minute."

Before he escaped the dimly lit room full of surveillance screens, Gordon stepped inside. "I have those rooms debugged and clean."

"Did either of my uncles check in yet."

"Not that I know of." Gordon dropped the extra key cards on the desk beside Julian. "Is there anything else you want to talk about?"

"After tonight, it'll all be clear."

If they survived the bust tonight. Hemming told Angie he'd be here at two, and it was already twelve minutes past the hour. He put through an encrypted call to Shanahan, who answered abruptly.

"Julian, I just checked in at the desk. We'll talk later."

"Yes, sir."

Another call came through from Tamara informing him of his uncles' arrival.

The person Julian hadn't heard from was Nick Lorenzo, who he'd called twice. He didn't like the way this was going down.

As he approached the barn, Waylon sauntered out to meet him. This area outside the barn wasn't bugged and didn't have camera surveillance, which meant it was one of the more secure places at Nick's. Julian asked, "What's up?"

"Yesterday I figured out that the real reason for Angie's riding lesson was to search for that little girl. Am I right?"

"How did you know about the girl?"

"I hear things now and then. Could be that little Cara told me." He shrugged. "I think that's it. Cara said something about her imaginary friend. I didn't know it was so important to find her."

Julian was irritated, mad at himself for not trusting the old cowboy with these secrets and hiding the truth from Waylon. "Do you know where she is?"

"No, sir, I sure don't. But I did. A couple of days ago, I could have taken you to her and introduced you. Not that the girl ever told me her name." He took off his hat and pushed his hair back from the accordion-pleated wrinkles on his forehead. "I'm real doggoned sorry I didn't speak up. Wasn't trying to trick you. Nothing like that."

"I believe you." Waylon's motives were innocent enough. He didn't want the little girl to get in trouble. "Tell me what happened."

"This here kid was hanging out in the barn. She'd dragged a blanket and pillow from the bunkhouse and made herself comfy in one of the horse stalls."

"That matches the story Cara told me."

"This little girl feeds me a sob story about how she got stuck here and her mama was coming to pick her up real soon. The mama, she said, was a princess."

Julian winced. Little Gigi wove a complicated web. "You let her stay."

"I didn't see the harm. Next morning when I checked in, she was gone. And she'd done a fine job of tidying up after herself. Heck, I wouldn't know she'd been here, except she left these drawings behind."

He handed over a few sheets of notepaper. The sketches weren't bad for a nine-year-old. Julian could tell that one was supposed to be Cara. Another was a standard version of a princess in a ball gown. There were also sketches of a horse, a dog and a barn. Each was signed in the right corner with a double initial: G. G.

"There's more writing on the back," Waylon said.

Julian turned over the sheets. The Cara sketch was labeled with her name. The dog was Pookie. And the princess was Marigold. "I'll be damned," Julian muttered.

He took out his phone to call Angie, but before she answered, he disconnected. Two of Valentino's dark blue vans raced toward the barn. He and Waylon jumped out of the way just in time. The door on the driver's side was flung open. Zapata lurched out.

Chapter Twenty-One

Frustrated that there wasn't more she could do, Angie flopped into one of the chairs at the table in Jane's suite on the concierge level. Jane placed a steaming mug of coffee in front of her and said, "You might as well relax. Fidgeting won't make the time go faster."

"I'm worried that Julian is going to get into trouble."

"It's like that when you're falling in love. Worry doesn't change anything. Trust and it will turn out fine."

"I hope so."

Though a change in schedule seemed unlikely, Angie feared a surprise switch. The trafficking operation would go into action before they were ready, and the witnesses would disappear. Julian's years of undercover intelligence gathering would be wasted as well as her own efforts. Lorenzo would—once again—evade criminal charges and continue living a charmed life in his Glass Palace.

She'd talked to Marigold and told her to come over here. Maybe she was asking her friend to jump from the frying pan into the fire, but if Marigold was at her side, Angie could protect her. As she raised the mug to her lips, she heard her ringtone. The caller ID showed that Julian was calling, but he hung up before she could answer. Not a good sign. "I wonder what that was about."

"You don't have to explain anything to me," Jane said,

"but I'm guessing that you and Julian have something going on."

"You could say that. He's my boyfriend."

"And something more." Jane cocked her head to one side. "I think you two are partners. Are you a cop?"

It was the second time she'd been asked that question in as many days. She must be losing her touch at maintaining an undercover identity. Since Marigold already suspected that Angie was in law enforcement, there didn't seem to be much point in further denial. Still, she put her index finger across her lips and pointed to Cara who was sprawled on the bed with a coloring book. "Let's talk about something else."

"Tell me all about you and Julian. I've never seen him with a girlfriend."

"We hit it off."

"When you're done with your work at Nick's, are you going to leave him with a broken heart?"

"That's not my intention." *What about me? What about my heart?*

"I hate to see him get hurt. He's a good man."

Cara had been coloring the same square of blue for the past several minutes. Clearly, she was listening to the grown-up conversation. Angie said, "It's complicated."

"How so?"

"My work can take me all over the country. Julian is based in Colorado, and this is where he's going to stay. If we make a commitment, one of us will have to leave our career, and I'm pretty sure that he'd want me to quit. That doesn't work for me. I'm not ready to settle down."

Jane nodded slowly. "Have you talked to him about this?"

"There's no need to talk or discuss. I'm sure he's thinking the same thing I am." Even more frustrated, she bounced to her feet, unable to sit quietly and allow fate to take its course. "We're very much alike, Julian and I. It's like we think with the same brain."

She heard the unmistakable snap of gunfire and ran to the window that gave a view of the barn. Cara had gotten there first and was staring. She saw the vans from Valentino's and armed men ducking for cover. They were under attack, and she was certain that Julian was in the middle of the assault.

She ran into the fourth floor lobby where Muscleman Matt sat at the concierge desk. "Go," she snapped at him. "Julian is in trouble by the barn."

"I'm on it. I'll get the others."

Her phone rang. The call was coming from Julian.

She answered in a flash. "What's going on?"

"A disagreement between Zapata and El Jefe."

"I sent Matt and the other concierge troops to the barn."

"Shanahan is here. He has more agents on the way. We can handle this."

She heard another blast of gunfire. "It definitely doesn't sound like you've got things under control."

"I talked to Lorenzo. He's looking for Marigold, and he doesn't sound happy. You need to warn her."

"Got it."

"There's something else I have to tell you. I wanted to do it in person. But this is what it is." More gunfire. "I love you, Angie." He cleared his throat. "Is there something you want to say to me?"

"You're nuts."

Chapter Twenty-Two

Julian disconnected the call and stared at the screen on his phone. That had to be the worst declaration of love in history! What kind of fool said something like that while dodging bullets? If he survived this, Angie was going to kill him.

He ducked behind the barn door and scooped up a semi-automatic rifle from a man who sprawled bloody and motionless against the side of the bakery van parked inside the barn.

Julian stepped out and sprayed a volley of bullets toward El Jefe, a man he'd never met. He gestured to Waylon. "Open the side door on the van. There are people in there. Get them to safety. Back in the horse stalls."

In spite of the limp, Waylon moved quickly. For an old guy, he got around well. He yanked open the van door and pointed the way to the stalls at the rear of the horse barn.

Two scrawny teenage boys came first, then four young ladies, then a kid. Waylon stepped back, gaping at the open door as Valentino came through. The Baker clenched his forearm around the throat of a pretty young girl whose eyes were as wide as saucers.

"Let her go," Julian growled.

"Then you'll shoot me."

"I don't want to hurt you, but if you don't release the hostage, I'll put a bullet in your brain."

The Baker craned to see around the van. The shooting escalated, and there were two explosions. Grenades? Valentino let go of the child. "Who the hell are those guys? A SWAT team?"

"CBI agents," Julian said with some satisfaction. He caught a glimpse of Hemming in his bulletproof FBI vest. "And the feds."

The Baker's eyebrows raised in disbelief. "You're a cop."

"Yeah."

His team was winning. He could only hope there had been no casualties.

ANGIE PUT THROUGH a call to Marigold, who answered on the first ring. "Almost there," she said. "Coming up the stairs to the fourth floor."

Angie braced herself in front of the door with the Exit sign above it. Marigold burst through. Following her was a girl with straggly brown hair. Marigold pulled the child in front of her, resting her hands upon skinny shoulders. Their eyes were the same tapered shape and greenish-gray color. Their button noses matched.

"This is my daughter," Marigold said. "Georgia Grant."

Two *g*'s equaled Gigi.

Cara—who had obviously been eavesdropping—dashed from her room and flung her arms around her mysterious friend. Both girls chattered like chipmunks as they scampered across the lobby and into the suite.

Angie remembered the call from Julian. "Lorenzo is after you."

"I know." She glanced over her shoulder as if she expected him to appear. "I'm hoping he won't look for me here. There's supposed to be something big going down."

Angie had about a million questions, but her number one priority was to keep them all safe. She poked her head into Jane's suite. "You have two minutes to grab everything you need. We're going to Julian's room on the seventh floor."

"Good plan," Marigold said. "I helped design this building, and Julian's suite is the safest place to be."

While Jane and the two kids gathered up their things, she turned to her friend. "Give me a brief explanation."

"When I was a teenager and Nick Lorenzo took an interest in me, I fell in love. He gave me expensive jewelry and clothes and cash. Just about the time he started to lose interest, I found out I was pregnant."

In her head, Angie did the math. It had been eleven years since she'd seen Marigold, and Gigi was nine years old according to Cara. "Go on."

"He shipped me off to live with a cousin in the mountains while I was pregnant. After the baby was born, we got back together, but he didn't want anything to do with Gigi. He arranged for her to be taken care of by a family in a small mountain town."

"Why didn't you go to the police?"

"Biding my time," she said. "He had enough to put me in jail, and he used Gigi's safety to control me. I was convinced that there was nothing I could do. I'd never be free. But then, I started collecting evidence on him."

"What kind of evidence."

"Documents, recorded conversations, photos. Trust me, there's a ton of proof. I can take down Nick, Zapata and most of his top guys." She dashed away an angry tear. "He wants me dead. And Gigi, too."

"That's not going to happen."

If they escaped in one piece, Hemming and Shanahan would be thrilled. Angie herded Marigold, Jane, Cara and Gigi into the enclosed stairwell and up to the seventh floor. The entire floor was devoted to only two luxury suites. The foyer was often used for receptions and cocktail parties. It was a huge space with a high glass ceiling in an A-frame design like the one on the first floor. Angie opened the door to Julian's suite using the code he'd given her.

She called his phone, expecting to leave a message. Instead, he answered.

"We're safe," she said. "In your suite."

"Stay where you are. I'm coming. We have Zapata and Valentino in custody, but Lorenzo just arrived in front. He went into the lobby."

She glanced at the door to the suite. At Valentino's bakery she'd seen the type of firepower these guys used. They could blast through the door. She took the Glock and two clips from the secret compartment in Julian's bedroom. As she stalked through the front room, she snapped out an order. "Stay here. Help is on the way."

"Where are you going?" Jane asked.

"I'm going to stall these creeps."

In the foyer, she took a position in front of the elevator. The digital numbers showed that the elevator was stopped on the fourth floor. No doubt, when Lorenzo was done searching there, he'd come up here. And she'd be ready. Her Glock was no match for his weapons, but she was smarter and more determined. For eleven years, she'd hated this guy. When she'd heard how he tortured Marigold and Gigi, Angie's loathing doubled. She wouldn't hesitate to shoot him.

The numbers on the elevator showed it ascending to the fifth floor, the sixth and here. When the doors whooshed open, she had the drop on Lorenzo and two henchmen, including Rudy.

"Get out," she said. "Don't get clever or I'll shoot."

Lorenzo gestured to the men standing behind him. "Do as she says. Angie is a reasonable woman. I'm sure we can come to an agreement."

Her gun didn't waver in her two-handed grip as she stared at this unspeakably dangerous predator. Shooting him would be a favor to humanity. "Drop your weapons."

Rudy and the other guy exchanged a smirk, but Lorenzo's face was blank. When he talked, his lips barely moved. His voice was pitched at a low baritone that was probably supposed to convince her that she had nothing to worry about. To Angie, he sounded like the warning castanets of a rattlesnake about to strike.

"I'm not going to hurt Marigold," he said. "I'm trying to do the right thing for her and for Gigi."

"Why should I believe you?"

"If I could, I'd let you talk to her social worker. Gigi is a runaway, a naughty little girl."

That was exactly what the authority figures said about her when she was a foster child desperate for understanding. "Your gun. On the floor. Now."

"You haven't got a chance. There are three of us and only one of you."

"If any of you—and that includes you, Rudy—make a move toward me, I'll start firing. I'm pretty sure that I can't get all of you, so I'll concentrate on one target. You, Lorenzo. Before your boys take me down, I can get three bullets into you."

He studied her for a moment with his cold, dark eyes. "I don't believe you. I don't think you're a killer."

Behind her back, she heard a door open and slam shut. Calamity Jane strode forward with her whip in hand. She wore the belt she used in her stage act—three throwing knives on each side. "What about me? Am I a killer?"

"This isn't your fight, Jane."

"You abused a child. I can't let that pass."

"Don't be a bitch." He stuck out his hand. "Give me the damn whip."

"You asked for it." She snapped the whip at his gun hand and disarmed him. His weapon clattered to the floor. "Now, you other two boys."

The whip flicked restlessly across the floor like a hungry serpent. The guy Angie didn't recognize set his weapon down and stepped back, but Rudy made a stand. He lifted his semiautomatic gun and prepared to shoot. Angie fired first. She wasn't a skilled markswoman and she wasn't familiar with Julian's Glock, but she managed to hit Rudy's gun and throw off his aim. A spray of bullets peppered the carpet near her feet. She felt a sharp sting in her lower leg and went down. She'd been shot.

Jane attacked with her whip, pinning Rudy's arms to his side. When she switched to her throwing knives, Lorenzo raised his hands over his head.

The other guy tried to flee, and Jane used her knife. It only took one hit in the wall in front of him to convince him to stop running and drop to his knees.

They'd won.

The second elevator arrived on the seventh floor. Julian and Muscleman emerged. If they were surprised, they didn't show it. Muscleman used zip ties to secure their prisoners.

Julian knelt beside her on the floor. He cradled her against his chest and gazed into her eyes. "Is there something you want to tell me?"

"For your information, the L-word doesn't count when bullets are flying, and you think you might be killed. And what's the point? No matter how we feel about each other, I'm not going to quit my job and stay in Colorado."

"I didn't ask you to do that." He pulled her closer. "Come on, Angie. Say it."

"Are you aware that I'm bleeding?"

"Who shot you? Was it Lorenzo?"

"Rudy."

"As if I needed another excuse to kill that traitor?"

She patted his cheek. "Maybe I do love you, after all."

Epilogue

The grand reopening of Nick's, which was now called The Double L—which stood for *Lucky Leif's*—was scheduled for December first, and it was the first time Angie had been back in Colorado since the joint FBI and CBI bust of Lorenzo's human trafficking network. Though their procedure had been thrown off by the change in timing, the final takedown was perfection with zero casualties and—thanks to perfect bookkeeping from Marigold—tons of evidence in the USA, Colombia and Mexico.

She'd spoken to Julian on the phone, talking for hours, but had only seen him twice.

Marigold had picked her up at the airport and was driving to the grand reopening. She zipped along the mountain roads, talking a mile a minute. "Are you sure you're okay? I love the cane, by the way."

"I don't really need the walking stick anymore. Wearing a cast was awful, but I'm a hundred percent fine."

"That's what Julian is going to say," she teased.

Angie didn't want to talk about herself. She was hyped to see her friends. "Tell me about the girls, Gigi and Cara?"

"Doing great. And we have a day care for the other kids of employees. The Double L is more family-oriented. Leif got rid of the casino but kept sports betting and OTB.

The Burlesque is a lounge with no nudity and lots of variety acts."

"I heard that Calamity Jane runs the place."

"She does that and special events. I do the decor and decorations."

"And Leif and Tamara are co-owners."

Soon they'd be married, which was wonderful. While they continued to chat, she couldn't stop thinking about Julian. He'd come to see her once in the hospital in DC. and one other time to make sure she got home and had everything she needed.

She still hadn't told him that she loved him.

Of course, she did. But she hadn't said the words.

A light dusting of snow covered the meadow leading to The Double L. Pretty as a postcard with hundreds of Christmas lights. At the entrance, valets in Santa hats took Marigold's car. Julian stood waiting at the top of the stairs.

When she stepped into his embrace, he lifted her off the ground and twirled her around. She wanted to tell him right now. The L-word was at the tip of her tongue.

Before she could speak, he said, "I have a surprise for you. I quit."

Was she supposed to be happy about this? "I don't understand."

"I like working undercover, but my career for the CBI is pretty much over. Half the criminals in the state know who I am and what I look like. But I can start over if I join the FBI."

"But you don't have the training."

"I took some special qualifying courses in Quantico. That's what I've been doing for the past six weeks when I wanted to be hovering at your bedside. I was learning to be a field agent."

"We can work together," she said. "We'll be partners."

"That's the plan."

She snuggled against his chest. "I love you with a capital *L*."

"And that, my darling, is no lie."

* * * * *

COLTON 911: DESPERATE RANSOM

CINDY DEES

Chapter One

"Honey! Are you ready?" Myles Colton's voice floated up the stairs.

Faith Colton yelled back, "Coming!"

Any time her husband tore himself away from the law firm and made time for a date night with her, she was going all out. She'd dropped off their four-year-old son, Jackson, at her mother's house and spent the rest of the afternoon picking out the perfect little black dress, debating the sexy-as-hell but torture-to-walk-in heels versus a lower, more practical shoe that wouldn't give her blisters—she went for sexy—and doing her hair, makeup and accessories.

She wanted tonight to be really special because she had something to talk about with Myles. Since Jack would be old enough to start pre-K next year, she wanted to go back to teaching full time. Myles had been against her going back to work, given that the outrageous cost of day care would have eaten up her whole paycheck, but that argument would be moot once Jack started school.

She was ready. Her one nonmommy purse in hand, a sleek black clutch with crystal trim with no sign of a Cheerio inside it, she marched downstairs. Or more accurately, she hobbled downstairs, already regretting her choice of shoes. But they made her legs look fantastic, and why work out for all those hours to get back her pre-baby body if she wasn't going to show off her legs a little?

Myles was waiting impatiently at the bottom of the stairs, looking at his cell phone. Probably scrolling through work emails. The man *never* stopped working.

She'd known intellectually that junior lawyers worked long hours, but she'd had no idea just how many early mornings, nights and weekends he would spend at the firm, doing whatever lawyers did. Myles rarely talked about his work at home, and truth be told, she knew very little about his clients or cases. He claimed that when he was off work he didn't want to think about any of it, but she knew better.

After the incident with gang members putting him in the hospital for convicting one of their leaders, and her freaking out over it, he'd stopped talking with her about his cases. Not that she regretted for one second insisting that he leave the district attorney's office and go into private practice.

She knew he didn't like practicing liability law anywhere near as much as he'd liked being a criminal prosecutor. But she'd been very pregnant and very scared when he'd been attacked, and she darned well didn't want to lose the father of her child to some pissed off defendant or his buddies out for revenge.

Myles looked up as she approached the bottom of the staircase, and those light green eyes of his that she'd been in love with since the sixth grade lit with pleasure. A flashback of coming downstairs for prom in high school washed over her. He'd been impossibly handsome then, too, tall and lean and athletic.

He was still tall and athletic, although he'd filled out

from that teen into the mature man smiling up at her. He still maintained a year-round tan from running, and it still set off his light brown hair and light green eyes like nobody's business.

"You look fantastic, sweetheart," he murmured.

She laughed a little. "The depth of the surprise on your face makes me wonder how bad I look the rest of the time."

He snorted. "You always were the prettiest girl in school. Why do you think I snatched you up so young and never let you go? I'm no dummy."

She smiled doubtfully as he gallantly held out an arm to her. She looped her hand around his muscular forearm and tottered out to the garage beside him, trying not to fall off her high heels.

She was tempted to ask him to wait for her to run back inside and get her mommy flats, but as she opened her mouth to speak, he commented, "We need to get a move on. Manchero doesn't seat patrons if they're more than ten minutes late for their dinner reservation. We'll be cutting it close."

"Your car or mine?" she asked. His was a sporty little number that was quick in traffic but low to the ground and horrible to get in and out of in a tight dress, stockings and heels.

"Yours," he replied. "The roads are wet and the mommy-mobile is safer on wet pavement."

She'd researched every car review she could find before she chose the vehicle she would drive her child around in. It had cost more than they could afford when they bought it, but it was the safest car on the market. Chicago's highways could be terrifying, particularly near the downtown area, and especially at rush hour. Out here in Evanston, the roads were saner, but a soccer mom late to pick up her kid from practice could be a menace, too.

Even though it was a weeknight, traffic was bad heading into the city. She didn't talk or ask Myles about his day as he navigated the congested roads back toward downtown and the posh restaurant at which he'd managed to finagle a reservation.

He'd said this morning when he called to invite her out on a date that he had something he wanted to talk with her about. To pass the time, she'd tried to guess what it was. Her money was on him finally getting promoted to partner at work. Goodness knew, he'd been working his tail off for it the past four years.

He'd promised her when he took the job with this firm that once he made partner he could cut back on his work hours, make a lot more money, and afford to enroll Jack in the outstanding private school she'd dreamed of getting their children into ever since they moved back to Evanston. She couldn't wait. She was ready to have her husband back. More than ready.

As Lakeshore Drive approached downtown, the traffic blessedly thinned, and Myles accelerated aggressively. He was obviously worried about missing their reservation. It made her nervous when he drove fast, but she got why he was doing it and said nothing.

The lights from the towering high-rises of downtown on their right sparkled off the pavement, still wet from the rain. The streetlights made pools of brightness in the dark, and even the traffic lights took on a festive air. It felt good to get out of the house, and as much as she loved Jack, a bright, high-energy four-year-old could be exhausting. She was looking forward to engaging in some actual adult conversation.

They turned onto Ontario Street to head for the trendy West Loop district, and with a glance at the dashboard clock, Myles stomped on the gas.

The light was green and the intersection clear when two things happened simultaneously. Her car beeped a cross-traffic alert, and out of nowhere on her right, a vehicle loomed in her side window. The vchicle was big, dark and had no headlights. It was coming fast. Way too fast.

She had a bare millisecond to register what was about to happen and for a single word to erupt in her mind. *No!*

A huge impact slammed her whole body to the left, blacking her out for a moment. But the painful rigidity of the seat belt yanked her back upright. She grunted as the front airbag smashed her face and the side airbag caught her body as it ricocheted back toward the ruin of her door.

It was all chaos, then. Spinning car. Musical crash of glass shattering. Tires squealing. Lights going round and round outside.

Then, stillness.

Pain.

Her chest felt cracked in half.

Can't breathe.

Can't breathe.

Panic hit her then, and she flailed against the terribly tight restraint of her seat belt, batting to one side the airbag now deflating away from her body.

Oh, Lord. Myles.

She tried to turn her head to the left, but her whole body protested. She spied Myles out of the corner of her eye, gripping the steering wheel with a trickle of blood running down his face. He was staring back at her, very much alive.

Thank God.

"Are you hurt, Faith?"

"Don't think so," she rasped.

He sagged in his seat for a moment, as if the relief of knowing she wasn't dead was too much to absorb. But then his shoulders straightened. Fury entered his gaze.

She watched, as if from a great distance, as he shoved open his door in slow motion and staggered out of the car. He stumbled around in front of the minivan to stare at something off to her right. She couldn't see anything through the hanging side airbag and crushed side door, but she heard Myles swear angrily.

And then time resumed its normal course. People ran over from their cars to poke their heads through her missing window and ask if she was okay. Phones came out, 911 calls were made. Someone told her not to try to move. Which was rich. She could barely breathe, let alone marshal the strength to drag herself across the mangled center console to crawl out Myles's door.

She felt disconnected from her body and emotions as this strange catastrophe unfolded around her.

All at once, the ability to draw breath normally returned. She gasped, a thousand knives of agony stabbed her chest, and then she exhaled carefully as her entire rib cage rebelled against motion of any kind. She panted in short, shallow breaths that were all her abused body would tolerate at the moment.

Myles was back, leaning across the driver's seat. "Faith. Baby. Where does it hurt?"

"Everywhere," she managed to croak.

"Are you bleeding?"

"Don't know—"

"Don't move, honey. An ambulance is on the way. Just stay still and stay with me."

She frowned. Where was she going to go? She was pinned in her seat—

Oh. He meant not to pass out. Or die.

"Is anything broken?" he demanded.

"How would I know?"

"Does anything feel broken?"

"Yeah. My whole chest. Breathing hurts."

She became aware of being leaned to the left with the whole passenger side of the vehicle plastered up against her right side. She thought that might be part of the armrest jabbing into her right hip. Whatever it was, it hurt.

"Are you seeing stars? How many fingers am I holding up?"

She didn't feel like fainting. She just felt as if she was floating slightly above and outside of her body. "Neck hurts. Don't wanna turn my head to count your fingers," she mumbled.

"Don't you faint on me," he said forcefully.

The sirens, when they came, were deafening and made her pounding head throb even worse. She squinted against the glare of spotlights suddenly pointed at her.

And then a fireman was right in front of her, his friendly, concerned face no more than a foot away. He spoke loudly and clearly. "Ma'am, can you hear me?"

"Uh-huh."

"We're gonna use the Jaws of Life and pull this car off of you, okay? I'm gonna put this blanket over you to protect you from sparks. It won't take long."

A heavy, suffocating blanket went over her head, torso and lap, shutting out his face and all the light. It felt as if she couldn't breathe through it. Suffocating. She was suffocating! She panicked, gasping frantically for breath.

A screamingly loud sound of metal screeching in protest made her go still. Good grief. They were ripping her car apart with her still in it.

The painful thing jabbing her hip went away all of a sudden, and then the fireman was back, peeling the blanket away from her face.

"Before we move you, ma'am, I'm just gonna give you a quick once-over for injuries. Tell me if you can feel me pinching."

He proceeded to rather painfully pinch her arms, legs and feet, and she yelped each time, on cue. He slipped his hand incredibly gently behind her neck and felt around under her hair. He announced over his shoulder, "Neck doesn't feel broken, but I want to immobilize her, anyway."

A stiff, plastic collar with not enough padding at the edges went around her neck and dug into her chin. Two firemen turned her carefully and lifted her out of the wreck of her car. As they swiveled her feet to the right, she caught a glimpse of the back seat. Jack's car seat was mangled.

As in, a twisted lump barely recognizable for what it was supposed to be.

And that was when she broke. Had he been in the car, he would've died for sure. Sweet, innocent, precious Jackson. Oh, God.

She began to sob, which did nothing to help her already rough breathing. She thought she might have hyperventilated, for when they laid her on a gurney and pushed her toward an ambulance, one of the firemen put a paper bag over her mouth instead of an oxygen mask.

It helped. By the time she was strapped into the ambulance and Myles had climbed in beside the medic, she could sort of breathe again, and the worst of the panic attack had passed.

The next two hours were a blur of bright overhead lights, X-ray rooms, and nurses poking and prodding her in pretty much every way they seemed able to think of. But at the end of it, a doctor with kind eyes came in to tell her she was a very lucky young woman and seemed to have avoided any serious injury.

"Good thing you and your husband were driving such a sturdy vehicle, Mrs. Colton," the doctor added casually. "Most people T-boned that hard wouldn't have survived."

Aaand…the panic attack was back.

She gasped ineffectively for air, any air at all. Myles lurched forward, obviously worried, but with no idea what to do. It was the duty nurse, a small, feisty, middle-aged woman named Mrs. O'Dingle who explained, "She's having a panic attack. Hug your wife until she calms down. But gently. *Gently, man.* She's going to be mighty sore for a couple of days."

He sat down on the edge of the bed and carefully wrapped his arms around her, holding her as if she was made of blown glass and the slightest squeeze would crush her. For all she knew, it might. They'd given her a shot a while back, a painkiller that had dulled everything to a distant ache. For now. But an ominous hint of pain to come hovered just over the horizon.

She was alive, though. They both were. And Jack was safe at home with her mother. Thank goodness.

It was taking forever to get her discharge paperwork compiled, and while she and Myles waited, a police officer stepped into the tiny room. "Mr. and Mrs. Colton? I need to take a statement from you regarding your accident earlier. Is now a good time?"

Now was most certainly not a good time, but the officer didn't sound as if he was giving them any choice in the matter.

Myles took the lead. He described driving west on Ontario Street, having a green light, and entering the intersection, a vehicle coming out of nowhere, moving south at high speed and slamming into the side of their car. He described her car giving a cross-traffic warning, then added, "But there was no time to swerve, no time to hit the brakes, nothing to do. It just slammed into us. Pushed us sideways all the way across the intersection."

"We didn't spin around?" she asked, frowning. "I remember lights spinning all around us."

"You were knocked half-silly. I expect you were dizzy and that made the lights seem to spin," Myles said gently.

"Oh."

The police officer spoke up. "Did you see the vehicle, Mr. Colton?"

"It was big and dark colored."

She gathered herself to offer, "It was a pickup truck. Black. No headlights. It had one of those winch things mounted on the front."

"No headlights, you say?" the cop said quickly.

"Correct."

Both men were frowning at her as if she'd grown a second head.

"It's a very dark night out. No moon, full cloud cover," the police officer said.

"I know," she replied tartly. "And the truck had no lights on. I may have imagined the lights spinning after the crash, but I know what I saw before it."

Both men were silent, their skepticism thick in the air. She knew what she'd seen, darn it.

"Did you hear brakes squealing before the truck hit you?"

She thought back. "No. Not at all."

The cop and Myles frowned heavily, and it hit her belatedly what that meant. Oh, my.

The cop cut across the sudden tension, asking, "Did either of you see a license plate, or maybe the driver?"

Now why would he ask that?

Myles answered, "As soon as I got my wits about me and saw that my wife was alive, I jumped out of my car to run around to see if I could catch a license plate number. But he was already too far away for me to see it. He backed up a hundred yards or so at high speed, did a Y-turn, and then peeled off in the other direction."

The other vehicle had fled the scene? Ahh. That must be why Myles had stood in front of their car swearing.

"Was an airbag visible in the truck?" the policeman asked.

Myles thought for a moment. "If it would have been white, then no. The cab of the truck was all dark."

"Hmm. Old vehicle or he must've disabled it."

"Looked like a late-model truck to me," Myles commented.

The cop stated, "That's what the witnesses said, too."

"Did any of them catch the license plate?" Myles responded quickly.

"Unfortunately, no witnesses could give us any detail that would identify the truck or driver," the officer said. "The department will try to track down some security camera footage or closed-circuit TV images of your hit-and-run vehicle. But don't hold your breath. We don't have much to go on."

"Did someone at least see if the driver was male or

female? Maybe a hair color? Basic description like beard or no beard?"

The officer shot her a wary look and muttered, "Witnesses thought the driver was wearing something over his head."

"Like a mask?" Myles blurted.

"Possibly. Like I said, we'll search for video to tell us more."

The policeman left quickly after that, and she turned to Myles to ask him more about the other vehicle fleeing the accident and what it could mean. But as she started to speak, he frowned and followed the policeman out.

She shamelessly tried to eavesdrop on their conversation, but they were speaking too quietly for her to hear anything more than a low rumble of sound. How frustrating!

The cop left, and Myles must have pulled out his cell phone, for he started to speak again. This time, she heard him well enough describing the accident to whoever was on the other end of the call, but then he lowered his voice again, and she missed the rest of the conversation. Darn it.

He stepped back in. "Who was that you called?" she asked.

"My boss."

"Why did he need to know about the accident right away? Shouldn't we call my mom first?"

"I'll call her next."

"What else did you say to your boss?"

"Nothing."

He was lying. But Myles never lied to her. Why was he doing so, now? What wasn't he telling her? With the powerful painkillers coursing through her system, her brain felt cloudy, her thoughts all blurry, and she couldn't summon a single sharp argument to confront Myles with.

He stepped into the hall again, this time to let her mother know they'd been in an accident but were both fine. That was another lie, but at least she saw the reason for this one. No need to panic her mom when there was nothing she could do to help them, right now.

Myles left the hallway altogether then, after muttering something about calling their insurance company and arranging a rental car for them.

She stared at the ceiling, hurting and scared. What wasn't he telling her about the accident? Had it been an accident at all or intentional? That was certainly how he was acting. But who on earth would try to hurt—or kill—them like that? And why?

Even worse than when she'd seen that truck barreling straight at her, terror tore through her now, along with a single thought replaying itself in her head over and over.

She'd almost died tonight.

Chapter Two

Myles ached from head to foot, but he wasn't about to complain, given the pounding Faith had taken in the accident. Bruises were already coloring her face from the airbag, and he didn't want to see what her rib cage looked like.

He took delivery of a rental car outside the emergency room entrance while Faith dozed inside, then he finished plowing through all the insurance and payment paperwork with the hospital. As an attorney, he made a habit of reading the fine print, and there was a lot of it on her discharge papers.

Finally, a nurse wheeled Faith out to the passenger side of the car and helped her into the seat. Seeing her hurt and in pain like that made Myles's fists clench around the steering wheel and his jaw tighten until it hurt.

Somebody was going to pay for hurting the love of his life. Faith was a gentle soul, kind and sweet with every cell in her being. He'd loved her forever, and right now, his protective instincts were in full afterburner.

The nurse passed him her seat belt, and he buckled it for her. Faith leaned her head back against the headrest and closed her green eyes, looking more exhausted than she had right after she'd given birth to Jackson. And she'd had a nearly thirty-six-hour labor with him.

"Drive gently," she said, sighing.

"And carefully," he added.

He headed for her mother's house. Knowing Faith, she would want to hug their son as soon as possible, and frankly, he wanted to do the same. That had been way too close a call tonight.

The insurance company's adjuster had received the preliminary pictures Myles had sent from his cell phone and echoed what the doctor and the cop had said, that the two of them were damned lucky to be alive. Only the sturdy make and excellent safety features of Faith's car had saved their lives—or at least hers.

He sent up a brief prayer of gratitude for caving in four years ago when she'd insisted on buying the expensive vehicle to protect Jackson. Sweet, scaredy-cat Faith. She always had been a safety girl. She was the kind of wife who explained why car insurance companies cut rates in half for men who got married. Not that she was a nag. But she did remind him when he got wild or reckless that he was a husband and father, now, and had responsibilities.

Responsibilities that weighed heavily on his shoulders tonight.

He had a sinking feeling that pickup truck plowing into them was his fault. He couldn't prove it, of course, but the law firm's private investigator, Hank MacDonald, was going to look into it. The guy had promised to call in a few favors, make a few calls, ask around on the street about a hit being put out on him.

Myles felt like crap for lying to Faith earlier and saying that he'd called his boss when he'd actually called Hank, but she was freaked out enough already. He didn't need to pile on to her terror by suggesting that the accident had been no accident at all.

Dammit.

Driving like a little old lady on the way to church, he merged cautiously onto Hwy 41 heading north out of Chicago toward Evanston, his mind racing. Cold, hard logic suggested that he assume the worst and take action accordingly.

Okay. Worst case: the driver of that truck had been out to kill him or at least send a strong message to him. The first order of business would be to secure his family and get them out of harm's way. He could plausibly argue that Faith should spend a few days at her mother's house where Jenny could look after her full time. Particularly since, with his big, new case about to go to trial, there was no way he could take the next week off.

That would get his family away from his home address, and Jenny Romans wasn't a name bad guys would know to associate with him. Faith and Jack should be safe at his mother-in-law's place while he and Hank tracked down that truck.

Next problem: identifying the driver. It didn't take a rocket scientist to connect the hit-and-run with his new case.

When his firm had asked him to take the super high-profile case suing a group called Anarchy Ink that ran around buying and selling weapons at gun shows, it had been a no-brainer to accept the case, given that he'd been a prosecutor specializing in gang crimes before he got hired at Whitney and Pierce.

The firm's partners had warned him the litigation could be risky. One of the two criminal trials against Anarchy Ink had ended in a hung jury that everyone believed to have been the result of juror intimidation by the gang. The second trial had been dismissed on a technicality. But everyone was convinced the gang was guilty.

The owners of Myles's firm had also suggested that if he won a big settlement, he'd get an associate partnership at the firm, a significant pay raise, a huge bonus, and be able to stop working eighty hours a week.

He'd judged it to be worth the risk. Because honestly, how much danger could swirl around a liability case? And he really, really wanted to make partner and get a semblance of normal life back for him and his family.

But then, this.

Now, what the hell was he supposed to do? He exited the highway and turned west. He couldn't back out of the case at this late date. He'd put in hundreds of hours preparing the case, not to mention he actually was the best equipped lawyer in the firm to go up against a hard-core bunch like Anarchy Ink.

Jury selection was due to start in a week. He couldn't just tell the bosses he'd changed his mind. Not without losing any chance at making partner anytime in the near future. But at what cost to his family? He glanced over at Faith, the curve of her cheek swollen and faintly purple in the reflected light of the dashboard.

He was damned if he did and damned if he didn't. He'd taken the case to provide for his family, but staying on the case could hurt his family. Frustrated, he turned onto the quiet residential street his mother-in-law lived on. Evanston was an upscale suburb of Chicago and boasted tree-lined streets with great architecture and grand old homes.

Jenny's house was a large brick colonial and decorated to the nines, but he'd always found it cold and overly formal. Uninviting. Not like his and Faith's cute little bungalow brimming with warmth.

Of course, if he and Faith expanded their family, they were going to need a bigger house. As it was, the three of them were bursting at the seams. Hence, the urgency for him to make partner and increase his paycheck significantly. It was time for them to stop living like broke college students.

He pulled into the Romans' driveway, and Faith opened her eyes. He murmured, "Let me come around and help you out."

"I can get out by myself—" She broke off, groaning a little as she shoved open the door.

"Like I said. Let me help you." She always had been fiercely independent. She often reminded him of a kitten, determined to be ferocious when she was really very soft and small.

He came around and took her elbow, helping lift her to her feet as she stood up. "How're you doing, sweetheart?"

"A little creaky around the edges," she confessed, which from her was a huge confession. She never, ever admitted to weakness.

"Let me go first. Your mom is liable to barrel out of the house and knock you over if I don't warn her first to go easy on you."

"Thanks," she said on a sigh.

It was a slow walk up the sidewalk and front steps. He rang the bell and, indeed, had to step in front of Jenny and grab her by both shoulders to stop her from launching herself at her daughter.

"Slow down there, Jenny. Faith is very sore from the crash. You'll need to treat her like a piece of crystal for a few days."

His mother-in-law glared up at him for a second but then huffed and nodded. She stepped around him more temperately and wrapped Faith in a hug that still had his wife wincing over her mother's shoulder.

"How are you feeling, darling?" Jenny cried.

"Like I went a few rounds with the champ, and the champ won."

"Champ? What champ?"

"It's a boxing analogy, Mom. The world champion boxer is often called the champ."

"Oh. I see. Well, come in, darling. Tell me all about it."

He trailed along behind the two women as they walked across the marble-tiled foyer.

"There's not much to tell," Faith said tiredly. "We were driving through an intersection and a truck slammed into my side of the car. The mommy-mobile is totaled."

"I don't give a fig for some car," Jenny replied fiercely, to her credit. "I'm just glad you're safe." The woman threw a damning look at him over her shoulder.

He threw up his hands. "The light was green. It was totally the other guy's fault."

"Is Jack in bed?" Faith asked.

"Yes. He should be asleep by now."

Faith looked disappointed. "I won't disturb him, then."

"Speaking of which," Myles said, "is there any chance Faith could stay with you for a few days while she rests and recuperates?"

"Why not let her rest at home in her own bed?" Jenny retorted.

"Unfortunately, I'm in the middle of a huge case, and there's no way I can take off work to look after her. And she really did get banged up. I'm worried about her doing too much if she's home alone with Jack."

Jenny harrumphed, making her opinion of him and his big case perfectly clear. "Of course, she can stay with me. Your old room is always here for you, darling."

Hell's bells. He and Faith had been married for seven years and officially dating ever since eighth grade. Jenny could let go already of the idea that he and Faith weren't going to work out.

Jenny was speaking again, solicitously and only to Faith. "Would you like a nice cup of tea, dear?"

"Actually, I'd love a bite to eat. We were on our way to a restaurant for supper when we got hit. I'm really hungry."

"Of course. Let me heat up some pasta primavera—"

"A peanut butter and jelly sandwich would be fine, Mom."

He noticed wryly that the offer of food was not extended to him. Jenny had never been his biggest fan, and since he'd joined Whitney and Pierce, his stock with her had dropped even further. Her husband, until their ugly divorce, had been a lawyer, and Jenny despised anything and anyone who had any association with that profession.

He murmured, "I'm going to pop upstairs and kiss Jack good night."

He retraced his steps to the front hall and started to jog up the curving staircase. But then his whole body protested. He hobbled the rest of the way as if he'd gone one too many rounds against his cousin Aaron, who was an expert boxer.

He had to give Jenny credit for being an enthusiastic grandma. She'd outfitted one of the guest bedrooms just for Jack, complete with a spaceship bed, glow-in-the-dark stars on the ceiling, and plenty of fun toys and books.

He pushed the door open and stepped in. A wedge of

light from the hallway fell across the low bed, illuminating Jack, sprawled on his back, all the covers kicked off, sleeping with the total abandon of youth.

He loved watching his son sleep. His face was so innocent and sweet, a mix of his features and Faith's. Everything was right with the world when he was with Jack like this, watching the rise and fall of his chest, imagining all the wonderful possibilities for his son's future, the laughter and triumphs awaiting him. If he could give Jack the world, he would happily do it, even if it meant working hundred-hour weeks.

His son twitched a little, obviously in the throes of a dream.

What was Jackson dreaming about tonight? Maybe playing soccer with his Saturday morning team, or wrestling with the puppy he kept bugging them to get? *After we get a house with a big fenced-in yard, buddy.*

He pulled up the covers gently and draped them over Jack, then leaned down and kissed his son lightly on the forehead. "I love you, little man," he whispered. "I'll keep you safe, always."

He backed out of the room quietly and headed back down to the kitchen. Faith was ensconced on a bar stool at the kitchen counter tucking in to a huge plate of pasta. Jenny's solution to every one of life's ills was food. The worse the problem, the more she tried to feed a person.

He didn't bother asking for a plate for himself. She obviously didn't think he rated her tender loving care.

"How about I run over to our place and pack a bag for you?" he asked Faith. "Is there anything special you'd like me to bring back for you?"

"Umm, no. Just loose clothing, I guess."

"You've got it." He dropped a quick kiss on her unbruised cheek and headed out. They lived only about ten minutes from Jenny, but the houses on their street were about one-quarter the size of hers. He and Faith had bought their Craftsman bungalow as a fixer-upper, and in his first few years as a lawyer, they'd worked together to repair it. But once he'd gone to work at Whitney and Pierce and his work hours had gone through the roof, Jenny had taken over all the home improvement projects. Nowadays, she hired a handyman when a job was too big for her.

He pulled into the drive of their cheerful home, crossed the stone columned porch and stepped into the front hallway. Every time he saw the original wood trim, plentiful throughout the cottage, he thought of the hundreds of hours they'd spent stripping paint and refinishing it all. They'd had so much fun doing it together—he missed those times.

He grabbed a suitcase out of the front closet and carried it back to their bedroom. Quickly, he tossed in clothes and toiletries. He filled up a second suitcase with clothes, toys and books for Jack. The boy had taken off reading recently and went through a dozen or more library books a week for early readers.

But then, Faith was an elementary school teacher. It made sense that their son would learn to read and do math early. She was a great mom and spent all kinds of time with him working on basic skills, visiting museums and the like. He often wished he could go on some of their outings with them. But…work. Always work.

He sighed and picked up the bags. He drove back to Jenny's house and delivered the suitcases. It was getting late, and Faith was wilting when he arrived. He stuck around just long enough to make sure she took her painkillers, tucked her into bed, and kissed her good night much as he had Jack.

"Stay with me?" she murmured sleepily.

"Your mother hates it when I sleep in the same bed with you under her roof."

"That was only before we got married."

"I'm not so sure about that," he replied dryly. "Besides, I don't want to bump into you during the night and hurt you. And I have an early meeting in the morning. I would disturb you with all my getting up and getting ready. You just rest, tonight."

"Okay." She sighed, sounding disappointed.

Remorse rushed through him. Screw his job, screw the promotion, screw the partnership. "If you need me, I'll stay with you. Or, I can pack up you and Jack and take you home right now."

"No, I'll be okay. I'm just a little sore. It'll go away soon enough, and your job is important to you."

He frowned and opened his mouth to argue, but she reached up and laid her fingertips across his mouth. "Really, it's fine. Go do what you have to do."

The last thing he wanted to do was pick a fight with her when she was hurting like this. "Okay, fine," he said, then sighed.

"I'll miss you," she murmured.

He smoothed her glossy auburn hair back from her pale forehead. A lavender blotch was already discoloring her fair skin on the right side of her face.

He whispered, "I'll miss you too, Freckles." He'd teased her mercilessly about the freckles across her nose when she was a kid. They'd faded as she grew up, and her skin was porcelain clear and softer than velvet, now.

He loved to trail his fingertips along her cheeks and jaw. But tonight, he refrained. "I love you."

"I love you, too, Viles."

They traded fond smiles and he bent down to brush his lips lightly across hers, being careful not to hurt her. "Dream of me."

"Always."

He headed down the stairs, lit only by a small lamp in the foyer—apparently, he didn't rate Jenny staying up long enough to see him out the front door—and he let himself out, locking the door carefully and checking it once he was outside.

As he trudged to his car, a wave of ominous premonition washed over him. This was a bad idea, leaving his family with his hostile mother-in-law and walking out on his wife like this. Whether she'd admit or not, Faith needed him, and he was abandoning her.

But he had no choice at all. It was this or risk their lives. And he would die himself before he let any harm come to Faith or Jackson.

Chapter Three

Faith started to roll onto her side and jolted awake as pain slashed through her entire body. She flopped on her back and groaned out loud. She felt as if someone had been bashing her with a baseball bat all night. No part of her body didn't hurt.

Oh, God. When the doctor had said she would be sore for a few days, she had no idea he'd meant *this*. Morning sunlight was streaming through her window, and on cue, her early rising son bounded into the bedroom and jumped onto the bed.

She groaned in spite of trying to bite it back. "Gently, Jackie," she mumbled. "Mommy's not feeling good."

"What happened to your face? It's all swelled and purple."

"Daddy and I were in a car accident last night. Daddy's fine. He had to go to work early."

"He always has to go to work early."

She had no response to that pithy observation. Jackson was not wrong.

"Is the car smushed?"

"Totally. Firemen had to rip it apart to get me out. It was really loud."

"Cool!"

Not exactly. But she wouldn't convince Jack of that. "Did you like getting to sleep all night in your rocket ship bed?"

"Uh-huh. I dreamed I was in space and all floaty. There was no gwavity." He demonstrated by standing up in the bed and flapping his arms up and down slowly. The bed joggled and she bit back another groan of pain. Where were those painkillers Myles had left for her?

She rolled carefully out of bed and shuffled toward the en suite bathroom. Spotting the brown plastic prescription bottle, she pounced on it in slow motion.

"Why are you walking funny, Mama?"

"I'm sore, baby."

"Why did we stay all night at Gwammy's house?"

"So I could rest, sweetie. Your daddy was worried he would bump into me in the middle of the night and hurt me."

"Oh. Can we have waffles?"

"You'll have to ask Grammy." Not that her mother ever refused Jackson anything he wanted. It was an ongoing argument between her and her mother that Jenny spoiled Jackson rotten. Jenny always retorted that it was what Gwammies did. The two of them were incorrigible, together.

"I'll race you to see who can get dressed fastest," she challenged.

"Mark. Get set, Go!" he shouted. He tore out of the room, and she wished for even a little of his boundless energy.

Painfully, she eased out of her nightgown and gasped at herself in the mirror. Huge bruises discolored her ribs, and a diagonal bruise showed clearly where she had slammed against the seat belt. Her neck ached like crazy, and she gave in and Velcroed on the thick padded neck cushion the doctor had sent her home with.

Now she abruptly understood the sympathetic noises the nurse had been making last night as she warned Faith not to do anything more strenuous for the next few days than lift a cup of tea. She couldn't do much more than that if she wanted to.

She walked slowly to the kitchen, where her mom was already making waffle batter and letting Jackson crack eggs into the mixing bowl. Without complaint, her mother fished out bits of eggshell as Jackson lost interest and headed out onto the back porch to pick up leaves. Where had this fun, nonjudgmental woman been when *she* was growing up?

Of course, Faith knew the answer to that. Her mother had been embroiled in a bad marriage and ultimately, a bitter divorce. Harold Romans was a prominent attorney in his day, not to mention an incorrigible womanizer. He'd thrown money at Jenny to keep her tucked away in her suburban housewife life while he'd lived his own life in the city. Faith had practically no memories of her father ever being at home. In fact, his death had barely touched her emotionally. She'd hardly known the man.

Jack shouted outside and she looked up in time to see him run and crash into the huge pile of leaves the gardener had left for him. Autumn's full glory was afoot in Evanston, and the backyard was ringed in shades of yellow, orange and deep red.

Jack tore back toward the house. "Look, Mama! I found a maple leaf!" He held up his red and rather bedraggled prize.

"If you find a few leaves you really like, I'll show you

how to iron them between sheets of waxed paper after breakfast."

Jenny looked up sympathetically. "You think you're going to feel up to lifting a heavy iron?"

Faith sighed. "Probably not. But I'm not used to being completely incapacitated like this."

"You just take it easy. I'll entertain Jackson for you. He and I have a great time together."

She smiled ruefully. "That's what worries me." Her mother had a tendency to never, ever, say no to him. Whatever he wanted, he got when Jenny was around.

Just because she and Myles would be able to afford to give Jackson anything he wanted as his life progressed didn't mean they ought to do so. She'd taught enough kids who, by third grade, were already spoiled, entitled brats to know that parents needed to set boundaries for their children and teach them not to expect to get everything they wanted when they wanted it.

Jackson bounded in through the French doors with a fistful of leaves in hand. "Look, Mama! They're as many colors as your face!"

"Gee, thanks, kid. You sure know how to give a girl a compliment."

"What's a compliment?"

"It's when you say something nice about a person to them."

"Oh. Can I have the first waffle, Gwammy?"

"Of course," her mother answered jauntily. The two of them launched into a discussion of what Jack wanted on top of his waffle, and Faith tuned out and pulled out her cell phone. She texted, Good morning, handsome. How are you feeling today? I spent all of last night thinking about my own discomfort, but you were in the accident, too. Are you sore?

Good morning to you too. I'm a little roughed up, but nothing a few aspirin can't take care of. How about you?

Truthfully... I'm not great. Good call to leave me at my mom's. Jack would've worn me out. I've been awake fifteen minutes and I'm ready for a nap.

Take one. You need rest to heal.

After breakfast. Have a good day.

Gonna be a busy one.

He always said that, and given how exhausted he was every night when he came home, she fully believed him. She was so proud of him making it into and then through law school and landing a job at such a prestigious firm.

She typed, Love you to the moon and back.

Love you to the stars and beyond.

She smiled at their little ritual and tucked her phone back in her pocket as her mother set a waffle in front of her. She didn't scrimp on calories this morning and slathered it in butter and syrup.

As she finished the last bite and pushed her plate back in satisfaction, her phone vibrated. She pulled it out and Myles had texted, By the way, don't tell anyone where you're staying.

Why not?

Just humor me, okay?

Um, okay. But...weird?

Just being safe.

Safe from what? She started to text back to ask him, but Jackson grabbed her hand and dragged her out to the back porch to watch how high he could go on the swing in the huge play set her mom had had custom-built for him this summer.

She took a blanket out onto the back deck and stretched out beneath it on a chaise longue to watch him play. She duly laughed and applauded Jack until her mother stepped outside to announce that Jack's favorite nature show was coming on TV. He tore inside, and she started to lever herself painfully to her feet.

"Stay," her mom told her. "Rest. I've got Jack."

Sometimes, she thought Jenny loved that kid more than her own daughter. Goodness knew, her mom had never been half so attentive to her when she was little. Jenny had been too busy being the perfect corporate wife, throwing cocktail parties, socializing with the other corporate wives, and social climbing. Always social climbing.

Faith's dad had risen quickly through the ranks at a major corporation to end up as VP in charge of the entire company's legal department. Like Myles, he'd never been home and had practically lived at his office. In fact, she and her mother found out years after the fact that he'd owned a ritzy condo in downtown Chicago where he'd entertained his many women.

Her parents had been estranged for as long as Faith could remember. Looking back now, as a married adult herself, she suspected her parents had had some sort of arrangement along the lines of him living his own life with no questions asked from Jenny, as long as he supported Jenny and Faith in fine style.

She didn't understand her mother accepting such an arrangement, but she reluctantly sympathized with her mother now that her own husband was gone much more than he was home, and she forgave Jenny a certain amount of her bitterness.

The painkiller she'd taken after breakfast started to kick in and her eyelids felt heavy. She closed her eyes and felt herself drifting off.

That black truck loomed in her vision, frozen in time while she stared at it. In her dream, she had plenty of time to register that it was going to slam into her, that it was going to hurt and that she might die. In that suspended moment of dreamed time, she thought back over her life.

The good times had mostly outweighed the bad. While her home life hadn't been especially happy, it also hadn't been particularly unhappy. Certainly not after Myles had come into her life. They'd met in their first year of middle school when several elementary schools' worth of kids came together in the sixth grade. He'd been a tall, good-looking kid who was popular, got excellent grades, and was quarterback of the football team.

Why he'd picked her out from all the other girls to have a crush on, she had no idea. She'd been quiet and studious, completely disinterested in the popular-kid social scene. She had a certain social status out of general principles simply because her family was rich and lived in a big house. But none of that had seemed to matter to Myles. He'd started sitting beside her in classes they shared, and before long he was sitting with her at lunch every day. He'd teased her until he forced her to come out of her shell and tease him back, and they'd been best friends by Christmas that year.

Their relationship had grown from there. He'd dragged her into his circle of friends, or more accurately dragged his friends to her, and she'd had a fun high school experience because of him. He'd been her bulwark against the drama of those years, and she supposed she'd protected him from peer pressure to party hard and play the field.

He'd shifted to wide receiver in high school, and she'd dutifully gone to every game, even though she neither understood nor liked football. Afterward, he'd collected her out of the stands and taken her to the postgame pancake supper the football moms put on every Friday night.

They'd decided to go to the University of Michigan together—it had an excellent education program for her, and a world-class law school for him. College had been a good time. They'd both done some growing up, briefly broke up with the intent to date other people, and had quickly gotten right back together.

She shuddered to remember the few dates she'd had with other guys. She'd spent the entire time comparing them to Myles, and not a one of them had come close to measuring up.

Her dream shifted, and she was back in the mommy-mobile in the first moments after the crash. She looked over at Myles, and he was slumped over the wheel with blood pouring out of his head.

"Myles. Myles!" she shouted. He didn't move. She

reached over to shake him and he slumped over lifelessly. His dead eyes stared up vacantly at her—

She lurched awake, breathing hard, with panic slamming through her. Oh, God.

A dream. It had just been a dream. But so danged vivid.

It was okay. Myles was okay. He hadn't been seriously injured in the accident. They were both fine. She repeated the assurances to herself over and over until her breathing calmed down and her pulse quit fluttering frantically in her throat like a trapped bird.

An urge to see Myles, to hold him and have him hold her, to spend time with him to make herself believe he was safe, overcame her.

She dug her phone out of her pocket and texted, lying, Had a nap. Feel much better. Will collect Jack and go home this evening. I'll cook us a nice supper to make up for missing our date last night.

It took a while for him to text back, which usually meant he was in a meeting. Can't make it home early. Stay with your mom.

No explanation. No apology. Just that terse message to stay with her mom. What on earth was up with him? Alarm sliced through her, sharp and painful.

One thing about having known Myles for most of their lives was she could sniff out when something was wrong with him like nobody's business. She knew him better than she knew herself. And right now, he wasn't telling her something.

Did whatever he was keeping from her have to do with what he'd wanted to tell her over a fancy dinner last night? Had she been dead wrong to assume he'd had good news he'd wanted to share with her and celebrate? Could it be the exact opposite? Did he have something bad to tell her and he'd wanted to get her out in a public space where she wouldn't kick up a fuss over it?

As far as she knew, the preparations for his big case were going very well, his job was secure, he was happy with his coworkers and bosses. Then what?

Had she done something to upset him? Was he mad she didn't want to go to the company Halloween party next week? She hated wearing costumes, and frankly, she had her hands full running Jack around to the Halloween parties his various activities were throwing, figuring out how to decorate the front porch to be spooky but not scary to little kids, and what kind of treat to offer that would be safe and fun, but also healthy—

No. Her gut said that wasn't it.

What wasn't he telling her? And why, for the first time in their many years together, was he keeping something from her? Was it possible? Was he having an affair?

Surely not. But what other explanation could there be for his abruptly closed and secretive behavior?

Stunned and afraid, she stared up at the ceiling. What was she supposed to do? How was she supposed to fight for her man if he wouldn't even come home to her?

Chapter Four

Myles looked up as Hank poked his head inside his office, saying, "Got a minute?"

"Yup." Uh-oh. The firm's private investigator closed the door behind himself. That wasn't good.

"I found a guy, a drug dealer, who was working that corner last night. He didn't want to talk to the police, but he talked with me."

"And?"

"And he thinks the driver of the truck was wearing a mask. A black thing that covered his whole head."

"Like a ski mask?"

"Exactly."

"He also confirmed that the headlights were off and that he heard no tires squeal before the impact."

Myles leaned back in his desk chair. *What the hell?* "So, it was definitely an intentional ramming?"

"Looks that way. My guy said he actually heard the truck's engine rev just before it hit you, like the driver hit the gas."

"Dammit." Myles shoved a hand through his short hair. "Any idea who it was?"

"I'm working on that. I've got a buddy in the police

department who says they're still pulling security camera footage. They hope to get a license plate number."

"Lemme know if they ID the driver, eh?"

"Will do. Oh, and the truck had a custom paint job. It was matte black all over, a heavy-duty model, and had some sort of contraption on the front fender. My informant said the truck didn't look damaged when it backed away from you. Makes me wonder if it wasn't a winch on the front of the truck, but instead some sort of ramming assembly."

"Seriously?"

Hank shrugged. "Do you have an idea if any of the guys in Anarchy Ink drive a vehicle like that?"

"No idea. But I'm damned well gonna find out. If those bastards came after me and my wife, they're gonna wish they'd never tangled with me."

"Easy, there, cowboy. Those are some bad dudes. You don't want to mess with them. Let law enforcement deal with them. They're mean, they're armed, and they've killed before."

"Yeah, and gotten away with it. That's why I'm suing their asses."

"How's the case against them looking?"

"Airtight. The FBI's forensic arson investigator says there's no question the fire started on Anarchy Ink's property outside Maple Bend. He thinks they were blowing up high explosives. There was a county-wide burn ban in effect because of a drought, and it was a windy day. Any reasonable person should have known not to mess with anything flammable.

"In the first criminal trial, ten of twelve jurors thought they were guilty, and everybody's convinced they bought off one juror and threatened the life of another one. In the second trial, they got off on a technicality, but in after-the-fact interviews, all the jurors said they were leaning toward conviction."

Hank snorted. "They need to pay for what they did. Four people died in the fire they started, and one of them was a kid."

Myles sighed. Eleven-year old Jordan Sweeting had ridden his bicycle to his elderly great-grandmother's home to warn her about the fire, and the blaze had caught up with them in her home. Neither had made it out. The other two victims had been a married couple without phones. They hadn't gotten the evacuation order and died in their bed.

"Have there been any threats against you?" Hank asked. "Any emails? Calls that hang up when you answer? A car or person following you?"

"Not that I'm aware of."

"Be careful, Myles. Keep your eyes open and your head on a swivel. These are seriously dangerous people."

He sighed. "I know. I've prosecuted gangs before."

"As gangs go these are the worst of the worst. They're not kids pushing a little weed on street corners. They're adult men engaging in illegal arms sales and smuggling. They're organized and well-trained. There's big money in it, and they're not messing around."

Myles nodded. "Keep me informed, eh?"

"Will do."

Myles reached for his phone out of habit to call Faith. He usually touched base with her during his lunch hour. Although recently, he'd been gulping down a sandwich his assistant brought him while he continued to work. He stared at his last text to Faith, and laid his phone back down.

She'd been so scared last night. He'd never seen her have a panic attack before. The nurse had warned him Faith would be in serious pain for the next couple of days, and he should do everything in his power to keep her calm. If he told her the accident had been an intentional attack on them, that would completely freak her out.

He hated keeping things from her, but it was for her own good. Worse, he would have to stay away from her, not only so Anarchy Ink couldn't hurt her again, but also because she knew him so damned well. She read him like an open book. Two minutes in her presence, and she would know he wasn't telling her something important.

The best thing to do right now was to stay far away from her and Jack. But man, it sucked.

Last night had scared the bejeebers out of him. He'd lain in bed for hours trying to imagine his life without Faith and Jack in it, and all he could see was a giant black hole where everything that mattered to him had been. They were his entire world. And he would be twice damned before he let anything bad happen to them.

THE NEXT FEW days passed in a blur for Faith. She had brief periods of alertness between doses of painkillers and spent the rest of the time napping. Gradually, the pain aged into a dull ache, and she tapered off on the meds and started to feel human once more. She had to admit, Myles had been right to insist she and Jack stay with her mother for the week. Without Jenny entertaining and caring for Jackson, she'd have been a seriously miserable camper.

She woke up Friday morning and was able to climb out of bed normally, get dressed, and make it downstairs without stopping once to gasp in pain. Hallelujah. She'd rejoined the living.

After breakfast, she texted Myles. Finally feeling better. Going home today. Jack has a soccer game tomorrow morning. Any chance you can make it?

Myles's reply dropped her jaw. Don't come home. Stay at your mother's house. I need complete silence to concentrate on this case, and I'm planning to work at home for most of the weekend. I'll try to make the game, but don't hold your breath.

She stared at her phone, aghast. He was ordering her not to come home? What. The. Actual. Heck?

A slow simmer of anger started low in her belly, little bubbles of fury tickling the edges of her gut. Since when couldn't he close the door to his office and work at home? She and Jackson had always been respectful of his privacy and were capable of being quiet for reasonable stretches of time. For that matter, she could take Jackson and spend the day at a museum or the zoo and leave Myles completely alone.

"Hey, Mom? Would you mind if Jackson and I shacked up with you a few more days? Apparently, Myles has a major case to prepare for and he'd like to have the house to himself to do it."

Jenny frowned. "Since when? He's never demanded to be alone before."

Faith saw the old pain in her mother's eyes. Recognition of the behavior. Yeah, she remembered, too. Her dad had been evasive and made strange excuses all the time to avoid being with the two of them. Faith had been a teenager before she figured out where her father spent all his time away from them, but Jenny had always known about the other women.

Surely, not Myles. The two of them had been unswervingly loyal to each other for basically their whole lives. No way would he cheat on her, now. Granted, practicing law at a big firm was a tremendous pressure cooker. But he'd always turned to her for stress relief in the past. Why change now?

Her mother tsked sympathetically. "Of course, you two are welcome here for as long as you'd like. This is your home, sweetheart. I'll always be here for you, no matter what that husband of yours gets up to."

Myles wasn't getting up to anything other than preparing for his case, but she wasn't feeling up to picking a fight with her mom over it. Besides, she was grateful her mom didn't mind putting up the two of them for a few more days.

Distracted and frankly irritated, she spent the morning playing board games with Jackson. He walloped her at all his favorite games and finally complained, "You're not trying, Mommy."

Her attention snapped to him. "Don't you like winning?"

"Uh-huh. But it's no fun if the other guy loses too easy."

Wise child. "What do you say to a movie marathon? You pick the movies. We'll pop popcorn and eat hotdogs and wear pajamas the whole time."

"But we're already dressed," her little pragmatist objected.

"We'll change back into jammies and put sleeping bags on the floor."

With a whoop, he tore upstairs to change clothes, and she headed for the kitchen to make snacks.

The remainder of the day passed with her four-year-old

pointing out every flaw in every classic superhero movie they watched. "You've got a promising future ahead of you as a film critic," she finally commented.

"I'm just telling the truth," he protested. "I'm always supposed to tell the truth, right?"

"Yes, sir. Life is a thousand times easier if you're honest."

Speaking of which, as Jackson cued up the next movie, she pulled out her phone to text Myles. What's going on? What aren't you telling me?

MYLES WINCED AS he read Faith's text. As he'd feared, she sniffed evasion from him. Even from afar, she knew him too well.

"Anything wrong?" Suzanne Pierce of Whitney and Pierce purred across the conference table at him.

She was in her early forties, sleek, fit, and expensively turned out. She was a hell of a litigator, single and had made full partner in her thirties—a title she'd earned on her own in spite of being the only daughter of one of the firm's founders—which meant she came by her confidence honestly. Were he not happily married to Faith, she was definitely a woman he would consider taking up on her flirtation. But as it was, he wasn't interested. At all.

They stayed late at the office, which had emptied out early on a Friday, with most of the associates going home by seven p.m. or so. Suzanne had volunteered to stick around, however, and help him practice his opening argument. Theatric oration was one of his favorite aspects of being a trial lawyer, and he enjoyed honing his presentation until it stirred the blood and sent shivers across jurors' skin.

She seemed to catch the hint that he wasn't looking for

romantic companionship, and with a smile and a shrug, got down to business.

Suzanne was tough, picking apart every sentence, challenging every assertion he made as she played skeptical juror. By about ten p.m. they were both satisfied that his opening argument was perfect, and they packed up, him with his script in hand to memorize over the weekend.

"Hungry?" Suzanne asked innocently enough. "We can swing by my club and grab a bite if you'd like."

"It's great of you to offer," he murmured. "But I'd better get all the rest I can this weekend. The next couple weeks are going to be killers."

"Maybe next time," she purred.

Honestly, there was nothing overtly sexual in her words or her voice, but there was just a vibe about her that she would definitely jump on any advance he made toward her. He was objectively complimented, but it wasn't happening. He loved his wife.

He smiled pleasantly and replied, "Have a good weekend."

"You, too. Call if you need any more help."

"Thanks for the offer," he responded noncommittally.

He headed down into the parking garage and climbed in his little sports car. He'd bought it used fresh out of his undergrad degree and restored it and rebuilt the engine in his spare time during law school. He was proud of her, and she had all the zip he needed on Chicago's crowded streets.

He headed north out of the city, driving through at a fast food restaurant to grab a sandwich and fries. And to think, people thought being a lawyer was sexy and chic. He approached his exit but surprised himself by staying on the highway one more exit and pointing his car toward the Romans's house.

This late at night parking spots were at a premium, and he ended up parking a half-block down the street with his mother-in-law's house ahead of him and across the street. He sat in the car to eat, since he had no expectation that Jenny would offer him food, and contemplated what to say to Faith.

How could he make things right between them without confessing that he was worried for her safety and without setting off a panic attack that would hurt her? Maybe she wouldn't freak out if he was straight with her—

Who was he kidding? She would totally freak out.

As he finished off the last crunchy little tidbits at the bottom of the fry bag, he noticed movement across the street from the Romans house. Someone was standing in the shadows of a big old tree with gracefully drooping branches that nearly touched the ground. The person was tucked inside the canopy, maybe leaning against the tree trunk.

Alarm flared in his gut. Was somebody watching Jenny's house?

He stayed put in his car, waiting tensely.

A lighter flared briefly, and then a tiny red pinpoint glow indicated that the person was smoking.

Son of a bitch. His wife and child were being watched! Please God, let it be Hank keeping an eye on his family.

Myles pulled out his cell phone and texted the PI. Any chance you're parked outside my mother-in-law's house watching my family?

Sorry, no. Not me. Call the police.

Myles swore hard and finally his brain kicked into gear. If he called the police, he would chase off whoever it was. Or, he could sit tight and try to figure out who the person was. If he'd learned one thing when he'd been an assistant district attorney trying gangs, it was that they only respected strength. Calling the police was a wimp move. Watching the watcher was the power play.

He sat in the dark for an hour, watching, waiting and wondering. How in the hell had these guys—for surely that was one of Anarchy Ink's men—found Jenny's house so damned fast? Had they researched his family? Maybe found Faith's maiden name online? Dammit. Tomorrow morning he would have to call the firm's computer guy and ask if there was any way to scrub all mention of Faith and Jackson off the internet. He recalled from his days as a criminal lawyer that the FBI was able to do that for testifying witnesses who needed to be inconspicuous for a while.

An upstairs light went on in his mother-in-law's house, and he spotted Faith walking across the window in the end bedroom. She must be tucking Jackson into bed.

He smiled briefly, but then the watcher moved suddenly, drawing Myles's full attention. The silhouette of a stocky man separated itself from the shadow of the tree and headed away from the Romans house.

Damn, damn, damn. The guy had to have seen Faith, same as he had. Was that the purpose of the dude's little surveillance operation? To verify where Faith Colton was staying?

Alarmed to the bottom of his soul, Myles waited alertly in his car to see where the guy went. The man got into a hefty muscle car and pulled away from the curb, the rumble of his engine loud in this quiet neighborhood.

Leaving his headlights off, Myles pulled out of his parking spot to follow. He let the guy turn the corner before he turned on his own lights. He raced to the stop sign and took a right, but the muscle car was gone. He'd lost the guy. Crap.

Myles headed for home. When he pulled into his own driveway, he texted what he'd seen to Hank, who texted back immediately, Leave the legwork to the pros. Don't mess with these guys, I'm telling you. Will call tomorrow.

Myles frowned. What did Hank know that he wasn't telling? The two of them were going to have a serious talk about who exactly Anarchy Ink was and what Hank knew about them that he wasn't sharing. As the firm's PI, he had a duty to share all the information he acquired pertaining to any active cases. The lawyers decided what to use in court and what to omit, not Hank.

Tired, he closed the garage door and trudged across the back lawn to the house. He opened the kitchen door and stopped, staring.

The kitchen was a wreck. Every drawer was pulled out and spilled, the refrigerator door was open, food on the floors, cabinet doors torn off the hinges. The kitchen chairs were overturned and broken, and the table smashed right in half. Looking through the dining room to the living room, both of those rooms were similarly trashed.

Swearing under his breath, he dialed the police and then called Hank.

The PI picked up and said a little impatiently, "I said we'd talk tomorrow."

"They ransacked my house."

"I'll be there in fifteen minutes. Don't touch anything and call the police."

"Already did." He hung up to the sound of the PI swearing.

Yeah. That.

Chapter Five

Faith stood on the sidelines, privately amused at the utter chaos that was a bunch of four-year-olds playing soccer. Every kid on the field ran after the ball, wherever it went, in a clumsy, adorable mob that resembled nothing so much as a pack of gamboling puppies.

The coaches shouted instructions that the kids completely ignored, and the parents cheered in between gossiping with the other parents.

About halfway through the game, a hand touched Faith's elbow and she turned. "Myles? You made it!" She threw her arms around his neck and he hugged her back tightly.

God, it felt good to really hug him. After the accident, they'd both been in too much pain to embrace. His body was hard and strong and so very alive. It was reassuring like nothing else that he was fine after the crash.

He murmured, "How are you feeling? Your bruises are, um, colorful."

She rolled her eyes and studied him back. He had dark smudges under his eyes and looked…haggard. She said softly, "You look exhausted. I don't care how important your case is, you have to sleep a little."

"Late night, last night." He looked out at the soccer field. "How's the game going?"

She glanced over at him. "Hilarious. It's more like herding cats than an actual sporting event."

He smiled beside her, but the expression didn't reach his eyes.

"What's got you so tense? Is it your case?"

"Yeah."

She turned her gaze back to the game. The other team had managed to kick the ball into the goal, and Jackson looked frustrated. He had a competitive streak as wide as his father's. She murmured to Myles, "Anything I can help with?"

"Actually, yes."

That made her turn to look fully at him. "I can help with your case?"

"Obliquely."

"Meaning what?" she retorted.

He sighed. "I was going to talk with you about all this over dinner on Monday. And this isn't exactly the best place to have a serious conversation."

"Do we dare try to go on that date again?" she asked wryly.

He pulled a face. Nope, he didn't want to challenge that karma, either.

"Just tell me what's going on, Myles. Blurt it out."

He huffed. "I believe the defendant in my case may be trying to intimidate me."

That made her stare at him. "Are you telling me the truck that hit us was someone trying to intimidate you? The driver almost killed me!"

"I know. That's why I wanted you to stay with your mother this week."

"You knew Jackie and I were in danger and you didn't say anything?"

"I didn't know for sure." He took a deep breath and added, "But I do, now."

"How?" she demanded. That simmer of anger that had been cooking in her belly all week long exploded into full-blown wrath. He'd been keeping this information from her for days. He'd been in danger—they'd all been in danger—and he hadn't thought that was important enough to share with his wife?

Myles was wincing beside her…and not answering. Her voice low, but vibrating with anger, she said, "You owe me the truth."

"Last night I went over to your mother's house, and before I could get out of my car, I spotted a guy watching the house."

"They were at my mother's house?" she squawked. She and Jackson *and* her mother had been in danger, and he hadn't bothered to tell her? Her chest started to feel as if there was an iron band around it, slowly tightening down until she couldn't draw a full breath.

"That, and when I got back to our place last night, someone had been inside."

She gasped. Someone had been in their house? "How do you know?" Oh, Lord. The band was so tight she could only pant in shallow gasps.

"Well, it was sort of trashed."

"Sort of? What does that mean?"

"Don't worry. The law firm hired a company to come in and put the house back together. I just wanted to warn you, though, that things may not be exactly the same as they were when you were last in the house."

"Exactly how trashed was it?"

"Very?"

"Myles Colton. What the hell is going on?" A few parents glanced over her way, and she lowered her voice, which had taken on a strident tone. "What aren't you telling me?"

He took her elbow and led her away from the cluster of parents toward one end of the soccer field. "Here's the thing. The firm picked up a really high-profile case. It's the kind that makes careers. Larry Whitney and Suzanne Pierce told me I'll be up for a partnership if I can win it. You and I will finally have all the things we've always wanted."

"What's the catch?"

He laughed ruefully. "You know me too well."

She merely stared at him expectantly.

"It's a wrongful death and property damage case. The defendants avoided penalties because of a technicality in the criminal trial, so the plaintiffs are going after civil damages for lack of any other recourse."

"And?"

He sighed. "The defendants are the members of a group call Anarchy Ink. They set a fire that burned a whole town and killed four people."

"Anarchy Ink? That sounds like a gang."

"It sort of is." He winced as he said the words. Obviously, he knew how she was going to react to that.

Far be it from her to disappoint him. She hissed, "You promised me! No more violent criminals! No more gangs! Myles, the last gang member you convicted almost got you killed!"

"Keep your voice down," he urged. "I can't draw attention to myself. I shouldn't even be here."

"Why the heck not?"

"I'm probably being followed. I drove around for an hour before I risked coming here to talk with you. I didn't see any tails, but I can't be sure."

"You led them to us?" The outrage in her stomach boiled over into an ugly, churning stew of fury.

"I had to see you. Explain what's going on. Look. I need you and Jackson to move to a safe house for a little while. The firm has offered to pay for it, of course. Hank MacDonald has found you an apartment downtown in a building with really great security. The head guard there is ex–Special Forces. And old friend of Hank's—"

"A *safe house*?"

"Just for a little while—"

"What about my mother?"

"She can come, too. Although, I doubt she's in any immediate danger."

"Speaking of which, how did these gang members know how to find my mother's house?"

"Hank thinks they got her address from your address book at our place."

Her jaw sagged. The bad guys had gone looking for her and Jackson specifically? Oh, God. This wasn't just about Myles's safety. She and Jackson were being targeted, too. "Just how much immediate danger are Jackson and I in?"

"Probably none. It's me they're after."

"It was me who nearly died in that car accident."

"I'm vividly aware of that. It's why you and I need to stay apart until this is over and I want to take extra security measures to protect you. I thought I would call my cousin Micha and ask if his security firm can provide some extra guys to protect you and Jackson around the clock."

"You promised not to take any more gang cases. You promised me, Myles."

"But my bosses offered me a partnership, Faith. I'll finally be able to slow down, and we can get a bigger house, put Jackson in North Hills Academy like you wanted. We can afford another child."

"None of that will matter if you're dead or if something happens to Jack or me."

"I know," he ground out.

"Walk away from the case. Now. Call your firm and tell them you quit it."

"I can't do that. Jury selection starts on Monday."

"Can't do it or won't do it?" she accused.

"Either. Both. I said I would take this case, and I'm going to see it through. These bastards are guilty as hell, and I'm going to take them down."

"If they don't take you down, first!"

"I'm being careful. And as long as I know you and Jack are safe, I'll be fine."

"Our house has been trashed and your family is in hiding. None of that is fine, Myles."

She stared up at him in anger and dismay. He'd *sworn* he wouldn't do this again. Had he forgotten being unconscious for a day and a half due to an attack by gang members? Lying in a hospital bed with a broken arm, broken jaw and a half-dozen cracked ribs? The long weeks of recovery from nearly being beaten to death? Good grief. His pain and suffering made her past week look like a walk in the park.

He stared back at her in what looked like frustration. With the situation or with her, she couldn't tell.

She said, "If I go along with you trying this case, will you say no the next time a big case comes along with a dangerous defendant? Or are we already headed down a slippery slide? Are you so addicted to criminal prosecution that you'll always find a way back to it? I told you I wouldn't stay married to you if you insisted on going after dangerous bad guys. I meant it then and I still mean it."

"Don't give me an ultimatum, Faith. It's not fair."

"What's not fair is you doing this to us, again. I can't believe you took the case. You didn't even talk it over with me!"

"I knew what you would say."

"And you did it, anyway. I'm so glad to know where Jack and I rate in comparison to your career."

"I took the case for you two!"

"Are you sure about that?" she challenged angrily.

"Yes!"

No way. He'd wanted this case and knew she would object to it, so he'd gone around her and taken it anyway. "I thought you were better than this, Myles."

"I thought you would understand that I made an exception this once so I can give you everything you've always wanted."

"I've never wanted a big, empty house and a husband who lies to me. I saw how unhappy my mom was with those. How unhappy I was growing up in that house. You know. You saw it, too."

"I've never lied to you!"

"You're going to try to convince me that omitting telling me about your case wasn't a lie? Really? We're going to split that hair?"

He shoved a hand through his hair, a sure sign of exasperation. Tough. He was wrong, and he knew it. He'd screwed up big-time, and now she and Jackson were paying for it.

He bit out grimly, "I'll have Hank pick you up and drive you to the safe house. He's a trained security professional and will make sure nobody tails you when he takes you there. You'll be perfectly safe."

"No thanks to you."

"I'm trying my best to look out for you guys. I don't want any part of this trial to touch you or Jackson." He added, "Or your mother."

"Oh, but it already has." She gestured at the bruises on the right side of her face.

"I'm so, so sorry about that."

"But not sorry enough to walk away from the case," she replied bitterly.

He exhaled hard. "That's a low blow. I had no idea they were even tailing me, let alone violent enough to put out a hit on me."

But he knew, now. And he was still determined to proceed with trying the case.

He continued, "The trial starts in less than two days. I've been preparing the case for weeks. *Weeks*. And there's a partnership hanging in the balance."

"I don't give a damn about your partnership," she snapped.

"I do give a damn about taking care of my family."

"Walk away from the case or walk away from me."

He stared at her a long time, the expression in his eyes turbulent. "I'm sorry you feel that way," he said quietly.

He turned and walked away from her.

Hot knives of grief and fury sliced her stomach into neat little bits, and terror seared their edges until her entire middle was an agonized mess as she watched him go. He never once looked back. Not once, as he climbed into his sports car and drove away.

What had just happened?

Blinded by unshed tears, she turned back to the soccer game as the final whistle blew. Jackson ran over to her, excited. "Did you see me, Mommy? I scored a goal and we won!"

Swearing silently at Myles for making her miss Jackson's big moment, she lied with a smile, "Of course I saw. You were awesome! How about a hot fudge sundae to celebrate?"

"Yay!" he cheered.

She waited while the coach gathered the kids to give them a little speech about winning gracefully and being good sports, and then Jackson's team ran over to their opponents and four-year-old hugs were exchanged.

She caught herself lingering in the ice cream parlor, among the last moms to collect her kiddo and pour him into her mother's car. Jackson didn't like the booster seat in her mom's car and whined about not being able to see outside all the way back to her mother's house. Poor kid was exhausted. What were the odds of getting him to go down for a nap after the giant bowl of ice cream she'd given him out of guilt for not seeing his big goal?

Not good.

Rats.

She pulled into the driveway of her mother's house and as she turned the corner beside the house to open the garage door, terror slammed into her. An unfamiliar SUV was parked back here, and a scary-looking bald dude with huge biceps stood beside it.

Panic flared in her gut and she reached frantically for the gearshift to throw the car into reverse. But the man waved frantically at her, and she rolled down the window cautiously. He called out, "Faith? I'm Hank MacDonald. Myles sent me."

Oh. Right. Undecided, she pulled forward once more, blocking his SUV in the paved area in front of the garage. She didn't get out of her car. "Can you show me some identification?"

"Of course." The man held out a driver's license and private investigator's license. She snatched them and took them into the car and gave them a hard examination. They looked legitimate. She passed them back.

"Okay. You're Hank MacDonald. Now what?"

"I've already spoken with your mother. She said she would pack bags for both of you. If you'd like to put that car in the garage, I'll go inside and tell your mother we're ready to go. I've got a man down the street and he says the coast is clear. For now."

For now. What had Myles gotten them all into? Furious at him, she parked her mother's car and unlatched Jackson from the booster seat. He started to run into the house to tell her mother about his goal, but Faith stopped him gently.

"Hey, buddy. You and Grammy and I are going on an adventure. I'm just going to move your booster seat over into Mr. MacDonald's car, okay?"

"Who's he?" Jackson demanded. "He doesn't have any hair."

"That's Mr. MacDonald. He works with Daddy."

Her mother came out of the kitchen just then, looking scared to death. Great. What had the private investigator said to her? MacDonald came out behind her, carrying two big suitcases. He loaded them in the back of the SUV while Faith installed Jack's booster seat, and then he went back into the house for Jack's blue roller bag with light-up wheels.

Jenny climbed in the front seat, and Faith piled in back beside Jack. Macdonald made a phone call saying merely, "Are we clear?" Then, "Roger. Rolling."

They pulled out of the driveway, and Faith noted a silver pickup truck falling in behind them. "Is that truck your guy?" she asked nervously.

"Yes, ma'am."

They drove in what seemed like circles for most of the next hour. The long ride did eventually knock out Jack, but within about five minutes of him crashing, they pulled into a dark underground parking garage, and he popped awake once more. Drat. She'd been hoping he would get a real nap, there.

"Where are we?" he asked sleepily.

"How about we go find out?" she answered jauntily.

MacDonald waved the all clear and she climbed out of the SUV, while her mother looked around fearfully. She knew the feeling. But she didn't want to scare her son. A new wave of anger at Myles for putting them all in this fix swept over her.

The man in the silver truck went into the building ahead of them and was back in a minute, waving at them to join him. A third man joined them when the elevator stopped at the lobby level. He put a key in the elevator panel and then entered a long number in a pad beside the elevator controls. The conveyance eased into motion and accelerated smoothly.

MacDonald said, "Mrs. Romans, Faith, this is Farley. He's the head of security for this building, and he'll be looking after you when I'm not here. I've known him a long time. He's a good man and will take great care of you."

Faith nodded stiffly. She added a belated smile. After all, it wasn't these men's faults her husband had put them in danger.

Hank continued, "I understand your husband's cousin will be sending over several men later this afternoon to supplement the security team. When they arrive, Rob will bring them up to introduce them to you."

The elevator ticked up through the forty-five floors of the building and finally stopped with no floor number showing on the elevator panel. "Is this the top of the building?" she asked.

"The penthouse, ma'am," Farley said. "If you'll follow me, I'll show you how to enter and exit and how to contact me and my guys. There are always two security men on duty in the building."

They stepped out of the elevator into a small lobby whose floors and walls were tiled with expensive looking white stone flecked with gold. A chic brass-and-glass table held a large vase full of fresh flowers. The space was understated, but shouted of money. Well, okay, then. Give Whitney and Pierce credit for not going cheap with their safe house.

The penthouse was as luxurious and sleek as its lobby, with a large living room completely glassed in on three sides. Along its only wall were three suites each with their own bedroom, and a professional kitchen. It was a very nice cage, but a cage nonetheless.

What made Jackson whoop with glee and Faith wince, however, was the long swimming pool on the deck outside.

Worse, her mom piped up with, "Good thing I packed your swimsuit, Jackie."

"Can I go swimming right now? Please, Mommy."

"I don't know if the water's warm enough. It's getting pretty cool these days."

Farley grinned at Jackson. "It's a heated pool, kid. You can swim out there if it's snowing."

"Awesome! I hope it snows while we're here!"

Faith scowled over Jackson's head at the security man. He shrugged. "He'd have dipped a toe in the water and figured it out, anyway."

The man was right. Faith sighed. "Fine, Jackson. Go put on your bathing suit."

While the boy was gone, the security man walked her and her mother through the security equipment discreetly installed in the apartment, pointing out cameras and other security features, including the panic buttons beside each bed, behind the bar, by the pool, and just inside the front door. Faith was dismayed when he showed her the panic room and how to lock its vault-like door, as well.

Jackson tugged urgently at her hand as soon as the door closed behind MacDonald and Farley. "C'mon! Let's go swimming!"

Jenny went out and sat with him beside the pool while Faith changed into the bathing suit her mom archly informed her that she'd packed. As she strolled out to the pool, she enjoyed the panoramic view of the city in one direction, and the midnight blue expanse of Lake Michigan in the other. This really was a lovely spot. Even if she was furious at being cooped up here.

She sat down on an upholstered chaise beside Jenny. "How is it you knew to pack swimming gear, Mom?"

"Mr. MacDonald mentioned there'd be a pool where we were going, dear."

"Did you pack yourself a suit?" Faith asked suspiciously.

"Oh, no. I don't like getting my hair wet."

"Uh-huh. Threw me under the lifeguarding bus, did you?"

Her mom laughed lightly. "I would never."

"Ha."

When Jackson was at the far end of the pool playing happily with a mask and snorkel from the box of pool toys Farley had shown him, Jenny asked under her breath, "Care to tell me why I got ripped out of my home and forced to come stay here with you? Even though that man from Whitney and Pierce was very nice about making me come here, he made it clear I had no choice."

Faith scowled. "Myles took on a dangerous case, and the people he's suing were seen outside your house last night."

"Does this have anything to do with your accident?"

Her mom never had been slow on the uptake. Faith sighed. "Probably."

"I knew it. I knew that boy wouldn't keep his promise to you. If I've told you once, I've told you a hundred times, it would come to no good, him going to law school. Lawyers. They're all the same. Can't be trusted—"

"Please, not now, Mom." She was too upset after her fight with Myles to have another one with her mother. Particularly since she knew Jenny would rehash all the same old gripes against Faith's dad and project all of her father's many flaws onto Myles. She couldn't handle the emotional assault just now.

"Look at me, Mommy!"

She smiled as Jackson did a cannonball into the pool and swam toward her, his neon green arm floats bobbing jauntily. Spotting the gleam in his eyes, she murmured to her mother, "If you don't want to get splashed, now would be a good time to beat a tactical retreat."

"Right. I'm out of here. But we'll talk about this more, later."

Oh, joy. With a sigh, she unwrapped her towel and headed for the side of the pool. Where was Myles, right now? Was he safe? As mad as she was at him, she certainly didn't wish him ill. She still loved him. She just wanted to strangle him, too.

As she dangled her feet in the surprisingly comfortable water and kept an eagle eye on Jackson, her thoughts wandered. The pool at the Grand Hotel on Mackinac Island where they'd honeymooned had been about this temperature, too. She hadn't been a strong swimmer and had lingered on the side of the pool dangling her feet until Myles swam over to ask her what was wrong.

In all the years he'd known her, he'd never figured out she was afraid of drowning. It was irrational, she knew, but it had persisted ever since she'd dreamed of drowning as a little girl and had woken screaming from the nightmare. It had been a recurring night terror through the years. She could still hear his teasing voice.

"Why aren't you coming in, Faith? The water's perfect."

"That's okay."

"No, really. You should take a dip. It was a long, hot drive."

The air-conditioning was on the fritz in his little sports car, and he couldn't afford to buy the parts to fix it, yet. So, they'd driven all the way to the junction of the Lower and Upper Peninsulas of Michigan with the windows down and baking heat from the concrete highway blowing through. If she ever was going to risk getting into a swimming pool, this was the moment. The sparkling turquoise water beckoned, and she was sticky and hot.

"I'd love to, but..." She trailed off.

"But what? We're married now, you know. You can tell me anything."

Funny, but marriage did change things between them, somehow. Even after all these years together—seven years of middle and high school, four years of college and three years of law school—she finally felt safe with him. He would never leave her, now. And that was immensely reassuring. Maybe she'd been more insecure about him because of her father abandoning her and her mother in everything but name and checkbook. And then her father had died last year, making it irrevocable.

She looked up at Myles, tanned and gorgeous, his mint green eyes glowing against his bronzed skin, his hair almost blond this late in the summer. His muscular shoulders flexed as he swished his arms back and forth in the water.

All at once, she blurted, "I'm afraid of drowning."

He tilted his head to study her. "Is that why you never go swimming? And why you refused to go out in the boat last month when we all went waterskiing?"

A bunch of his law school buddies and their significant others had gone on a class picnic at a lake, and waterskiing had been involved. She nodded, embarrassed.

"Huh. How did I not know that about you?"

She glanced up. "I never told you."

"Well, can you swim?"

"Sort of. I refused to take swim lessons after my nightmare."

"What nightmare?"

Haltingly, she told him about the recurring dream

of dark closing over her head, of being weighted down, seeing a light above and knowing if she didn't reach it she would die.

"Aww, honey, that's awful!" He came over and rested his elbows on her knees. "You do know I'll never let anything bad happen to you, right?"

She smiled down at him. "What would I do without you?"

"Well, you'd be holed up in some room somewhere with your nose buried in a book, not enjoying yourself half as much as you do with me."

She had to laugh a little. He was not wrong.

"How about you put your hands on my shoulders and ease off the edge of the pool? I'll hold on to you. If it's too much, I'll lift you right back out. Think of it as an experiment."

She gazed into his earnest, warm eyes, and in that moment, knew she trusted him with her life. "Um, okay. I guess it wouldn't hurt to try. Worst case, I at least get wet and cool off a little."

He reached out, and his hands went around her bare waist. His palms were cool against her skin, but warmed up quickly. His fingers were strong and spanned a lot of her waist as she leaned forward tentatively and placed her hands on his wet shoulders.

"Look at me, Faith. Just stare into my eyes. Listen to my voice." As he spoke soothingly, he lifted her a bit and pulled her forward. Her body slid into the cool embrace of the water. When it hit her armpits, she started to panic, but then her toes touched the bottom of the pool and the terror receded.

Myles wrapped his arms around her, pulling her close, and the warmth of his body was a sharp contrast to the chill of the water. She looped her arms around his neck and floated in his embrace until her body started to relax. They'd had sex a thousand times before, but today was different. This delicious hunk was her husband now. That yummy body was hers.

She relished the washboard hardness of his stomach against hers, and the hardness developing rapidly in his crotch. She pressed her breasts more firmly against his chest, and he grinned knowingly.

"You're doing great, baby," he murmured. "I'm so proud of you. You're so much braver than you know."

If only.

"Ready to go for a walk around the pool? I'll stay in shallow enough water so you can stand up anytime you want. Okay?"

She nodded, eyes wide as he stepped backward, away from the edge of the pool.

The water flowed across her skin in eddies and whorls that felt nice. Really nice. And all the while, his arms had held her close, surrounding her in safety and protection. She concentrated on releasing the tension in her neck and didn't die when she did it. Huh. Maybe she could try relaxing her shoulders? Bit by bit, she relaxed, releasing years' worth of pent-up terror.

He kissed her then, and she abruptly understood the appeal of sex in hot tubs. The movement of the water against her skin was sensual as his mouth moved lazily across hers, his tongue laving hers in warmth and desire.

Ah, Myles. He kissed away her fears and replaced them with joy and trust. She would be a neurotic mess without him in her life. Over and over since that day at the Grand Hotel swimming pool, he'd uncovered her fears with compassion and warmth, gently showing her that she could overcome them and that everything would be okay—

A splash of water smacked her in the face and she jolted. “Hey! No fair!” she called out to her laughing son. She kicked her feet vigorously, sending up waves of water and splashing both herself and Jackson liberally.

She prayed the security measures Hank MacDonald had put into place and her own mommy bear impulses were enough to keep Jack safe from harm. If she could roll him up in Bubble Wrap and hold him in her arms, never letting him go, she would. But Jackson needed to grow up and become independent, and smothering him would only make him fearful and nervous, the way she’d been as a child. Better to swallow her parental terror and let him embrace adventure and exploration.

But it was hard to bite her tongue sometimes, particularly with fear clawing at her ribs from the inside out.

What she wouldn’t give to have Myles wrap her in a big hug right now and tell her it was all going to be okay. But no. He was mad at her and tied up with his stupid legal case. He had no time for her or Jackson.

And she felt utterly alone for the first time in a very, very long time.

Chapter Six

Myles tossed and turned in the unfamiliar bed. Hank had insisted he stay in a hotel under an assumed name, possibly for the duration of the trial, depending on the mood of the Anarchy Ink members in the gallery watching the proceedings.

The mattress was too hard, the pillow too soft, and it was weird not sleeping beside Faith. Her gentle breathing soothed him at night and her warmth felt like home.

He replayed their fight at Jack's soccer game, thinking of all the things he should have said, all the better ways to have brought up the lawsuit that wouldn't have set her off, all the calming things he should have told her to allay her fears.

Problem was, her fears were entirely reasonable. He rubbed his right side absently where the gang members had cracked four of his ribs the month before Jackson was born. Even now, he got stabbing pains there from time to time. Whether they were caused by guilt or merely remembered pain, he couldn't tell. Maybe a little of both.

He had to talk to Faith again. Reason with her. Make her understand that he hated this as much as she did, but that he still thought it worth the risk to set up the rest of their lives in comfort. Why she couldn't see the logic in that—

Logic. Yeah. Not how Faith rolled. She saw the world first and foremost through the lens of her feelings. Which was why they made a great match. She kept him in touch with his empathetic side, and he tempered her gut-feel decision-making with a solid dose of common sense.

He rolled over, punched his pillow, and closed his eyes. *Sleep, self.*

Nope. Not happening.

His mind drifted over the particulars of the case. He was totally prepared for *voir dire* tomorrow, better known as jury interviews and selection. He knew exactly what sort of jurors he was looking for. Not only had the firm done an exhaustive analysis of its own, but he'd tried enough gang cases as a prosecutor to have a great nose for jury members who would see gang activity as a serious threat and be inclined to convict. Of course, all he really needed for this case were twelve people willing to sympathize with the loss of lives and property the good folks of Maple Bend had suffered because of the Anarchy Ink wildfire.

Eventually, he tired of thinking about the case, and his mind turned back to his estranged wife. He hoped that was too strong a term for their current disagreement, but a niggling whisper in the back of his mind said it was exactly accurate.

Good Lord willing, this trial would fly by at the speed of heat. A day for jury selection, two, maybe three, days for testimony and cross-examination, and then a quick verdict could put him home with Faith and Jackson by the weekend.

But he was probably being naive to hope things would

go that smoothly or quickly. This trial could drag on for weeks if the gang's attorneys wanted to get cute.

He picked up his phone and texted Faith, Are you asleep?

I'm not now.

Still feeling prickly was she? Not that he blamed her. I'm sorry about earlier. I hate arguing with you, and I feel like crap for upsetting you.

No answer from her. He sighed and tried, Is the apartment nice?

It's a penthouse. It's fabulous.

Do you feel safe?

I feel like a houseplant locked in a bank vault.

He smiled at his phone. If she was being sarcastic, then she wasn't too afraid. That was a good sign, at least. He sighed. Tell Jack I love him.

He went to bed hours ago.

Tell him in the morning. I love you, Faith.

Then drop this case.

Still pretty irritated at him, was she? He supposed he shouldn't be surprised. But it did beg the question of how massive a gesture he was going to have to pull out of a hat to make up with her. She responded best by far to expressions of affection. But how to do that grandly enough to impress her now? He fell asleep without any answers coming to him.

No solution had come to him by the time Hank arrived at his door, handed him a baseball cap and sunglasses, and hustled him out the service exit of the hotel into a bland sedan with blacked-out windows. They drove to the rear entrance of the courthouse, and he removed his disguise as they stepped into an elevator.

"How are Faith and Jackson?" he asked as the elevator lurched into motion.

"Jackson is in love with the swimming pool. Your wife is…less thrilled. And your mother-in-law is on the warpath. The whole time I was with them yesterday, Mrs. Romans hardly quit bad-mouthing you once."

"That sounds about like Jenny. She never has liked me much."

"Haven't you and Faith been together since you were, like, kids?"

"Yeah. Since sixth grade."

"Hard-core, man."

He shrugged. "When you've met the one, you've met the one. Whether you're thirteen or thirty, or eighty for that matter, you just know."

Hank snorted and stared at the numbers flashing by on the control panel. The elevator dinged and he said, "Here we are. Let me get out first and clear the hall."

"Surely, the Anarchy Ink guys wouldn't attack me in a courthouse," Myles blurted.

Hank shrugged. "It's all about a show of force. If I'm aggressively protective here, they'll know I'm that much more protective outside the court."

It seemed like overkill, but Hank knew his job. The

hall was clear, and they made their way to their assigned court without incident.

Myles stepped into the courtroom and waited through the routine questioning of the juror pool by a bailiff of various reasons jurors would be disqualified—knowing any of the defendants, knowing any of the victims of the fire, any prejudice that would prevent them from being objective.

And then the actual juror interviews began. It became clear in approximately two minutes that the Anarchy Ink lawyers were going to be a nightmare. They were condescending, argumentative and borderline belligerent. Personally, he thought it was a huge mistake for them to alienate the jurors the way they were, but it would make his job easier.

He made a point of being low-key, respectful and pleasant as he sorted through the jury pool. It was a long day, and after getting very little sleep last night, he was tired and in no mood for shenanigans as court recessed with only part of the jury seated.

Hank collected him and herded him out to the elevators, and the Anarchy Ink ringleader, a man named Aric Schroder, came up to stand beside them.

Without looking in Myles's direction, Schroder commented, "Your wife is pretty. Cute kid you've got, too."

Myles froze as rage exploded in his gut and raced outward to fill his entire body with a trembling need to bury his fist in the man's smug face. He felt Hank tense beside him. If he knew the guy, Hank was poised to tackle him instead of Schroder. If Myles attacked a defendant, it could very well cause a mistrial to be declared.

It took every ounce of self-discipline he had, but Myles said in a pleasant voice, "If you or any of your boys go anywhere near my wife again, that will be the last anyone ever sees of you."

"Are you threatening me?" Schroder exclaimed gleefully.

"Not at all. Just making a casual observation. I make no claim whatsoever of knowing how it would happen or who would do it. We're just speaking hypothetically, here."

The elevator door opened and he and Hank stepped in. As Schroder started to move forward, Hank bit out, "Wait for the next one."

"Are you threatening me, now?" Schroder demanded.

Myles stepped forward to stand beside Hank in the front of the otherwise empty conveyance. "This elevator is full."

Shoulder to shoulder, he and Hank stared down Schroder. Just as the doors were closing, the guy's stare finally fell away. Rage and embarrassment were obvious on his face.

The dude had better get used to it. He was going to shred Schroder and his gang, and that was a promise.

"Not a great guy to antagonize," Hank murmured.

"Neither am I. He messed with my family, Hank. I will take him out if he tries to hurt them."

"I feel you, Myles. If he hurts your family, I'll be right there with you helping make that jerk disappear. But don't say what you just said to me where anyone else can hear you, okay?"

"I'm not a moron. I would never threaten him in public. I refuse to give him the satisfaction or the ammunition." He glanced over at the PI as they stepped out of the elevator, and their gazes met in grim understanding. The line in the sand was drawn, and if anyone from Anarchy Ink stepped over it, he and Hank would not be taking any prisoners.

"How sure are you that you're going to win this case?" Hank asked he drove out of the parking lot.

"It should be a slam dunk, but you never know with a jury. It's why cases go to trial at all. You have to play out the arguments and roll the dice."

"What happened to my stuff from the room last night?" Myles asked a little while later as they pulled up in front of a new hotel.

"One of your cousin's guys packed it up and brought it over here this afternoon. After he searched it for tracking bugs and listening devices, of course. So, don't freak out if your stuff looks as if it's been rifled through."

"One of Micha's guys?"

"Yep. Sharp outfit your cousin runs. Good bunch of guys."

"That's good to know," Myles commented. "I mean, I like him a lot. He's actually my cousin-in-law, I guess. My actual cousin, Carly, is crazy about him."

Myles asked as they headed toward the elevators, "Who's paying for all this security, anyway? I'll empty my savings account to keep my family safe, of course. But so many security people must be expensive."

"The firm is footing the bill. Let's just say it's costing them a crap-ton of money."

Myles nodded. "I've been impressed at how Larry and Suzanne have stepped up to protect me. I just hope they're getting their money's worth."

"You'll be safe. I promise you that."

"I don't care about my safety. Put all the men on my family."

"Most of them already are."

Thank God. Just a little while longer, and then he and Faith and Jackson could resume their normal lives. He hoped.

The next few days passed in a blur. The jury was seated, the judge instructed them, and then opening arguments began. Myles walked the jury through the mountains of evidence, much of it tedious, some of it gruesome, painting a picture of how the gang had purchased a hundred acres just west of Maple Bend, built a fort-like compound, and then blown up a bunch of dynamite, for which they had no permit, on a day with winds gusting over forty miles per hour, in a drought. Dry grasses had caught fire and a wildfire ensued, growing to overrun the entire town of Maple Bend, several dozen surrounding farms, and most of a two-thousand-acre state park before finally being brought under control.

He outlined to the jury how he would show gross negligence and reckless disregard for safety, and that the entity known as Anarchy Ink and its individual members should be penalized to the maximum extent of the law for the financial losses, grief and suffering they had caused all the victims of the fire.

He spent an entire day acquainting the jury with all the people who'd lost property, crops, livestock, or their actual lives in the fire. Using a white board, he kept a running tally of the financial toll of the fire with each new victim he introduced. By the end of that day, the total cash loss ran well over a hundred million dollars, and that didn't take into account the value of the four human lives lost.

They adjourned for the weekend, and as he piled into the back of an SUV one of Micha's ex-military buddies drove, he leaned his head back and closed his eyes. A day like this was draining, even for him. The sheer scale of suffering and loss caused by the fire was still hard to wrap his head around, and he'd been living with it day and night for weeks.

Man, he was tired. He really could stand to see his family right about now. Hug his wife and play with his son.

"What are the odds I can see my family this weekend?" he asked the driver.

The guy eyed him critically in the rearview mirror. "Not good. Why?"

"I could really use a mental break. That, and my wife and I didn't leave things in a great way the last time we saw each other."

The driver made a sympathetic face. "I'll mention it to Hank. Can't promise anything, but maybe we can work something out."

C'mon, Hank. Come through for me. I'm wrecked, here.

And if he was this bad a mess, he couldn't imagine that Faith was doing much better. This week apart was the longest they'd ever been separated, and he desperately hoped it was the last time they were ever apart this long.

Otherwise, he was completely and irrevocably hosed.

Chapter Seven

Faith was losing it. As beautiful as the cage might be, she was still vividly aware of being trapped. The walls were closing in on her, and she was seriously considering ways to murder her mother. Jenny would not shut up about how all of this was Myles's fault and how she'd known all along that he would one day show his true stripes and turn on his family.

For crying out loud, she and Myles had been together since they were kids. If he had any hidden stripes to show, surely they would have become visible long before now. She was probably there when he formed whatever stripes he had. She knew every detail of pretty much his entire life, and he knew every single moment of her life, as well.

Jackson threw a huge tantrum when Faith regretfully informed him that he had to miss his soccer game this Saturday. He was too young to understand why they had to stay cooped up in this penthouse.

Jackson had cried himself out and settled into sullen silence by lunchtime, refusing to speak to anyone, when Hank showed up.

"Hey, Jackie boy," Hank said jovially, "I have a surprise for you tonight. I want to make up for you not being able to go to your soccer game, so I'm taking you and your mommy someplace really special."

"Where?" Jack mumbled, interested in spite of himself.

"It's a surprise. But it's the coolest ever."

Faith made eye contact with Hank, and he stared back significantly. Unfortunately, she couldn't read his mind the way she read Myles's, and she had no idea what he was trying to convey to her. She finally settled on murmuring, "What time should we be ready to go?"

"Nine o'clock."

"That's after my bedtime!" Jackson exclaimed. "Do I get to stay up late?"

"You get to stay up really late, kid," Hank replied, grinning. "In fact, you'd better take a big nap this afternoon because I'd hate for you to fall asleep just when it's getting really awesome."

Jackson interrogated Hank for the rest of lunch with a single-mindedness and ferocity that Myles would have been proud of. But the PI didn't give even the slightest hint as to what the big outing was going to be.

She popped Jackson into the pool for a big play as soon as his stomach had settled after lunch and then sat with him in the attached hot tub until he was almost asleep. She carried him inside and laid him in his bed, murmuring for him to sleep hard so he could stay awake really late tonight.

She backed out of his room as he squeezed his eyes tightly shut and made a face too adorable for words as he tried really hard to go to sleep. Smiling, she headed out into the great room, considering a nap herself.

Jenny was seated with a book in front of the long

quartz fireplace with gas flames flickering up through a bed of blue glass stones.

"Can I make you a cup of tea, Mom?"

"That would be lovely, dear. Any word from that husband of yours?"

"That husband of mine has a name. And just because I'm mad at him doesn't give you any right to be mean about him. He's still the father of your only grandchild."

"Donating genes to a baby doesn't make a man a father," Jenny snapped.

Oh, how she knew that to be true. "Myles is nothing like my dad. He spends every minute he can with Jackson and is a loving and engaged parent."

"Then where is he now? I don't see him engaging with and loving with his son."

"This is a short-term separation—"

"Are you so sure about that?" Jenny interrupted. "What if this is just him pushing you two away so he can spend all his time at the office, build up his career, and have his own life? How do you know he's not tired of you?"

She stared at her mother, appalled. That had always been her worst secret fear of marrying her childhood sweetheart. They'd been together forever and never seriously dated anyone else. What if there *was* someone better out there for Myles? What if he wondered the exact same thing? What if he decided to take a look around? Play the field? There was no guarantee he would come home to her and Jackson.

Jenny barreled on, apparently unaware, or at least uncaring, of the dagger she'd just buried in Faith's chest. "That boy always was the one to break away from you. Every time the two of you had a fight or things weren't going exactly his way, Myles bailed out and took off, leaving you behind crying your eyes out. I'm telling you, Faith. You did yourself no favors taking him back over and over like you did—"

"Enough, Mom. You've never liked Myles, and you've always tried to break us up. I'd really appreciate it if you'd get over whatever problem you have with my husband and stop trying to interfere in my life."

Jenny flounced out of the great room without bothering to collect the cup of tea Faith had steeping for her on the wet bar.

An urge to sit down and cry nearly overcame her. But she dared not break down. Not yet. She had to stay strong, for Jackson and for herself. At least until they were past this threat to all of them and they were safe once more. Then, she could cry to her heart's content.

She'd almost managed to get her act together when her cell phone rang. She jumped violently, her heart pounding anew. *Please don't be Myles. The sound of his voice will destroy whatever shreds of composure I'm hanging on to.*

"Hello?" she said cautiously to the unknown number.

"Hey, Faith! It's Lila. I'm calling from London on Carter's British phone. How the heck are you?"

"Hey, Lila!" She was Myles's older sister and had been more or less the sister she'd never had since she'd started dating Myles and half-lived at their house. "I'm okay. How are you? How's Carter?"

"He's amazing. Fantastic. Perfect. Hot—"

"I get the idea." Faith laughed at her sister-in-law's enthusiasm.

"I just talked with Myles, and he sounds like crap. He wouldn't tell me what's going on, but he seemed really upset."

"So you figured you'd go behind his back, call me, and get the scoop?" Faith asked.

"Well, yeah. We Coltons have to look out for one another, you know."

"Ah, the famous Coltons-united-against-the-world pact."

"Exactly," Lila replied, laughing.

Faith huffed. She had no idea what she was and wasn't allowed to say to Myles's sister about being hidden away from a bunch of bad guys. The problem with saying anything to a Colton was they all shared everything with everyone in the clan. It was wonderful under normal circumstances, but she doubted Myles would want the gossip network going into high gear over this threat to his family.

"So…spill, Faith."

"I don't know what to say."

"I know Myles has been spending way too much time at the office and that you two have been basically apart for months. Is everything okay between you? How are you holding up?"

Intentionally ignoring the first question, Faith answered, "I'm surviving. I mean, raising a bright, high-energy four-year-old more or less by myself is hard. But Jackson goes to school next year. Then I'll have a little more time for myself."

"To do what? Have you talked with Myles yet about the idea of you going back to teaching full time? I know how much you miss being in the classroom."

"We haven't had a chance to talk about it," she admitted.

"Why not? Just grab him by the nose and blurt it out to him. He loves you. He'll listen to what you want."

Maybe. Maybe not. He'd been one hundred percent focused on his career for a while, now. And it was handier for him to have her at home full time holding down the household. Not only was she raising Jackson mostly alone, but she also made sure food got cooked, the house got cleaned, errands run, repairs made, suits dry-cleaned and picked up—she even scheduled Myles's dentist appointments for him.

"Wow. That was a loaded silence," Lila commented. "How bad *are* things between you?"

"I don't want to put you in the middle between us. He's your brother—"

"And you're my sister from another mother, so you can stop with that right there. I love both of you equally."

Faith smiled a little. "You're the best."

"And you're still dodging my question."

She sighed. "He's been working more than ever. I feel…abandoned. It's as if he's zigging every time I want him to zag. We're totally out of sync."

"I'm so sorry. Is there anything I can do to help?"

"From London? Maybe say hello to the royal family for me if you bump into them?"

Lila laughed, and thankfully, the remark seemed to sidetrack any further inquiries into the state of her and Myles's marriage.

"What's this I hear about your house getting broken into?"

"How on earth did you hear about that?" She had barely registered that her home had been broken into since she hadn't been back to see it since it had happened. Hank mentioned a few days ago that the people hired to put her house back together after the break-in were finished and that everything was good as new.

Lila answered, "My mom was trying to get ahold of Myles and he kept dodging her calls, so she drove over to your place. She was worried something had happened to you."

Faith rolled her eyes. Great. Her mother-in-law, Vita, was awesome and loved her family fiercely, but sheesh. Nosy much?

Lila continued, "Mom found a bunch of strangers repairing stuff in your house and she freaked out. Apparently, she left a bunch of messages for Myles and complained that your phone wasn't even taking messages."

Faith winced. She'd turned off her voice mail when she tired of ignoring messages from Myles to call him. She asked reluctantly, "Did Myles get in touch with Vita and calm her down?"

"Eventually. Apparently, he's in the middle of a big case or something?"

"Yes. He is."

"What kind of case?" Lila asked.

"I don't know the details, other than it has taken him a lot of time to prepare for it," she said evasively.

"Good luck and Godspeed with the whole being a lawyer's wife thing," Lila grumbled.

Faith snorted. "As if Carter's career is any less demanding, running around catching art thieves and forgers. You can have the danger, thank you very much."

Lila laughed. "It's not usually dangerous."

"Spoken by Miss Nearly-burned-to-a-crisp-by-an-arsonist," Faith replied tartly.

"Okay. That was scary. But Carter saved us both."

If only Myles would save his family, too. In a blatant bid to change subjects, Faith asked, "So how's the rest of the Colton clan doing? I've been swamped getting ready for Halloween and haven't spoken with anyone in a while."

"Crazy year the family's having, what with finding about all our new cousins and Carin's lawsuit over Grandpa Dean's will."

Faith noted that Lila didn't call Carin Pedersen grandmother. Not that it was a big surprise. She, herself, had only met Carin a few times over the years at major family events like weddings and funerals. Myles had always been much closer to his stepfather, Rick Yates, than with his birth father, Axel Colton, who was one of Carin's twin sons.

While Myles got along great with his various Colton cousins, he shunned his bitter, angry birth-grandmother. Carin had been Dean Colton's mistress barely long enough to get pregnant with twin boys, and he'd supported her for decades afterward, but she'd been livid at not being included in Dean's will.

Dean's estate was worth about sixty million dollars, and Carin had sued for half of all of it. The case still had not been settled and hung over the whole family like a gooey black scum of old scandal. One thing Myles was not wrong about: he always said money brought out the mean in people, and it had sure brought out the mean in Carin Pedersen.

"So, where are you, now?" Lila asked, interrupting Faith's wandering thoughts. "You're obviously not staying at your house."

"Oh. Um, a friend is letting us stay at his place while he's out of town."

"That's handy. How's Jackson doing?"

"Fabulous. This place has a swimming pool, and he's

living in it. I think he's growing a dorsal fin and starting to speak dolphin."

"Give my fave nephew a hug for me, will you?"

"Of course. How long do you guys plan to stay in jolly old England, oh nomadic wanderer?"

"No idea. Carter just wrapped up a case for an art gallery out here, and we're relaxing and doing a little sightseeing before he picks up his next assignment."

"Sounds heavenly."

"When's the last time my brother took you on a vacation? A real one that departed Illinois?" Lila demanded.

"Um…our honeymoon?"

"That was seven years ago! That constitutes criminal neglect! I'm going to call Myles right this second and tell him to get off his lazy behind and take you on a proper vacay. Goodness knows you've earned one if you've put up with him for all this time!"

"There hasn't been time. Law school, then his new job, then a baby—"

Lila cut her off. "There's no excuse for him not taking proper care of his marriage. Couples need time alone together now and then to reconnect."

"And you know this how, Miss Independent?"

"Hey. I'm following my man all over creation for a year. I assure you, a change of scenery now and then is good for a person…and great for a couple. And I'm telling Myles that in no uncertain terms!"

Faith deeply appreciated Lila's loyalty to both her and Myles. It would be easy for his sister to take sides with him in this disagreement of theirs. "Good luck getting through to him, Lila."

"I'm serious. I'm hanging up now and calling him to give him a piece of my mind!"

"Okay, then."

"Bye!"

Faith said goodbye, but Lila hung up before she could finish the word. She dearly loved her sister-in-law and hoped she would have better luck getting Myles to step back from his work to spend a little more family time with her and Jackson.

Until then, she was stuck here, staring at these four walls and praying that all of them would come out of this mess in one piece.

Guiltily, she turned her phone's voice mail function back on. Next time Myles called to bug her, she would have to pick up the call, like it or not, and tell him to quit harassing her. She didn't get angry often but when she did, he knew full well that she wanted to be left alone until she calmed down and could discuss the situation rationally.

Truth be told, she wasn't there yet. In fact, she was afraid it might be a good long time before she was ready to talk about it calmly with him. He'd endangered Jackson, and for that, she was going to have a very hard time forgiving him.

Chapter Eight

Myles waited impatiently in the darkness, shifting from foot to foot. It hadn't occurred to him that Faith might refuse to come see him, but she was late, and he was starting to worry about just how mad she was at him. She'd threatened in the past to leave him if he ever went back to prosecuting gangs. Had she meant that literally?

The sound of a car approaching him made him shrink back in the shadows instinctively. Man, the Anarchy Ink leader's threats had him on edge. He believed Aric Schroder when the man hinted he would go after Faith and Jackson. His gang was hard-core and worth tens of millions in weapons, ammunition and military grade equipment. They sold it at gun shows all over the United States legally and no doubt sold much of their inventory illegally out of the bunker on their compound. That, and they were flat mean.

They'd been surly in the courtroom and had spent a fair bit of their time staring down jurors until the whole jury squirmed with discomfort. Personally, he thought it was a dreadful tactic. If they'd been his clients, he would've told them to cut it out and stop trying to intimidate the jury. As it was, the court had sequestered this jury as a precaution and put them under around-the-clock guard in a hotel.

Several car doors opened and closed and nervousness exploded in his gut. A familiar silhouette loomed outside, and he exhaled in relief. *Hank.*

Then a small shadow raced around Hank and launched itself at his thighs. He bent down and scooped up his son in a big hug. “Hey buddy! I’ve missed you!” Jackson’s body was small and warm and wiggly, and a wave of pure adoration rolled through him.

“I missed you, Daddy. We have a pool, and I swim in it every day, and I can swim without floaties all by myself but only when Mommy watches me, and I’ve got a TV in my bedroom, and I can watch it whenever I want, and I’m going as a dinosaur for Halloween. A big scary one with claws and big teeth. A carnivore.”

He grinned and buried his nose in Jackson’s hair as the boy chattered on at auctioneer speed. A willowy shadow approached, and he looked up sharply, meeting Faith’s wary gaze.

“Thank you for coming,” he said quietly.

“How did you arrange for this particular meeting place?” she asked curiously as he turned and headed into the building.

“I didn’t. Hank pulled strings and got permission for us to meet here in the Adler Planetarium after hours. I told him you love stars and maybe we could arrange to meet at night where you could see them. Hank ran with it from there. I’m sad to say I can’t take credit for this.”

Faith smiled warmly at the private investigator. “I had no idea you’re such a romantic, Hank. Thanks for this.”

Myles’s jaw clenched, but he forced himself to relax. It was his own damned fault his wife was seeing a lot more of another man than him. But jeez, it bugged him to no end.

Hank was speaking. "No problem, ma'am. How about Jackie boy and I take a look around the exhibits while you two do some grown-up talking?"

Myles winced to see his son, laughing and chattering, grab another man's hand and drag Hank to look at pictures of planets on the walls. He turned back to his wife. "How are you holding up, Faith?"

"All right. The penthouse is lovely, and I feel like I'm living in Fort Knox."

"Good. I told Hank to put all the security guys on your protection detail."

"Is anybody looking out for you?" she asked quickly, alarm tightening her face.

He shrugged and started walking toward the planetarium. "I've got a guy for after hours. They're moving me to a new hotel every day. It's a pain, but we seem to be staying ahead of the Anarchy Ink crew."

"How's the trial going?"

"Excellent, actually. The jury hates the Anarchy Ink guys."

She rolled her eyes. "I get that part of trials is a popularity contest, but how's the case itself proceeding?"

"Great. Their lawyer has failed at all attempts to exclude damning evidence. The judge is obviously torqued off that this case made it to trial. About once a day he asks their lawyer why this case wasn't settled out of court."

"Sounds like you've got a sure winner going."

"Let's hope so. I want this thing over with so I can get back to you and Jackson."

She frowned and went silent.

"What?" he asked quickly. The last thing he needed

was for Faith to clam up and refuse to talk to him for another week. She did that only when she was really upset and trying not to say something she would regret and could never take back. "Talk to me, baby," he urged.

She sighed. "How long after this trial is over am I going to have to look over my shoulder, lock the doors and never take my eyes off Jack? How long are these guys going to hold a grudge against you, and by extension, your family?"

"I can't answer that. But I can tell you, we're going to strip absolutely everything they own from them. They're going to lose their homes, their cars, their stash of weapons, their land, everything. They never bothered to incorporate and set up any separation between themselves personally and their business entity. Big mistake."

"Can you get some sort of injunction against them that, I don't know, throws them out of Illinois permanently?"

"No. But I can certainly get an order of protection for you and Jack."

"Is that like a restraining order?"

"Yes. It'll make it a crime for them to get anywhere close to you or him. And believe me, prosecutors all over this state will seize on any excuse to throw these guys into jail. If we can't put them in prison for burning down Maple Bend and killing those folks, we'll happily put them in jail for something else."

"Like Al Capone going to jail for mail fraud?" she asked.

"Exactly."

He opened the door that led into the big, darkened dome of the planetarium, and Faith stepped inside. She gasped as she looked up and realized the star projector was turned on. He'd asked the museum guards if any of them knew how to turn it on and one of the men did. The fairy dust strip of the Milky Way arced overhead through the depiction of stars that would be visible in the Chicago night sky if the light pollution downtown didn't wash them out.

"It's beautiful," she breathed.

He stared at her, her sweet face turned up to the starlight, and murmured, "Yes, it is."

"You know what I've always wanted to do in here?" she said suddenly.

"What's that?"

"Lie down on the floor and gaze up at the stars."

"Let's do it." He strode to the middle of the room next to the double globed star projection machine and lowered himself to the carpeted floor. "Join me?"

She smiled and sat down, then lay back. He joined her on his back. From this angle, the arcing rows of empty chairs weren't visible, and it was as if they lay in a northern field, or maybe on a deserted beach, with the universe arrayed in all its glory before them.

"Do you suppose there's anyone out there gazing back at us?" she murmured.

"Absolutely. And I'll bet someday our descendants get to meet them."

"How exciting," she replied. "I wish I could be there to see it."

He smiled a little. She was such a dreamer. They lay side by side in silence for a while, just staring up at the wonder of the sky.

Eventually, he broke the silence. "Faith, I'm so sorry about everything. I never, ever meant to upset you or hurt you. I was only trying to do the best thing for my family. If I could give you the whole universe—and not just a pretend one like this—I would. You know I would."

She was quiet a long time. "I appreciate how hard you work to provide for me and Jackson. I really do. But I hope you know that's not why I love you. I miss you. And so does Jack."

"This will be over soon. Maybe another week."

"I'm not talking about that. I'm talking about the last four years. When you went to work at Whitney and Pierce, you all but disappeared from our lives."

"That's how a law career goes."

"That's how the law career of someone who can't say no goes."

"Faith, I have to do the work they give me. I would lose my job if I refused to work the long hours."

"Are you telling me there's nowhere you can work as a lawyer that doesn't involve working eighty or a hundred hours per week?"

He bit back an angry retort and counted to ten. Then he reminded himself he wasn't here to fight and that she had good reason to resent how much time he spent at the office. He said calmly, "I agree with you. I don't like how much time I've been away from my family. I feel left out when you and Jackson do fun things, and I worry that I'm not as close with him as I should be. I want to change that."

Faith turned her head to stare at him, and even in the faint starlight, he saw the quick flash of hope on her face before a more cautious expression took its place.

"This has been a rough mountain to climb, but we're almost there. Please don't give up on me now. When I win this case, the partners have basically guaranteed me a partnership. And then everything will change."

"You promise?" she said in a small voice.

"I promise," he replied firmly.

He rolled on his side facing her and gathered her into his arms. She snuggled close against him, and he let out a massive sigh of relief as her body went soft against his. He tilted his chin down and, thank God, she lifted her chin to meet him.

Their mouths touched, and everything else fell away. All the arguing and tension, the fear and strife. This was Faith. His one and only true love. Her mouth moved against his, brushing lightly across his lips. He let her set the pace, not pushing her or asking for anything.

She seemed prepared to take her time and simply enjoy being with him. And, although it had been too long since they'd slept together and his body was rapidly tightening with need, he told himself to cool it. She'd had a terrible scare in the car accident.

"I forgot to ask," he murmured against her soft lips. "How are you feeling after the car accident? Any lingering discomfort?"

"I'm fine. I've been sitting in the hot tub every day, and it has worked out the last of the kinks."

He leaned back to look down at her and ran his fingertips lightly across the fading bruises that appeared like faint yellow smudges in this dim light. "I'm so sorry." He leaned down and kissed her cheek lightly, trailing kisses down the side of her face to her jaw, following the line of bruises the impact of the side airbag had caused.

She turned her head and lifted her chin, giving him access to her neck, and he kissed his way down it to her collarbone and back up her neck to nibble on the velvet soft lobe of her ear.

He whispered, "I'll never forget that first instant after

the crash. My one and only thought was to pray that you hadn't died. And then I looked up at you and you looked back at me. That is the single most relieved moment of my entire life."

"Same," she mumbled. Her arms slipped around his neck and he rolled onto his back, taking her with him.

He stared up at her, memorizing her face, even though he knew every inch of it better than he knew his own face. He'd watched this face lose the plumpness of childhood, mature from a girl's face into a woman's, then into a wife's, and into a mother's face. He'd seen all the passages of her life reflected in Faith's dark green eyes. And he'd been privileged to go through them beside her.

"I love you so much," he murmured.

"To the moon and back," she replied, her mouth curving into a smile.

"To the stars and beyond." He slid his hand into her silky auburn hair and ever so gently suggested she lower her head, bring her mouth to his, and let him show her just how much he adored her.

She exhaled, her breath a wisp of magic, soft across his skin like morning fog, and then her mouth touched his again. She deepened the kiss, her mouth opening on his, and her tongue slid across his fleetingly. He groaned in relief that in this, at least, they hadn't lost their connection with each other.

Her hair fell in a wavy curtain around them, blotting out the stars, and leaving only her eyes shining above him. They were all the stars he needed.

She moved restlessly on top of him, her legs tangling with his, her belly rubbing across his muscular torso, and he groaned again. "You're so tempting, and there's nothing I can do about it here."

She sighed in disappointment.

"Agreed," he murmured, rolling over to tuck her beneath him and kissing her deeply.

She smiled against his mouth and wrapped her legs around his hips in blatant invitation.

He said, "If I knew we'd have this place to ourselves for another half hour, I would totally take you up on that. But as it is, Jack and Hank could burst in here at any moment."

"The price of parenthood," she said, sighing. "No privacy."

As if on cue, he heard a door opening close by. He rolled away from Faith onto his back and stared up sightlessly at the blur of the stars.

"Whatchya doing?" Jack demanded. "Are you taking naps?"

Myles laughed. "No. We're stargazing, silly. This is how it's done properly. Come join us."

Of course, Jack wiggled in between him and Faith, and Myles slid to the side to make room for him. Jack grabbed Myles's hand, and if he had to guess, also grabbed Faith's hand. "Ohh," Jack said in the innocent wonder of a child. "Pretty. Is that the Milky Way?"

"You're so smart," Myles murmured. "That's exactly what that big stripe of stars is."

"If I become an astronaut, can I fly to it someday in a spaceship?"

"Maybe. You'd have to invent a way to fly very fast, though." He didn't think his four-year-old was quite ready to hear about the difficulties of achieving faster than light travel just yet.

"I'll build the fastest rocket ever!"

Faith said, "But I would miss you so much if you flew away into the stars, Jack."

"I'll take you guys with me," Jack announced indignantly. "And if we get a puppy, I'll take it, too!"

Myles chuckled. "You never miss an opportunity to lobby for a dog, do you, kid? You'd make a great attorney if you decide to pass on being an astronaut."

Jack was quiet for a moment, then said, "I don't want to be a 'torney. You work too much."

"You're right, son. I'm going to try to work less in the future."

"Yippee!" Done with stillness, Jackson jumped up and ran over to take a closer look at the star projector.

"Don't touch it," Faith said quickly. "It's very fragile."

She jumped up to dart after Jackson, and Myles stood up more slowly.

Hank strolled over to him. "Work anything out?"

"Maybe. At least she's speaking to me now."

"After this is all over, you should take her on a nice long vacation. Just the two of you."

Myles glanced over at the PI wryly. "My sister just told me the exact same thing but not nearly as nicely."

"Your wife has really been through it the past few weeks. She's been worried sick."

"If only that worry was about me," Myles muttered.

Hank looked at him, his head tilted to one side. "She is worried about you. She's crazy about you. I mean, yeah, she's been ticked off at you, but she hasn't stopped loving you. Anger isn't the opposite of love. Apathy is. If she's mad at you, she's still fully in a relationship with you."

Myles stared at Hank, startled by the pithy wisdom of that observation. "And how do you know that?"

"Because I had a wife who left me. Spec Ops careers

tend to make that happen. Long deployments, her never knowing if I would come home alive or dead, never being able to be counted on for anything with the family. They take a toll on a marriage. Mine didn't end in fireworks. It just…faded away."

"I'm sorry," Myles murmured.

"Long time ago. I'm in a better place, now." Hank paused, then said low, "If you won't take offense at me saying it, your wife is one of the good ones. You should fight to hang on to her. And your kid is great, too. You're lucky to have both of them."

Myles sighed. "Yeah. I am. Damned lucky."

Hank said briskly, "I only told them I needed this place for an hour. It's time for us to go. Sorry y'all can't stay longer."

Myles said sincerely, "No apologies. This has been great. I think all three of us needed this more than I realized."

"That's me. PI extraordinaire and saver of marriages."

Myles gave Hank a grateful squeeze of the shoulder and headed for his son. "When my trial's over, do you want to come back here with Mommy and me and see the star show here?"

"Yeah!" Jackson shouted.

"It's a date—" Myles looked up at Faith "—if you'd like to."

She smiled warmly at him. "It's a date."

Chapter Nine

Faith stared down at the cheap phone in her hand. “And I need a burner phone why?”

She looked up at Hank, who shrugged. “Call it a little preventive paranoia. The burner phone doesn’t have a GPS locator in it, and nobody can track your location with it. You can use that to call Myles and he can call you on it. I’ve preloaded both of your phones with a couple hundred minutes of call time. When you run out, let me know and I’ll reload minutes in the phone.”

“Why do I need this now? It’s not as if I’m going anywhere,” she asked.

“Trial’s going to end soon, and the Anarchy Ink guys are going down in flames. They’re going to be mighty pissed off.”

“How soon?” she asked quickly.

“Myles thinks closing arguments will wrap up this afternoon and the jury will be given its instructions. They’ll start deliberating tomorrow. Could be a day, could be a week. Depends on how long they spend reviewing the testimony, and how long they take making a decision.”

“Thanks,” she said doubtfully.

“I’ll need your regular cell phone, ma’am.”

“Why?” She hated the idea of giving up her cell phone.

It had been her lifeline to the outside world for the past two weeks. Not only did it hold all of her contact names and phone numbers, but she got news from it, read books on it, scrolled through her stored pictures, played stupid games to occupy her hands when she got fretful—

"I'm going to show you how to replace the SIM card if you absolutely have to use this phone," Hank said, interrupting her silent tantrum at having her phone taken away.

"Fine," she said, sighing. She watched closely as he used a paper clip to open the SIM card drawer and took out the tiny chip. Hard to believe that teeny bit of plastic and metal stored so much information on it. Practically her whole life.

He wrapped the SIM card in a piece of tinfoil and taped it to the back of her cell phone. "You just open that little slider drawer, pop in the card, then turn on the phone. It'll take a second to load data off the card, but then you'll be right back in business."

She nodded and slipped her phone in her purse, along with the new burner phone. "How much longer until we can go home?"

"Give me a few days after the trial ends to gauge the mood of the Anarchy Ink folks. If they seem prepared to accept the verdict and get on with their lives, you'll be back to your real life very quickly."

"And if not?" she asked soberly. "If they're looking for trouble?"

Hank shrugged. "Let's cross that bridge when we come to it. I've found that borrowing trouble never does anything but cost me sleep."

"Ha. You say that as if I'm sleeping now!"

"Don't you worry, ma'am. The guys and I will keep you safe."

Lord, she hoped so. Her family had to get back to normal *sometime.*

THE CALL CAME in late the next afternoon. She jumped at the unfamiliar ringtone emanating from her purse and picked up the burner phone cautiously. "Hello?"

"Hey, Faith, it's me."

Myles.

"We won! They were found liable on all counts!"

"Congratulations!" she exclaimed.

"Larry Whitney and Suzanne Pierce have invited you and me to a celebratory dinner with the whole legal team that worked on this case and a bunch of the junior partners. Please tell me you'll come. It's the biggest win of my career. Hank will bring you over. It's going to be in a private dining room at a private club. Totally safe. You're the only person I really want to celebrate this with."

"All right already," she laughed at his full-court press to get her to go to dinner with him. "I'll come. Cocktail dress, I assume?"

"Wear something sexy. For me."

"Hmm. We'll see about that," she murmured. She fully planned to get all dolled up, but he deserved to be kept in suspense after what he'd put the whole family through.

"Wear a burlap sack if you want. I just want to celebrate with you. We did it, Faith. You and me. We made it over the hump. Life should get better from here on out."

If only. He always had been the flaming optimist of the two of them. She was the one who anticipated all the problems, planned for contingencies, and argued for caution in their lives.

She got off the phone with Myles and immediately yelled for her mother. Jenny poked her head out of her bedroom in alarm. "What's wrong, dear?"

"Nothing. Myles won his case, and he's invited me to dinner with his firm's partners."

"Oh, darling. That's wonderful. They're going to offer him a partnership. What are you going to wear? I'll babysit Jack, of course. Do you have anything appropriate to wear for an important dinner party?"

"No," she wailed. "The dressiest thing I have with me is my good yoga leggings."

Jenny rolled her eyes. "Quickly. Ask one of those bodyguards to take you to Saks Fifth Avenue. I'll call ahead and have a professional shopper meet you. You're going to need help getting everything pulled together fast that you'll need for tonight."

"I can do my own shopping, Mom—"

"Trust me. Shoo! Go find a security guard to drive you." Jenny literally pushed her toward the door, picking up Faith's purse and thrusting it into her hands. "Hurry. You've only got a couple of hours to get ready."

Cripes. How long did her mother think it took for her to become presentable?

Hank's security guard was none too pleased at the prospect of taking her out in public, but when Faith made it clear she was going shopping with or without his protection, the guard gave in.

They drove in a blacked-out SUV to the big Saks Fifth Avenue in the Magnificent Mile of downtown Chicago. A second security man hustled her inside the store while the other guy drove away in the SUV. They'd barely made it inside the store before a posh woman stepped forward and said pleasantly, "Mrs. Colton? I'm Patricia. I'll be your personal shopper, today. Your mother called ahead and gave me your sizes. If you'll follow me, I've already pulled a selection of dresses and put them in a dressing room for you."

Faith blinked, startled. Was this how the other half lived? She was thankful her mother wasn't here to make any snide comments about Faith not knowing how to embrace privilege.

"This way, Mrs. Colton. We'll have you ready to take over this town in no time."

Faith felt like a paper doll as she basically stood still and let Patricia dress her from the skin out. They tried on a half-dozen dresses, every one more stunning than the last. She hated to think what the price tags were on the designer fashions.

And then Patricia dropped a simple red dress over her head and zipped up the side. The fabric hugged her body in all the right places, with raised seams that emphasized her slender height and slim curves to absolute perfection. Granted the knee-to-shoulder foundation garment that felt like a full body girdle smoothed out a world of small imperfections. But dang.

"That's the one, isn't it?" Patricia said softly.

"Um, wow. I had no idea I could look like this."

"It's all in a good cut and fit. Now, how comfortable are you in heels? I have just the shoes for you if you can take a little height."

"Let's go for it," she said gamely. This dress was so spectacular she would tolerate any amount of pain in her feet to do it justice.

Patricia brought in a sleek pair of tall stilettos that added a good four inches to her height. And just like that, she went from average to tall and sexy.

"What are we thinking in jewelry?" Patricia asked. "Maybe a dangling earring to draw attention to your lovely neck? Honestly, I would leave the dress bare. Let your body be the attraction."

"I'm putty in your hands," Faith murmured. "I have no idea what I'm doing with a dress like this."

"I'm thinking we'll pull your hair up on the sides and let it hang long in the back. It's so lovely. Is that auburn your natural color?"

"Same as the day I was born."

"You lucky, lucky young woman. Okay. Take off the shoes and I'll have someone rough up the bottoms a bit so you don't slip on them tonight. If you'd like to take off the dress for now, I'll take you upstairs."

"What's upstairs?"

"The salon. Your mother said to turn you out from head to toe. We're under orders to send you out of here ready to wow."

Stunned, she followed the woman to an elevator. "If you don't mind my asking, what's this all going to cost?"

"Your mother said to put it on her Saks card. It's her gift to you."

Wow. Her mother could be a pill, but every now and then, she pulled a stunt like this, and Faith was reminded that underneath her tart, sometimes bitter, exterior, her mother loved her fiercely. Either that, or Jenny was just determined to see Faith climb the same social ladder she had.

Thing was, unlike her mother, she was happy with a husband and son, a modest but loving home, and her teaching. She didn't need more than that to be happy. Her mother had always been about the big house, the prestige car, the designer labels. Of course, Jenny had grown up desperately poor and craved financial security above all else.

Maybe that was part of what motivated Myles. His family had gone through more than one really rough financial patch before his mother married Rick Yates. She couldn't fault Myles for craving the financial security he hadn't had as a young boy.

The elevator door opened and a team of stylists whisked her into a chair, told her to sit still and close her eyes, and they went to work.

An hour later, they declared her finished and let her open her eyes. She stared at the woman in the mirror in shock. She was sophisticated, adult and terribly sexy. She had never in her life looked like this. The slender rows of cut crystal teardrops dangling from her ears sparkled against her fair skin and made her neck look a mile long. Her auburn locks swept up from her face at exactly the right angle to make her cheekbones look cut from marble, and her eyes had been treated to a smoky look and sweeping liner that made them look huge and mysterious.

"If I come back here someday, would you show me how to do this eye makeup?" she asked in wonder. "I could never look like this on my own."

The makeup artist laughed. "Of course. But you already have the bone structure and eye shape. The makeup is the easy part."

"Uh-huh," she responded skeptically. "When I do my makeup, I either look like the mommy I am or a vaguely frightening clown."

Patricia helped her don the dress carefully and zipped it for her once more while Faith stepped into the high-heeled shoes. "There you go, Mrs. Colton. You're ready for your big night."

"I feel like Cinderella after the fairy godmother got done with her."

Patricia smiled widely. "Then go get your prince."

Faith took the garment bag holding the clothes she'd worn to the store and walked carefully to the elevator. When the doors opened on the ground floor, Hank was waiting just outside.

"Whoa!" he exclaimed. "I mean you look nice, ma'am."

She smiled shyly. "Here's hoping Myles reacts like that."

Hank cleared his throat. "He'd be insane not to." He held out his forearm to her gallantly. "Shall we go?"

She was glad for his arm to balance on as she got the hang of walking in these exceptionally high stiletto heels. The ride to the private club was short, and Hank walked her inside quickly. They rode an elevator to a high floor of the skyscraper and stepped out in the lobby of a dark, wood-paneled restaurant that dripped of wealth and exclusivity.

"The maître d' will take you back to the private dining room," Hank murmured. "I'll be just outside."

She nodded and followed the maître d' down a side hall without ever passing through the main restaurant. He opened a door for her, and she stepped inside a private dining room.

The entire room fell silent as she stepped inside. Alarmed, she searched the faces until she found Myles's familiar visage. He was staring at her like he'd seen a ghost. Oh, God. Was she wildly overdressed? She did look like a clown, didn't she? She took a step backward and started to turn to flee the party when Myles stepped forward quickly and captured both of her hands in his. He leaned forward to kiss her cheek.

"My God. You're stunning," he murmured.

"Why is everyone staring?" she mumbled back in panic.

"Because you're spectacular. I've never seen you look more beautiful. Come. Let me introduce you to Larry Whitney. It's been a while since you met him. You remember Suzanne Pierce, don't you?"

Faith replied *sotto voce*, "The blonde barracuda who always looks at you like she wants to eat you? Yes. I remember her."

He laughed under his breath. "That's her."

The elderly, surviving founder of the firm, Lawrence Whitney, was effusive in his greeting, praising Myles for having such a stunning wife and keeping her under wraps all this time. Faith was glad when Myles answered smoothly and casually placed a hand in the small of her back. She knew her husband well enough to know that, not only was he making sure every male in the room knew she was his wife, but he was also silently offering her support and reassurance.

As the meal was served and everyone moved to the table, she muttered to Myles, "Kick me under the table if I make a fool of myself."

He threw her a quizzical look. "You do realize everyone in the room is intimidated by you, right?"

"That's kind of you to say, but—"

"Myles. Why didn't you tell me your wife is such a tour de force?" Faith looked up to see Millicent Whitney, Lawrence's wife, smiling warmly at her. "Faith Romans Colton, isn't it?" the woman said.

"That's correct. It's a pleasure to meet you, Mrs. Whitney. I so admire your work raising money for the city's after school programs. I'm a teacher, and some of my students have benefited from your work directly."

"I'd like to hear about them. Perhaps lunch next week?"

"That would be lovely, ma'am."

"Please. Call me Millie."

"If you'll call me Faith."

Myles held her chair for her, and as Faith sank into her seat, she was vividly aware of the other partners' wives staring at her. She leaned over to Myles. "Why are they all staring at me again?"

"Because Millicent Whitney is a fire-breathing dragon who's never nice to anybody."

"Oh. Oh my. Why me?"

"Because you're perfect, of course," he said, smiling back.

"Flatterer," she murmured as she unfolded her linen napkin and laid it across her lap.

"I haven't begun to flatter you yet," he replied low.

Their gazes met warmly, and her tummy fluttered in anticipation. For once in her life, she didn't feel like a plain brown sparrow next to his striking good looks.

She made it through the meal without using the wrong fork or dropping her napkin on the floor, but then, her mother had always been a stickler for proper etiquette. She supposed she owed her mom a very belated thanks for preparing her for an event like this.

As dessert and coffee were served, Larry Whitney and Suzanne Pierce stood up at the head of the table.

Whitney spoke. "As you know, we won the largest liability settlement in the history of the firm today. Congratulations to all of you for your hard work on the Maple Bend case." There were cheers and applause, lubricated by the cocktails that had been flowing freely since she'd arrived.

"I'd like to propose a toast," Suzanne Pierce said when the din died down. She raised her glass, and everyone followed suit. Expectant silence fell, and into it she said, "Here's to the newest associate partner at Whitney and Pierce. Everyone, please give a well-deserved welcome to Myles Colton."

"Hear, hear!" the group called out.

Faith turned to Myles and caught his exultant gaze. He leaned toward her and she toward him. "Congratulations," she murmured just before he kissed her.

Everyone cheered and they broke apart, startled by the noise.

"Speech! Speech!" a number of the partners yelled.

Goodness, these lawyers were boisterous when they got some liquor in them. Or maybe it was the millions of dollars in legal fees they'd earned today that was making them all so enthusiastic.

Myles stood up. "First of all, I would like to thank all my team members for the long hours and hard work all of you put in on the Maple Bend case. Second, I would like to thank Larry and Suzanne for believing in me enough to give me a shot at the case. Third, I would like to thank all the jurors wherever they are tonight for seeing things my way." That got a laugh. "And last but not least, I would like to thank my lovely wife for her exceptional patience with me over the past few months, and her saintly understanding through all the things she's had to put up with while we tried this case."

She smiled up at him while everyone clinked their glasses and drank around them. His gaze was more relieved than anything else, and she, of all people, understood why. This case had been hard on him, too. Their routines had been disrupted, their house upended, their family split apart. She was as eager as he was to get back to normal and put their lives back together.

The party didn't go on too much longer, and she and Myles spent the remainder of the celebration fielding congratulations from the other associate partners and invitations for her to do lunch at country clubs, play tennis, and various other activities way, *way* outside of her usual list of activities. Her social circle until now had been largely dictated by Jack. The moms of his friends were her friends, and she met them at play dates, soccer games, and the playground of the park near their house.

Finally, she and Myles walked out of the restaurant with the Whitneys and Suzanne Pierce. Hank hung back discreetly as they stepped out onto the sidewalk. Valets brought around their cars, and as the partners drove off, she and Myles were left alone beside his little sports car.

"Can I come home with you, or do I have to go back to the penthouse?" she asked Myles.

He glanced over at Hank, who shrugged. "How about I take you over to the house to show you the repairs, and then I'll drive you back to the penthouse in a bit? Does that work for you, Hank?"

The PI replied, "Do you think you can spot a tail if anybody follows you from your house?"

"Sure."

Hank frowned. "I suppose it's okay. We'll be moving your family in a couple of days, anyway."

"Moving us?" she said quickly. Alarm spiked in her chest.

"Well, yes. The Anarchy Ink crew left Chicago immediately after the verdict and headed back to their compound near Maple Bend. As long as they stay gone, you should be able to resume your normal life."

"How will we know if they stay gone?" she asked.

"I've got a couple of my guys keeping an eye on them."

"Is a couple of guys enough? Aren't there a lot of them?" she replied, not convinced that leaving the safety of the fort-like penthouse was a great idea.

"There are about a dozen core members, and they all live in the same compound. For now. They'll be evicted fairly soon when the property is seized by the state."

She frowned, unconvinced.

Hank said soothingly, "Don't worry, ma'am. It's my job to keep you and your boy safe."

Myles's arm went around her waist, and she looked at him in concern, asking, "Are you okay with this?"

"Sweetheart, it'll be fine. I'll be with you and Jackson, and Hank will still have a guy watching our place, won't you, Hank?"

"Absolutely."

She nodded nervously. "But we'll just go have a look at the house tonight? We won't stay?"

A frown flickered across Myles's brow as if he'd planned to do more than just show her the house, but he murmured in agreement evenly enough.

She hadn't paid a whole lot of attention to the fact that their house had been broken into before now. Frankly, she'd been more concerned about Jack's and her mom's safety. But all of a sudden, now that she was finally returning home, the fact that the sanctity of her house had been violated smacked her between the eyes.

Myles drove slowly, but she looked around carefully as they approached every intersection right along with him.

Hank followed them in the big SUV, but when they

parked in the driveway of their house, he parked across the street and stayed inside the vehicle. Myles helped her out of the car and opened the front door for her. She stepped past him and stopped cold.

"What happened to all our stuff?" she blurted. The home was stripped bare of everything that had made it their house. The walls were a bland cream color, the furniture was new. Even the rugs on the wood floors were new. None of Jackson's toys that usually littered the living room were visible, let alone scattered all over. All their books, mostly well-worn paperbacks, were gone from the recessed bookshelves on each side of the fireplace, and slick, chic knickknacks replaced them.

"You don't think it looks nice?" Myles asked. "The firm hired a designer to redecorate it."

"I liked it decorated the way it was," she grumbled as she walked through the living room and into the dining room. "A whole new dining room set? What the heck, Myles?"

"The damage was extensive. The designer had all the pieces repaired that she could, but the rest had to be replaced."

"The only piece I recognize so far is the bar, and it's built-in. Where's all of *our* stuff? My china. Our books. Jack's toys."

"Like I said. The intruders vandalized everything pretty badly."

"Are you telling me they broke all our plates, tore up all our books and broke all of Jack's toys?"

"Pretty much. The bill to repair or replace everything cost more than we paid for the house."

"You didn't tell me!" she accused.

"You were freaked out about having to go into hiding. I wasn't about to scare you even more."

"And you seriously think we're in no more danger just because a verdict came down? A verdict that will take everything these people own from them? If they were willing to do this to our home before, what on earth will they want to do to us now?"

He sighed rather more loudly than usual. Tough. When he said someone had broken into their house, she hadn't realized they'd *destroyed* it.

"At least come upstairs and see the rest of the house," he said.

The sleek new master bedroom and bathroom she could live with. But then she stepped into Jackson's bedroom. All signs of the room belonging to a little boy were gone. It was painted charcoal gray, and the single bed—far too high for him to sleep in safely—had an orange duvet. She hated gray and orange as a color palette for a little kid!

The desk by the window was also far too big for him, and the only concession to a child living in the room was a framed poster of a NASA rocket.

"Myles! You can't possibly think Jack would like this room. Maybe when he's fourteen, but not four!"

"Obviously, it needs toys and books and more kid stuff in it."

She turned to stare at him. "It's hideous, and you know it."

"Okay. So, this room is hideous and will need to be redone. But we can do that. We've done bigger makeovers."

"We? You mean me."

"Well, yes. You're the one with the eye for design."

She just shook her head and left the room. She walked

downstairs in silence and reached for the front door handle, now a square, modern, brushed brass atrocity that looked awful on the home's original, oil-rubbed Douglas fir Craftsman door.

"Where are you going, Faith?"

"Back to the car. I want to leave."

"It's not late. I thought we might spend a little time alone together..." He trailed off, obviously hinting that he wanted sex.

She declared, "For the record, counselor, I won't sleep in this house. I won't have sex in this house. And I certainly won't live in it. Not like this. Put it back the way it was or forget it."

She headed outside and nearly broke her neck going down the front steps. In her ire, she'd forgotten about the teetery high heels she was wearing. Thankfully, she caught herself without looking too much like a clumsy giraffe and made it to his car without any more stumbles. She climbed in the passenger seat and waited in silence while he moved around the house turning out lights and locking the place up.

He was silent as he drove her back to the penthouse, which was just fine with her. How could he have let that happen to their home? She wailed and shouted silently in her head, but clamped her mouth shut against letting any of it out. She knew the answer, anyway. He'd been too busy with his precious trial to pay any attention to what the decorator had done to their cozy home.

He pulled up in front of the skyscraper downtown and reached out to lay his hand on hers as she started to reach for the door handle. "Don't leave me like this, Faith. We had a really good evening until the house. I hate to end things on such a negative note. I'll pay whatever it takes to have the designer put the house back the way it was."

"Don't bother. What made our home special was that it was decorated with love. We did it together. We made it ours. I don't want some designer trying to create some pale, fake imitation of that."

He replied heavily, "What do you want me to do, then? We can't live apart forever."

She pursed her lips, declining to reply. "You do whatever you want to. That's how you've been living the past four years. Why stop now?"

On that rather snarky note, she let herself out of the car and hurried into the lobby of the building. The security guard at the front desk looked up and then did a hard double take. "Um, good evening, Mrs. Colton. I barely recognized you."

Oh. Right. Clown suit and makeup.

"I'll see myself up to the penthouse. Don't leave your desk unattended."

"Call me when you get there, ma'am?"

"Fine." She added belatedly, "Have a good night." No need to be rude to the man because her husband was an ass.

"You too, ma'am."

Not bloody likely.

Chapter Ten

Myles hit both fists hard on the steering wheel. Dammit. Things had been going so well between them, and then Faith had freaked out at how the house had been redone. When he saw it through her eyes, he could understand why she was upset. But the designer had been adamant that redoing it in a sleek, clean, modern decor would massively increase its resale value.

But Faith had stormed out of the place before he could broach the idea with her of selling it and buying their forever home, big enough to raise their whole family in, maybe close to the private school she wanted to send their kids to, closer to his office, and ideally farther away from her mother. Much farther if he had any say in the matter.

Hank had cleared him to stay in his own house if Myles wanted to give it a go, but after the fight with Faith, he had no desire to go back just now. He'd checked out of the last hotel they'd stashed him in, though, and his suitcase and garment bag full of suits was in the trunk of his car. Where to go, now?

With a sigh, he headed for his mom and stepdad's place. They had a big house with plenty of spare room for kids and grandkids. He passed the Yates' Yards Plant Nursery, which was dark at this hour. The greenhouses were mostly dark, with only the end of one glowing lavender with plant lights suspended over a new batch of seedlings. The big two-story farmhouse came into view past a stand of fruit trees, and he sighed in relief as he always did at the sight of home.

This was where he'd found happiness and peace as a kid. When the whole world was going to hell around him, he could always find a friendly ear and a warm hug here. Maybe that was what had drawn him back here tonight. The Yates home was his bedrock.

This was exactly the kind of home he wanted to build with Faith if she would just get over being mad at him and agree to resume their life together as a family. The windows were dark, and he let himself in the back door quietly, using his old house key.

Too frustrated to sleep, he made his way to his stepfather's liquor cabinet and poured himself a shot of Rick's smooth aged whisky. He carried it to the kitchen and sat down at a bar stool to sip on it and try to figure out what the hell he was going to do next.

Did he dare even take the partnership at the law firm? Would that be the final straw that broke Faith's back? Sure, the pay raise was great and his work hours would go down, but would she see it as an act of ultimate selfishness for him to take the offer?

A floorboard squeaked behind him and he turned quickly, startled.

"Hey, son. What brings you here at this time of night to raid my bar?" Rick Yates was illuminated in the soft light of the stove hood, his hair sticking up in every direction.

"Hi, Dad. Sorry. Didn't mean to wake you up."

"Need some company to drink with?"

"Sure."

"Mind if we move to the living room? If I'm going to enjoy a good single malt scotch, I prefer to do it in my favorite chair."

Smiling, Myles followed Rick into the living room. The house was comfortable and not the least bit pretentious. The wood trim was plentiful, as were pictures of the entire Colton clan. Vita lovingly covered her walls with framed photographs of her children and grandchildren.

He sank down in a comfortable armchair beside Rick's recliner, teasingly referred to as Dad's throne by Myles and his sister, Lila.

"What brings you home, Myles?" Rick asked casually.

Myles had to smile. His stepfather had a talent for putting his kids at ease and making it easy for them to open up to him. "I checked out of my hotel room this afternoon, and I didn't feel like going back to my house alone. I figured you wouldn't mind if I shacked up in my old room tonight while I decide what I'm doing next."

"What does Faith think you should do next?"

"She's not too happy with me at the moment. I expect she thinks I should go jump in Lake Michigan."

Rick chuckled. "The lake's pretty cold at this time of year."

Myles sighed. "I messed up pretty bad. I mean, I thought I was doing the best thing for Faith and Jackson, but that's sure not how Faith sees it."

"Tell me about it."

He poured out his troubles to his father and finally fell silent, staring morosely into his whisky. Somehow, it felt better just getting it all off his chest. He still didn't see the path through to the other side of this, but at least the burden had lifted enough for him to think more clearly.

"Is Faith right that you've been prioritizing your career over your family?"

"Of course, she is. She's always right." He sighed.

Rick laughed. "You're well on the way to a happy marriage if you can acknowledge that your wife is smarter than you and knows better than you."

He rolled his eyes. "I don't know what to do about the partnership offer. It's what I've worked all these years for, and it'll make our lives materially easier. But I don't want to lose my wife over it."

"Have you told her that?"

"We haven't even talked about the partnership yet. She was so mad over the redo of the house that she stormed out and gave me the silent treatment all the way back to where she's staying."

"Yikes. That doesn't sound like Faith."

"She's not normally the type to hold a grudge."

Rick said soothingly, "Give her a little time. She's had a lot thrown at her the past few weeks. And maybe next time you two talk, you can do most of the listening?"

"Yeah. You're right. Lila gave me the what-for about not having taken Faith on a real vacation since our honeymoon."

"Since your—" Rick broke off. "Oh, man. You're way overdue to pay some quality attention to your wife without Jackson around. Why don't you leave Jack with me and Vita for a week or two and get out of Chicago? Go somewhere warm and sandy and reconnect with your wife."

"I don't know if she'd even go with me at this point."

"She'll go. Trust me. That girl is crazy in love with you. You just have to remind her why."

"I am due some vacation time after the trial. I could take a week or two before I pick up another case."

"Sounds like a plan. What say we turn in and get some sleep? I've got a big landscaping job kicking off tomorrow, and I'll need to be there bright and early to make sure my crew doesn't dig up the wrong plants. We're redoing that mansion over on Elm Street. The one with the giant hydrangeas overtaking the whole front of it?"

"You've been itching to redo that place for years. How'd you finally get Mrs. Merriweather to agree to it?"

"I wore her down with my charm, of course. That and I gave her a good deal on the bid. We're doing a historically accurate formal garden. Should be a stunner when we're done. She's going to let us put up a sign for the nursery in her yard for a month after it's finished."

"That should bring some nice jobs your way."

"That's the idea."

Myles carried their glasses to the kitchen sink and padded upstairs after his father. He loved this old house. Even the squeaky floors sounded like home. He stripped and fell into his bed in his old room, breathing deeply of the faint leather smell of his varsity jacket and baseball glove, both hanging on the coat rack in the corner. His old sports trophies still collected dust on a shelf over his desk, and the bulletin board still had all his best memories of high school and college tacked to it. Funny how all of those memories were tied to Faith in some way.

She was the heart and soul of his entire life. Always had been. Always would be. His dad was right. He just needed to take her away somewhere and let her know that. A plan in hand, he fell asleep quickly for the first time in weeks.

LARRY WHITNEY WAS all over him taking a vacation with Faith, and shocked Myles by offering up his condo in the Turks and Caicos Islands for them. Myles made a quick call to his mom, who delighted at the idea of watching Jack for a week, and then he booked a pair of plane tickets to the island chain south of the Bahamas and northeast of Cuba.

He made a quick call to Hank, who thought it was a great idea for the two of them to leave Chicago for a bit while the Anarchy Ink crew cooled off. The PI's hope was that the gang members would move away from this part of the country, ideally splitting up and going their separate ways, sooner rather than later.

Everything was taken care of. Now, to convince Faith to go along with his plan.

He left the office a little before lunch and headed over to the penthouse. He stepped out of the elevator and knocked on the door.

His mother-in-law opened it. "Oh. It's you. What are you doing here, Myles?"

Wow. Cold much? He bit back a sharp retort. Jenny never had been a warm person, and putting her daughter and grandson at risk surely hadn't endeared him to her in the least. "Is Faith here?"

"Where else would she be? We've been locked up here for weeks."

It had only been two weeks, and at a glance this place looked pretty palatial.

"Daddy!" Jackson raced inside from some sort of rooftop deck and launched himself at Myles.

He caught his son up in a big bear hug and spun him around until the boy squealed with laughter. A little dizzy himself, he grinned as Faith came inside more slowly.

"Myles? What brings you here? Is it safe for you to be here?"

"Well, since I'm hoping you'll let me kidnap you and take you out of here, it should be okay that I'm here this once."

"Can I be kidnapped too?" Jackson piped up.

"You bet, squirt." Over his son's head, he said to Jenny, "Hank has given you the all clear to go home."

Jenny nodded stiffly, not looking all that thrilled to return to her big, ugly house. Not that it was his problem she had no friends or family to share her life with other than her daughter and grandson.

"Where are we going?" Faith asked warily.

He met her gaze wryly. "Not back there."

Relief passed across her expressive face. "I'll go pack, then."

"Can I help?" he offered quickly.

"Why don't you pack up Jack? Can you two boys handle that all by yourselves?"

"Yeah!" Jack shouted.

"Yes," Faith corrected, smiling.

Jackson wiggled to be put down, and Myles obliged. "Show me your room, kiddo. What do you want to bet we can get you packed faster than Mommy can get her stuff packed up?"

"Mark. Get set. Go!" Jack shouted, tearing off toward an open door off the living room.

Myles gathered that was Jack's room and followed at a more leisurely pace, grinning at his wife. "You're toast, you know. You have all that girl goop to pack up."

"Ha. You haven't seen all the toys Jackson insisted on bringing with him."

Laughing, Myles stepped into his son's room, where

Jackson was busy piling all of his possessions in a haphazard jumble on the bed. "Whoa, there, son. We have to get out your suitcase and fold all this stuff."

"Awww, man," Jackson complained.

"Here. I'll show you how. We'll still beat Mommy by a mile."

It took nearly an hour to collect all of their belongings, check and double-check the suite for anything left behind, and to load Jenny in Hank's SUV. While the pair left for Jenny's house in Evanston, he buckled Jackson in the minuscule back seat of his sports car, which turned out to be just about the right size for his young son.

"Whee! I get to sit in a big boy seat and not a booster!" his son crowed.

"Drive carefully," Faith murmured nervously.

"Always," he rcplied, guiding his car toward Wheaton and his parents' house.

"Are we going to stay at your folks' place?" Faith asked as they neared the Yates Nursery.

"Jackson is."

"What about me?"

Myles grinned. "It's a surprise."

"I don't like surprises," she declared.

He snorted. "Yes, you do. You like them almost more than Jack."

"Fine," she conceded. "But I'm not sure I like this one."

He laughed. "Trust me. You'll love this one."

They pulled up beside his parents' house and Jack took off as soon as he was released from the back seat, racing up the porch into the kitchen to see if Gramma Vita had baked his favorite chocolate chip cookies for him. Myles didn't even have to smell the scent of warm vanilla to know she had. She spoiled the kid possibly worse than Jenny did, and that was saying something.

He carried Jack's and Faith's suitcases inside and traded out Faith's for the one he'd packed at their house this morning for their trip. He sincerely hoped he'd remembered everything she would need in a tropical paradise. He carried his bag and hers back out to his car and then gathered in Jack close for a secret meeting.

"Will you help me kidnap Mommy?"

"Sure!"

"I want you to have her close her eyes and then you lead her out to the car. Okay? I'm taking Mommy on a trip, and she doesn't know anything about it."

"It's a s'prise?"

"A big one. Will you be okay hanging out with Gramma and Grandpa this week like a big boy?"

"Can I help water the plants?"

Myles laughed. "I'm positive you can. And you can eat all the cookies you want, too."

Jackson nodded vigorously. "Deal."

"Deal." Myles hugged his son tightly. "I'm so proud of you, Jackie. You're growing into such a good boy. I love you this big." He held his arms out as wide as they would go.

"I love you even bigger!"

"Go get Mommy. And tell her no peeking. Not a word to her of what's up, okay?"

"Uh-huh." Jackson raced off to collect Faith, and he jogged inside to grab her small suitcase that he knew she packed her toiletries and girl goop in. He made it outside just before Jackson led a laughing Faith carefully down the porch steps.

"What on earth is going on?" she demanded, her eyes screwed tightly shut.

"Daddy and me are kidnapping you!"

"You are? Where are you taking me?"

"To Daddy's car?"

"Then where are we going?" she asked, obediently letting Jackson lead her by the hand to his car.

Myles opened the passenger door for her and helped her sit down in the car. "Thanks for the help, Jackson! You're a great kidnapping buddy."

Jackson waved enthusiastically as Myles backed up the car and turned it around.

"Can I take off the blindfold now?" Faith asked.

"I suppose. But no questions."

"I can't even ask where we're going?"

"Nope. This is a kidnapping."

"What are you up to, Myles?"

"Reminding you why I'm the love of your life and why you're the love of mine."

"Hmm." She leaned back, her arms folded skeptically, but he thought he spied a smile hovering around the edges of her mouth.

When he took the exit for O'Hare International Airport, she exclaimed in surprise. "What on earth?"

"No questions," he reminded her.

The smile became more visible as he parked the car and they rode a shuttle into one of the giant terminals. He told the ticket agent when he handed over their passports and checked their bags not to mention their destination because it was a surprise, and the woman played along, smiling broadly as she told them to have a nice trip.

He spotted Faith taking a hard look at the luggage tags, but he doubted the letters PLS would mean anything to her. They were the code for Providenciales International Airport in the Turks and Caicos. So far, so good.

They made it through the security checkpoint and strolled into the huge terminal. He'd gotten here plenty early so they would be in no hurry. This trip was purely about relaxing and winding down. Truth be told, he probably needed that as much or more than she did.

"Coffee? A bite to eat?" he offered.

"How long until our flight leaves?" she asked.

"It won't start loading for another hour. We've got time to sit a bit."

"You mean like grown-ups?" she asked.

He laughed. "The four-year-old is with my folks. We don't have to be grown-ups, here. We can be adults."

"What a thought," she said, sighing.

"This trip is about just the two of us," he murmured. "It's high time we reconnected."

"Did your sister tell you that?"

He winced. "In no uncertain terms. She chewed me up one side and down the other."

"Can we afford this trip of yours?" Faith asked anxiously.

"Larry Whitney is letting us use his vacation place, and he insisted on paying for the plane tickets."

"Wow. The firm must really be pleased with their chunk of the settlement from your case."

He shrugged. "It'll run close to thirty million dollars."

"Whoa. I had no idea."

"Biggest settlement the firm has ever landed."

"Congratulations."

He couldn't tell if she was being sarcastic or not, but he chose to take her at face value. "Thanks. I wasn't kidding when I said the case would make my career. This morning, the firm has already had inquiries from a couple of big money clients looking to hire us."

"And they're letting you go away for a vacation?" she blurted.

"Larry and Suzanne are commanders in chief of schmoozing new clients and putting them on retainer. I'll undoubtedly pick up a case or two when we get home, but there's time enough for that later."

"That's so…non-wage slogger of you."

"Gee. Thanks. I haven't been that bad for the past four years, have I?"

She rolled her eyes. "You've been worse."

Remembering Rick's advice last night to listen more, he sighed. "Tell me about it. How bad has it been for you?"

"Seriously?" she asked.

"Yes. This trip is about us reconnecting. I want to hear what your life has been like."

She spent the hour before they had to board talking honestly about how hard it was sometimes to have to do everything around the house by herself and how overwhelmed she felt sometimes having to parent Jackson alone. He felt like a heel by the time he finally said, "It's time for us to board the flight."

She let out a big breath. "Thanks for letting me get all that off my chest. I didn't realize I was hanging on to so much of it."

He hugged her close. "I love you, Faith. I'm sorry I haven't been there for you. But that changes, starting now."

She hugged him back for a moment, but then stepped back. "C'mon. Let's go board our plane. I'm dying to know where you're taking me."

He grinned and led her to their gate.

She squealed when she saw the destination on the monitor behind the ticket agent. “I don’t even know if there’s a bathing suit in my suitcase! Or sunblock!”

“Yes to both. And anything I forgot to pack for you we can buy there.”

She threw her arms around his neck in excitement. “Oh, Myles! A real vacation in an island paradise! Beaches. With sand!”

He laughed. “Most beaches do have sand, yes.”

“C’mon! They’ve called our group. Let’s board!”

“Man. You’re worse than Jackson, Miss Impatient.”

She grinned over her shoulder at him. There she was again. The fun loving, exuberant girl he’d fallen in love with. Yep. This trip had been a fantastic idea. He made a mental note to thank Lila expansively the next time he talked with her.

Chapter Eleven

Faith looked around in disbelief that this morning she'd been in chilly Chicago, and now she was on this tropical beach with a warm breeze rustling her hair, the soft swish of the ocean soothing her, and the warm glow of the candles lighting their table on her face.

"What a magical place," she said softly.

Myles smiled across the table from her. "It's pretty nice."

"So, this is how the other half lives, huh?"

He smiled. "We can be part of this other half if you'd like. All I have to do is accept the offer of a partnership at Whitney and Pierce."

"What will being a partner entail, anyway?"

"Well, there's a buy-in. But that will be taken out of my bonus for winning the Maple Bend case. After that, I'll share a percentage of all the earnings the firm makes, on top of whatever I make from my own billable hours. And, as a partner, I can charge more per hour, so I'll make more money regardless."

"How much more?"

"My take-home pay should nearly double," he answered.

Whoa. That was a substantial pay raise. "What would we do with all that money?" she asked, startled.

"Save some of it, of course. Invest some and put some in Jackson's college account. Beyond that, I thought maybe it's time to buy a new house. A bigger one we can raise our family in."

She stared, shocked. "Already? I thought it was going to be a few more years before we could afford that."

"Normally, it would've been a few more years. But the Maple Bend case pushed the timetable forward. That's why I took the case."

She sighed. "Now that it's over and nobody's dead, it's okay for you to say the risk was worth it. But I stand by my original opinion that your safety—and mine and Jack's—were not worth taking such a chance."

Myles was uncharacteristically silent. He'd been quick to argue in defense of his decision every time they'd talked about it before now. Or more accurately, fought about it. Eventually, he said slowly, "I see your side of it. It was a stupid chance to take. No amount of money or partnerships is worth your safety. I'm immensely grateful that it all worked out. However, I won't be doing anything like that again."

"For real?" she blurted, startled.

"Not without consulting you and getting your full approval."

"And if I refuse to go along with such a dangerous decision?" she asked cautiously.

"I'll abide by your wishes," he answered.

She frowned. Since when? "What's the catch?"

"No catch, Faith. I mean it. There's nothing else I want from my career that would require me to do anything so risky again."

"What if another case comes along that's ten times the

size of this one? That will put you on the national news and make you internationally famous?"

"If it puts you and Jackson at risk, I'll walk away from it," he answered firmly.

"Forgive me for being skeptical," she replied.

He exhaled audibly. "What do you want from me? I'm trying to give you everything you want."

It was her turn to sigh. "I'm not asking you to give up all your ambitions and dreams, Myles. I know how important your career is to you. I'm just asking you to put your family first."

"Fair enough. I'm putting you guys first."

She heard the words, but she wasn't sure she truly believed them yet.

"How's your food?" he asked.

She looked down at the remnants of the lobster thermidor on her plate. "Out of this world. Yours?"

He pushed back his plate, which had held a surf and turf meal. "Amazing. I didn't know when Larry offered us his condo that the meals were included. I may go back to Chicago the size of the Michelin Man if all the meals are like that."

"We can walk off the food on this gorgeous beach," she murmured.

"Speaking of which, would you like to take a stroll in the moonlight by the sea?"

"I would love to."

It felt decadent to get up from the table, totally ignoring the dirty plates and walk away without cleaning up after the meal. By the time they reached the dark strip of wet sand about a hundred feet away from the covered gazebo where they'd eaten, she noted that a server had already moved in to clear the table.

Myles reached out and entwined his fingers with hers. They'd gone down to the gazebo barefoot, and the sand was sugar soft between her toes. As they reached the water's edge, it became cold and firmer, easier to walk on. The last bits of a wave washed over her feet and then retreated.

The beach arced gently in front of them, curving toward a distant point marked by an outcropping with a stand of trees clinging tenaciously to it. The ocean was dark to her right, the lights of the resort twinkling brightly to her left.

"This really is paradise." She sighed.

Myles smiled. "It's paradise because I'm here with you."

"Aww, shucks, you smooth-talking romantic," she teased.

"That's me."

That was what she was afraid of. He had always been able to talk her into just about anything. He was so smart and so persuasive she always caved to him. It was what made him a great attorney, but sometimes it made her feel steamrolled.

Tonight, however, he was being much quieter than usual. They walked in silence until the resort was a tiny white strip in the distance behind them. She let the soothing whoosh and hiss of the waves wash away all the stress of the past few weeks. Heck, of the past few years. She couldn't remember the last time she'd been this relaxed. Maybe never.

They turned to head back toward the resort and she asked, "What's on your mind that's got you so quiet?"

"Actually, I'm waiting for you to talk to me. My dad

pointed out to me recently that I possibly haven't been listening to you very well."

"Did he, now? God bless Rick."

"I haven't been that bad, have I?" Myles asked quickly.

"You've been worse. You've totally ignored my needs and wants for a long time."

"Like what?" He sounded startled.

"Well, I told you the night of the car accident that there was something important I wanted to talk over with you at supper. But you've never once asked what it was."

He looked chagrined. "I really have been a jerk, haven't I? What was it you wanted to talk about?"

"I put together a whole rational, logical argument to present to you over supper of why it was a good idea for me to go back to work."

"Teaching?"

"Yes, teaching. I love it, and I miss it."

"But Jack—"

"Jack is old enough to attend pre-K right now. The only reason he's not doing it is because I'm still at home full time with him. He's a social and outgoing kid. He could benefit from being with other kids and getting familiar with the structure of a classroom environment."

"You don't think he'll be bored out of his mind? I mean, he's already reading up a storm and doing math. It's not like he needs to spend all day reciting the alphabet and counting to ten."

She sighed. "The pre-K program at the North Hills Academy is geared toward the gifted child who's already at Jack's level or beyond."

"And how expensive is this pre-K?" Myles asked.

"Does it matter? I thought we're going to be rolling in money when you go home."

"We are. I'm just trying to budget in my head."

"North Hills is going to have an opening next year for a third-grade teacher. I was thinking about applying for it. If I get it, Jackson could attend the school for free, anyway."

"You've already been searching for job openings?" Myles asked quickly, accusingly.

"No," she answered defensively. "Jack's friend Max at soccer has an older sister in the third grade at North Hills, and Max's mom was lamenting that Christie's teacher is retiring at the end of this year."

"Ah." Myles walked on in silence.

She trailed along beside him until they were almost back at the resort before pressing him. "What are you thinking, Myles?"

"To be honest, I was thinking about asking you if you'd like to have another baby, soon."

"A...baby?" she echoed blankly.

"Yes. You know. Small, screaming, proto-human pooping machine? Eventually grows into a child?"

She laughed in spite of herself. "Yes, I'm familiar with what they are, thank you. Do you want another one?"

"I do. And I thought you did, too."

"Well, I do. I just wasn't thinking about having another one right now..."

"Then when? How big an age gap do you want between Jack and another child?"

"Not too much. I'd like them to be close enough in age to at least talk with each other."

"Then shouldn't we get cracking on having another one?" Myles asked reasonably.

She frowned. "But if I have another one, I might have to put off going back to teaching again."

"Which is a problem why?"

"At some point I'll have been out of teaching long enough that my skills and education will be outdated. I won't be able to go back at all. Ever."

"You could always go back to college and get a master's degree. Update your skill set, as it were."

"And when would that happen?" she asked.

"After we've had all the kids we decide to have."

"Just how many children are you envisioning us having?" she blurted.

"I don't know. Maybe a couple more."

"Three kids? I thought we agreed on two."

"That was when we couldn't afford more than two."

They reached the beach in front of the resort and she turned to face Myles. "You do realize I'm basically a single parent, right? I can't raise three kids and hold down a full-time job."

"I'll be around more in the future—"

She cut him off. "You won't be there all day to change diapers and chase toddlers and drive kids around to activities, not to mention keeping the house clean and preparing meals and doing the other stuff that crops up. I'm *busy* all day long as it is, just with Jack. And you want to add two more kids to that mix?"

"Once they're school age, things will slow down."

She snorted. "No, they won't. Then I'll pick up after school activities and homework and school events and social stuff."

"Are you saying you don't want to have any more kids at all?" Myles sounded surprised and disappointed.

"I'm saying it's a big decision, and I want to think about it before I commit to anything."

"Fair enough." He led her off the beach and onto the boardwalk that crossed the dune prior to the elegant resort.

They'd almost reached their door when he said, "By the way, you do realize we'll be able to afford a nanny, right?"

"A…what?"

"A nanny. Someone who can take care of a baby during the day while you work, run errands, cook, maybe help out after school with running kids around."

"Um, wow. I'd never considered that."

He smiled a little. "You're the one who grew up wealthy."

"My mom had no life, whatsoever. She lived to take care of me and clean her house. She didn't want or need help."

"I just wanted to throw out the idea while you think about what you'd like to do regarding more kids or no more kids."

She stopped and turned to face him in the moonlight. "This isn't solely my decision. We're a couple. We're supposed to decide these big things together."

He gazed down at her seriously. "Okay. Let's decide this together. We've got a few days to talk it over and examine our options with no outside distractions. But for now, let's just relax and enjoy this beautiful place, shall we?"

"What do you have in mind, counselor?"

"How about we dig out one of those bottles of your favorite white wine and take it out to the hot tub. We can drink it under the stars."

"Wow. Sounds romantic," she murmured.

"That's the plan."

"You have a plan?"

"Oh, yes," he replied, a smile playing around the corners of his mouth.

While he headed for the wine refrigerator in the kitchen, she hurried to the master bedroom and changed out of her clothes, jumping into the skimpy bikini Myles had packed for her. She hadn't worn the thing since Jackson had been born, but fortunately, she'd spent the past year working hard to get back into prebaby shape. Still, she was nervous as she pulled it on and looked at herself in the mirror.

Her breasts were bigger than before she'd nursed a baby, and a little softer, but still nice, she supposed. Her hips were a little wider, but it gave her rather narrow frame more of an hourglass shape than she'd had in college. At least her stomach was flat and firm these days. She silently thanked her Pilates instructor who'd been a five-foot-tall tyrant, for making her do all those crunches and planks.

She grabbed a couple of the fluffy white beach towels the resort provided and headed out to the patio facing the beach. Myles was already lounging in the deep tub, bubbles foaming around his chest, his shoulders glistening with wetness in the light of the rising moon.

The surf, only a few hundred feet away, serenaded them rhythmically, its soothing rise and fall calming all the way down to her soul. The night air was cool as she slipped into the steaming hot water. Myles held an arm out and she slid over next to him, half-floating against the lean hardness of his body. Myles ran on a treadmill and lifted weights in the firm's fitness room every day at lunch to work off stress and think about his cases, and a couple of times a week, he went to his cousin Aaron's gym to box.

"Mmm, you're warm," she murmured.

"That's just the water. I'm a coldhearted, black-hatted lawyer, remember?" he joked. "We're the bad guys."

"You did the right thing in the Maple Bend case," she said softly. "You weren't the bad guy, then."

"Not to the people of Maple Bend, but I was the bad guy to you. I'm sorry I took the case without talking it over with you. But I was debating telling you about it at dinner the night of the accident."

"Did they ever catch the driver of that truck?" she asked.

"Nope. The police theorize it was one of the Anarchy Ink guys trying to scare me off of the case. They pulled stuff like that during their criminal trial but aimed at jurors. Maybe if we had found anything to link the gang to the crash we could've gotten a search warrant and looked for a truck matching the description of the one you saw. But in the absence of a link, there's nothing the police can do about it."

"Thankfully, we have good insurance, and the car will be replaced. And you and I walked away from it."

"Barely," he muttered. Myles's arm looped around her shoulders and drew her around to sit on his lap facing him. She felt weightless in the water.

"I don't ever want to come that close to losing you again, Faith."

"Nor I you." She looped her arms around his neck and stared into his light green eyes, which were gray in the moonlight. His short hair was wet and made little wet spikes on the side of his head. The hair on top of his head slicked back from his handsome features only highlighted how good-looking a man he'd grown into over the years.

"I sure got lucky," she said softly.

"Lucky how?"

"Well, when I fell for you in the sixth grade, I had no idea you'd turn out so hot. I would never have tried to go for a guy as good-looking as you in college if I hadn't already been with you."

He laughed, a low rumble in his chest that vibrated through the water to caress her skin. "If I hadn't met you until college, I'd have been scared to death of you."

"Me?" she exclaimed. "I was a mousy bookworm who had no idea how to flirt with any guy but you!"

"You were so gorgeous in college it hurt to look at you. You still are, you know. You keep getting more beautiful with time, Faith." He pushed her hair back from her face with a wet hand. "You're one of those women who'll be stunning at seventy and elegant at ninety."

"Let's hope we both live long enough to find out if you're right."

He grinned. "I don't know about you, but I'm aiming for one-hundred-ten-years old before I kick the bucket."

"Not me." She grinned back. "You'll be the death of me long before then."

"Aww c'mon. I'm not that bad."

"When you're not working day and night, you're not."

He nodded as the smile faded from his face. "I promise. No more hundred-hour weeks. At least, not often. I might still burn the midnight oil right before a case goes to trial, but I won't make a habit of it anymore."

"I'll hold you to that," she replied.

"Seal the deal with a kiss?" he murmured.

"Is this how you seal all your deals?" she teased. "No wonder Suzanne Pierce eyes you like you're a grade A prime piece of tenderloin steak."

"Suzanne? Nah."

"Ha. Don't lie to me. You know she's after you. I'll bet she's even made a pass at you by now, hasn't she?"

Myles grinned. "A little. She invited me out for a late supper a few weeks ago. But I declined."

Faith laughed. This was the part of having known Myles for so long that she loved the best. They could tell each other anything. The trust between them ran so deep that she could casually ask about another woman, and he could just as casually admit that the woman had made a run at him.

Faith said, "I hope I look as good as her in ten more years."

Myles's arms tightened around her waist, pulling her tight against him. "You'll look ten times better, and you won't have shark teeth for me to worry about."

"Shark teeth?"

"I'm fairly certain she mates with her men and then eats them."

"So…she's not your type?"

Myles laughed heartily. "Not at all. I like my women… woman…soft and sweet and gentle. Warm-hearted." He added wryly, "In fact, I'd settle for warm-blooded."

Faith smiled. "Well, I'm glad I have such a low bar to attain. I think I can manage warm-blooded."

She closed the remaining distance between their mouths and kissed him then, tasting the faint salt of the night air on his lips. That and the crisp sweetness of the white wine he'd been sipping before she joined him.

"Mmm. That wine is nice. Can I have some, too?"

Myles reached off to the side and brought a wineglass next to her. She was surprised when he didn't give the crystal glass to her, though. Instead, he took a sip and then looked at her expectantly.

Smiling, she leaned forward and licked the wine off his lips. "Mmm."

"My turn." He held the glass to her lips and she let the cold, bright wine slide into her mouth. With notes of both sweet and sharp, the white wine made taste buds all over her tongue tingle. And then Myles's lips and tongue were there, stealing the flavor and soothing away the bite of it.

She surged against him in the water and he slid his hands down her bare back to the tie holding her top on. She felt a brief tug and then the triangles of cloth hung loose around her neck. Another tug under her hair and the scraps fell away altogether. Her breasts felt light and buoyant in the bubbling water, their higher curves emerging from the foam to gleam pale in the moonlight.

Myles leaned back, reaching between them to cup her breasts lightly. His thumbs stroked across her nipples, and she gasped, surprised at how intense it felt. It had been a long time since they'd done this, and she was unused to how strongly she reacted to him.

Eager to return the favor, she reached down into the water and slipped her hand down the front of his bathing trunks. As foreplay went, it was direct and simple, but effective.

Myles groaned, and she felt the thickness and hardness of his reaction to her immediately. Using her free hand, she pushed back from him, off his lap. She reached for her bikini bottoms, and he reached for his trunks.

In a big hurry, they came together again, their bodies fitting perfectly. Floating in the middle of the hot tub now, Myles lightly supported her weight while she wrapped her legs around his hips.

"It's been so long," she murmured.

"Too long," he groaned, guiding his erection to her body.

She squeezed his hips, urging him forward, and slowly, gloriously, he came home at last. She could've sobbed in relief when he finally filled her with his familiar, wonderful, pulsing energy. His hands cupped her buttocks and rocked her forward, seating him even more deeply inside her.

"I've missed you so much, Faith."

"I've missed you, too. Let's never be apart again."

"Deal."

And then the talking ended and the sex took over, all surging flesh and splashing water and bubbles dancing across her skin. They'd never made love in a hot tub before and it was fun. It was also noisy, and definitely messy, as they sent water all over the patio in waves that overtopped the edge of the tub in time with their surging lovemaking.

And then Myles buried his face in her neck, groaning in release while she hugged him close, shuddered along with him as release claimed her in a tingling storm that went all the way to her toes and fingertips, and went limp in his arms.

The tsunami of their lovemaking stilled, and only the quiet whir of the hot tub's motor and the swish and hiss of the surf were audible. That, and their breathing slowly returning to normal.

"I don't know about you, but I'm hot. I'm ready to get out of this thing and cool off," Myles commented.

"Me, too." Had she not been submerged nearly to her neck in water, she suspected she would have been covered in perspiration.

Myles climbed the steps up and over the edge of the

tub, his magnificent physique glistening like marble carved by one of the old masters. The muscles in his back and legs were sharply defined by moonlight and shadows, and she smiled in appreciation.

He turned around to help her out and caught her smiling. "What?" he asked.

"I was thinking about how you look like a statue by one of the ancient Greek sculptors."

He smiled a little. "Thanks. I try to look good for you. Your turn to come out of the hot tub looking like Venus rising from the sea."

"I don't know about that," she said doubtfully.

"You're gorgeous. I appreciate how hard you work out. It shows."

She laughed. "Good recovery. I was going to be disappointed if all those Pilates classes hadn't paid off at least a little."

"Don't knock fluffy. It would look good on you, too. You're a naturally beautiful woman, and I'll think you're sexy no matter what shape you are." He held out a hand and she used it for balance as she climbed out of the tub to join him on the patio.

She patted his cheek as she passed by him on the steps. "Nice try, Slick. But I will hold you to that."

He grinned. "Feel free."

He kissed her long and leisurely as he pushed her wet hair back off her shoulders and neck. She wrapped her arms around his hard waist and confessed, "My legs feel like noodles."

Myles grinned against her temple. "Mine, too. We must be out of practice."

Laughing, she replied, "Thank you for not following

that up with some smarmy remark about how we'll have to get back into practice."

"Ah, sweet Faith. We have the rest of our lives to practice making love. It's one of the best things about being married to you. I'm not in some panicked rush to grab all the sex I can before you dump me. I know you're mine forever, and I'm yours forever."

She tilted her chin up and smiled as his lips came down to meet hers. "I love you, Myles Colton."

"And I love you, Faith Colton."

He leaned down and she squealed in surprise as his arm swept behind her knees. He lifted her off her feet, cradling her in his arms. He turned to carry her inside, pausing only long enough for her to lean down and push open the sliding glass door for them. He strode into the bedroom and over to the bed, where he deposited her on top of the covers.

"We're all wet!" she protested.

"Then I guess we're sleeping down by the beach on towels tonight," he replied as he followed her down to the mattress.

"I like how you think. Now how about we practice some more? I think we could improve on last time if we try hard."

"Ever my perfectionist," he murmured against her belly button. His mouth slid lower, tracing a path of heat and destruction of her ability to form coherent thoughts. "Let me know when I get this just right."

"Oh, I will," she gasped, already feeling her body tightening and tingling, building toward release again. He knew her far too well, and could take her right to the edge and hold her there, teasing her until she begged for mercy. And she loved every second of it. Of course, the good news was, she knew how to do the exact same torture to him, and they had an entire week to do it to each other…

Chapter Twelve

Myles woke up with a jolt as the airplane banged down to the runway at O'Hare. Faith roused beside him, lifting her head from his shoulder and unwrapping her arm from across his waist.

This past week had been good for them. More than good. Great. They'd reconnected like they hadn't in years. He'd forgotten how much he enjoyed talking and laughing with her, sharing his thoughts about anything and everything and hearing hers. She was smart and observant, and she made him laugh at the world and at himself. Recently, he'd forgotten how to really enjoy life. But Faith had reminded him how to savor the small moments and make choices based on what he would like rather than what he should do. She was the perfect foil to his tendency to take life too seriously.

"Ready to return to the real world?" he murmured as the plane taxied toward a gate.

"No," she wailed under her breath. "Can we just stay on the plane and go back?"

"If only. I promise, it won't be so long between vacations next time."

She smiled up at him. "I'll hold you to that."

"Please do. Don't let me lose myself in my work again.

It sucked being wrapped up in legal cases 24/7. I forgot how to breathe."

"I won't ever let you suffocate again," she declared as she stood up.

He pulled their hand luggage from the overhead bin and followed her down the narrow aisle toward reality. Responsibility. Adulting.

As he moved up beside her on the jet bridge, he caught her wistful look back at the plane. "At least we get to see Jack, soon," he murmured.

That wiped the sadness from her eyes. Her whole face lit up, in fact. "Do you think he'll like the idea of having a little brother or sister?" she asked.

"I'm sure he'll let us know his opinion when we ask him," Myles replied, laughing.

"He's like his daddy. Knows exactly what he does and doesn't want."

Myles replied, smiling as they entered the terminal and headed toward customs and the baggage claim area, "He's also like his mommy. He's good at expressing his feelings."

"It's cool how he's a mix of both of us, isn't it?" she commented as they wound their way through the customs line.

"Yes. It is. But I do hope the next one is a little girl who's the spitting image of you," he replied.

She smiled warmly at him. "I wouldn't mind another little guy like Jackson, though. He's been so much fun."

"You do realize Jackson is the perfect child who was sent by the universe to trick us into having the next one, right? My mom always said Lila was such a good baby that it didn't dawn on her a terror like me could exist."

"Aww, you grew out of being a terror by the time you were twenty-two or so," Faith commented.

A crack of laughter escaped him. "You've been warned. No complaints out of you when our next kid makes you crazy."

She grinned back at him. "You forget. I'm a teacher. I've seen every kind of kid there is."

"Ooh. You did not just say that! You just jinxed us to get the one kind of kid you've never encountered before and who completely confounds you as a parent."

She laughed at that. "I'm up for it. Are you?"

"If it's our child and we can raise him or her together, I'm up for any child we get."

She stopped in the middle of the giant concourse and stood on tiptoe to kiss him soundly. "Another Colton grandbaby coming up, sir."

"Maybe not right now," he said in alarm. "We still have to sell the old house, find a new one, move, get me settled into my new job, and see if you get hired to teach at North Hills next year. That'll affect the timing of when we try to get pregnant—"

"There's my cautious lawyer."

"This isn't about caution. It's about doing all the things we agreed to in a logical and sensible order."

"Like I said. Welcome back, counselor."

He scowled, shocked to realize he didn't want to be that guy again. Not yet. He liked this other side of himself that Faith brought out much more than the lawyer side of himself. There would be time enough to shift into attorney mode come Monday morning.

They collected their bags, lugged them out to his car and made the short drive across the north side of Chicago to Evanston in blessedly light traffic. How long would it be until he wasn't tense anytime he was driving with Faith in the car? A thought of getting into another accident with her, or heaven forbid, Jackson, made his knuckles go white on the steering wheel. If nothing else, the crash had made a much more defensive driver of him. He watched every other car on the road like a hawk, now.

They pulled into his parents' driveway, and he sighed in relief, turning the steering wheel loose. Wow. His hands actually ached.

But then Jack came racing out the front door and Myles leaped out of the car to intercept his son, scoop him up and toss him high in the air.

"You grew while we were gone!" Myles exclaimed. "You're getting so tall! What did my mother feed you while we were gone!"

"Super-duper grow big pancakes!" Jack shouted.

Faith laughed as she rounded the car. "Do I get a hug?"

Jackson wiggled and Myles set him down, watching fondly as his son tore around the back end of the car to half-strangle Faith who'd knelt to meet him. As a family, they walked up the sidewalk to where Vita stood waiting in the front door. She looked highly approving of the whole show of affection that had just transpired. The Coltons were big huggers, after all.

"How was your trip, dear?" Vita asked Faith.

"Amazing. Just what the doctor ordered."

Rick just nodded and smiled at Myles, who smiled back.

Vita already had Jackson packed, and they collected his toys and suitcase and were out of the house in under a half hour. While they drove home, Faith called her mother to let Jenny know they were back. He did notice that Faith chose not to share any of the big decisions they'd made in the past week, including the fact that they were going to sell their house nearby to buy one farther away from Jenny and closer to his work and the school Faith wanted Jack to attend. She didn't mention the idea of her going back to work or of them having another child, either. Interesting.

While he would never try to drive a wedge between Faith and her mother, a little more distance, physical and emotional, between his wife and his hostile mother-in-law would not break his heart.

He drove back toward their house, and as he turned onto their street, he glanced over at Faith. Sure enough, her face had tightened and stress lines were visible at the corners of her eyes.

"It's just temporary," he murmured. "Think of it as the house being staged and ready to sell. We'll only be there long enough to get it sold, and then we'll create a new home for our family."

She reached across the center console and gave his hand a grateful squeeze.

"Hey, buddy," he said, glancing in the rearview mirror at his son. "Mommy and I have a proposition for you."

"What's that?"

Myles had to grin at the suddenly cautious tone and sharp interest in Jackson's eyes. His son had the instincts of a lawyer all the way.

"Mommy and I were thinking it might be fun to buy a new house. A bigger one close to where you'll go to school next year."

"And?" Jackson prompted.

Faith clapped a hand over her mouth not to laugh aloud, and he fought back a grin. "Well," he continued, "we were thinking that our new house should have a fenced-in backyard—"

Jackson cut him off, shouting, "So we can have a puppy!"

"Correct. But you have to promise to help take care of it, and help feed it and train it to be a good dog."

"Can it sleep in my bed with me?" Jackson asked eagerly.

Faith looked alarmed. He answered, "That'll depend on how big your bed is and how big the dog is, I suppose."

"I'll sleep in a big boy bed and everything," Jackson said eagerly. "Can we name it Ringo?"

"Ringo? When did you become a Beatles fan?"

"Huh? Like the rings around Saturn, Daddy."

"Ah. My bad."

Faith did laugh aloud, then. "Feeling old, yet?" she murmured.

He rolled his eyes as he parked the car and turned off the ignition. "Before we go into the house, Jackson, there've been a bunch of changes inside. It's painted different colors and has new furniture, and we'll have to keep it very neat and clean for the next few weeks. It's not any fun to live in, but it looks very fancy. That's so people can come look at the house and decide it would be a very nice place to live."

Jackson replied indignantly, "I watch TV with Gwamma, Daddy. I know what staging a house is."

Myles threw up his hands, laughing. "I stand corrected." As Jackson ran ahead to the front porch, he looked over at Faith wryly. "That kid's a chip off the old block."

"Your block or mine?"

"Both, I fear."

The remainder of the weekend was hectic, unpacking, entertaining Jackson without messing up the house, and trying to keep everything clean. The good news was the Realtor who came over on Sunday afternoon swore the house would sell in a week and quoted a significantly higher price than Myles had hoped for, which meant they could afford to look for exactly the kind of house Faith had always dreamed of, spacious and on a big lot where kids could run and play.

Monday morning back at the office was equally hectic. He took care of the pile of small crises that had stacked up during his week off and finished the day upstairs, meeting with Larry Whitney and Suzanne Pierce. They had the paperwork prepared for him to sign that would officially make him an associate partner of the firm.

He took a deep breath and signed the documents. Relief washed over him that had nothing to do with career success and everything to do with feeling great about knowing he could provide for his family in exactly the way he'd always dreamed of doing.

He texted Faith before he left the office to let her know the paperwork was moving on his partnership. And when he got home, she and Jackson had prepared his favorite supper, homemade lasagna, a tossed salad and garlic bread. Jackson announced proudly that he'd buttered the bread all by himself.

They ate together, and he relished being home in time to eat with them for once. As they meal concluded, he murmured to Faith to sit and that he would clear the table.

"Well, this is nice," she commented.

"And there'll be a lot more of this going forward."

"Will you tuck me into bed tonight, Daddy?"

"Sure will. After your bath, pick out a book you'd like me to read to you."

Jackson tore out of the room and Faith smirked. "You do realize he's going to pick the longest book he owns. Trade off having him read to you and you reading to him. It tires him out faster. Maybe you'll get out of there in less than an hour."

"Noted." He tossed a dish towel over his shoulder and grinned at her. "Man, this feels good."

"We were here the whole time."

"I'm glad I found you again."

He leaned down to kiss his wife and just as their lips touched, Jackson yelled from the bathroom, "My bath is ready, Daddy! Come play submarines with me!"

"Submarines?" he murmured between kisses.

"Plastic windup toys that putt-putt around the tub."

"Got it. You relax a bit while I do the bedtime routine."

"I think I may go change into something a little more comfortable," she replied suggestively.

"I like the sound of that." And when he'd duly engaged in submarine races and staged an underwater naval battle between the plastic toys, read Jackson three chapters of a book on what colonies on Mars would look like and kissed his son good-night, he made his way down the hall to his and Faith's bedroom. She was already in bed, reading a book and wearing a scandalous lace teddy.

"Why, Mrs. Colton. You look like you might freeze in that scrap of lace."

"Then why don't you come on over and warm me up?"

Stripping off his tie and unbuttoning his shirt, he placed one knee on the mattress beside her and kissed her thoroughly. "In case I haven't told you recently," he murmured into the sweet valley between her breasts, "you make me the happiest man in the world."

She tugged at his hair and pulled his mouth up to hers. "Right back atchya. Now turn out the lights and get naked before I do the job for you."

FAITH WOKE LAZILY the next morning, stretching out a few random aches from last night's lovemaking with Myles. He'd always been an athlete, and he still was insanely fit. Which meant he'd exhausted her thoroughly.

Speaking of which, she glanced over at the bedside clock and gasped in alarm. It was nearly ten a.m. *Jackson!*

She bolted out of bed and ran for the bathroom, but stopped cold when she saw the note taped to the bathroom mirror. *Jack and I got up early and went out for a guys-only breakfast. Your mom agreed to watch him this morning so you could sleep in. Oh, and I forgot to tell you. Your new car was delivered while we were on vacation. It's in the garage. Keys are on a hook by the back door.*

Wow. Myles was pulling out all the stops to be a great husband, these days. She could get used to this. She took a leisurely shower, dried her hair, and dressed. She headed out to the detached garage and squealed in delight at the brand-new minivan parked inside. It was the same color as her last one—a dark, cherry red—with even more safety features and gadgets. She spent nearly a half hour just sitting in it, familiarizing herself with the various features. When she was satisfied she knew her way around the vehicle, she drove it out of the garage.

As she backed out of the driveway, she noticed a man

lounging across the street. He was youngish, fair and lean, but that was about all she caught as she accelerated away from the house. Must be one of Hank's men keeping an eye on her and the house.

Inspired by all the great changes happening in their lives, she decided to drive over to North Hills Academy for Gifted and Talented Children. The receptionist was helpful and friendly, and gave her both an application for Jack to attend the school and an application for her to teach there. Excited at the prospect of both, she headed over to her mom's house.

It was a beautiful, sunny day, the last gasp of Indian summer before the dreary months of winter set in, and she took the opportunity to drive Jack over to their favorite park. While he ran around like a maniac with the other kids, she looked over the job application.

It was pretty straightforward, and she made mental notes of the materials she would need to collect to accompany it. Résumé, performance reviews from her last school, letters of recommendation from principals at various schools she'd substitute taught at recently, an example curriculum and teaching modules. She would send them science and math modules, not only because they were particularly strong subjects for her, but also because schools were desperate to provide top-notch STEM instruction these days.

The other kids started to drift home toward lunch, and she looked up from the paperwork in search of Jack. That was when she noticed the lean man lurking a little ways from the playground, watching the kids crawling on the equipment.

"Jack!" she called. "Time to go!"

"Aww, Mom!"

"I'm making macaroni and cheese for lunch!" It was his favorite.

Thankfully, Jackson came running without any further protest. The man moved away from the playground as Jackson raced to her, and she lost sight of him as he faded behind a stand of trees. She would have to ask Myles to thank Hank for keeping an eye on them like this.

The afternoon passed with her and Jack having to leave the house a couple of times for showings to prospective buyers. She only had time to throw together hamburgers for supper, but was delighted when Myles made it home a second day in a row to eat with her and Jackson.

"By the way," she commented near the end of the meal, "please pass my thanks to Hank and Micha for having a man keeping an eye on us."

Myles frowned a little. "Yeah, sure."

They did the dishes together and adjourned as a family to watch a little television before Jack's bedtime. They tucked him in together, and then Myles said regretfully, "I actually do have a little work to do this evening. But I'm happy to read in bed if you are. Forgive me?"

She smiled at him. "I didn't expect the vacation to last forever. I knew you would have to actually work, sometime. Speaking of which, I picked up an application to teach at North Hills today."

"That's great! Good for you."

Around eleven o'clock, Myles closed the last folder. "I'm ready to call it a night whenever you are."

She turned out the lamp on her side of the bed and met Myles in the middle of their bed in the dark. "Thanks for all your effort to make things better, Myles. I was getting really scared there, for a while, that I was losing you."

"I was scared, too. I don't know what I'd do without you and Jackson."

Chapter Thirteen

Seated in his brand-new office the next morning, Myles stared at Hank MacDonald in consternation. "You're absolutely sure? None of your guys have been tailing Faith and Jackson?"

"I'm positive."

"And it's not Micha's guys?"

"I just got off the phone with him, Myles. None of his guys are watching your family."

"Then who in the hell is tailing Faith and Jackson?" he burst out.

"I don't know. Obviously, I'll get on it right away."

"If this is the Anarchy Ink guys, I'll slap them with a restraining order so fast their heads will spin—"

"Speaking of which," Hank interrupted gently, "you're expected down in Maple Bend tomorrow when the compound is officially seized from our favorite gang. Just in case they try any stunts, the local sheriff asked us to send a lawyer down who's familiar with the case and the disposition of it."

Myles shoved a hand through his hair. If those bastards were threatening his family again, or heaven forbid, harmed Faith or Jackson, he was going to *hurt* someone. "I'll be in Maple Bend bright and early," he said grimly.

In time to have a word with the leader of the bunch and make it clear that Aric Schroder and his guys had better damned well stay away from his family. Far, far away.

As he drove home from the office, he debated with himself. Should he tell Faith or not that she hadn't seen Hank's men, but rather Anarchy Ink's men watching her and Jackson? She would freak out if he told her, but she might freak out worse if he didn't.

He hated to frighten her, but what choice did he have? He needed her to be aware of the threat and take precautions not to expose herself or Jackson to unnecessary risk.

Dammit. Just when they'd been getting past the Maple Bend trial. Things had been going so good between them. And now, this. Cursing, he pulled into the garage and walked reluctantly into the house.

He'd learned his lesson from not telling her right away about taking the Maple Bend case and didn't beat around the bush, tonight. "Hey, Jackie. Mommy and I need a minute to talk about grown-up stuff. Any chance you could go find your soccer ball? I'll kick it around with you before supper if you'd like."

"Yay!" His son tore out of the kitchen.

"What's up?" Faith asked quietly. Soberly. Man, she read him so well.

"Whoever has been tailing you isn't Hank or Micha's guys. Hank himself is going to keep an eye on you for the next few days, so if you see him, don't be alarmed. Well. Don't be alarmed by him."

She sat down at the table abruptly. The color drained from her face. His gut clenched in response. He'd known she was afraid over the weeks in hiding, but seeing her terror for himself like this was awful. Visceral. A primitive, and violent, need to defend his mate and take out whoever had scared her this bad roared through him.

Forcing himself to speak calmly, he continued, "Hank wanted me to ask you if it was the same guy you saw or if there seems to be more than one guy tailing you."

"He's lean and has light brown hair. Average height, I'd guess." She paused then asked in a rush, "Does this mean we have to go back into hiding? We were just starting to get back to normal. To be a family, again."

He shared every bit of her frustration and paced the kitchen, unable to contain it. "Hank says to go on with your regularly scheduled life. We'll catch these guys and throw the legal book at them."

Jackson tore back into the kitchen carrying a soccer ball, and as much as he wanted to stay and comfort Faith, fatherhood called. He went outside into their tiny backyard and kicked around the soccer ball with Jack until Faith called out, "Supper's ready!"

She was quiet over the meal, and he carried the conversation with Jack, interviewing his son on anything he might want in a new house. The boy wasn't too picky beyond a backyard for a dog and his own bedroom… with bunk beds.

Myles shooed Faith out of the kitchen, and he did the dishes. Maybe some time hanging out with Jack would settle her a little. But as soon as the boy was tucked into bed, she came downstairs and nervously closed all the curtains and blinds in the living room.

"I doubt they're watching us right now," he said low so Jack wouldn't hear them. "We're home for the night, and I'm here. In case you hadn't noticed, I'm a big, athletic guy. I might not win against them in a fight, but I'd be hard to take down and deal enough collateral damage to give them pause."

She shuddered, an all over body shiver, and she'd gone pale again. "Why is this happening to us?"

"Come here, baby." He held out an inviting arm, and she settled beside him on the couch, plastered against his side. He turned on a random television show on a home improvement channel that Faith watched sometimes.

Gradually, she relaxed against his side. But it took an entire home renovation and sale for a massive profit to do the job.

"I'm sorry I had to be the bearer of bad news," he murmured, "but I did promise you there would be no more secrets between us."

"I appreciate it. Not the bad news, but the honesty."

"How was your day otherwise?" he asked.

"Not bad. North Hills Academy called and they want to interview me."

"That's fantastic!" he exclaimed. "When's the interview?"

"Day after tomorrow."

"Wow. That's fast. Good thing you already worked up the example teaching modules, then."

"That's me. Ms. Preparedness."

"Don't knock it. My mom always says an ounce of prevention is worth a pound of cure."

She smiled ruefully. "My mom was more to the point. She always told me not to be stupid like my father."

He recalled Faith's tough teen years when her parents were estranged and fought bitterly whenever they were together. He hugged her a little tighter and turned to kiss her. "I love you, Faith. I'll always be there for you."

She kissed him back, seeking comfort and reassurance, which he was glad to share with her.

"Bed?" he mumbled against her delicious lips.

"Uh-huh," she mumbled back.

They headed upstairs, and because it was early and Jack had gone to bed recently, made love as quietly as possible. When they'd fallen back to the pillows breathing hard, he leaned over to murmur, "That reminded me of sneaking sex in your mom's house when we used to come home from college to visit her."

Faith giggled. "It reminded me of when we used to sneak up to your bedroom in your folks' house to make out."

"Note to self—the master bedroom in the new place has to be on the other side of the house from the kids' bedrooms."

"Definitely. Speaking of which, will you have time in the next few days to do a little house hunting? The Realtor thinks we're going to have a couple of offers come in on this house any minute. She advised me to get rolling with finding a new place so we don't end up homeless."

"We'll never be homeless. Not with your mom and my folks rattling around in big houses with lots of extra room."

"You know what I mean."

"I have to go to Maple Bend tomorrow to supervise the property seizure. But day after tomorrow? What time is your interview with the school?"

"Eleven a.m."

"How about after that? Maybe we can do lunch and then meet the Realtor? I'll take the afternoon off."

"Wow. You get afternoons off now?"

"I'm almost officially a partner, baby."

"Well, okay then." She rolled over smiling and sprawled on top of him, kissing him until it became clear they weren't going to be sleeping for a while, still.

FAITH STAYED HOME the next day, not only because she hated the idea of being stalked, but also because she actually had a lot to do before her job interview. She set up Jack with a movie marathon and worked at the kitchen table until she perfected her presentation. Then, she flopped onto the living room floor with Jackson and watched movies for the rest of the afternoon.

Before supper, she carried a bag of trash out to the garage and was jumpy as heck, her head on a swivel. She should've carried a baseball bat out here with her, for crying out loud. She felt naked and exposed in the gathering dusk.

As she turned to head for the house, she spied a movement in the cluster of small pine trees that formed the corner between their yard and the next door neighbor's. Was that a man in there? Oh, God. Terror roared through her until she could hardly breathe.

She cowered in the doorway of the garage, shaking with fear, eyeing the long walk to the back door of the house with deep alarm. Where was Hank? No doubt he was parked out front, across the street. She swore as she remembered she'd left her cell phone on the kitchen counter. Fat lot of good it did her there, darn it. Maybe she could scream for help. But at this time of day, the street was busy and Hank probably wouldn't hear her. She was on her own.

She eyed the trees warily. The clustered pines with their thick, fluffy branches and deep shadows between them were perfect for concealing a human. If she squinted and stared hard, she could just make out a human-shaped shadow standing in the midst of the trees, silently staring at her house.

And then the silhouette moved. The man had shifted weight. No doubt about it. That was a man out there!

Adrenaline screamed through her veins. Her whole body went hot and trembled with need to flee as fast and as far as she could run. But she couldn't leave Jack. She would never abandon her son. She had to get to him. Even if that meant sprinting for the house in utter terror.

All at once, something inside her cracked.

She was so sick of this! She just wanted her life back. Was that too much to ask? Her terror shattered and fell away, replaced by rage. It flowed through her sharp and bright. She'd had it with cowering in the shadows hiding from these jerks. And nobody—*nobody*—was messing with her child.

She looked around quickly in the garage and scooped up one of Myles's golf clubs, a nice, heavy iron with a long shaft. Cocking it back like a baseball bat, she charged out of the garage and stormed over toward the stand of pine trees furiously.

"Hey! You! Quit following me and my family! You hear me? You mess with me or my son, and I'll take you out! You hear me? I'll kill you. And when I'm done with you, if you're still alive, my husband is a lawyer and will put you away for a good long time! Get out of here and don't come back!"

Without warning, a tabby cat shot out of the bushes near the trees.

She lurched violently, brandishing the golf club in terror, ready to clobber anything or anyone who got near her.

The cat raced across the neighbor's yard with a yowl.

The noise shocked her out of her unreasoning rage. She stared as the terrified cat tore around the corner of the neighbor's house and disappeared. Faith burst out laughing. Welp, she'd sure told off that cat but good.

Shaking her head at her foolishness, she headed back to the house and jogged up the steps. As she turned in the kitchen to close the back door, though, she happened to glance toward the stand of fluffy pines, and darned if she didn't see a man-size silhouette fade back farther into the shadows of the trees.

Well, hell. Maybe she wasn't crazy after all.

And just like that, the fear was back, crawling up her spine, lizard-like, with sharp nails that dug into her flesh and sent painful chills tingling through her entire body and across her scalp.

She agonized over whether or not to pull down the blind over the window behind her kitchen sink. If she closed it, nobody outside could see in. But that man could also approach her home unseen. Frozen in indecision, she stared at the window for far too long.

"Mom! I can't find the next movie!"

She leaned the golf club by the back door and hurried into the living room to queue up the next movie for Jack.

Sitting down on the sofa behind him, she stared sightlessly at the television screen, her mind racing. That had definitely been a man in the trees. What was she supposed to do now? Call the police? Call Myles? She pulled out her phone and texted Hank's number. *I saw a man in the trees at the back of our yard. Was that you?*

Hank's response was immediate. *Stay inside. Lock your doors. I'll check it out. Am across the street.*

God bless him. She waited, tense, for about ten minutes before her phone beeped another incoming text from Hank. All clear.

Surely she hadn't imagined that silhouette. She'd seen him, clear as a bell, lurking in those trees. In spite of that cat, the shadow had definitely been man-size. She wasn't crazy, darn it.

But she was jumpy and tight until she heard Myles's car pull into the driveway as she was tucking Jack into bed. She hurried downstairs to meet him.

"How was your day, honey?" he asked cheerfully as he came in the back door.

"Scary. I saw a man in the pine trees at the back of our yard. I texted Hank and he checked it out. He didn't find anyone, but I'm dead sure of what I saw. I'm not imagining things!"

Myles swore quietly and wrapped her in a tight hug.

"I swear. I'm not making this up."

"I believe you, sweetheart."

"I just tucked Jack in. If you want to go up and say good-night to him, I'll warm up some food for you."

Myles nodded and left the room. She scooped up a serving of the chicken potpie she'd made and heated it in the microwave. She set it on the table and sat down to wait for Myles.

He returned in a few minutes and sat down with her. "While I was in Maple Bend today, I had a little conversation with Aric Schroder. I explained to him very politely what would happen if any of his guys come anywhere near you again. He made it clear to me that he fully understands and will see to it his crew stays out of the Chicago area entirely. You shouldn't have any more trouble with them. The guy in the trees today was undoubtedly the last of it. Schroder has called off his goons. Their plan is to leave this part of the country entirely. I overheard a couple of Schroder's guys talking about Idaho, in fact."

"Poor Idaho."

"I'll alert the authorities out there to keep an eye on the Anarchy Ink crew." He reached across the table to squeeze her hand. "You're safe, now, Faith."

She heard his words and wished more than anything that they were true. But something deep in her gut still clenched with terror. Call it intuition, or maybe pure paranoia, but she didn't feel safe. Not yet.

MYLES LAY IN BED, staring at the ceiling, listening to his wife sleep fitfully. Her breathing hitched and sped up frantically, then slowed down, only to race in panic again. He considered waking her from the troubled dreams obviously gripping her, but figured she would rather sleep badly than not at all, especially with her big interview tomorrow.

Had he done enough to keep his family safe? Would Schroder follow through, move his crew out of state and never darken their doorstep again, or was he being naive to take the man at his word?

Schroder had been surly with him but had snarled that his guys didn't attack women and children. At least not intentionally. There was the whole bit about his guys starting the fire that had killed four people, including two women and a child.

This morning, he'd been inclined to believe the guy. Schroder was a borderline crackpot and came across as close to homicidal much of the time, but he seemed to have good control of his men.

Case in point, the moment the verdict had been handed down in court, Aric had turned around and said something quietly to his men seated in the first row of the gallery behind him. The whole bunch had instantly stopped all their staring and glaring to scare the jurors and shifted one hundred percent into looking contrite and remorseful. The posturing had been fully orchestrated and controlled by Schroder.

No doubt about it, though, he purely hated entrusting his family's safety to a man like Aric Schroder.

He tossed and turned through much of the night until Faith turned in her sleep and sprawled across his chest. The weight of her body, her warmth, and the clean scent of her hair finally soothed him enough that he drifted off and got a few hours of decent rest before his alarm clock went off.

"What time is it?" Faith mumbled in the predawn darkness.

"It's early. I'm going in to work to get in a few extra hours before I take the afternoon off with you. Go back to sleep. Your alarm isn't set to go off for a while." He kissed her gently, loving the warm, sweet scent of her.

He tiptoed around in the dark, showering, shaving quietly, dressing and slipping out of the bedroom. He brewed himself a quick cup of coffee, grabbed a couple of the blueberry muffins Faith had baked yesterday and headed out.

Perplexed, he spied his 3-iron leaning by the back door. How did that get there? Faith must have brought it in. Was she really that terrified? Stricken, he left the golf club where it was and headed for the garage. He, too, took a hard look at the pine trees where Faith had spotted the guy yesterday. The branches were still and dark now, undisturbed by any human shapes.

Her paranoia was rubbing off on him, now. He hated

all of this nervousness and worry for his family. Faith had been right all along. It had been a terrible mistake to take the Maple Bend case. He spent the entire drive to work berating himself for being a fool.

But then, he parked in his new reserved parking space, said hello to the half-dozen junior associates already hard at work at their desks and headed into his new office with a window. Waiting on his desk was an envelope holding the receipt for a payment to him in the sum of one million dollars.

He stared, stunned. He'd never seen such a large number in his life. At least not on a check with his name on it. The firm had already withdrawn and paid his federal income taxes on the amount, and as they'd agreed yesterday, subtracted the quarter-million-dollar buy-in fee to the firm. The remainder, just shy of five hundred thousand dollars, had been deposited in his checking account overnight.

Wow. That would make for a huge down payment on their dream home.

Maybe it hadn't been that big a mistake, after all, to take the Maple Bend case.

FAITH WAS GROGGY when she woke up, as if she'd barely slept at all and hadn't gotten the solid eight hours of sleep that she had. She slammed back a big cup of coffee, fed Jackson breakfast and dropped him off at her mom's house early, then headed for a coffee shop across the street from North Hills Academy to do her final rehearsal for the job interview.

She'd been there about a half hour when she happened to glance out the front window. She stared through the glass in shock. There he was again. The lean, light-haired guy.

She swore under her breath and dug in her purse, snatching out her phone to take a picture of the guy to prove to Myles and Hank that she wasn't making up being tailed. But by the time she pulled up her camera app and pointed her phone at the window, the guy was gone. Had he even really been there? Or was she just being paranoid?

As she did her final preparations for her interview, she kept looking outside, but she never saw the guy again.

The job interview went better than she could've hoped for, and she walked away excited that she might actually have landed a job at the prestigious school.

She kept an eagle eye out as she made the short drive to a cute diner close to Myles's office. Nobody seemed to be tailing her, and she saw no sign of the light-haired guy.

She must have imagined seeing him. In her anxiety over the interview, her mind had played a trick on her. Either that, or some other random guy of the right build and coloring had walked by. She'd been looking through a dirty window and across a busy street, after all. And Myles said the leader of Anarchy Ink had promised to call off his crew. It was no secret that she was prone to being a bit nervous and fearful.

She parked her car and walked to the diner without looking over her shoulder once and without scanning the crowded sidewalks at all. Proud of herself for getting control of her paranoia, she sat down across from Myles and told him all about the interview, leaving out her imagining bad guys where there were none.

As the plates were cleared away and cups of coffee set in their place, Myles smiled expectantly and passed her an envelope. "This was waiting for me on my desk this morning when I got to work."

She opened it and stared in disbelief at the receipt for his bonus. "Ohmigosh, Myles. You did it. Everything you've ever dreamed of is coming true."

He reached across the table and took her hand in his. "Sweetheart, everything I ever dreamed of came true when you agreed to marry me and the day Jackson was born. There could be no zeroes at all on that check, and I would still be a happy man whose fondest dreams have all come true."

She smiled softly at him, and then teased, "Yes, but all those zeroes don't hurt one bit."

"No, they don't. What say we go find ourselves the house of your dreams?"

"The house of *our* dreams."

Everything they'd ever worked for was finally coming together. She ought to be ecstatic, but as they stepped outside, a cloud passed over the sun and an abrupt shadow darkened the day. A frisson of premonition whispered across her skin, raising goose bumps on her arms and tightening her stomach muscles.

Everything was too good. Too perfect. Something was about to go terribly wrong, and no matter how hard she tried, she couldn't see it coming. But she felt it in her bones.

As they climbed into Myles's car to go meet the Realtor, she commented, "This morning, I thought I spotted the guy from yesterday standing outside the coffee shop. I tried to take a picture of him, but he disappeared before I could get my camera out."

Myles jolted. "Did you tell Hank?"

"No. He disappeared before I could pull out my cell

phone to take a picture of him, and I figured it was just me being paranoid." She refrained from mentioning that it was his fault she was still being followed. But it was there in the air between them.

He swore quietly and pulled out his cell phone, texting quickly, striking the face of the phone angrily. After a few seconds, his phone buzzed an incoming response. Myles announced grimly, "Hank's going to have a guy follow you around the clock until we catch this joker. I've had it with you being harassed like this. I don't want to see fear in your eyes ever again, dammit."

She reached across the car and laid her hand over his in gratitude. "Thank you for taking such good care of us."

"I haven't been doing a very good job of it recently. But I'll stake you out myself, if I have to, until we catch this bastard."

"I'm sure Hank's guy will handle it. I met a bunch of his and Micha's guys when we were at the penthouse, and they all seemed extremely competent. They told me about their backgrounds, but I didn't understand any of it past the words *special forces* and *commandos*."

"Good." He threw his car into gear and pulled out into traffic. "This crap ends now."

Chapter Fourteen

"This is the one," Myles announced, standing in the middle of the spacious breakfast nook. The floor-to-ceiling windows looked out on a huge fenced backyard with plenty of room for kids and puppies to play and grow up.

The rambling home was over a hundred years old but had been completely renovated recently. It was bright and spacious but also warm and friendly. It was exactly the kind of place he wanted to raise his children in.

"I love it, Myles, but it's pretty expensive. Can we afford this?"

"No problem. Even if you choose not to go back to work, we'd be fine on just my salary."

"I don't want you to have to work sixteen hours a day to pay for this. I'd rather have less house and more time with you."

He swept her up in a hug. "I'm not ever taking a chance with losing you again. No more eighty-or hundred-hour work weeks for me." He especially liked the gated entrance to this neighborhood and the full-time security guards who manned the gate and patrolled the neighborhood. He couldn't promise never to upset a legal adversary enough that his family was jeopardized.

"Well," she said slowly, "if you think we can afford

this, I'm on board. This place is perfect for us. A perfect blend of old and new, casual and formal. Let's do it."

She kissed him soundly, and he kissed her back to seal the deal. Her mouth was soft and warm and sexy against his. He couldn't wait to christen this house with her, alone in their master suite on the opposite side of the house from Jack's bedroom. The exultation filling him was hard to contain. Life was coming up roses in every possible way for them.

"Where do you suppose that Realtor has gotten off to?" he asked, reluctantly peeling his mouth away from hers.

Faith giggled. "I think she beat a discreet retreat when we started kissing."

"Let's go find her and get an offer started."

"This is so exciting!" she burst out.

"Do you think Jack will like it?" he mused.

"One word—puppy."

He laughed. "Well, there is that."

They followed the Realtor back to her office to fill out paperwork for submitting the offer, and he read the fine print carefully. He wasn't a real estate lawyer, but he'd studied enough contract law in law school to understand most of what he read.

It was late afternoon by the time they left the Realtor's office, their fingers crossed for a quick acceptance of their offer. It was too late for him to go back to the office and put in a few hours of work tonight. Besides, this was a special day, and he wanted to spend it with his wife.

He glanced over at Faith, glowing with excitement in the car beside him. "What say you and I go out for a celebratory supper? Just the two of us. I still owe you a date night, I believe."

"You just bought us the house of our dreams. I'm willing to let a missed date night slide."

He grinned at her. "Fine. I admit to being selfish. Sometimes, I like having you all to myself for a few hours. And Jackson adores your mother. He won't mind getting spoiled rotten by her for a little while more."

"Let me give her a call and make sure it's all right." Faith reached for her cell phone.

He snorted. It wasn't as if Jenny did anything else with her life. She had no hobbies, no volunteer work, no friends to speak of. The woman sat in her perfect house with its perfect furniture and lived her perfectly empty life.

He would feel sorry for her if she wasn't so nasty to him most of the time. But the woman seemed never to have forgiven him for taking Faith away from her. At least he and Faith had given Jenny a grandson to dote over.

Faith disconnected the call. "Mom says it's fine for us to leave Jack with her for the evening. She told us to have a good time."

"Did you tell her about the new house?"

Faith winced. "I thought I would wait until it's a done deal. That way if she throws a hissy fit that we're moving too far away from her, there won't be anything we can do about it."

"Don't you mean when she throws a hissy fit?" he replied dryly.

Faith rolled her eyes. "She means well."

"Sure, she does," he commented sarcastically.

They drove in silence for a bit until Faith asked, "Where are we going?"

"I thought we might try to get a table at True, tonight." His cousin Tatum on the new side of the family owned the upscale farm-to-table restaurant that was the talk of Chicago. She swore that there was always room for family in her restaurant, but apparently it was becoming harder and harder to get a reservation to eat there. He and Faith hadn't been there since shortly after the place had shut down over a drug bust of a few kitchen staff. It had just been starting back up the last time they went, and the dining room had been half empty.

"Myles! We only go there for special occasions!"

"Does it or does it not serve your favorite food in all of Chicago?"

"But it's expensive."

"Honey, we can go to it on more than just special occasions now. And besides, we just found our forever home. I'd say that's a special occasion deserving of proper celebration."

"We don't know if we got the house—"

"There have been no other offers, and the bid we put in was extremely competitive. They'll accept our offer. Worst case, they'll come back with a reasonable counterbid."

"I hope so," she said fervently. "It's only a few blocks from North Hills Academy. In nice weather, Jack and I can walk there. Assuming he gets in and assuming they hire me."

Myles laughed. "Jack is the smartest four-year-old I know."

"He's the only four-year-old you know."

"Name me any eight-year-olds you taught who are smarter than him."

She shrugged. "Point taken."

They got to the trendy restaurant before the main dinner crowd hit and were able to get a table in spite of not having a reservation. His cousin Tatum came out of the kitchen herself to take their orders, in fact. Not that she gave them much choice in what they ate. She promised to whip up something special for them herself and disappeared into the kitchen.

They ate slowly, savoring a salad course of fresh greens and savory herbs, followed by fresh trout in a delicate butter sauce. An entire course of roasted root vegetables and roasted apples came out, and then slices of aged beef tenderloin so tender they could be cut with a fork were served.

As their dinner plates were finally being taken away, his cell phone vibrated. He glanced at the caller and gulped. "It's the Realtor," he told Faith.

"Well, pick it up! See what she has to say!"

Grinning at her impatience, he took the call. "Hello, this is Myles Colton."

"Good evening, owner of a new house," the Realtor said gaily.

"For real?" he blurted.

"What? What?" Faith asked, practically bouncing in her seat as the Realtor confirmed that the seller had accepted their offer.

Relishing torturing his wife just a little, he kept a straight face until he got off the call. Then he looked up at her and said, "Well, we got the house."

"Ohmigosh!" Faith launched herself out of her chair and came around the table to kiss him enthusiastically.

"See? We weren't wrong to treat ourselves to a celebration dinner."

She sat back down, grinning from ear to ear. He loved seeing her so happy.

"Shall we go for dessert?" he asked. "To cap off a perfect day?"

"I like the way you think."

He grinned. "Let me guess. The chocolate mousse?"

They took their time enjoying the confection, which was so airy and silky it almost evaporated in their mouths. How Tatum did that with chocolate and cream and eggs was beyond him, but he savored every mouthful nearly as much as his chocoholic wife did.

Finally, stuffed to the gills, they left the restaurant to head home. He'd been careful not to drink too much wine to drive safely, but he still felt relaxed and expansive as he guided the car toward Evanston.

As they turned onto Jenny Romans's street, Faith asked, "Should we tell Jack tonight that he's getting his puppy?"

Myles shrugged. "If he's not already asleep. Realizing, of course, that he'll be awake another two hours once we give him the news."

"I'm okay with that. It's a special day for us. It should be special for him, too."

He turned into his mother-in-law's driveway and frowned. "What on earth?"

The front door was open. Light spilled from the foyer across the front porch and onto the front lawn.

"Do you suppose they're waiting for us?" Faith asked, sounding startled.

It was completely unlike his mother-in-law to wait to welcome them home. Unless Jack had instigated some sort of doorway vigil. The little tyke was wildly intuitive at times and might have sensed they would have good news for him. Not to mention, Jack knew they'd spent the afternoon out looking at houses. Although the boy wasn't particularly interested in the new house, he was obsessed with the new puppy that would come with it.

Myles pulled his car around the circle drive in front of the house and got out. Faith had already jumped out by the time he got to her side of the car and was hurrying up the front steps. He followed along behind her, vaguely alarmed. It was a complete anomaly for Jenny to leave her front door open for any reason. The mosquitoes that would get into the house were reason enough for her to never do something like this.

Faith disappeared inside in front of him.

Her scream pierced the night, and he bolted forward in panic.

Sprawled on the white marble floor of the foyer with a small pool of blood under her head was Jenny Romans. The woman looked unconscious as Faith knelt and shook her mother's shoulder.

"Does she have a pulse?" he asked tersely, fumbling for his cell phone.

"I don't know." Faith jammed her fingers under her mother's throat as he jabbed 911 on his phone.

"Nine-one-one. What's your emergency?"

"I need an ambulance." He rattled off his mother-in-law's address and then elaborated, "My mother-in-law is lying on her foyer floor with the front door open."

Faith stated, "She's got a pulse."

He continued to the operator, "She's alive but unconscious. Hit her head. There's a lot of blood."

"You said the front door is open, sir. Was the house broken into?"

Holy crap. He hadn't even thought about that. "Uh, I don't know." And then it hit him. *Jack*.

"Wait a minute. My son is upstairs asleep."

Myles bolted up the stairs, taking them two at a time, and sprinted down the long hall to Jack's bedroom. He burst into the room and breathed a sigh of relief when he spied a lump under the blankets.

"He's in his bed—"

Myles stepped forward to wake Jack and lurched. He wasn't in his bed. He reached for the comforter and tore it back. A couple of pillows were turned sideways to look like his son. What the hell?

He swore. "My son's not in his bed. This is a big house. It'll take a minute to find him."

"I'll stay on the line with you, sir. See if you can spot anything missing. Any other signs of a break-in or foul play besides your mother-in-law's injuries. I've dispatched police to your location, as well. They should arrive in the next four to five minutes."

"Um, okay."

He poked his head into Jenny's bedroom. On rare occasions, Jack had nightmares and tended to crawl into bed with whatever adult was watching him. Jenny's bed was undisturbed, neatly made.

He checked the bedroom he and Faith usually slept in as well, but that bed was also unoccupied.

"Faith!" he yelled down the stairs. "Where's Jack?"

"He's not in his room?"

"No!"

"I'm putting pressure on my mom's head where she hit it. It's still bleeding a lot, so I can't move. Come look for Jack down here. He's probably asleep in front of the TV."

Myles tore down the stairs, a sick feeling settling in the pit of his stomach. Something very, very bad was happening here. He just didn't know what it was yet.

He raced past Faith and her mother toward the back of the house. "Jack!" he called. "Where are you, son?"

He burst into the family room, and saw a blanket lying on the floor in front of the sofa. An abandoned pillow lay on one end of the big couch, as if Jack had been tucked in there, watching television. But he wasn't in the room now.

Running frantically, Myles tore into the kitchen. No Jack.

Dining room. Empty.

In desperation as he exhausted places in the house where Jack could be, he bolted out into the backyard. It was dark and silent. There was no sign of movement out here. No sign of Jack at all.

He remembered the cell phone in his hand and shouted at the 911 operator, "My son is missing! He's four years old and there's no sign of him. Send *all* the police. Put out an alert for him!"

"What's your son's name, sir?"

"Jackson Colton."

"What does he look like?"

"He's blond. Light green eyes. He's three-and-a-half-feet tall and I think he weighs about forty pounds."

"What was he wearing when you last saw him?"

"I don't know. He could be wearing blue pajamas with rocket ships on them." He sprinted for the foyer and Faith. A sound of sirens was just becoming audible in the distance.

"Faith. What clothes was Jack wearing when you brought him over here today?"

"Why? What's wrong? Where's Jack?"

"His clothes, Faith," he said forcefully, cutting through her burgeoning panic.

"Um, blue jeans and a red T-shirt."

He relayed that to the 911 operator.

"The police and an ambulance should be there momentarily, Mr. Colton. Have you checked in front of the house? Up and down the street? It's possible he wandered out the front door."

"He's a bright kid. He wouldn't wander away. Particularly if his grandmother was hurt."

"Did he go to a neighbor's house for help?" the operator asked.

That gave him pause. "Possibly."

"Why don't you check with the neighbors, sir, while you wait for the police to arrive."

He raced toward the front door and Faith called after him, "Where are you going? What's happening?"

He couldn't tell her yet. He had to fix this. Had to find his boy. If he told her Jackson was missing, Faith would lose her mind. And right now, he needed to focus all his efforts on finding his son while she dealt with her mother's injury.

He sprinted to the nearest house. It was agonizing waiting for someone to come to the door to answer the ring, and he shifted his weight from foot to foot, chanting, "Be here, be here, be here."

A silver-haired man came to the front door. "Can I help you?" he asked cautiously.

"I'm Jenny Romans's son-in-law. There's been an accident at her house. She fell and hit her head while babysitting my four-year-old son. Jackson isn't in the house right now, and we thought he might have run to a neighbor's house for help. You haven't seen him by any chance, have you?"

"No." The man turned to call over his shoulder, "Sharla!"

An attractive gray-haired woman came into the entry.

The man quickly explained what had happened, and she volunteered to call all the neighbors and ask if Jackson Colton had come over to their house for help.

After blurting a quick thanks, Myles headed back out to the sidewalk. Lord, it was dark outside. If Jackson was out here alone, he would be cold and scared.

Myles ran faster than he'd ever run before, heading up the street, then down it, shouting Jackson's name. With every step, every shout of Jack's name, the knot in Myles's stomach pulled tighter. The panic got so bad he finally had to stop and catch his breath as he hyperventilated.

Coherent thought wasn't even possible. His entire being screamed with need to find Jackson. That single drive overwhelmed everything else. *Everything else.*

But there was no sign of his son.

Jackson was gone.

Chapter Fifteen

Faith looked up gratefully as a pair of paramedics burst into the house through the open front door. One of them demanded, "What happened, ma'am?"

"I don't know. She was like this when we got home. Unconscious with a pool of blood under her head."

The second paramedic looked at Jenny's position in the middle of the foyer. "Doesn't look like she fell down the stairs."

Faith frowned. Now that he mentioned it, the guy was right. Her mother was at least fifteen feet from the stairs and off to one side far enough that she couldn't have possibly tumbled down the stairs and landed here. Weird.

The first paramedic shoved her aside gently to examine her mother. "Trauma on the back of the patient's head. Bleeding from a deep cut. Swelling is forming around the point of impact. Looks like it'll need stitches. Give me a sterile pad."

The second medic ripped open a paper packet and passed over a large gauze pad, which the first guy pressed directly onto the wound as he continued talking. "Possible shock. Let's get her to the ambulance and start a saline drip. She'll need an X-ray to check for skull fracture. Bring the gurney."

The second guy jogged outside and returned in a few seconds with a rolling gurney.

Faith watched anxiously as the two men efficiently lifted her mother onto the wheeled bed. Her mother was pale, her skin clammy, and she didn't even move, let alone show any signs of consciousness. What on earth had happened to her?

As the men lifted the bed up and long, wheeled legs extended, Faith gripped her mother's hand tightly and walked along beside the gurney, talking encouragingly. "You're going to be fine, Mom. These men are taking you to the hospital, and they'll get you fixed right up. When you wake up, I'll be there, and you can tell me how you got knocked out. I love you. Be strong, Mom—"

The men pushed the gurney into the ambulance quickly, leaving her standing behind the vehicle, unsure of what to do next. "Should I come along?" she asked. "Or, I don't know. Follow you?"

"Do you have your mother's identification and medical information?" the guy climbing out the back and heading for the driver's door asked.

"Um, I can get it. I'll go inside and find her purse—"

"We need to roll. If you'll meet us at the St. Francis Hospital's emergency room with that information, it'll help the admissions folks."

"Okay. I'll run inside and find her purse and meet you there."

The paramedic nodded and hopped in the truck. She watched the vehicle pull out of the circular drive and started to turn for the house when she saw Myles coming up the driveway.

Oh, God. That was right. Jackson wasn't in the house. She searched for his little silhouette beside his father's larger one but didn't spot him. Although, knowing Myles, he'd arranged for whatever neighbor Jackson had run to for help to babysit their son so they could go to the hospital with her mother.

As Myles drew near, she said quickly, "If you'll get the car, I'll run inside and get my mother's purse and then we can go to—"

"Faith," he interrupted her.

"We need to take my mother's insurance information to the hospital—"

"Faith," he interrupted more strongly.

"What?" she snapped, turning around on the front steps to face him.

"Jackson is missing."

Her legs threatened to buckle and she grabbed at the porch column beside her. "Missing? What do you mean, missing?" Blank denial filled her mind with a white fog that defied comprehension of the words Myles was saying.

"We don't know where he is."

"What do you mean we don't know where he is?" Her voice rose with every word. "He went to a neighbor's house for help when my mom fell—"

"None of the neighbors have seen him. In fact, most of them are out looking for him right now. And the police are looking, too. They told me to come back here and wait with you. They're sending someone to question us."

"About what?" Even to her own ears, her voice sounded perilously close to a screech.

"About where Jackson might be."

"He should be here! He knows not to go running off!" She was starting to shake, an allover quaking that made breathing nearly impossible. Her legs started to go out from under her.

Myles leaped forward, catching her and hauling her up against his chest. But the constriction of his arms around her was too much. She freaked out, struggling and hitting at him to let her go. She was screaming, now. "Where's Jackson, Myles? Where's my baby?"

"Let's go inside."

"You said Jack's not in the house!"

"No, he's not. But let's search it one more time, just to be sure."

She ripped free of him and sprinted into the house, determined to find her son. He *had* to be here somewhere. It simply wasn't conceivable that he wasn't here. He *must* be hiding.

Going room to room, she searched every nook and cranny that a four-year-old boy might possibly squeeze himself into. Truth be told, she searched every nook and cranny a mouse could squeeze into.

Myles worked beside her in grim silence, as if he already knew what the outcome of this search would be. But she kept at it doggedly. He had to be here, somewhere. He *had* to.

But he wasn't.

"This is because of your case, isn't it?" she accused Myles.

His face was already pale but went a ghastly shade of gray at her words.

She spun away from him angrily, starting yet another fruitless search of the house. She was too panicked to sit still.

She was just heading downstairs to search there when

a half-dozen police officers in uniforms and several in street clothes piled into the foyer.

"Mr. and Mrs. Colton? I'm Detective Caruso. I understand your son is missing under suspicious circumstances."

Faith snapped, "If you call coming home to my mother's house and finding the front door wide open and my mom unconscious in a pool of blood suspicious, then yes."

The man took her attack calmly and replied, "Can you tell us anything about how your mother came to be unconscious on the floor?"

Faith frowned. "The paramedics said she didn't fall down the stairs."

"Can you show me exactly where she was lying? I mean, I see the pool of blood. That was where her head was, right? Where was her body?"

Faith quickly described where her mother had been sprawled awkwardly, and the detective looked around the foyer in confusion. He asked one of the other men in a civilian suit, "Do you see anything she could've hit her head on?"

"Nope."

"Where was the wound on your mother's head, ma'am?"

"She was bleeding from the back of her head, here." She touched the middle of the back of her head a couple of inches above the nape of her own neck.

Detective Caruso and the second detective traded frowns. "What?" Faith demanded quickly.

Caruso ignored her, telling the second man, "Call the ER and get confirmation from the attending physician."

The second man moved off to one side and started talking into his cell phone.

"What is going on?" Myles demanded. "Where's my son?"

"We've got a dozen men out searching the neighborhood and more on the way. It appears at least a dozen of your neighbors are also out searching for the boy. He's too young to have gone far. I'm sure we'll find him before long," the detective said soothingly.

"And if the search party doesn't find him?" Myles demanded.

Faith looked at her husband in horror. "What are you suggesting?" That blank wall of denial was dropping over her brain, again.

"Detective, I'm an attorney," Myles said tersely. "I just tried a huge fraud case against a bunch called Anarchy Ink, and I took them to the cleaners. They're a weapons smuggling and sales group out of—"

"I know who they are," Caruso interrupted.

Myles nodded. "They've intimidated jurors and threatened lawyers in the past. Their leader threatened my wife and son at the beginning of the trial. We were in a car accident that might have been somebody hitting us intentionally. Is it possible that they..."

He trailed off, and Faith's hyper-alert imagination filled in the rest.

"Oh my God," she wailed. "They've taken Jackson? Myles! My baby! *What have you done?*"

"Now, ma'am. Don't be jumping to any conclusions. It's far too early to tell what happened here."

"My. Son. Is. Missing." She ground out the words from between clenched teeth. "Maybe you should be jumping to conclusions faster."

"We're already treating this as a missing person's case. We've waived the twenty-four-hour waiting period, given the child's age and the circumstances of the crime scene. An Amber Alert will be issued shortly."

"*Crime* scene?" she echoed. "Just what do you think happened here?"

"It appears someone may have entered your mother's home. Possibly assaulted her. Possibly took the child."

Faith's legs did collapse then, and she sank to the cold marble floor in agony. An urge to tear at her hair nearly overcame her as scream upon scream upon scream stacked up in her chest, demanding to be let out.

Myles knelt beside her. "You've got to be strong, Faith. Hold it together for Jackson. We need to help the police figure out what happened."

His words registered vaguely beneath the deafening din inside her skull. It took a moment for her to make sense of their meaning, but belatedly she nodded. He lifted her to her feet, and she let him, but her body felt disconnected from her brain, a limp rag doll thing that was only the vessel for her breaking heart.

Not her baby. Not bright, funny, loving Jackson.

"He's a baby," she moaned. "Just a baby."

"We'll find him. I swear. We'll find him," Myles groaned low.

"You can't promise that, and you know it." Unreasoning rage at him exploded in her gut. Although, maybe it wasn't so unreasoning after all. She turned to glare at Myles. "This is your fault. You did this to our son."

"What?" Myles looked stricken as what little blood that remained in his face drained out, leaving him a ghostly white.

"You took the Anarchy Ink case. You knew they would come after us. And you took the case anyway. This. Is.

Your. Fault." She emphasized her words with pokes in his chest with her accusing finger.

"Ma'am. Please. Now is not the time for recriminations," Caruso said. "We need to focus all our energy on figuring out what happened and finding your son." She glared at the detective, not caring if he was right. Her rage was so overpowering it was a miracle she didn't scratch Myles's eyes out.

"I'll have the Chicago PD gang unit contact their Anarchy Ink informants immediately. See if they've heard anything." The cop got on his phone and talked quickly.

Myles went over to the stairs and sank down on the second step, shoving a hand through his hair.

In all her life, Faith had never seen Myles look so utterly ravaged.And she didn't care. He deserved to be completely wrecked. If something had happened to Jackson, she would never, *ever* forgive Myles.

As suddenly as the rage had consumed her, it drained away, leaving her trembling so violently she wasn't sure she could make it to the nearest chair. She reached out blindly, and a uniformed officer rushed over to her and led her into the living room to seat her on the sofa.

She realized that tears were streaming down her cheeks and had been for some time. She hadn't even registered them.

"Is there someone we can call, ma'am?" the police officer asked her. "A family member or friend?"

Her only living relative was unconscious in the hospital right now. "Lila. Lila Colton. My sister-in-law. No. She's in England. Um, I don't know."

"Why don't you give me your phone and I'll see if I can find someone?" the man asked gently. She opened the phone and passed it to him numbly. In some distant place that didn't quite reach her, she heard his voice speaking into the phone. "Mr. Yates? This is Officer Jones of the Evanston Police Department. There's been an incident at the home of Mrs. Jenny Romans. Do you know her? Could you or someone close to Mr. and Mrs. Myles Colton come over here?"

The cop handed her phone back, and she took it blindly.

Time passed, but she had no idea how much or how little. But another police officer came to stand in front of her. "Is there any chance you'd be able to find us the insurance information for your mother and maybe some identification?"

"Hasn't she regained consciousness?" Faith asked. She'd just assumed that once her mother got proper medical care, she would wake up.

"No, ma'am. She's in guarded condition and remains unconscious. They've admitted her."

Moving like a robot, she forced her body to stand. Watched it walk across the living room and head for the kitchen. Jenny usually left her purse on the desk just inside the mud room and garage.

Detective Caruso followed her into the kitchen and frowned as she dug in her mother's designer purse and pulled out Jenny's wallet. "Does your mother keep much cash in her purse?"

"I don't know." She picked up her mother's wallet and opened it. She felt as if she was invading her mother's privacy to do this, but the detective looked as if he would do it if she didn't. "Um, there are several hundred dollars in here. And of course her credit cards."

"What kind of credit cards?" the detective asked quickly.

"Premium cards with no credit limits," she answered

absently, looking for her mom's insurance card. "Ha. Here it is." She pulled the insurance card out of its slot along with her mom's driver's license and passed them to Caruso.

The detective examined both and then passed them to the uniformed officer who'd asked for them. That guy left the kitchen quickly, presumably to take them to the hospital.

Caruso asked, "Any credit cards missing?"

She looked. "I don't think so. The two main ones she uses are right here."

"Hmm. Any jewelry in the house?"

"Yes."

"Would you mind checking to see if it's still here?"

The detective followed her up the stairs to her mother's room. Faith opened her mother's jewelry box and did a quick inventory. "I don't see anything missing here, either."

"Is any of your mother's jewelry particularly valuable?"

"Yes. This emerald necklace is worth a lot. And this ruby ring. Oh, and her diamond bracelet. It's here."

"I think it's safe to rule out a robbery, then."

She heard a commotion downstairs and recognized her father-in-law Rick Yates's deep voice and the softer tones of her mother-in-law, Vita Yates. "Anything else, Detective?" she asked.

"No. That's all for now."

She nodded and headed back toward the stairs. As the foyer came into sight, she lurched to a stop. Good grief. It was full of people. Apparently, the entire Colton clan had been called in as reinforcements.

As she stared down from the shadows, she saw her

mother-in-law, Vita, wrap Myles in a fierce, motherly hug. His head dropped to his mother's shoulder in a moment of agonized grief.

Faith had never seen him in such pain. For an instant, her heart softened toward him, and an urge to race down the stairs and comfort him herself rushed through her. But then she remembered this was all his fault. Her son was in danger, missing, because of him. She could find no shred of forgiveness for Myles in her heart.

The rage she'd felt before surged forward once more, cloaking her in its cold armor. Stonily, she walked down the curving staircase.

Vita rushed forward and wrapped her in a hug before her feet hardly hit the marble floor. "Oh, sweetie. I'm so sorry. What can we do to help?"

"Find Jack. We have to find Jack." She realized as the words came out of her mouth that they sounded far away. As if she were in another room, separated from her voice. Shock. She must be in shock. Which was fine. She welcomed the numbness. It was a blessed relief from the tearing agony of this nightmare.

"Cruz and Sean are here," Vita said kindly. "They're both with the Chicago Police Department, and are already working on coordinating search parties and police response from all the police departments in the greater suburban area."

In the past year, a whole new branch of the Colton clan had come to light—the legitimate children of Myles's grandfather, Dean Colton, as it turned out. With them had come a whole slew of new Colton cousins. Tatum and January Colton, daughters of Alfred and Farrah Colton, were both in relationships with cops. As Faith recalled, Cruz was a narcotics detective and Sean was in the homicide division. She sincerely prayed she didn't need either of their professional services any time soon.

Aaron Colton and his fiancée Felicia rushed over to hug her, followed by Myles's cousin Damon and his fiancée, Ruby. Damon, a DEA agent, was grim but wore a determined look.

He murmured as he hugged her, "Be strong. All the law enforcement resources in this part of the state are being thrown at finding your boy. BOLOs have been issued, Jackson's picture has been sent to every cop, on or off duty, at every police department for a couple hundred miles around. The Feds have been called. Even fire departments and emergency rooms have been put on notice. Someone will spot him."

"What's a BOLO?" she mumbled.

"It stands for Be On the Look Out. It means every cop in northern Illinois, southern Wisconsin and northwest Indiana are looking for Jackson."

She nodded against Damon's shirt and fought back an abrupt and overwhelming need to sob. She preferred the shock to this.

As the blanket of fog settled over her once more, Damon's fiancée and a nursing student, Ruby, hugged her and then leaned back to take an assessing look at her. "You're in shock, Faith. Why don't you come sit down and let me get you a glass of water?"

At the mention of a drink, Faith was suddenly aware of being so thirsty she could hardly think about anything but getting a drink. She let Ruby lead her to the family room and bring her a big glass of water. She downed the whole thing and Ruby brought her a refill. "Sip at this, Faith. And give me your wrist. I want to check your heart rate."

As Ruby stared at her watch and counted to herself,

Faith became aware of her pulse fluttering against that finger pressed into her wrist. Wow. Her heart was really racing.

"If you feel light-headed at any time, go ahead and lean forward to put your head in your lap. Or, you can stretch out flat on the sofa. But don't try to get up and walk around, okay?" the future nurse said.

Faith nodded her understanding.

Sara Sandoval, an employee at the Yates' Yards Plant Nursery came over and said kindly, "Can I get you more water, Faith?"

"That would be great. Thanks."

She appreciated how everyone was trying to do things to make her feel better, but the only thing that would take away the ten-ton anvil sitting on her chest was the safe return of her son.

Carly Colton, another one of the new cousins, came in and had a brief, quiet conversation with Ruby. Faith dimly recalled that Carly was some sort of nurse. Maybe a pediatric nurse?

Carly sat down beside her. "A bunch of the family and most of the police here at the house are going out to join the search party. Detective Caruso is going to stay here along with my cousin, Damon, just in case."

"Just in case what?" Faith asked blankly.

The two nurses exchanged glances around her. "What?" she demanded. "Tell me."

Carly sighed. "In case a ransom demand comes in."

"Oh, God," she whispered. The reality slammed into her with the force of a freight train at full speed. Jackson had been *kidnapped*. Strangers had her son and could be treating him terribly. He had to be scared to death.

He might be young, but he was frighteningly smart. He would understand full well what was happening to him.

Spots danced in front of her eyes, and her entire scalp felt hot as the room began to spin around her.

"Breathe, Faith," Carly said quickly. "Do it with me. In. Hold. Out slowly. *Slowly.* Hold, there. Now in again."

It took a dozen full breaths for the room to stop whirling and her vision to clear.

"Where's Myles?" she demanded strongly. "The kidnappers will call him."

"He's still out looking for Jackson. But his cell phone is here at the house. The police have it. Speaking of which, it might not be a bad idea to give them your phone, too, in case the call comes to you."

She surged to her feet, swayed, and the two nurses jumped up on either side of her to steady her. When she had her balance, she nodded and made her way to the living room, where an impromptu command post appeared to have been set up.

Detective Caruso and Ruby's fiancé, Damon, sat in front of laptops set up on one of Jenny's prized French antique side tables that had been hauled into the middle of the room. Both of them were speaking into phones as she rounded the corner.

She waited until they'd both hung up, then held out her cell phone to them. She noticed Myles's cell phone lying on the table with a cable connecting it to one of the computers. "Do you guys need my cell phone, too?" she asked.

Caruso answered, "It wouldn't be a bad idea. Also, I'll need your email address and password. We'll be monitoring your email and your husband's email for possible communications."

"So, you're sure Jackson was kid—" Her voice broke. "Kidnapped?" she managed to ask without throwing up. Although it was a close call.

"It seems logical. We're going to proceed on that assumption until your son is found. Better to hit the ground running right away rather than give a kidnapper a big head start."

"Are you looking into the gang my husband tried? They threatened me and Jackson—"

Caruso interrupted gently. "We've got the Chicago PD gang task force looking into them, and the Feds have been called in. They'll undoubtedly be tapping their various informants to find out what Anarchy Ink is up to."

The unreasoning rage she'd felt toward Myles earlier threatened to erupt once more, and she spoke quickly to stop herself from screaming incoherently. "Will you raid the Anarchy Ink compound? Obviously, that's where they'd take Jack." Maple Bend, Illinois, was several hours southwest of Chicago in the heart of rural Illinois. If the police got going, they could be there not long after midnight.

"The Anarchy Ink compound was seized by the state of Illinois a few days ago. They won't be there," Damon said gently.

She swore under her breath. "Then where are they now?"

"We're looking into that urgently, ma'am," Caruso answered.

"What am I supposed to do now? I can't just sit here doing nothing."

"Actually, Mrs. Colton, that's exactly what we need you to do. We need you to stay out of our way and let us do our jobs. Police departments train to respond to cri—" He broke off. "To situations like this all the time. We know what we're doing. Be with your family. Rest if you can."

She snorted. As if. No way was she sleeping again until Jackson was home safe and sound.

And he would absolutely come back to them safe and sound. Any other alternative was completely, utterly unthinkable.

But cold fingers of dread crept around her heart and were beginning to squeeze, slowly but surely, warning that this wasn't going to end well.

Chapter Sixteen

Myles came back to Jenny's house cold, wet and filthy. He'd spent the past few hours crawling through hedges and bushes throughout the neighborhood around the Romans' house in search of Jackson. But he hadn't found a single footprint, not even a thread on a thorn to indicate that his son had run outside to hide from whoever had attacked Jenny. His cousin Micha, who had Special Forces training in tracking, had also been out there with him and spotted nothing.

Exhausted and heartsick, he stepped into the kitchen, took the cup of hot, black coffee someone handed him and gulped it down, only vaguely registering its bitterness.

How was he ever going to face Faith again if they didn't get Jack back? It would be his fault. All his fault.

As the caffeine hit, he heard a familiar sound coming from elsewhere in the house. Faith's cell phone ringtone.

He tore through the house and into the living room where a cadre of police had set up computers and phone lines to coordinate the search and wait for a ransom demand. At this point, he would almost be relieved to get a ransom call because at least it would mean Jackson was alive somewhere and not hurt and half-frozen in the woods somewhere by himself. The temperature had dropped into the low forties and was forecast to dip into the midthirties by morning. A little boy outside in thin cotton pajamas wouldn't likely survive the night.

Detective Caruso was listening to whoever spoke at the other end of Faith's phone. As soon as the man disconnected the call, Myles demanded, "Well?"

"That was the hospital. Mrs. Romans is starting to come around. They were calling to notify her daughter."

"Should we go over there?" Myles asked. "I know Faith is going to want to see her mother. But do you guys want to question her?"

"Oh, yeah. I definitely want to talk with her," Caruso replied. "Maybe she can shed some light on what happened here this evening. If you and your wife would like to meet me out front, I'll drive you over."

"I have my car—" Myles started.

"Let me drive. You and your wife are in no condition to be behind the wheel. You're distracted and have to be exhausted."

The detective was not wrong. "Let me go get Faith."

He found her lying on the sofa in the family room. All the Colton women had clustered there and were curled up in chairs or on the floor. They'd brought down pillows and blankets and appeared to have made a slumber party out of it.

He touched Faith's shoulder and she jolted, panicked. Her eyes were wild as she looked up at him, and she didn't have to speak for him to know the first thought in her mind.

"No news on Jackson," he murmured. "But your mother's waking up. Would you like to go over to the hospital with me and Detective Caruso to speak with her?"

"What if a ransom call comes in?" she mumbled.

Myles answered, "The police can forward it to Detective Caruso's phone. Once the call comes in to one of our phones, they'll still be able to trace it, even if they forward it to us."

Faith nodded and reached for a pair of tennis shoes sitting on the floor. Sometime in the evening, she'd changed into a pair of yoga pants and a sweater he didn't recognize. Someone must have raided Jenny's closet for her.

She brought the blanket she'd been huddled under with her and wrapped herself in it, then curled up on the far side of the back seat of Caruso's car, as far away from Myles as she could go. He sighed and didn't offer her his arm or his body to cuddle up to, even though he desperately needed a hug.

His new cousin Simone, a psychologist, had explained to him earlier that everyone dealt with stress of this kind differently. While he wanted physical comfort from loved ones, Faith was dealing with her terror by hiding behind a wall of anger.

Simone had warned him to let her have her anger and not to attempt to reason past it. She also said that no matter how in control of herself Faith looked, she would be balancing on a razor's edge of losing it completely. The last thing Simone had said to him before offering him a long, tight hug was not to hold Faith's anger against her. It was purely a coping mechanism and would go away once Jackson was found.

But he wasn't so sure about that. When she'd lashed out at him earlier, blaming him for Jackson's kidnapping, she'd sounded completely rational and completely convinced all of this was his fault.

Thing was, he didn't disagree with her. If Anarchy

Ink had, indeed, lashed out at him and his law firm by taking his son, he would never forgive himself. And he surely didn't expect Faith to forgive him.

For an instant his mind spun forward, envisioning a future without Faith and Jackson, without his family. Alone. Shunned. A pariah. He would have to leave Chicago. He wouldn't be able to stand to look at anything that reminded him of his home. Of his lost family—

"Mr. Colton?" Detective Caruso said, startling him out of his misery.

He looked up. They'd pulled into the hospital parking lot, beside the emergency room entrance. He climbed out of the car and went around to let out Faith. She brushed past him without saying a word, and he stepped back silently. But God, it hurt not to reach out, put his arms around her, and share his grief and guilt and terror with her.

For his entire life, she'd been the one he turned to in bad times. She had always been his rock. The one person who anchored his world. But with her ignoring him and giving him the cold shoulder like this, he felt cast adrift, tossing on stormy seas. No lifeboat. No land in sight. Just him all alone. Drowning…

He lurched into motion and hurried to catch up with Caruso and Faith as they strode into the garishly bright emergency room. Caruso went over to the high counter and flashed his badge. The three of them were immediately escorted by a nurse to an elevator and led down a series of hallways into what looked like an ICU unit or something darned close.

They were passed off to another nurse who said, "Mrs. Romans is this way. The doctor is with her now. She's starting to rouse."

Myles followed Faith and the detective into a room full of monitors and tubes and wires. His mother-in-law looked pale and old, dwarfed by all the medical equipment in here.

A man in a white lab coat looked up. "I was told you needed to get a statement from Mrs. Romans as soon as possible?"

Caruso replied, "That's correct. Is she alert enough now to answer yes or no questions?"

"Maybe. She's been squeezing my hand and struggling to speak, but she's not fully conscious."

Detective Caruso waved Faith forward. Which was actually decent of the guy. Faith leaned over her mother. "Hi, Mom. It's me, Faith. I'm here with you, and you're safe. You're going to be fine. But we need you to wake up and tell us what happened. We need to find Jackson."

The words had a definite effect on Jenny. The beeping of the various monitors sped up markedly, and her mother's eyelids fluttered. Jenny made several sounds akin to gagging, and then turned her head slowly to one side and then the other, appearing to take in her surroundings. Her eyes drifted closed once more.

Detective Caruso stepped forward. "Ma'am, I'm a police officer. I need you to open your eyes." He was markedly more forceful than Faith had been as if maybe he had experience questioning barely conscious crime victims when time was of the essence.

"Gently," the doctor murmured.

Screw gently. They needed to know what had happened! Myles was relieved when Caruso rolled his eyes at the doctor and said loudly, "Mrs. Romans. Look at me."

Jenny's eyes opened slowly. She seemed to recognize Faith and opened her mouth, but no sound came out. Caruso stepped directly into Jenny's line of sight. "What happened tonight, ma'am? You were in your house with your grandson."

"Doorbell," she rasped.

"The doorbell rang?" She nodded and he continued, "You opened the front door, and then what happened?"

"Man. Mask." She paused for a moment to catch her breath and then continued, "Pushed inside. Hit me." She frowned. "Can't remember..."

"One man? Or were there more?"

"Two," Jenny gasped.

"Do you remember what the other man did?" Caruso demanded, his voice rising in volume as Jenny seemed to fade a little.

"Up the...stairs," she breathed on a labored exhalation.

"Did they take Jackson?" Caruso all but yelled as her eyes started to close. "Did they kidnap your grandson?"

"Don't...know..." The monitors went crazy as Jenny's eyes drifted all the way shut, but her heart rate and blood pressure appeared to spike alarmingly.

"I think that's all you're going to get out of her right now," the doctor said. "Do you want to stick around and try again in a few minutes when she comes back to us again?"

Caruso shook his head tersely. "I have enough for now. She confirmed a home invasion and said nothing about her grandson fleeing. Which means the boy was kidnapped as we surmised. Do you two want to stay with her?"

Faith looked reluctantly at Myles where he stood at the foot of her bed. "I'd like to stay with her."

"I'll go back to the house and hold down the fort

there," he replied grimly. Faith looked relieved that she wouldn't have to be in the same room with him. It was a dagger straight to his heart, but he absorbed the blow in silence.

Caruso said briskly, "I'll have an officer come over here and stay with you, Mrs. Colton. Whenever you're ready to come home, he'll bring you."

"You'll call if there are…developments?" she blurted.

Caruso glanced at him as if he expected Myles to field his wife's question. "Of course, sweetheart. The second we hear anything, I'll let you know. Take care of your mom for now, and get some rest if you can."

She turned her back on him to lean down over her mother, and he sighed. "I love you," he murmured, unsure of whether or not she heard him or if she cared. He didn't expect a reply, and he didn't get one.

Glumly, he followed Caruso back to the elevator.

"Give her time," Caruso commented, staring at the door. "People respond in all kinds of whacky ways to a crisis like this. She'll come back to you when this is over."

"Maybe," he bit out.

"Have some faith."

Huh. Faith was the one thing he didn't have right now. Not the religious kind and not his wife.

When they got back to the house, Caruso gave him a short speech about needing to conserve his strength and urged him to try to get some sleep. Right. With his son missing? Not a chance.

Someone forced a sleeping pill on him around four a.m. and he went upstairs, crawling into the bed he shared with Faith when they stayed over here. It felt cold and empty without Faith beside him. No way was he going to sleep…

SHOCKED, HE OPENED his eyes to see bright sunlight streaming in the window. He registered the sound of the shower running in the attached bathroom and frowned. Who was that?

He rolled out of bed and pulled on his dirty clothes from last night. Maybe somebody would be willing to go over to his and Faith's house and bring back a change of clothes for them. He finished tying his shoes and looked up to see Faith stepping out of the bathroom, dressed in more of her mother's clothes, her hair hanging wet down her back in dark strings the color of an old penny.

"Did you get any sleep?" he asked quietly.

Faith answered relatively civilly, "I caught a nap in the chair in my mom's room."

"Was she able to say any more?"

"Not much. She remembers a man in a black mask pushing in the front door and hitting her. As she went down, she saw a second man come in behind him. That's it. She passed out after that."

"Is she going to make a full recovery, then?" he asked.

"Doctor is planning to release her this afternoon."

"That's good news," he responded.

Faith volunteered, "The doctors are treating two head injuries. One is on the side of her head where they think the intruder hit her with a heavy blunt object. The other one is from where she fell and hit the floor. She's got a concussion, but no skull fracture."

"That's good news."

She walked over to the door and stopped, her hand on the knob. A look of panic crossed her face. He knew the feeling. He didn't want to face what this day had to bring, either.

Hesitant to disrupt the fragile truce that seemed to

exist between them, he nonetheless murmured, "I don't want to go down there, either. But we have to be strong for Jackson. I'm here for you if you need anything from me, Faith."

She glanced over her shoulder at him, and for an instant, the unbearable agony she was feeling showed in her eyes. Then she shut it all down, leaving nothing but a wall of cold blankness. Thank God Simone explained last night what was going on with her. Otherwise, she would be scaring the ever-loving hell out of him, right about now. As it was, he was still terrified he was going to lose her because of this.

He added quietly, "If you need to rant or rage or scream at someone, I'm here for you. No matter what you say or do, no matter what happens, I love you."

Staring at the door panel, she drew a single sobbing breath. Then, she squared her shoulders, lifted her head and walked out the door into whatever new horror today brought.

God, the strength that had taken. She was made of sterner stuff than he'd ever dreamed of, that was for sure. The least he could do was match her courage. He took a deep breath of his own and headed downstairs, profoundly relieved that they'd had at least a tiny moment of peace between them. It wasn't much, but it was something to build on.

He jogged down the staircase and stared in surprise. A whole new crew of law enforcement professionals crowded the living room, this batch all wearing civilian clothing, suits mostly.

He stepped forward to join Faith just as she stopped in the doorway to the living room. He recognized one face in the entire room, and it belonged to Brad Howard,

Simone's fiancé. He was an FBI agent. So. The Feds had arrived, had they?

"Hey, Myles, Faith." Brad took both of Faith's hands and kissed her on the cheek. "How are you two holding up?"

Faith didn't answer, so Myles jumped in. "About as you'd expect. Lousy."

Brad murmured, "I'm not here in any official capacity. As a family member, I can't work on this case. Conflict of interest."

"Too bad," Myles replied. "I'd trust you to find Jackson and bring him home safely."

Brad smiled a little. "I can, however, act as a liaison between you and my FBI colleagues. I can translate the acronyms and jargon and generally keep you updated on what's going on, if you'd like."

"What is going on?" Faith asked hoarsely.

"The Evanston Police Department has officially turned the investigation over to the FBI. We're taking point on the investigation. We've got agents out, right now. They're en route to pick up Aric Schroder and bring him in."

"I'd like to be there when they question him," Myles said quickly.

"That's not standard procedure—"

"Put me behind a mirror in an observation room," Myles interrupted. "I just spent two weeks in a courtroom watching every nuance of that man's body language and expressions. I saw him tell the truth, but more importantly, I saw him lie. I know how he acts when he's not telling the truth."

"Huh. Interesting," Brad said noncommittally.

Myles leaned on his cousin a little harder. "I can be of

use to you guys. Let me do something to help." He added in desperation, "Please."

Brad shrugged. "Let me see what I can do."

"And nobody's contacted us yet?" Faith asked. "Is there a chance Jackson fled from the bad guys and got lost?"

Brad replied gently, "Search teams scoured every square inch in a three-mile radius of this house. It's all suburban yards with only a few tiny patches of brush and one park. I think we can safely say that Jackson did not flee this house or end up anywhere outside."

"But how can you be sure?" Faith demanded.

"Your mother was questioned this morning, and she claims not to use a housekeeper. Is that true?"

Faith frowned at Brad. "Yes. That's correct. She's a stickler for doing things herself. That way everything is cleaned just the way she likes it. But what does that have to do with anything?"

Brad nodded briskly. "When the forensics guys dusted the room your son stays in, they picked up two sets of prints. One of them popped up as belonging to a man with a rap sheet a mile long of minor criminal offenses."

Faith staggered beside him, and Myles put an arm around her shoulders to steady her. They both stared at Brad. Myles bit out, "Do you have a name?"

"We do. And yes, we have guys staking out his last known address. We'll have a warrant within the hour to search his place. But the special agent in charge will want to be the one to tell you the details. Come on. Let me introduce you to her."

Myles and Faith followed him over to a woman who looked to be about forty years old. She glanced up as they approached, and the no-nonsense sharpness of her gaze eased slightly.

"Myles and Faith Colton, this is Senior Special Agent Mary Baker. She's in charge of the investigation of Jackson's kidnapping."

"So it's officially a kidnapping, now?" Myles asked.

"It is," the woman replied briskly.

Brad said, "I told them about the fingerprints in Jackson's room, but I left the details to you, Agent Baker."

"Right. Two sets of prints. First set belongs to a guy named Donald Palicki. Any chance either of you have heard of him before?"

Faith shook her head in the negative right away, but Myles was slower to reply. "I'm a litigating attorney, so I'll have to ask my current firm and the Chicago district attorney's office where I began my career to check out the name, but I don't recognize it."

Faith studied him intently. "It's not the name of one of the Anarchy Ink members?"

He shook his head. "No. And believe me. I know all of them, not only by name, but by face."

Brad dived in again. "As you know, ma'am, Myles just finished suing Anarchy Ink. He spent two weeks in court studying Aric Schroder and thinks he can tell us if Schroder's lying when we pick him up and question him."

Myles added quickly, "I know I can't and shouldn't be in the room when your people interrogate him, but I'd like to observe from behind the glass. I know how to read him and his body language."

"I'll take that under advisement," Agent Baker said evenly.

"For the love of God, let me do something to help," he said low.

She tilted her head in acquiescence. "I'll let you know when we have Mr. Schroder in custody. In the meantime, I need the two of you to stay here in the house. We usually get a ransom demand within the first twenty-four hours after an abduction. When the call comes, I'll want whichever one of you whose phone gets the call to answer it. I'll have one of my negotiators brief you on what to say and what not to say in a few minutes, now that you're both awake and rested."

Myles wouldn't exactly call himself rested after four hours of fitful sleep, but he wasn't as exhausted as he'd been when he fell into bed in the wee hours. Faith couldn't have gotten much more rest than he did sitting in a hospital armchair.

"Do you have a cryptocurrency account, Mr. and Mrs. Colton?" Agent Baker asked.

"No," he answered, surprised.

"I'll have one of my guys walk you through setting one up."

"Why?" Faith blurted.

"The vast majority of kidnappers demand that ransom be paid to them in a cryptocurrency. It's anonymous and untraceable and tends to be how bad guys conduct their other business beyond kidnapping."

"You think terrorists or drug dealers snatched my son out of his bed in my mother-in-law's house?" Myles exclaimed. "That seems a little far-fetched, don't you think?"

Agent Baker stared him down until he looked away. Then she answered evenly, "I'm not ruling out anything, Mr. Colton. I think it's much more likely that someone who knows you and your wife took your son. This has all the hallmarks of a personal vendetta. However, I'm also not going to be caught unprepared if that turns out not to be the case. And since you're the person who floated the early theory that Anarchy Ink might be involved, I should point out that they do much of their illegal arms trading via cryptocurrency."

"Fair point," Myles conceded.

He spent the next half hour or so setting up a crypto-trading account with the help of an FBI computer technician who walked him through the process. At the end of it, the guy said, "Don't ever get on the dark web by yourself, okay? You have to have all kinds of special programs to protect yourself from being hacked and having your identity stolen. And the stuff that floats around on the dark web…well, it's not nice."

Myles snorted. "The way I hear it, criminal activity, porn and terrorism abound."

"You would not be wrong, sir."

"Now what do we do?" he asked the tech.

"Now, it's a waiting game. I'm set up to trace any calls that come in. The profiler is waiting to hear what the kidnappers say, and we'll put together a plan based on how the call goes and what the kidnappers demand."

Myles jumped on that. "Kidnappers plural?"

The agent shrugged. "The vast majority of kidnappings for ransom are carried out by groups, not individuals. Lots of moving parts to a good kidnapping. A resource heavy crime—" He broke off. "I'm sorry. I can be a bit of a crime statistics geek."

Myles tried and failed to smile at the guy. His son was not a statistic. He was a little boy. An innocent caught up in something Myles didn't yet understand. What was he missing? Agent Baker said it was a personal vendetta against his family. Who hated him or Faith bad enough to kidnap their young son?

He racked his brains but came up with nothing. Everybody loved Faith. As for him, he obviously had stepped on some toes in his legal career, but he couldn't think of any past cases where the defendants had not only been angry enough but also had the resources and hate to take a child.

"Mr. Colton?" another agent said from behind him.

He turned around to face a man who looked about as rumpled as he felt. "Yes?"

"I'm Dr. Philbin and work as a profiler and psychologist. I'd like to brief you and your wife on what to expect in a ransom call."

Myles went over to the sofa and sat down beside Faith. Philbin pulled up one of Jenny's delicate Louis XV chairs and sat on it facing them.

"First order of business—the call will be recorded and we'll put it on a speaker so everyone in the room can hear it. Don't worry if you don't remember what's said so you can repeat it. We'll have a full recording of the whole thing."

Myles nodded along with Faith beside him.

The psychologist continued, "Expect some sort of voice synthesizer or voice alterations. It may not sound like a human you're talking to, and you may not be able to discern the caller's gender. Don't worry about that. I'll figure it out from speech patterns. The caller will ask who you are. Tell them. Then, before they can say anything more, I want you to ask for proof of life."

Faith gasped beside him and Myles reached out to squeeze her hand.

"Ask to speak to Jackson on the phone or tell the kidnapper you want a picture texted to you of Jackson with today's newspaper. Expect the kidnapper to get angry and try to regain control of the conversation."

Myles and Faith nodded. "Then I want you to listen carefully to what he or she says next. It's usually the demand itself and instructions for how to deliver it. I want you to repeat those both back to the kidnapper to confirm them. Repeat back each instruction slowly and individually. Wait for confirmation that you've got it right, and then repeat the next piece of the instructions."

"Is that a delaying tactic to keep him on the line longer so you can trace the call?" Faith asked.

"The computer technician will be working on that, and yes, the more time he has to triangulate a location, the better. I'll be analyzing speech patterns and stressors, among other things. But I need to hear the kidnapper speak as much as possible. Your goal is to draw the conversation out as long as possible and to get the kidnapper to say as much as possible. With me so far?"

Myles and Faith nodded.

"Don't make any emotional outbursts. This is a business call. Keep it impersonal and professional as much as you can. He or she is counting on you being desperate and emotional. Don't give him or her that. The more frantic you sound, the more they will press to have their ransom demands met before they return your son to you. Can both of you do that?"

Myles nodded, but Faith was slower to agree.

"Mrs. Colton, if you feel yourself losing control, pass the phone to your husband. And vice versa. If you're losing it, Mr. Colton, pass the phone to your wife. Although the call won't probably last long enough for this to matter, it's fine if you have to hand off the phone to each other more than once."

Faith's fingers tightened around his as Myles glanced over at her. She looked ghostly pale. "We can do this," he murmured to her. "For Jackson."

"Right. For Jackson," she mumbled.

"I'll be right beside both of you," Dr. Philbin said. "We can mute the call so the kidnapper can't hear us, and I can give you quick instructions if you forget what to say next or the call happens to go off script." But the profiler sounded skeptical that it would.

Which made Myles feel marginally better. This was obviously not the profiler's first rodeo with coaching frantic parents through a kidnapping. "Anything else?" he asked reluctantly.

"Go get something to eat if you're hungry. Both of you need to keep up your strength. Rest and eat when you can. This situation could last for several days."

Myles frowned. "I thought most kidnappings of young children end within twenty-four hours?"

"In this case, we believe your son's kidnapper may have some sort of agenda. It's unusual for a kidnapper to break into a home to take a child. Usually, kids are tricked or snatched off the street or outdoors, away from their parents."

"What agenda?" Faith beat him to ask out loud.

The profiler shrugged. "I can't say for sure. Not yet. That's why getting the kidnapper to talk as much as possible during the call will be helpful."

"Guess," Myles bit out.

The profiler sighed. "I'm not ready to give you a full profile yet. But I can tell you this. It sounds as if this kidnapping has been carefully planned. The incidents with being followed indicated to me that the kidnappers have been waiting for an opportunity to commit this crime for at least several days, if not longer. They have a plan, and they have a clear reason for doing this. Which indicates that they're organized and have a goal in mind."

"What goal?" Faith blurted.

"That, I don't know yet. I expect a ransom call will tell us much more about that."

"Stop saying that as if we may not get a ransom call," Myles snapped. "We'll get a call. We have to."

The profiler shrugged enigmatically. "I need both of you to be patient. We're operating on the kidnapper's schedule right now. I know how frustrating that sense of not being in control is. But we'll regain control of the situation as soon as we can."

The prospect of having to wait for days to get their son back made Myles want to vomit. He had to fix this mess. His entire life—his family, his marriage—depended on it.

He stood up and rushed out of the living room, heading for the front porch and deep gulps of fresh air. He couldn't do this. He had to do this. *Think of Jackson. Picture him healthy and happy and playing with his new puppy.*

When his stomach finally calmed down, Myles headed for the kitchen and the smell of bacon cooking. His mother was standing at the stove, flipping pancakes as a big sheet of bacon crisped up in the oven.

"Coffee?" Vita asked. "I made a proper pot of it, not that battery acid the police made last night."

"Thank God." He poured himself a cup out of the coffee pot, doctored it to his liking and leaned against a counter to sip it.

His mother glanced up from the griddle. "How are you holding up, Myles?"

"I'm not. I'm faking it as best as I can."

"I'm so sorry about all of this. Does the FBI have any idea who did it?"

"They have a name from a fingerprint they pulled from Jackson's room. Guy named Donald Palicki. Does that name ring a bell to you?"

As the long-time bookkeeper of the Yates' Yards Plant Nursery, she was familiar with most of their long-time clients. "No, dear. That name doesn't sound familiar. I'll have Sara look it up in our financial records, though."

"How's she working out?" he asked. Sara Sandoval was the new marketing assistant Rick had hired a few months back.

"She's great. She has all kinds of terrific ideas for increasing traffic to the nursery and growing our client list."

"Where is she now? I thought I saw her sleeping on the family room floor last night."

"She's at the police station."

"The police station? Does she know something about the kidnapping?"

"No. The Evanston police showed up at the yard this morning to question all the employees. Since she was here and they missed her at the yard, they called and asked her to go to the police station. Of course, she went right away. She wants to help in any way she can. We all do."

He swiped a piece of the bacon already out of the oven and munched on it absently.

Vita asked, "Who is this man whose fingerprints the FBI found?"

"Donald Palicki. Small-time criminal. Bar fights, DUIs, and petty thefts. If he's involved in the kidnapping, he's not the guy in charge. He's hired muscle."

"You mean somebody's hiding behind this Palicki fellow?"

Myles nodded. "Agent Baker didn't say so, but it's clear that's what she's thinking."

"We're all praying for Jackie, Myles. I called my church, and the pastor has the entire congregation praying. And Jack's face is all over the news. The whole city is looking for him and praying for him. He'll be okay. I know it."

"From your lips to God's ears," Myles murmured.

"Call it an intuition. The police will figure this out—"

From behind Myles a phone rang. Faith's cell phone. He slammed the empty mug to the counter and took off running.

Chapter Seventeen

"Take a deep breath, Mrs. Colton. Are you ready? Remember everything I told you earlier. Keep the kidnapper talking."

She looked up fearfully at Dr. Philbin, who smiled reassuringly at her. And then she reached for her phone. The number was blocked on the screen, and the FBI seemed sure this was The Call.

She noticed Myles careening around the corner just as she said, "Hello?" Rats. Her voice wobbled a little, and Philbin said not to show emotion. She felt Myles move over to stand behind her and was grateful when his hands landed lightly on her shoulders in support.

An electronically generated voice said, "Hello, Mrs. Colton. I have your son."

"Oh, thank God," she interrupted quickly. "We were worried he'd gotten lost outside somewhere. Can you bring him back to us or should we come to your house to pick him up?"

Myles's cousin Simone had suggested a ploy of deliberately misunderstanding the kidnapper to fluster him or her, and Dr. Philbin had liked the idea.

"No," the kidnapper blurted. "I have your son. I kidnapped him."

That urge to scream was back. *Be strong. No emotion.* Myles's hands tightened convulsively on her shoulders.

"Oh. Really? Well then. That changes things," she replied. "I'm going to have to ask you to prove you have my son, then. Put him on the phone and let me speak with him."

"He can't talk to you right now."

"Why not? Isn't he with you? Do you really have him?"

"Yes, I have him! He just can't talk right now. He's asleep."

Terror blossomed in her belly. Surely the kidnapper hadn't killed him. Ohgod, ohgod, ohgod. Her breathing accelerated dangerously and spots of light began to swim in front of her eyes. She realized she was panting and resorted to the breathing exercises she'd been taught before she'd given birth, concentrating on short, sharp exhales.

The kidnapper seemed to be at a loss for what to say, so she spoke into the silence. "If he's asleep, you can still take a picture of him, right?"

"Uh, yes."

"Great! I know what you can do. Get a copy of a newspaper put out today. Any paper will do as long as it was published today. Put a copy of it by him and take a picture of both of them. Then you can send it to me. I can give you my email address and you can send it to that." She spelled out her email address and repeated it again. "Or, you can just text the picture to this phone number, I suppose. Oh, I should have thought of that before. I guess I'm nervous. This is my first kidnapping after all. Is it yours?"

"Uh—" The kidnapper broke off.

For all the world, it had sounded as if the kidnapper

was about to say yes. A glimmer of hope ignited in her chest. If this wasn't a hardened criminal, maybe Jackie would get out of this okay. Dr. Philbin nodded encouragingly at her. They'd wanted her to extend the phone call, to keep the kidnapper on the line and talking.

"How is Jackson doing? That's his name, by the way. Or you can call him Jack."

"I told you. He's asleep."

"Is he warm? Does he have a blanket? You took him in his pajamas."

"Yes. He has a blanket and a pillow. He's in a bed. Now, shut up and listen."

"Um, okay. What do you want to say?" She felt like a blithering idiot chattering on like this.

"We have your son. If you want to see him alive again, you'll give us thirty million dollars in cash."

"Thirty million!" she exclaimed. "My husband and I don't have that kind of money! Both of our families combined don't have that kind of money!"

Philbin made a frantic hand gesture for her to keep talking.

"If we all sold everything we own and took out loans, we couldn't come up with that much. I think you've mistaken the Colton family for someone else."

"No, I haven't. I know you have that much money. You have twice that much money."

Philbin pressed a button on the recording machine in front of her, apparently a mute button for her phone because he said quickly, "Ask if they'll accept a lesser amount."

"Will you accept some lesser amount?" she asked the kidnapper. "My husband and I can scrape together about a million dollars if we liquidate everything we own. Will you take a million dollars?"

"Is that all your son is worth to your family?" the kidnapper spit out. "Thirty million. I'll call to tell you when and where to deliver it when you've got the money."

"Not without proof of life!" she retorted. "Send me that picture of my son or no deal."

The words felt like acid tearing at the back of her throat as she forced them out. She would rob a bank and get the thirty million if she had to. This was her son. He was worth giving up her life for. She would go to jail, but he would be safe—

"Little bitch," the kidnapper snapped.

The line went dead and she sagged back in her seat, exhausted.

People talked urgently around her. "Did you get the trace?"

"Yes. Burner phone in a two square block area in west Chicago," a technician answered. The same fellow rattled off a series of street names, and a police detective relayed them quickly to someone, presumably the Chicago Police Department, which would dispatch cruisers to that location.

She sagged in the chair. Please, let it have been enough. Let the police have learned enough to find her baby.

Dr. Philbin talked over her head at someone behind her. "Definitely an amateur kidnapper. Which means this is a personal vendetta. Someone who knows the family."

Cousin Simone replied from behind her, "Why thirty million dollars, specifically? Does the kidnapper know that one side of the Colton family has sued the other side for exactly that amount? The exact amount of the lawsuit was never printed in the newspapers, was it? Myles, do you know?"

He spoke from directly over her head. "No, it wasn't published. But are you saying a member of our own family kidnapped Jackson?"

"That's crazy," Myles's mother declared from the doorway.

An urge to scream in frustration as everybody talked at once and talked over her head as if she wasn't sitting right here, nearly overcame Faith. Goodness, she was fighting an urge to scream a lot these days.

Dr. Philbin responded to Vita, "Although it's not unusual for a family member to abduct a child, usually that happens when there's some sort of custody dispute. In this case I surmise that it's someone who knows a member of the extended Colton clan. Someone who's talked with a family member about this lawsuit or overhead a mention of it."

Agent Baker stepped forward. "I'm going to need each Colton to write down a list of everyone they can remember talking to about this lawsuit. And I need all the details on who's suing who."

Myles fielded that one. "My grandfather, Dean Colton, had twin sons with his wife, and another set of twin sons with his mistress. When he died, he left his estate to his legitimate sons and their kids. Ernest and Alfred, the legitimate twins, were murdered earlier this year, and their heirs will inherit the Dean Colton estate in its entirety. With me so far?"

Agent Baker nodded.

Myles continued, "Dean's mistress, who is my grandmother, Carin Pedersen, has sued Ernest's and Alfred's heirs for half of the Dean Colton estate, which is valued at roughly sixty million dollars."

"Well, that does make a demand for thirty million in ransom money sketchy as all get out, doesn't it?" Mary Baker commented lightly.

Faith surged out of her seat and turned to face Myles. "What are we going to do? We can't come up with thirty million in cash! Even if everyone in your whole extended family chipped in, each one of us would have to come up with over a million dollars apiece. Not only do we all not have that kind of money, we can't ask the entire family to bankrupt itself."

"We'll figure something out," he replied grimly.

"So, if this isn't about your job, it's about your family?" she demanded.

His gaze met hers in anguish, but she couldn't stop the gush of hurtful words. "This is all your fault."

He wrapped his arms around her and she stiffened. She desperately wanted to be hugged and comforted, but she felt so close to breaking that she was terrified the slightest touch would shatter her into so many pieces she could never put herself back together. And right now, her son needed her in one piece.

Myles's arms fell away from her, and she took a careful breath.

Rick and Vita were talking somewhere nearby. Something about calling a family meeting at their house this evening.

"We can't ask them to do this," she mumbled.

"We'll find another way," Myles replied low. "Give us all some time to think, and for the FBI to do its analysis. Also, we need the kidnapper to send us that picture of Jackson before anything else happens."

"Stop being a lawyer for once. This is our son you're talking about. He's not a thing to be haggled over—" Her voice broke. Haggling was exactly what they were going to do over Jackson. They were going to have to argue over what her priceless son's life was worth and what the family was willing to pay for him.

She felt a crack starting in the middle of her chest. It was expanding with every breath. Crud. She was going to fall apart right here, in the middle of all the FBI agents and Myles's family.

"I'm losing it," she whispered. "I can't do this anymore."

Myles swept her out of the living room and up the stairs to their bedroom without stopping to talk to anyone, without answering any of several questions that were thrown at them.

The door closed behind them in the nick of time and the dam inside her burst. For the first time since Myles had told her Jackson was missing, she cried.

Although, the gulping sobs, runny nose, and ugly tears probably qualified as more than mere crying. She let out her fear and grief and guilt and whatever else had accumulated in the toxic stew of emotions in her gut. And it all came pouring forth. She raged and screamed and cried for several minutes, only vaguely aware that Myles was saying nothing, doing nothing to stop her. He merely stood by, silent witness to her grief and agony.

Eventually, the reservoir of emotions emptied, leaving her utterly drained. She fell silent and spent.

Myles's arms went around her and he picked her up. He carried her over to the unmade bed and laid her down in it, then followed her down, stretching out beside her.

"Please, Faith. Let me in. He's my son, too. There will

be time later for blame, but right now, he needs both of us to be strong for him. Can you try to put aside your anger at me until we get him back?"

He was right. And she'd finally released enough of her terror to admit it. She nodded against his chest.

They cried together then, quietly, clinging to each other and pouring out their fear and sorrow. They were each lost in their own agony at the moment, but there was comfort in knowing he was suffering as much as she was. Even if there was no relief to be had from this nightmare, at least they were going through it together.

They lay there together for a long time. The sobs racking their bodies gradually subsided, and stillness settled over them both. Or maybe it was just exhaustion. Either way, she finally slept a little, and she thought Myles did, too.

They didn't sleep for long, but this short nap was a hundred times more rejuvenating than the several hours of sleep last night had been. Probably had something to do with the emotional release that preceded it.

At any rate Myles roused when she did and pressed his forehead lightly against hers. "This doesn't feel real," he said low.

"It's a terrible, terrible dream. But I don't know how to wake up from it."

"We'll get him back somehow. I don't know how, but we'll find a way."

"Promise?" she murmured.

"I promise."

An awful, sick certainty settled in her belly that if they didn't get Jackson back safely, the two of them would not make it as a couple. Despite all their years together and everything else they'd been through in their lives, their marriage would not survive this. For the rest of their lives, when they looked at each other, they would see Jackson and recall only this searing pain.

Myles sighed. It was a heavy sound, laced with reluctance. She knew the feeling.

"Ready to go back into the fire?" he asked.

"No. But we have to go anyway, don't we?"

"Afraid so. But we'll go together, okay?"

She nodded, gathering the shredded remnants of her emotional armor around herself once more.

He sat up, saying, "Any time you need to let go or freak out, you let me know, and I'll pull you out. I'll bring you somewhere quiet and private so you can lose it."

"Thanks." She rolled out of bed and came to her feet. She felt a hundred years old and ached from head to toe. Never in her life had she gone through anything remotely this taxing. She trudged toward the door unwillingly.

"Before we go back out there," Myles murmured, pausing with his hand on the doorknob, "I'm sorry I took that case. Even if the Anarchy Ink guys have nothing at all to do with this—" his voice broke and he cleared his throat "—I had no idea what it would be like to put you and Jackson in this kind of danger. I'll never, ever, do anything to put you two in harm's way again. I swear."

She had no answer for him. This was hell, pure and simple. And until they knew for sure that Anarchy Ink wasn't involved, she couldn't forgive him, anyway.

She followed Myles downstairs, and they walked in on a conference between Agent Baker, Dr. Philbin, Simone and a couple other FBI agents. They were playing back the recording of her phone call with the kidnapper and dissecting it, apparently.

"Have you guys figured out anything?" Myles asked, his arm still looped lightly around Faith's shoulders.

Agent Baker looked up. "We have. We've done a detailed analysis of word choices, syntax, intonation—the works. We're convinced the kidnapper is an amateur."

"How?" Faith blurted.

"A pro would have read off a script and not allowed you to take over the conversation the way you did." The agent added, "And, of course, there's the specific demand for thirty million dollars. That appears to confirm our supposition that the kidnapper knows someone in the extended Colton family."

"Anything else?" Myles asked.

"Most importantly, we don't think the kidnapper intends any harm to your son. We can't be certain of that, of course, but the kidnapper's insistence that Jackson is asleep leads up to believe that perhaps he's sedated. And the only reason you sedate a child is to keep them quiet or not to frighten them. Given that your son is plenty old enough to be threatened into silence, we think it's possible the kidnapper isn't out to scare Jackson. That also goes along with the theory that a family acquaintance is behind this. If you put all of that together, it adds up to a kidnapper who's not planning to kill Jackson at this time."

Faith bit back a sob. Just hearing the word kill in the same sentence with her son's name was hard to bear. Still, the analysis gave her a faint glimmer of hope.

"Any luck raiding Donald Palicki's place?" Myles asked.

"He's not at home. Doesn't appear to have been there for at least twenty-four hours. The Chicago PD is staking the place out. Maybe he'll show up, but I'm skeptical." Agent Baker shrugged.

"Why are you skeptical?" Faith asked.

"If he's involved in the kidnapping, he's undoubtedly with his coconspirator. Maybe he was babysitting Jackson while the kidnapper made the call."

"Did you find the caller?" Myles demanded. "What about the trace?"

The woman FBI agent replied, "We found a burner phone in a trash can. We think the call came from it. The phone is being processed by an evidence team as we speak. Maybe they can pull some DNA off it."

Faith felt like swearing, but refrained in the interest of not losing her very thin self-control. And, after her recent meltdown, she had a much better understanding of just how thin her control really was.

"What else have you guys gleaned from the phone call?" Myles asked.

Dr. Philbin spoke up. "The amount of the ransom, thirty million dollars, is symbolic. This person wants to hurt the Colton family. We don't think collecting the ransom is actually all that important to the kidnapper."

"Which means what?" Myles followed up.

Agent Baker shrugged. "We think we'll be able to negotiate some lower final ransom settlement, as long as we make it clear that whatever amount your family comes up with will cause the whole family a lot of financial and personal pain."

Myles snorted. "The family has already suffered immeasurable personal pain just by Jackson having been kidnapped."

Agent Baker jumped in. "How would your family feel about doing a press conference? We would need the whole clan to participate, and we would need them all to show lots of suffering and grief. Would they be willing to go along with something like that?"

From across the living room, Rick Yates said strongly, "Every member of this family will do anything and everything to get our boy back."

Myles said, "I'll have to ask the other side of the family if they'd be willing to play along. I'm guessing you people will want both sides of the family represented in a show of unity and mutual misery?"

Agent Baker made a rueful face. "Yes. We would need all of you."

Rick spoke up again. "We're having a family meeting this evening at the nursery. We'll ask everyone then."

The FBI agent in charge nodded briskly.

Faith looked around. Now what? There didn't seem to be anything pressing for her to do. All this waiting was making her crazy. She headed for the kitchen where Sara Sandoval was busily drying dishes and hunting down where all the pots and pans were normally stored.

"Need some help figuring out where to put stuff?" Faith offered.

"Sure. How are you holding up?" the young woman asked.

"Beneath this facade, I'm screaming my head off," Faith answered honestly.

"The whole family's that way," Sara said sympathetically. "You're lucky you have such a big, close family. They'll stick by you no matter what."

"We'll see. The kidnapper wants thirty million dollars, which will bankrupt the whole lot of us."

"They'll do it in a heartbeat, you know," Sara murmured, putting away a baking dish. "They'll sell their businesses and homes, and they'll empty out their savings accounts for your son."

"I feel weird asking it of them, though," Faith con fessed. "They're Myles's family. Not mine."

"The way I hear it, you practically grew up in the Colton family."

Faith smiled a little. "Myles and I met in the sixth grade. We've officially been a couple since eighth grade."

"Wow. Childhood sweethearts. That's so cool."

"I know all of his teen dirt, and he knows all of mine."

"You don't strike me as the type to have much scandal in your past."

Faith's smile widened. "Sadly, I'm pretty boring."

"Mrs. Colton?" Faith looked up quickly as one of the FBI agents, whose name she couldn't remember, poked his head into the kitchen. "We need you in the living room. A picture has come in."

Oh, God. Jackson.

She raced toward a large computer monitor with a crowd of people in front of it and pushed her way through unceremoniously. There he was. Jackson. Wearing his blue rocket jammies, sleeping on his belly, his hair sticking up every which way. Were it not for the fact that the plain single bed he slept in was not his own, he could've been right upstairs, crashed exactly like that.

A moan escaped her throat and she slapped her hand over her mouth.

A newspaper was spread out on top of the blankets covering Jackson's torso, the front page plainly visible.

Agent Baker turned to her. "That's today's newspaper. We have proof of life. Your son was alive at the time this photo was taken."

Irritated at the woman's use of the past tense, Faith

snapped, "How can you tell he's alive? He could be—" She broke off, unable to make herself say the word *dead*.

"There's color in his cheeks, ma'am. He's definitely alive in this photograph."

Myles rushed up beside her just then and stared at the screen. "Thank God," he breathed. "Now what?"

Dr. Philbin answered, "Now, we wait. The kidnapper will have to call back to arrange for delivery of the ransom and delivery of your son back to you, since he or she didn't get around to telling you that in the first phone call."

Agent Baker added, "And, we need your family to figure out exactly how much cash it can pull together in the next twenty-four hours or so."

"You're planning for us to actually pay the ransom?" Myles blurted.

Agent Baker made a face. "That's not usually how cases like this work out. But I need whatever amount of ransom we offer the kidnapper to sound reasonable. This person obviously knows enough about your family to have some idea of the Colton family's wealth. I need an amount the kidnapper will buy."

Myles nodded. "I'll get you the number."

"How long until the kidnapper calls us back?" Faith demanded.

Dr. Philbin shrugged. "Hard to tell. Kidnappings usually run really fast. With small children, they tend to be over within about twenty-four hours. But in cases where ransom actually ends up being exchanged, the kidnappers typically wait a day or so—sometimes up to a week—to let the family gather the ransom money." He frowned. "However, this yahoo doesn't know what he or she is doing. The kidnapper might call in the next few minutes or he or she might wait a few days. It depends on how much planning went into this abduction. The kidnapper may or may not have already worked out when, where and how to make the exchange of ransom for your child."

"And?" Faith prompted.

"If the kidnapper acted on impulse and has yet to work out the final details, it could be a few days before we hear back."

Myles responded, "But if two men attacked Jenny, they must have planned this out in advance. Particularly if you think Palicki was just hired local muscle."

Faith looked at the FBI agents clustered around them. These people weren't telling her and Myles everything. "What? What aren't you telling us?" she demanded.

"We're telling you everything we know," Agent Baker said soothingly.

"What are you guessing at that you haven't told us?" Faith challenged.

"We're telling you everything we can, ma'am. I promise."

Ha.

At Agent Baker's suggestion that her team had work to do and could use some space, Myles guided her out of the living room.

Faith turned to him angrily in the foyer. "I'm telling you. They know something they're not telling us!"

Myles's cousin Brad stepped into the foyer beside them. "Come with me," he muttered.

They followed him into the family room and turned to face him expectantly. He said low, "Mary's team is going through various rescue and assault scenarios. They've figured out from the photo of Jackson that he's being held in a house. It's undoubtedly someplace local. They're starting to plan a tactical assault and don't want to scare the hell out of you two. Also, everything they're discussing right now is hypothetical, anyway. Think of it as advance preparation for various possible outcomes."

"They're not planning to provoke a shootout with my baby in the middle of it, are they?" Faith blurted, alarmed.

"Absolutely not," Brad soothed. "But even if they did, Jackson could be sitting in a chair in the middle of a gun battle and not one FBI bullet would touch him. These tactical units are phenomenal."

Cousin Micha strolled into the family room from the kitchen, holding a sandwich. "Sorry. Couldn't help but overhear you guys. Brad's not wrong. We did hostage rescues in my Spec Ops unit, and we never once hurt a hostage."

Faith glared at him. "But the bad guys can always kill hostages rather than let them be rescued, can't they?"

Micha shrugged. "It happens now and then. But mostly, kidnappers think of their hostages as human shields. They're no good to the kidnapper if they're dead. They try hard not to kill the hostages."

"He's right," Brad said quickly. "Please. Just let the FBI do its job. We're very good at handling situations like this."

"What percentage of kidnapping victims get returned safe and alive?" Faith demanded of the two men.

Brad and Micha exchanged cryptic glances, then Brad answered carefully. "Statistics can't tell the whole story. Each case is unique."

"The percentage is terrible, isn't it?" she challenged him.

Brad threw up his hands. "Agent Baker is optimistic

that she can get Jackson back for you. This kidnapper doesn't seem to have any immediate interest in killing your son. Normally, kidnappers threaten to kill the hostage right up front, but no mention of anything like that was made in the phone call. We need for you to stay positive and let us do our job. Okay?"

Faith exhaled hard. "Okay. Fine. But I can't promise to stay sane for much longer. I want my son back. Alive. Got that?" She poked a finger at Brad's chest. "The FBI had better not do anything to jeopardize my baby."

Chapter Eighteen

Myles headed over to the police precinct to observe the questioning of Aric Schroder by the FBI. The Anarchy Ink leader had been picked up by the sheriff's department down by Maple Bend and driven up to Chicago this morning. Apparently, he'd been cooling his heels in the lockup for several hours.

Myles stood in the observation room, behind a piece of one-way glass, watching Schroder closely. The guy's posture was defensive, but the look in his eyes was closer to confusion. As if he didn't know why he was here.

Detective Caruso stepped into the interrogation room. The plan was to start with the local police and escalate the interrogation with FBI agents if Schroder didn't co-operate immediately.

"What's this all about?" Schroder demanded the second Caruso sat down in front of him.

Ignoring the question, Detective Caruso informed Schroder of his right to have an attorney present and told the man the interview was being recorded. Then Caruso said briskly, "Did you or your people kidnap Jackson Colton?"

"Kidnap? Colton? As in Myles Colton? Who's Jackson Colton?"

"Jackson is Myles Colton's four-year-old son. He was kidnapped yesterday."

"Son of a bitch." Schroder shoved a hand through his military crew cut hair. "Nah. We don't kidnap people. And we definitely don't mess with little kids. Not on purpose."

"You sure? The way I hear it, your boys have dispersed. How can you be sure none of them got the bright idea to get even with the lawyer who confiscated everything your crew owned?"

Schroder leaned forward and snarled, "Because I'm in charge of my crew. They do what I say, and I told them not to mess with the lawyer's family."

Caruso pushed a picture of Jackson across the table. "Ever seen this boy?"

To his credit, Schroder studied the picture before answering, "No. Never." Then he added gratuitously, "I'm telling you. I don't countenance kidnapping."

Myles frowned. Dammit, the guy's body language was open and relaxed. No hunching of his shoulders, no shifting looks, no frozen posture, covering his mouth, or shuffling feet. And the biggest tell of all, Schroder wasn't biting his lips. Without fail during the trial, when Schroder or one of his guys said something on the stand that Myles knew from other sources to be a lie, Schroder gnawed on his lower lip.

Caruso hammered at Schroder for nearly an hour, but the Anarchy Ink leader never wavered. He denied any knowledge of Jackson's kidnapping and swore steadfastly that he and his crew had nothing whatsoever to do with it.

And Myles believed him, dammit.

Caruso seemed to as well, for he left the interrogation room and joined Myles in the observation room as the FBI took a turn with Schroder. Although the FBI had a few tidbits of information to shake up Schroder with, undoubtedly tidbits gleaned from informants, Schroder never wavered once in his insistence that he and his gang had nothing to do with Jackson's kidnapping.

In fact, as the FBI agent declared Schroder free to go, the man actually turned to the mirror and said, "If you're back there, Mr. Colton, I swear to you. We didn't take your boy. If there's anything we can do to help find him, you just let me know. We don't mess with kids, and I mean that. My word of honor, man."

Caruso uttered, "Bastard sounds sincere. Do you buy it?"

"Yeah. I do. He chews his lips whenever he's lying, and he hasn't done that once. And you guys have put him under plenty of pressure. He would've shown a tell of lying if he weren't being truthful." He sighed heavily. "He and his guys didn't do this. Which means we're back to square one."

"Not exactly. We've got Donald Palicki's life under a microscope and are tracking down all of his known associates. Plus we have the link to your family with that specific ransom demand. Something will pop up."

Despite the detective's optimism, Myles wasn't convinced. He said, "If you don't mind, I need to head over to my folks' place for our family meeting."

"Need a ride?"

"That would be great."

A POLICE CRUISER dropped him off in front of his parents' rambling house. Every light was on downstairs, and cars filled the driveway, spilling over into the nursery's parking lot. It looked like all of the Coltons, old and new, had shown up. He registered a moment's gratitude that they'd all cared enough to be here tonight. He just hoped Carin Pedersen's lawsuit didn't throw a monkey wrench into the whole works.

She might be the jilted mistress who felt snubbed by being left out of Dean Colton's will, and she seemed to have convinced her twin sons, Erik and Axel to get on board with the lawsuit, but none of Erik and Axel's children had expressed any interest in taking money from their newfound cousins.

At least that was how it had been until now. Who knew what would happen when the whole clan got together? Well, almost the whole clan. Erik and Axel were estranged from their children, and Myles had specifically asked his mother not to invite either of them to this family meeting. It went without saying that Carin wasn't invited. Not only did she barely show up at family weddings and funerals, but her grandchildren disliked her possibly more than her greedy, shallow sons.

He jogged up the front steps and slipped inside. It seemed as if every square inch of floor space was taken up by the crowd milling around, chatting. The mood was somber, but everyone was taking the opportunity to catch up, it seemed. More importantly, everybody seemed to be getting along. Thank God.

As he made his way across the living room, he froze, staring. "Cousin Valerie?" He rushed over to his favorite cousin. They'd worked summers in the nursery together in high school, and he was closer to her than any of his other Colton relatives except for his sister, Lila. "I thought you were living in Ohio!" he exclaimed as she threw her arms around his neck.

"I am," she replied. "But this is a family crisis. I had

to be here to lend you moral support. I'm so sorry about your son."

He nodded, choked up that she'd come all this way for him. His family really came together great in a crisis. And it meant more to him than he could say.

His father spotted him from across the living room and waved him over. Myles wound through the crowd, which took a minute, because everyone he passed wanted to stop him and offer their sympathy and support.

Finally, he made it over to his stepfather's side. Rick raised his voice. "Everyone? Can we all take a seat and get started?"

As people found a spot or claimed a chair, Rick asked him quietly, "Do you want to do this, or shall I?"

Myles sighed. "I'll talk. He's my son."

Rick gripped his shoulder hard for a moment and Myles nodded back, his throat tight. The room fell silent, and he took a deep breath.

"As you all know, Jackson was kidnapped yesterday evening. What we know so far is two men broke into my mother-in-law's home, knocked Faith's mother unconscious, then went upstairs and abducted Jackson from his bed. Jenny's home from the hospital now and resting. She has a serious concussion but no fractured skull."

Murmurs of relief rose from the group.

"The Evanston police, Chicago PD and the FBI have been called in. Quite a crew of them are parked in the living room of my mother-in-law's house as we speak."

More nods.

"Late this morning, we received a ransom call from the kidnapper. The voice was electronically altered, so I can't tell you if it's a man or a woman. At any rate the kidnapper demanded thirty million dollars in cash."

As he expected, an exclamation went up at that, and everyone talked at once. He let the hubbub wind down before he continued.

"The FBI believes the amount of the ransom is no accident. They think the kidnapper knows at least one member of the family and is familiar with the amount in Carin Pedersen's lawsuit." He paused for effect and then said seriously, "I need each of you to think back. Who have you mentioned the lawsuit to? Anyone at all. The FBI needs you each to write down *all* of those people's names so the FBI can check into each person. One of them is probably the kidnapper. It's vital that you not leave anyone out. You don't have to show your list to anyone else, and I'm begging all of you not to blame anyone in the family for anyone whom they might have mentioned the lawsuit to."

Vita started moving around the room with sheets of paper and pencils, which she passed out to everyone.

"Jackson's life may depend on all of you remembering everyone you've talked to about the lawsuit," Myles added grimly.

The room went quiet, and the next several minutes were spent with everybody staring into space and jotting down names.

After about ten minutes, Vita went around the group again, collecting all the folded papers. When she was finished, everybody seemed to breathe a collective sigh of relief.

Myles stood up to speak again. "As if that wasn't uncomfortable enough, now I'm going to have to ask you something even more uncomfortable. Again, I'll pass out pieces of paper and feel free to fold them up. As an attorney, I swear to keep all of your answers confidential. Only the FBI and I will see what's written on them."

His cousin Aaron responded, "Holy crap, Myles. You're not going to ask which ones of us have done drugs or had affairs, are you?"

Everybody burst out laughing, and he smiled gratefully at his cousin for breaking the tension like that.

When the laughter had faded Myles said, "So, here's the thing. The FBI doesn't think the kidnapper is particularly interested in collecting the thirty million. They think the kidnapper is most interested in causing the Colton family pain and suffering."

That caused an angry murmur.

He let it settle and continued, "The FBI is advising Faith and me to negotiate with the kidnapper for a lower ransom amount that we can reasonably collect. Unfortunately, because we believe the kidnapper is at least somewhat acquainted with our family, this person will likely have a decent idea of our collective net worth. Hence this request from the FBI—they would like for each of you who own a business or own a home to write down what you think the approximate net worth is of each."

Heath Colton, the president of Colton Connections—the invention and patent firm that comprised the bulk of the Colton fortune—spoke up. "Are you asking us if we'd be willing to sell all our various companies and homes to raise the ransom cash for your son?"

Myles looked him in the eye. From the short time he'd known Heath, the man was a stand-up guy. He suspected Heath might actually be willing to liquidate his company to save Jackson's life. "I sincerely hope it doesn't come to that. The FBI doesn't think it will."

"But it's possible?" Heath said quietly.

Myles answered heavily, "I hate to say it, but yes."

Multiple voices spoke up at once. "I'll sell."

"So will we."

"And us."

"If it were my child, I'd sell my house, so I'll sell mine for Jackson."

"Yep. Count me in."

Myles was so overwhelmed he couldn't speak. He was utterly humbled by the generosity of both his old family and new one as they unanimously expressed willingness to liquidate lifetimes' worth of investments in time, money and sweat in an array of businesses, while others offered to sell large homes and buy smaller ones, donating the difference to a hypothetical ransom fund.

Eventually, his throat relaxed enough for him to speak once more. "Don't put your homes and businesses on the market just yet. There are still some major issues to work out with this ransom demand."

"Like what?" someone asked.

He replied, "For one thing, asking for thirty million dollars in cash is completely unrealistic. That much money, even in hundred-dollar bills, would weigh over six hundred fifty pounds and take up half a cargo pallet. In small bills, it would weigh over a ton and fill a small truck."

A chuckle rippled across the crowded room as everyone realized the kidnapper obviously hadn't thought that one through very well.

Myles continued, "We're hoping to do some sort of electronic funds transfer of a much smaller amount in the next day or two. If the kidnapper seriously wanted all of us to sell our homes and businesses, that would take months. The FBI highly doubts the kidnapper wants this situation to drag out that long. Their analysts hope that if we make the *offer* to liquidate everything, that will satisfy the kidnapper's desire to make all of us squirm."

Heath waved the second blank sheet of paper Vita had handed him. "So right now, you're only asking us to write down the net worth of all our assets so you can use that combined number as a negotiating tool?"

"Correct," Myles answered.

"No problem." Heath's head went down, and he wrote quickly on his own sheet of paper. The others in the room followed suit. There were a few conferrals as couples debated the value of their homes, and joint owners in business ventures discussed current valuations.

The second set of folded sheets of paper were collected and passed to Myles. He said, "I'll treat these with full attorney-client confidentiality and will destroy them as soon as this situation is resolved."

Several voices called out in unison, "Is there anything else we can do to help?"

"Funny you should ask," Myles said dryly. "The FBI would like all of us, everyone in this room, to go on television. They want Faith and me to give a press conference pleading for the return of our son, and the Feds want all of you standing behind us, looking worried and upset. The goal is for the kidnapper to see the suffering and pain he or she is causing all of us."

"Where do you need us to go for this press conference?" Farrah Colton, Alfred's widow, asked.

Her twin sister and Ernest's widow, Fallon Colton, chimed in, "Just say when, and we'll all be there." Farrah and Fallon were the matriarchs of the other side of the Colton clan.

Thankfully, there were nods and murmurs of agreement all around.

Myles responded, "I'll text my mom the time and place, and she can distribute it to all of you. Now, if you don't mind, I need to get back to my wife and the team of FBI agents who are waiting for a call from the kidnapper to tell us when and where we're supposed to deliver the ransom."

He waded out through the sea of sympathetic hugs, expressions of support and exhortations to stay strong. He had to admit, it was reassuring to know that the entire clan had his family's back like this. Now, he just prayed he didn't need their help…or their homes.

His cousin-in-law Brad gave him a ride home, and blessedly, the FBI agent seemed to understand he wasn't in a talkative mood. The ride was silent for the most part. He put his head back and closed his eyes, but it wasn't as if sleep would come to him easily. He was too tense for that.

Brad parked in front of the house, and Myles climbed out of the car reluctantly. As much as the family meeting had lightened his heart, walking back into Jenny's house was still almost more than he could face.

He stepped inside and the command center in the living room was quiet. "I take it there's been no more communication from the kidnapper?" he asked the room at large.

Agent Baker wasn't present, and another FBI agent, a man, looked up. "No, sir. Nothing, yet."

"Where's my wife?"

"Upstairs, resting. A medic gave her a sleeping pill about an hour ago."

It was barely eight o'clock, but he was glad she was getting some sleep. Even if it had to be drug-induced.

Myles wandered into the kitchen. Apparently, neighbors had been dropping off food all afternoon, and the island was crowded with casserole dishes, snack trays and desserts. He grazed unenthusiastically, not tasting anything he ate.

He lurched when his cell phone rang in the distance, and he slammed down his plate and tore into the family room.

"Caller ID says Erik Colton," the technician monitoring the phones said quickly.

Myles sagged and swore under his breath. What did his birth father want? "Can I answer it?"

"Yes," the tech guy replied. "Your phone has call waiting, so if another call comes in, we can transfer you over to it."

Myles picked up his phone. "Hello, Erik." He'd stopped calling the man dad, or thinking of the man as his father, a very long time ago. Rick Yates was all the father he needed.

"Hello, son. I hear there's a problem with your boy. A kidnapping?"

"That's correct."

"Why didn't you tell me? I can help."

"How can you help, Erik?" he snapped. "Do you know who kidnapped Jackson?"

"No. Of course not. But I'm family. The boy's my flesh and blood."

He was *not* going to get into an argument with his birth father over his woeful disinterest in his first grandchild. Myles took a deep breath and said evenly enough, "There is something you can do for me."

"Anything."

"Who all have you told about Carin's lawsuit?"

"Why? That's a weird question."

He didn't trust Erik Colton farther than he could throw him, and his gut told him not to explain any further. "Have you told anybody about it?"

"Not that I recall off the top of my head. It was in the news, so it's not any big secret, though."

Yes, but the amount that Erik's mother was suing for had never been in the papers. Rather than tell that important detail to Erik, he said, "There's something else you can do for me, then. Convince Carin to drop her lawsuit. She's not going to win. That copy of Dean's will she produced isn't going to hold up to scrutiny, and it's going to be proved fraudulent in court. She's wasting everybody's time."

Erik sighed. "Yeah, but what if it does hold up? Our family will be rich. Don't you want to be able to give Jackson anything he wants?"

"My son has been *kidnapped.* I don't know if he'll be alive tomorrow, let alone in a few years. I don't give a damn for Dean's money."

"And my mother dropping her lawsuit will help you get Jackson back how?" Erik demanded truculently.

Myles huffed. He was not going there with Erik Colton. The man didn't deserve to know anything about the family he'd abandoned or their family business. "The lawsuit is wrong, and you know it. Don't be an ass, Erik."

On the other end of the line, Erik started to bluster. Myles cut him off sharply. "I need to get off this phone in case the kidnapper calls back. We're waiting to find out how to deliver the ransom. Goodbye, Erik." He hung up on the man who'd donated DNA to his life but not a whole hell of a lot more.

The FBI technician was looking at him sympathetically. Myles rolled his eyes. "Family. Can't live with 'em, can't kill 'em, right?"

The technician smiled. "Guy sounds like a piece of work."

"He and his twin brother, and their mother for that matter, are all pieces of work. Thankfully, my mom divorced him and married the man who raised me and became my real dad."

"Rest of your family seems real nice."

"They are."

Agent Baker, wearing slacks and a casual sweater, came into the living room just then.

Myles made eye contact with her. "I thought you'd gone home to get some rest."

"Not me. I'm here until this case is resolved. I just ran out to wash up and change clothes. How'd the family meeting go?"

"Very well. Here are the lists of names of people they've told about the lawsuit and this pile is everybody's rough net worth. I haven't looked through them yet. I grabbed a bite to eat first." Truth be told, he was hinky about learning what every single member of the family was worth, and he'd been avoiding the job.

"I'll compile the information, Mr. Colton," Agent Baker said as if she understood his hesitation.

"We may have a problem, though," Myles said. "My birth father just called. Erik Colton. He's Carin Pedersen's son. I asked him if he's told anyone about his mother's lawsuit, and he was evasive with me. It's possible he or his brother or Carin herself have been spewing information about the lawsuit to anyone who will listen."

Agent Baker stared at him thoughtfully. "In the morning, I'll send some folks around to interview all three of them. We'll get the names out of them of who all they've blabbed to."

He smiled a little, relishing the FBI shaking down his least favorite relatives. "Tell your agents not to be too nice, eh?"

Agent Baker grinned. "Unfortunately, we usually get better results in nonhostile interrogations."

"Too bad," he replied dryly.

"It's getting late," Baker said. "I doubt the kidnapper's going to call us tonight. If you want to get some rest, we'll be manning the phones overnight. We'll wake you if we need you. Now, it's a waiting game."

Chapter Nineteen

Faith woke with a jolt. She looked at the bedside clock, and it was almost six a.m. Whoa. She'd slept for ten hours. That sleeping pill the FBI doctor had given her had really packed a punch. She swung her feet to the floor and Myles sat upright in bed abruptly.

"What? What's happened?" he mumbled, sounding more asleep than awake.

"Go back to sleep," she murmured.

"Nope. Can't," he said more alertly, as if the nightmare had already crashed back down on him. "Stay with me for a few more minutes," he added gently.

She lay back down beside him and he gathered her in his arms. She stiffened but then forced herself to relax.

"I watched the cops and the FBI question Aric Schroder yesterday. He swore on a stack of Bibles that his guys had nothing to do with kidnapping Jackson, and I believe him."

"Of course, you'd believe him. It's in your interest that he not be involved—"

Myles cut her off. "The police and FBI don't think he's lying, either. He even offered to do anything he and his guys can to help find Jack. Anarchy Ink isn't behind this."

She absorbed that for a minute, then pushed up on Myles's chest to stare down at him. "Then who?"

"We're back to someone close to the Colton family who wants to see all of us suffer."

"Like who?"

"If I had the answer to that, I'd be pounding down that person's door right now."

She exhaled hard. "You're sure this has nothing to do with your case?"

"Positive."

She knew Myles well enough to be certain he was telling her the truth.

The ice around her heart shattered all at once, and she dissolved in tears. She buried her face on his chest, soaking the T-shirt he'd worn to bed.

Eventually, he murmured, "What's wrong, Faith? Talk to me."

"I've been so mad at you. I was so sure this was all your fault. I've been horrible to you."

He laughed a little and rolled to his side, gathering her close against him. "Simone told me you were using anger to shield yourself and that I should let you. I haven't taken anything you've said to heart. I meant it when I told you that no matter what you said or did, I would love you."

The remorse twisted its sharp blade even harder in her chest. "I don't deserve you."

His lips were warm and resilient on hers, cutting off any more mea culpas from her. Fine. If he wouldn't let her talk, she would show him how sorry she was. She looped her arms around his neck and relaxed against him, loving how hard and flat his stomach was and how strong and gentle his arms were around her. She undulated invitingly against all that lovely muscle and was gratified when he groaned in the back of his throat.

They stripped off their clothing quickly and came back together under the covers, naked and needy. His skin was hot against hers, and she relished running her palms through the silky hairs on his chest.

Myles rolled her onto her back and pushed away from the headboard, sliding down her body, kissing as he went, down her neck, between her breasts and then to one side to capture a nipple between his teeth. As she gasped and arched up into the slightly painful tug, he let go, laving the bud with wet swirls of his tongue until she gasped again.

He slid his palm down her torso, across her stomach, and then lower, easing between her legs. She opened eagerly for him, loving how his fingers stroked and teased at her most sensitive flesh, drawing forth a powerful reaction from her. She groaned as well, arching into his hand hungrily.

One of these days, they would have to really take their time and make love for hours, exploring and relearning each other's bodies inch by inch. But today was not that day. She reached for his erection, which was pressing against her thigh, and guided Myles home without any further ado.

He filled her as perfectly as he always did, and she sighed in relief as the stretching fullness promised her sweet relief from the desire clawing at the inside of her body, seeking escape.

He started moving then, and she held on to him, wrapping her arms and legs around him and pulling him close. Her hips rose to meet his, and they found a rhythm together very quickly. In the dim predawn light, she looked up at him and he gazed down at her, and they came together in shared pain and shared grief, seeking a moment's escape from all of it, and maybe a brief affirmation that if they were still alive, their son must be, too.

As her body responded to the sex, she let herself get lost in it, let herself just feel for the moment. Waves of pleasure sloshed back and forth within the fragile vessel of her body, threatening to break free at any moment, and she relished the rocking of their bodies, the rolling of that building tide of glory, and the way her entire being stretched taut with anticipation as the power of it drew ever closer to breaking free.

Myles arched hard against her, burying his face in her neck and the pillow. With a muffled shout he found release, and that raw sound was just enough to tip the scales for her. An almighty orgasm ripped through her, exploding through her entire body and shattering into a million tiny, shimmering pieces of sensation. Gradually her senses settled as they passed, weightless, through her flesh, and fell in a lazy, floating flight toward her soul.

The rightness of being with her husband like this, of taking this one moment of affirmation and renewal for themselves in the midst of the madness roaring around them, sunk into her bones. They'd needed this. And if they were to be strong together for Jackson, it was good that they'd reconnected at this deep, visceral level. She would not feel guilty about stealing a moment's joy in the midst of this agony.

"Are you okay?" Myles asked carefully.

"I am. You?"

"Yes," he said, sighing. "I needed that more than I realized." He added hastily, "Not the sex. The closeness with you."

She smiled gently at him. "I understood what you meant. I needed to connect with you, again, too. I'm sorry I was so mean to you."

He leaned on one elbow and used his free hand to push her damp hair back off her forehead. "I deserved it. If Anarchy Ink had been involved in this catastrophe, it would have been my fault. I put you guys at risk because I was selfish. I could've never forgiven myself."

"I'm past caring whose fault it is. I just want my little boy back—" Her voice caught and she couldn't continue.

She stared up through a haze of unshed tears, and she thought Myles's eyes were suspiciously watery, too.

He murmured, "Brad told me last night that the FBI is optimistic about this case. It's not a typical kidnapping, and they think there's a decent chance we can get Jackson back safe and unharmed."

"How?" she wailed softly. "We don't have anywhere close to thirty million dollars."

"We'll find a way. I don't know how, but we'll find one."

They lay together in silence for a few moments.

She sighed. "I suppose we should go downstairs and see if there's any news."

Myles groaned under his breath. "Is it just me, or are you a little afraid of Agent Baker, too?"

Faith giggled. "She is kind of scary, isn't she?"

"Kind of?" Myles rolled his eyes. "Care to share the shower with me?"

"I'll scrub your back if you'll scrub mine," she replied.

"Deal."

It didn't take long for them to shower and get dressed, and they walked down the stairs hand in hand to face the new day and whatever fresh horrors it brought.

MYLES GRABBED A cup of coffee and joined Faith on the back porch where, surprisingly, she was talking into what looked like a cheap burner phone.

He interrupted, asking, "Where'd you get that?"

"Hank gave it to me while I was in hiding. I'm talking with Lila, by the way."

"Hi, sis," he called.

"Let me put her on speakerphone," Faith said. "There. Now we can all talk."

Lila said, "Carter's here, too. I put this end of the call on speaker, as well. What's going on back there? Mom said Jackson's been kidnapped?"

Faith said, "I've filled them in on everything so far. They offered to pitch into the ransom fund."

Myles grumbled, "What I really need is a small and portable way to give the kidnapper something that looks worth thirty million dollars, but that's actually a fake. Something like fake diamonds. Except any reasonably observant person can probably tell when diamonds aren't real."

"Easy," Carter said. "Give 'em a fake painting."

"Where would I even get one of those?"

Carter snorted. "I'm an art fraud investigator, my dude. I know everyone who's anyone in the art forgery world, and I happen to know where some excellent fakes are stored or displayed."

"Do you know of any paintings worth thirty million dollars or thereabouts that happen to have a fake of them sitting in Chicago?"

"Actually, I do. Although I think the real painting is worth north of forty million by now."

Lila piped up. "What are you talking about, Carter?"

"A collector tried to sell a Picasso to the Art Institute of Chicago a couple of years back—an alleged sixth painting in his *Les Femmes d'Algers* series. It was a late cubist piece. Phenomenal forgery, actually. The price tag was shy of forty million dollars, as I recall. My firm proved it to be a forgery. Too bad, actually. Another painting in the series sold not long ago to a Saudi collector for just under two hundred million dollars. It would have been a steal for the museum at forty million if it had been real."

"Two hundred million for a painting?" Myles asked blankly. "Dang. I'm in the wrong business. I gotta learn how to paint!"

Carter laughed. "You'd have to change your name to Picasso and become an innovative great master, while you were at it."

"Any idea where the fake Picasso is now?" Myles asked, not holding out much hope that this idea would be feasible.

"As far as I know, the Art Institute of Chicago still has the forgery. They don't display it, of course."

Excitement bloomed in his gut. "Any chance they'd sell it to us to pay the ransom for Jackson?"

"Can't hurt to ask," Carter replied. "Stay on this line while I make a quick call."

Myles and Faith waited on pins and needles, while Lila talked about sightseeing in London to distract them. In about five minutes, Carter was back. "The curator would be delighted to give you the forgery if it'll save your son's life."

"Wow. That's generous!" Myles exclaimed.

"Even better," Carter added, "the curator is willing to throw in the forged provenance documents. It'll take an art fraud expert like me to tell it's not the real thing.

If your kidnapper is clever, he or she could probably get away with selling the painting on the black market."

"I don't care what the kidnapper does with it as long as I get my son back," Myles retorted.

Carter laughed. "Personally, I rather enjoy the idea of ripping off the kidnapper and the rube he tries to sell the forgery to. Either way, it's a win for me. A bad person loses their shirt over greed."

"Let me run this by the FBI, and then we'll have to convince the kidnapper to go for it, of course."

"Good luck. Let me know if there's anything more I can do to help. I'll send you the curator's private phone number and I'll email him to expect a call from you," Carter said.

"You're the best, Carter," Faith chimed in.

"Hey, I'm an honorary Colton now. And I'm told we Coltons stick together."

Myles and Faith traded tentative smiles. Here was hoping the family's intense loyalty was enough to see them all through this crisis and bring Jackson home safely.

Chapter Twenty

A headache pounded in Faith's temples. The gathered Colton clan was loud, the crowd of press in front of her and Myles was louder, and the camera lights were blindingly bright. She felt stretched paper thin. One millimeter more and she would tear into tiny little pieces and blow away.

She could do this. Jackson needed her to be strong.

She repeated the mantra over and over in her head as the last sound checks were completed and the stagehands stepped back into the shadows.

The press conference started, and the members of the family went quiet. No doubt they were dabbing at tears and looking devastated as they'd been instructed by the FBI to do, and as they actually were. Jenny had insisted on joining the Colton family and stood directly behind Faith, sniffling loudly.

It had been decided that Faith would read the prepared statement the FBI's profilers had written. She looked over at Agent Baker, who nodded for her to start.

Faith started to read aloud, but the words coming out of her mouth didn't register as having any meaning. She knew it was a plea for anyone who knew anything about her son's kidnapping to contact the FBI or any police department, and a statement that the entire Colton family had pooled all of its financial resources to gather the ransom money. She thanked anonymous donors who'd also donated money and resources, and then she begged the kidnapper to return her son safe and well to her and Myles. She choked in the middle of the last sentence, her voice breaking. Oh, God. She was losing it. She couldn't do this.

Jackson. Be strong for Jackson.

Using every ounce of willpower she had, she gathered herself and started over, repeating the plea for Jackson to be returned safely to her and Myles.

And then it was over. The whole statement took no more than a minute. Her legs threatened to buckle, but she dug deep again. One minute at a time. One tiny action. She could do this. Stay upright. For Jackson.

Agent Baker swept forward and took over the podium while Brad Howard and another FBI agent escorted her and Myles swiftly off the stage. Thankfully, Brad had her by the elbow and helped hold her upright as he whisked her off the dais and into an empty hallway.

She was startled when she and Myles were swept right on outside and into a black SUV. The driver stuck a siren on the roof over his head, and they tore across Chicago and back to her mother's house.

"Why the rush?" she asked as they streaked onto a highway.

"The kidnapper will see the recording of you when it goes on the noon news. We need you two at home and by your phones by then."

"Why?" Myles asked. "Do you expect the kidnapper to call us in response?"

Brad answered from the passenger's seat. "We just

made it clear you've gathered the ransom money and are ready to make the trade. We also made it clear your family is suffering gravely, which is exactly what the bastard wants. The kidnapper will call immediately after the broadcast of your statement."

"Let's hope you're right," Faith said fervently. "But… I'm scared."

Myles reached across the back seat to squeeze her hand. He seemed to understand her dilemma. On the one hand she wanted this over as quickly as possible. On the other hand, she dreaded the outcome so much she frantically didn't want the end of the crisis to come. Jackson had to be all right. He *had* to.

She closed her eyes and tried to reach out with her mind, or her mommy intuition, or divine grace, to sense Jackson. She'd been trying to do this ever since Myles had first told her he was missing, but she'd never sensed anything from her son. She didn't get the feeling he was dead, but she also didn't get the feeling he was afraid or angry or anything else. And that scared her worst of all.

If possible, she stretched even a bit more thinly, that much closer to the breaking point. She closed her eyes and concentrated on drawing her next breath. And the next one. And the next. The grief and terror and agony loomed over her, giant, crouching monsters waiting to rip her apart and devour her in their drooling maws. She felt their hot, fetid breath on the back of her neck. They were coming for her. And she wouldn't be able to hold them off much longer.

One more minute.

One more breath.

They pulled up at her mother's house and climbed out of the vehicle. Woodenly, she allowed herself to be rushed inside. Dr. Philbin met them at the front door and started speaking immediately. She fought like mad to concentrate on his words. To make sense of the sounds he was making. But it was a struggle. She was at the end of her rope.

"We expect a phone call any minute. Regardless of which cell phone the kidnapper calls, we want you to answer it, Mr. Colton. You'll explain to the kidnapper that you've obtained a painting worth thirty million dollars, and that its mate just sold for close to two hundred million. You're proposing the painting as the ransom in lieu of bulky, heavy, traceable cash. You can have the painting in a few hours."

"What if the kidnapper refuses to take the painting instead of cash?" Faith blurted, startled that she was even able to form a coherent question.

Myles looked at the psychologist. "Should I lay it on thick that the family has bankrupted itself buying this painting? That we pulled in a huge favor to get the owner to sell it to us for what he paid for it?"

"Exactly," Philbin said. "I'm counting on you to sell the idea to the kidnapper. A painting is light, small and portable, and this particular painting is potentially worth much more than thirty million dollars."

Myles nodded. "I'll treat the kidnapper like a jury I'm trying to convince."

"Don't lay it on so thick the kidnapper suspects you're lying," Philbin responded.

Myles grinned. "This is my job. I sell ideas to people for a living."

Faith followed the men into the living room and sent up a silent prayer that Myles was as good a lawyer as she thought he was. Their son's life depended on it, right now.

The grandfather clock in the corner of the room struck noon. Its last, clear chiming of the twelfth hour had barely faded away before Faith's cell phone rang. If she wasn't mistaken, the ringtone sounded angry. Eager. Which was silly, of course, but this was it.

She leaned against the back of the sofa and tried not to hold her breath. Her face felt hot, and adrenaline rushed across her skin.

The technician nodded his readiness, and Myles nodded his. Dr. Philbin murmured for the tech guy to put the call through.

"Hello?" Myles said calmly.

Faith heard the tension in his voice, but she knew him very well.

"Do you have the money?" the kidnapper rasped without preamble in that creepy electronically altered voice of his or hers.

"I have something better than cash," Myles replied.

"I told you thirty million in cash!"

"How are you planning to transport so much money?" Myles asked. "In hundred-dollar bills, that much cash would weigh well over six hundred pounds and take up a couple of large steamer trunks. And in small bills, thirty million dollars would weigh a ton-and-a-half and fill a small truck." Without pausing to let the kidnapper get a word in edgewise, Myles continued, "Look. The entire Colton family has bankrupted itself. We sold houses fast for cash, emptied bank accounts, even sold businesses. We took out loans and got donations from all over the country, and we came up with the money you demanded. And we used that money to buy you a painting."

"A painting?" the kidnapper squawked.

"Not just any painting," Myles cut in. Faith smiled

faintly. She knew the technique. Myles had practiced it on her when he was a young prosecutor. He steamrolled over someone and distracted them, getting them to forget what they were originally going to say and pushing them to say what he wanted them to, instead.

"It's a Picasso," Myles said excitedly. "One of his *Les Femmes d'Algers* series. I don't know squat about art, but the person who sold us the painting paid thirty million for it about a decade ago. One of its mates just sold at auction for two hundred million dollars. It will probably appraise for a lot more than thirty million, but we can absolutely guarantee it's worth at least that much."

It sounded like the kidnapper tried to say something, but Myles barreled on, "It's light, and easily portable. It has been professionally removed from its frame and rolled into a tube for transport. Also, it comes with all the provenance paperwork, which will make it easy and legal for you to sell it. All you have to do is take it to any major auction house in the world—Sotheby's, Christie's—or any art museum, for that matter, and they'll take care of selling it for you. You can remain anonymous, and the money can be wired to a numbered bank account. It's the cleanest and easiest possible way to get the ransom money to you so you have full access to it and can spend it legally."

He fell silent, and the other end of the line was also silent.

Oh, God. Had the kidnapper hung up? She lurched toward Myles in panic, but he waved her to silence. Dr. Philbin was nodding in approval. They seemed to think the kidnapper was mulling it over.

"You paid thirty million for the painting?" the kidnapper asked.

"Thirty-one million," Myles answered. "It was all the money the entire family had. But it was the only way we could think of to make this transfer go smoothly. You obviously didn't want us messing around with cryptocurrencies or bank transfers, which can be traced and blocked. You needed something tangible. We considered diamonds, but they're hard to sell and capricious in value. The Picasso seemed like the best option."

"Very well," the kidnapper said.

Faith sagged in relief and had to reach for the back of the sofa to steady herself.

"Bring the painting and the papers that go with it to the LaBagh Woods. Start walking on the North Branch Trail. Someone will meet you there and ask for the Picasso by name. When you hand over the painting, they'll tell you where to find your son. Be there in two hours."

"I'll be there. How will your messenger know me?" Myles asked.

"He'll know you," the kidnapper snapped.

The line went dead.

"Interesting," Philbin murmured. "The messenger will recognize you on sight. This is definitely being run by someone who knows you, Mr. Colton."

Across the room a flurry of agents on phones were relaying the ransom exchange details to Agent Baker and to a host of other FBI agents and law enforcement agencies.

Brad Howard stepped forward and said to Myles, "We don't have much time. Take off your jacket and shirt."

Faith frowned as Myles started to strip down. "Are you putting a microphone on him?"

Brad winced. "No. A bullet resistant vest."

Oh, God.

She couldn't lose Myles.

Not Myles *and* Jackson.

The room swayed. Spun around once. And then everything went dark.

MYLES LEAPED FORWARD as Faith fainted and caught her under the armpits. He wasn't able to stop her from going down, but he broke her fall and lowered her gently to the floor.

She came to quickly, blinking up at him in surprise. "Why am I lying down?"

"You fainted, sweetheart."

"Oh."

"Do you want to go with us for the exchange, or would you rather—"

"I'll go with," she said quickly.

He smiled a little. "It's time to go, then. We have to pick up the painting and get over to the drop-off spot."

He helped her out to the SUV, with his cousin Brad driving and Agent Baker sitting in the front seat. He and Faith had the back seat to themselves. He held out his arm and she dived against his side, huddling there, trembling. Lord, he hated seeing his wife suffer like this. What had the two of them ever done to deserve this agony? A spear of rage stabbed him. Once they had Jackson back home with them, somebody was going to pay for doing this to his family. He just wished he knew who was behind it.

Eyes narrowed, he focused on the task ahead. He would get a good look at one of the kidnappers in a little over an hour. The cavalcade of SUVs drove to the Art Institute of Chicago, and Brad and another agent hurried inside to pick up the forged Picasso. They were back in under ten minutes with a long, black tube that conveniently had a shoulder strap attached to it.

Brad passed the tube to Myles. "Provenance papers are inside, with the canvas. There's a tracking burr in the tube, and another one on the painting itself. Their batteries are good for about a week. And the museum staff is mighty amused to be passing off a forgery on a bad guy, by the way."

Myles smiled tightly. It was time to put on his game face.

They drove toward the LaBagh Woods at the south end of the North Branch Trail complex. But as they neared the wooded area, the vehicles turned off the main road and parked behind a local police precinct. There were only about twenty minutes left before he was supposed to walk down that trail. What was wrong?

"What's happening?" Faith asked nervously.

"Everything's fine. We'll wait here until it's time to go," Brad said soothingly. "We're just doing one last check in with all the agents in the field. Making sure they're in position in the woods before we send in Myles. This is all perfectly routine."

"Will the kidnapper come in person to pick up the painting?" Myles asked. If so, he had no problem jumping the bastard himself.

"Definitely not," Brad replied. "But he may be nearby, watching the exchange."

Faith blurted, "Myles won't be all alone out there with the bad guy, will he?"

Brad grinned. "Oh, no. There are close to a dozen FBI agents already in place. They moved the minute we got the location for the drop-off. We'll tail the guy to wherever he takes the painting."

Brad used a tablet computer to pull up a map of the trail Myles would be taking. "You'll start here, at this parking area. You'll walk to this trail marker and start down the path. It's a bike and hike trail, so it's fairly wide in most spots. It narrows here where it follows a bend in the Chicago River and then widens out again. We think the kidnapper's guy will be past this spot. It puts the hand off out of sight of casual observers. While you're on the trail, our guys will put tracking devices on every vehicle in the parking lot. No matter which car he uses to exit the hand off, we'll be able to track him."

Myles nodded. "How long do you need to plant the trackers on the cars?"

"About two minutes. Once you meet with the kidnapper's guy, try to keep him talking for that long. Ask about Jack's condition, repeat back any instructions or addresses he gives you about where to go to get Jackson. Maybe repeat your conversation from before about how and where to go to sell the painting."

"Got it."

"All right. It's time to go. Are you ready?" Brad asked quietly.

"Let's do it."

He reached for Faith's hand, and she scooted over close beside him, murmuring, "Be careful. And don't do anything heroic, okay? I couldn't bear to lose both of you."

"You're not going to lose either one of us, baby. I've got this. I'll hand off the painting, and then we'll go get Jack. Sound like a plan? We'll be together by suppertime."

"Promise me," she said softly.

He knew she wasn't talking about them being together. She was asking him to promise not to do anything heroic that would get him killed.

He sighed. "Okay, fine. I promise."

She smiled up at him, but the expression didn't reach her eyes, which were dark with worry. "I wish I could come along."

"Not me," he blurted. "I need to know you're safe."

"I'll be in an armored car full of FBI agents," she retorted.

"Good."

The vehicles pulled out, and Faith fell silent beside him, pensive. He knew the feeling. It was a short drive to the parking area, and Faith leaned over to kiss him. "For luck," she whispered.

Good Lord willing, he wouldn't need any.

He climbed out of the SUV and headed for the wooden sign marking where the trail passed by this spot. Maybe it was just his imagination, but he felt eyes watching him. No doubt the plentiful FBI agents sprinkled around the woods. He glanced around furtively but didn't spot anyone nearby. Dang, they were good at camouflaging themselves.

He walked around the gate blocking cars from accessing the wide trail and turned north. It was a gray day with low clouds scudding by on a sharp wind. He slung the tube over his left shoulder so it hung down his back, out of his way as he walked. The wind was knocking down a lot of leaves today, and the air fluttered thickly with yellowed leaves twirling on their flight toward the ground. He thought idly that it was a pretty way to die.

He reached the narrow spot in the trail and tensed as he walked around the bend. He expected someone to be there waiting for him, but the trail stretched away from him, empty.

Huh. He kept walking.

He walked perhaps ten more minutes and had covered

the better part of a mile when the trail narrowed again. Trees crowded in close, and the trail narrowed to little wider than a sidewalk as it swooped close to the shore of the river running cold and black beside him.

Without warning, something sharp stabbed him high on the right side of his back. It hurt—a lot—as if a wasp had stung him.

"Oww!" he yelped.

He took a few more steps and realized the trees were spinning all of a sudden. He stumbled. Barely caught himself. What the hell?

He fell to his knees. Had he been drugged?

He heard a clicking noise behind him and with great effort, turned his head to look over his shoulder. A bicycle was coming up behind him fast. A thin guy with light brown hair rode it, but his face was fuzzy as Myles blinked several times hard to clear his eyes.

The bicycle slowed and Myles pitched forward onto his hands and knees. The tube fell off his shoulder to the ground beside him. The bike slowed.

"Gimme the Picasso," the bike rider hissed. Myles watched stupidly as the guy stopped, leaned down to scoop up the tube, and then jumped back on his bike. As Myles pitched forward onto his face, he saw the bicycle speed away to the north.

"WAKE UP, MYLES," a male voice said urgently. Someone slapped his cheeks hard enough to make his eyes sting. "C'mon, buddy."

He groaned and forced his eyelids open. "Wha' happ'n?"

"You were shot with a tranquilizer dart. A kid on a

bike snagged the painting and took off up the trail. We don't have any agents out here on bicycles to follow him."

The brain fog was clearing rapidly. "Did you get a look at him?" he asked urgently. "Are you tracking him?"

"Yes to both. We think the bicycle rider was Donald Palicki. If you think you can walk, we'll get you back to the SUV and catch up with the other vehicles who are following the painting."

He would stand and walk if it was the last thing he did. With Brad's help, he rose to his feet. The trees were still spinning, but he concentrated fiercely on putting one foot in front of the next.

With every passing minute, his mind grew sharper and his steps more confident. After about five more minutes, he looked over at his cousin. "I'm good to run if you are."

"Let's go, coz."

They took off running, and it became a race to see which of them could reach the parking lot first. It was close, but Myles edged out his cousin. They piled into the SUV, panting.

"What happened?" Faith cried, flinging herself across the back seat at him as the SUV lurched into motion. "They said you were shot!"

"Apparently, the bastards used a tranquilizer dart on me," he bit out.

Brad filled her in. "Our guys think the shooter was on the other side of the river. Looks like he used an animal dart. Myles went down in about sixty seconds, and then he came around about as fast."

"Where are we headed?" Myles asked.

"West. Toward Aurora."

Myles listened while Brad gave directions to the FBI agent driving the vehicle, then asked, "Where's Agent Baker?"

"When you went down, she left me here to deal with you while she hopped into another vehicle to track the bicyclist. She and the other carload of agents are about ten minutes ahead of us. Apparently, the biker is cutting through parks and giving them fits trying to follow him in cars."

"Smart guy," Myles commented.

"If the biker is Palicki, he's not known to be a rocket scientist. Which means the main kidnapper probably planned the hand off and the bicyclist's escape route."

"How long till you guys catch the biker?" Myles asked impatiently.

"Could take a bit. We'll stay back from him and let him go wherever he's planning to go before we close in and arrest him. The hope is he'll lead us to his partner in crime and to Jackson."

Faith was practically bouncing up and down in her seat with impatience, and he shared her anxiety. A single thought kept running through his brain. It was about his son. *Please be safe. Please be safe.*

Chapter Twenty-One

Faith wasn't sure she could stand this waiting. They were cruising slowly toward a residential area well west of downtown Chicago, while a net of FBI agents slowly closed in on the locator beacon inside the painting's carrier tube.

The bicyclist had transferred to a car and then drove south toward the sprawling suburbs of Chicago, obviously trying to lose anyone who might be following him. He made illegal turns, doubled back on his route, even parked and sat in a shopping center parking lot for ten minutes or so. But the whole time, the FBI hung back, out of sight of the driver, trusting their tracking technology to tell them where the guy was.

The tracker had stopped moving again about five minutes ago at a house. The FBI was waiting out the driver again to make sure this was not another ruse to draw them out.

"How long till you guys move in?" she asked Brad impatiently.

He shrugged. "Agent Baker will make that call. Could be five more minutes. Could be an hour. She'll get eyes on the house before too much longer and will make that determination. You'll hear her come up on the radio soon."

Sure enough, in about five minutes, Baker's familiar voice said, "An infrared scan of the house shows two individuals inside, one downstairs, one upstairs. Both are stationary. As long as this situation remains static, let's give this a little more time to see if anyone else shows up."

Faith groaned. More waiting.

Myles put his arm around her shoulders and drew her close to his side. "Not much longer," he murmured.

"I can't take this," she complained.

"You're so much stronger than I ever knew. You've held up through this nightmare like a rock."

"I don't feel like a rock. I feel like a sponge."

He dropped a kiss on her temple, and she lowered her head to his shoulder. He was warm and solid and steady, her own bulwark against any storms life threw at her. She prayed then, like she'd never prayed before. And she'd been praying pretty fervently the past three days.

How long they were silent together, each lost in private prayers for the safe return of their baby, she didn't know. But all of a sudden, the interior of the SUV filled with Agent Baker's voice. "That's it. Let's go in. Tactical team Alpha, you are greenlighted."

A deep voice said merely, "Roger. Going in."

The driver of their SVU started the engine and pulled out into traffic without waiting to be called in. Thank goodness. She couldn't stand one more minute of inactivity.

"How long will breaching the house take?" Myles asked.

Brad snorted. "About sixty seconds. And that's if they're taking their sweet time."

Their SUV parked across the street from a totally normal-looking house, where two more big black SUVs were parked across the driveway, and a big step van parked directly in front. The front door of the house stood open, and a man dressed in all black military-style body armor stood in the front door, wielding some sort of assault weapon.

Voices started calling out over the radio in a cascade.

"Clear left!"

"Clear right!"

"Clear hallway!"

"I've got a body."

Faith jolted and Myles stiffened against her side.

"Kitchen clear!"

The voice that reported the body said, "Looks like Palicki. He's dead."

Dead? Faith's eyes opened wide and she looked at Myles in horror. He stared back at her, ashen.

"Stairs clear."

"Front right, clear."

Then, "I've got a child."

Faith jolted so hard she banged the top of her head into Myles's chin.

"It's the Colton boy. Unconscious, but breathing."

Faith registered that she was sobbing, but her relief was so profound she didn't feel her tears nor hear her own voice. She was fumbling at the door handle, tumbling out of the vehicle and running toward the house before she was even aware that she'd moved. Myles was right on her heels. Brad bolted out of the SUV as well and somehow managed to beat them to the front porch.

"You can't go in yet," he said forcefully. "It's an active tactical scene."

The guy in the body armor moved across the front door menacingly, as well. Faith briefly contemplated bowling him over, but then Brad froze, as if listening. He broke into a big smile and said, "They're bringing Jackson out."

Faith spied red lights flashing behind her and glanced over her shoulder to see an ambulance coming around the corner, its lights on, but with no siren.

And then a man dressed in black tactical gear came out of the house. She saw familiar blond hair. Blue rocket pajamas. And Jackson's beloved face. It was him. It was really him.

She kept pace with the guy carrying Jackson as he hustled over to the ambulance, and Myles did the same on the man's other side. The boy was so tiny on the adult-size gurney. An EMT examined Jackson quickly and allowed her to brush the hair off his forehead gently.

Myles spoke to him from beside her. "Hey, buddy. It's Mommy and Daddy. Can you wake up for us?"

The EMT glanced up. "He appears to be sedated. We're going to take him to the hospital for a more thorough examination and blood work."

Myles said dryly, "No power on earth is moving my wife or me out of this ambulance or away from our son's side, you realize."

The EMT grinned and shrugged. "I get that. You just got him back." He looked toward the driver. "Let's go."

The ride in the ambulance was short, and they walked in on either side of Jackson as he was wheeled into the emergency room. Faith held her son's limp hand the whole time, silently begging him to wake up and to be okay.

The doctors shone lights in his eyes and drew vials of blood to test for various chemicals in Jackson's system. It was a tense wait, but finally, the doctor came back in.

Myles put his arms around her waist from behind and she leaned back against him, terrified of what the doctor would have to say.

"Your son has been given a heavy dose of sleeping pills. He's got way more in his system than I'd like to see in a child of his age, but once he wakes up, he should suffer no lasting harm."

Faith turned in Myles's arms and sobbed against his chest. The relief flooding her was too profound for words. That FBI agent who'd carried her son out and given him back to her and Myles had given them back their life. Jackson—their little family—was their life. Nothing else mattered.

It was going to be okay. Everything would be fine. Myles had found his way back to his family, and now Jackson had found his way back to them, as well. Her family was safe.

Myles whispered into her hair, "I'm never letting anything bad happen to you or Jackson—or any of us as a family—again."

"Amen," she whispered back. "Amen."

Chapter Twenty-Two

Myles looked around at the gathered Colton clan. Unlike the last time they'd gathered like this to discuss how to raise the ransom money for Jackson, this time they were laughing and talking and gossiping, and doing all the wonderful things big, noisy families did. Kids tore around, causing chaos, and he smiled fondly as Jackson tore around with his cousins, as well.

He'd had to spend a night in hospital while the sedation the kidnapper had used wore off. The good news was he had no memory at all of the kidnapping. Apparently, the kidnappers had knocked him out with something like chloroform before they took him from his bed, where he'd already been asleep. He'd woken up in his hospital room, confused about how he'd gotten there, but none the worse for the experience. It was a minor miracle.

But it did beg the question of who would go to so much trouble to make sure Jackson wasn't traumatized while being kidnapped. Myles was privately more convinced than ever that someone very close to the Colton family was behind the kidnapping. But who was anybody's guess.

Unfortunately, the kidnapper had found the tracking device sewn into a seam at the edge of the canvas and removed it from the painting. The tracker had been found in a trash can at the house where Jackson was found, and all trace of the kidnapper had been lost.

Faith strolled over to him, smiling sexily as their gazes met. "Hey, hot stuff."

"Right back atchya, sexy mama," he murmured.

"How late were you thinking about staying tonight?" she asked.

"Not late. Ringo will need to go outside before long. His puppy bladder isn't that big yet. And besides, I was thinking about turning in early with my wife."

"Are you tired?" she asked, surprised.

"Not in the least. You?"

She smiled widely. "Nope. I had a nap. I'm bright-eyed and bushy-tailed."

"Good thing. I'm planning on keeping you up very late, Mrs. Colton."

"I'm counting on it."

He kissed her lightly. "Congratulations again on getting your dream teaching job, sweetheart. I'm proud of you."

"I'm looking forward to it," she responded. "I love you—"

"Mommy! Daddy! Tell Cousin Valerie that Ringo isn't named after a bug! He's named after a planet!"

Myles grinned at his son, who'd had a big growth spurt in the two weeks since he'd been back home. "Kid's right, Val. Ringo's named after the rings of Saturn, not the Beatles."

Valerie ruffled Jackson's hair fondly. "You're too smart for a four-year-old. I think you're actually a puny nine-year-old."

"Am not! I'm four-and-a-quarter."

Valerie wandered off with Jackson, quizzing him on if he knew how much a quarter was. Myles grinned. Jackson definitely knew his basic fractions, already.

"You sure you're ready to have a couple more just like him?" he asked Faith. "He's a handful."

"Just like his daddy. And if I can handle the two of you, and I can surely handle a few more. But I secretly hope the next one is a girl."

He smiled fondly. "So do I. If I'm lucky, she'll look just like you and have your gorgeous auburn hair."

Faith smiled archly. "Do you remember how hard my mother tried to chase you away from me when we were first dating?"

He snorted. "All too well."

"You think you're up to the task of doing that with your own daughter? I can't wait to see this." She laughed up at him, her entire being glowing with happiness. She'd never looked more beautiful. Her sweet soul shone from the inside out.

Somehow, someway, he'd found his way back to Faith, and he was never, ever letting her go again. It had been a close call, there, for a while. But they'd stuck together, and the entire Colton clan had stuck with them through one of the worst nightmares any family could go through, and the power of love, the power of family, had seen them through it all.

He had to say. It wasn't half bad being a Colton. Not half bad at all.

His front pocket vibrated, and frowning, he fished for his phone. It was a weekend and the firm wouldn't be calling him. Pretty much everyone else in the world that he loved and cared about was in this room, right now.

"Hello?" he said into the phone.

"Myles, it's your father."

Wow. He hadn't spoken with his birth father since their last contentious phone call. It was a bit of a mental whiplash to hear from him. But, given the resolution of the recent family crisis, he supposed it made sense. Someone must have mentioned his son's return to Erik. His father had never been the kind to avoid drama. In fact, if there was a commotion to be had, the man usually was in the middle of it, stirring it up.

"Erik? Why are you calling me?"

"We've got a problem. A *family* problem…"

* * * * *

COMING SOON!

We really hope you enjoyed reading this book. If you're looking for more romance, be sure to head to the shops when new books are available on

Thursday 11th November

To see which titles are coming soon, please visit

millsandboon.co.uk/nextmonth

MILLS & BOON
A ROMANCE FOR EVERY READER

FREE delivery direct to your door

EXCLUSIVE offers every month

SAVE up to 25% on pre-paid subscriptions

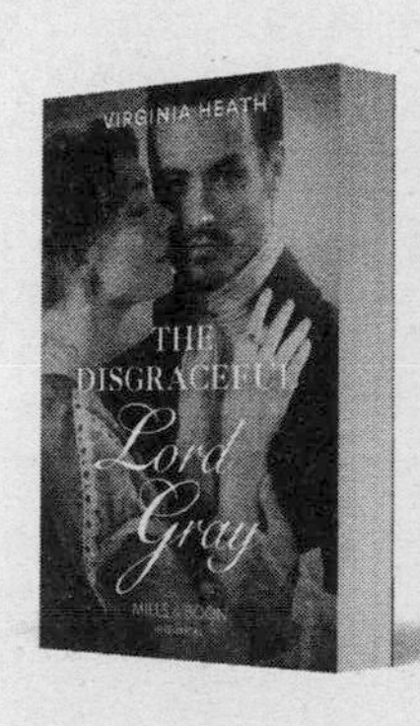

SUBSCRIBE AND SAVE

millsandboon.co.uk/Subscribe